T0290205

Joy Dettman was born in Echuca, Victoria. She spent her early years in small towns on either side of the Murray River. In the late sixties, she and her husband moved to the outer suburbs of Melbourne, where they have chosen to remain. Joy is an award-winning writer of short stories set in country Australia, which were published in Australia and New Zealand between 1993 and 1997. The complete collection, *Diamonds in the Mud*, was published in 2007. Joy went on to write the highly acclaimed novels *Mallawindy*, *Jacaranda Blue*, *Goose Girl*, *Yesterday's Dust*, *The Seventh Day*, *Henry's Daughter*, *One Sunday*, *The Silent Inheritance* and the Woody Creek novels.

Joy returns to Woody Creek for the final time in *Trails in the Dust*. She says that she owed herself and her readers a more satisfying end to her epic tale.

Also by Joy Dettman

Mallawindy
Jacaranda Blue
Goose Girl
Yesterday's Dust
The Seventh Day
Henry's Daughter
One Sunday
The Silent Inheritance
Diamonds in the Mud

Woody Creek series
Pearl in a Cage
Thorn on the Rose
Moth to the Flame
Wind in the Wires
Ripple on a Pond
The Tying of Threads

Joy Dettman

TRAILS IN THE DUST

MACMILLAN
Pan Macmillan Australia

First published 2019 in Macmillan by Pan Macmillan Australia Pty Ltd
1 Market Street, Sydney, New South Wales, Australia, 2000

Copyright © Joy Dettman 2019

The moral right of the author to be identified as the author of this
work has been asserted.

All rights reserved. No part of this book may be reproduced or transmitted by any
person or entity (including Google, Amazon or similar organisations), in any form
or by any means, electronic or mechanical, including photocopying, recording,
scanning or by any information storage and retrieval system, without prior
permission in writing from the publisher.

Cataloguing-in-Publication entry is available
from the National Library of Australia
http://catalogue.nla.gov.au

Typeset in 12.5/16 pt Adobe Garamond LT by Midland Typesetters, Australia
Printed by McPherson's Printing Group

This is a work of fiction. Characters, institutions and organisations mentioned
in this novel are either the product of the author's imagination or, if real,
used fictitiously without any intent to describe actual conduct.

MIX
Paper from
responsible sources
FSC
www.fsc.org   FSC® C001695

The paper in this book is FSC® certified.
FSC® promotes environmentally responsible,
socially beneficial and economically viable
management of the world's forests.

*For my brother Jack who has gone to
tend the gardens over the rainbow
7.4.1938–3.3.2019*

PROLOGUE

'Stand up and walk,' she said. It was the same advice she'd been offering herself for the last half hour. Had she been able to see a hand before her, she may have taken the advice. Couldn't right now. That pale scythe of a wintery moon had slid in beneath its blankets and left her in the dark.

There'd been pockets of stars winking down at her when she'd run. They'd deserted her too. She'd walked through rain for an hour. There was no shelter to be had out here. Anything that scratched a living from this land was stunted. Just scrubland and no end to it.

She'd thought she'd find a fence, a house, sheep, something. Her foot had found a dead branch. It tripped her.

'It could have been worse,' she said. 'You could have broken an arm, a leg.'

Her shoulder had taken the worst of her fall. It didn't feel good but she could still move it. Should have got straight up and kept on walking. The logical side of her brain had told her to get up; the other half had told her to rest her legs, just for five minutes. She'd been sitting for so long now her legs were too cold to move.

Her body wasn't cold. She could thank her parka for that, could thank it for a lot. She'd wiped blood from her brow with a crumpled tissue found in one of its pockets, had been sucking on peppermint Life Savers, also found in that pocket. Only had four left.

'Get up and go back to that goat track,' she said.

She was in wild pig county. She'd seen three fighting over roadkill before he'd made her turn off the bitumen road. Too much traffic on it. He hadn't liked traffic. He hadn't liked towns. He was running from something.

She'd seen wild pigs on television but until last night had never seen one in the wild. That's where she'd been attempting to walk back to, that road, those pigs — until she'd tripped.

This scrub was probably riddled with pigs, not that they'd find much roadkill beside that last track. She'd seen one vehicle on it, a big twin-cab ute that came out of nowhere, then disappeared into nowhere.

'It was travelling too fast not to be going somewhere,' she said. 'Taking a short cut home, maybe.'

Should have walked that way. Maybe where he'd been going would have been closer than that bitumen road.

'You make your choices and you have to stick to them — and I could be closer to those pigs and that road than I think.'

He'd carjacked her, not for her car and money but for a driver. She hadn't seen his bare and bloody foot at the time. She hadn't seen much — other than the gun he'd shoved in her face. They'd been doing it in America for a while now, carjacking. It went without saying that they'd start doing it over here. Australia had been following America's lead forever.

'He's long gone,' she said. 'Get your feet beneath you and go back to that track. It will be easier walking.'

He could have been long gone. He could have been parked in the dark waiting for her to come out of the scrub too. He was crazy.

She'd always been a walker. She'd walked in the rain before tonight. Her parka was shower proofed and she was wearing a sweater and cardigan beneath it. Wasn't wearing much beneath her slacks, and they felt damp.

Had no idea where she was. She'd crossed over a rattling old bridge to get him away from one town. He'd liked that bridge less than the town, and on its far side there'd been another town. BAR-something. That's all she'd seen of the sign.

There'd been farms on the outskirts of Bar– and more farms and farmhouses beside that bitumen road. When she'd taken off from the car, she'd expected to find a farm, but what farmer in their right mind would want this land? It was worn out, dead.

'And if you don't get up soon, you'll be dead.'

PART ONE

PART ONE

CARA

She was running blind through smoke-filled rooms, attempting to scream Morrie's name, but her throat would produce no sound. She was opening doors, different doors but always the same door, seeking that red room. In dreams, she always found him in that red room.

Her heartbeat woke her, and her lungs whooping for air. He was beside her, sleeping the deep sleep of the just. Dreams rarely disturbed him, his or hers.

Easing herself away from his warmth, she got out of bed, then, her hands before her, feeling her way, she walked through to the bathroom, closed the door silently, then hunted the last of that nightmare away with a flood of white light.

For thirty years she'd been dreaming that house dream. At times it was Amberley, at times it was Langdon Hall, on occasions it was Georgie's crumbling old house, but wherever her nightmare took her, there was a red room, and since the night of the fire, the houses were burning.

She blamed Cathy for tonight's dream. They'd spoken late – late in England, morning in Australia. Cathy and Gerry were flying over for Elise's wedding in October. It was a gruelling twenty-six-hour flight, which Cara and Morrie had sworn never again to sit through. When they'd spoken last night, Cathy had likened the flight to childbirth – agony at the time but once the baby was in your arms, the pain faded fast. She'd know. She'd given birth six times before she'd got her daughter. Cara had given birth once – or for twenty-eight hours she'd attempted to give birth the natural way – until a surgeon took pity on her and cut Robin free. To this day she remembered the agony. They'd adopted their girls.

The shower turned on, she stripped off the t-shirt she slept in, tucked her hair beneath a plastic shower cap, then stepped under the hot spray. Once a week her hairdresser washed and straightened her hair, which remained that way until the next appointment – if she didn't get it wet between shampoos.

Had never concerned herself with shower caps when she'd worn her hair short and natural. It had been short when, for a week, her photograph had been plastered all over the media. She would have packed up and flown with Morrie then, but hadn't been free to fly, or Tracy hadn't. Until the adoption was finalised, she'd had to remain in Victoria. It had taken seven months, long enough for her hair to grow. She'd had it bleached and straightened in Melbourne, had it cut in a chin-length bob, and every time she'd shown her passport during her escape to the UK, it had raised eyebrows.

They'd been a mixed and matched bunch that day. Robin had been registered as a Grenville-Langdon – by Cara's parents; Tracy had been made a Grenville by her adoption, Cara's passport, issued in her maiden name, said she was Cara Jeanette Norris. Only Robert had got through without questions, her father. He'd flown with them, if unwillingly.

She turned off the water, dried herself, and then slipped on a towelling dressing gown before removing her plastic cap. Apart from the hair at the nape of her neck, the rest had remained dry.

She combed it then crept back to the bedroom, where the small windows were now allowing a little light to enter, enough for her to see Morrie's head still buried in his pillow.

She envied his sleep as she'd once envied Cathy's – her best friend by default. They'd been thrown together by room allocation at college, vociferous Cathy, silent Cara, unlikely friends. Their relationship had continued, perhaps assisted these last years by that twenty-six-hour flight.

Cathy had been the first to uncover Cara's secret vice. They'd been in Sydney, sharing a bedroom at Amberley, when she'd helped herself to a partial draft of *Angel at My Door*. Her demand to know how the story ended had added fuel to Cara's youthful pencil and paper obsession. It was Cathy who'd presented her with her first rattle-trap typewriter, who'd first planted the idea of a pseudonym – twenty-three books ago.

'You'll need to marry someone with an interesting name,' she'd said. 'Cara Norris sounds like the author of a book about brussel sprouts.'

She'd turned the conversation to brussel sprouts – and weddings – the night they'd sat around her dining-room table in Ballarat, wading through the legal jargon of Cara's first publishing contract.

'Cara Grenville-Langdon sounds like a writer's name,' she'd said.

'Of hysterical romance,' Cara said. She hadn't written a romantic novel.

The Author has written an original work at present entitled 'Rusty' herein called the Work. To Cara, the only words of importance in that contract had been *'Author'*, *'Rusty'* and *'Publisher'*. For years she'd pursued publication.

Morrie had added his vote for 'Grenville-Langdon'. He'd wanted them to remarry before he had to fly home.

'C.J. Langdon,' Gerry suggested. He'd been Morrie's friend before he'd become Cathy's husband. 'It's a name that could be male or female.'

'C.J. Langhall,' Cara had said, her promise that she'd join Morrie at his Langdon Hall when she was free to, and when she'd printed *C.J. Langhall* on that contract, it had looked right.

They'd remarried, in Ballarat, but not until after *Angel at My Door* had been published.

The bedroom windows looked down on a huge old tree, which may have been as large when Henry Whitworth Langdon had walked this land. Cara wasn't fond of the monstrosity she called home but she loved that timeless tree. It had seen it all, had stood through the battles and the blood, through the births and deaths of generations of Langdons.

All gone now. Robin had dropped the Langdon name when he'd married. His son was registered as Richard John Grenville. Cara's hairdresser called her Mrs Grenville. Her passport and driving licence still claimed that she was Cara Norris. Her readers knew her as Ms Langhall. Being spilled nameless onto a kitchen floor and left to her fate by her birth mother may have had some bearing on her confusion of names.

'What are you doing up at this ungodly hour?' Morrie asked.

'Thinking?'

'Thinking what?'

'Cathy. She raises memories.'

'They're the by-product of leaving half of our lives on the wrong side of the ocean,' he said. 'It's easy enough to cut ties, but no one has yet invented a cork to hold back memories. Come back to bed.'

'My hair is damp at the back. If I lie on it, it will go frizzy. What do you think about when you think of Australia, Morrie?'

'You,' he said.

'Full points for a safe reply. You spent seventeen years of your life there. What do you think about when you remember those years?'

'Houses,' he said. 'Lots and lots of houses.'

'How many?'

'Balwyn, Cheltenham, Frankston, Bendigo, Ballarat, Kew –'

'That Kew house belonged to Lorna. You never lived with her.'

'She lived with us. Mum and Pops moved into the Kew place for a time. I was at a school nearby.'

'What do you remember about Armadale?'

'Your dogbox.'

'I meant when you were a kid. You went to school at Armadale Primary for twelve months.'

'Come back to bed,' he said.

She slid in beside him, and he kissed her and told her she smelt of toothpaste.

Right or wrong, she loved him, loved his face, loved the scent of him, and if one day she stood before her parents' god for judgement, she'd point to her daughters. Robin may well be an added sin, but not the girls. As a twelve-month-old baby, Elise had been found in a park, strapped into a stroller. The authorities never found her mother. Cara had known Tracy's birth mother, Raelene King, an addict, a thief, who'd given birth in prison. Cara had fostered tiny mop-topped Tracy – until Raelene was released and attempted to add kidnapper/murderer to her resume.

She'd come in the night, with the mongrel she'd run with. They'd taken Tracy from her bed, drugged her, sealed her into a cardboard carton, then left her to die beside a farm fence. She'd survived that nightmare night. Raelene hadn't.

They'd shielded Robin from the aftermath and the media – or believed they had. He'd been eight at the time. He was in high school when Cara realised how badly they'd failed.

A dawn call from Cathy had woken her, but before she'd silenced the bedroom telephone, Robin, who slept downstairs, had picked up the family-room phone. Cara heard his voice on the line.

'He's definitely dead, Aunty Cath?' he asked.

'Dead as a dodo,' Cathy had replied. She was into church and God in a big way and not the type to celebrate a death, but her voice had sounded jubilant. Without need of a name, Cara had known who was as dead as a dodo.

'A pregnant woman got him with a shovel,' Cathy said. 'Tell your mum he was dead on arrival at the hospital.'

'She'll want to hear it from you. Hang on and I'll wake her,' Robin said.

They met on the stairs, Cara and her pyjama-clad golden son, she halfway down, he halfway up, both holding telephones. 'Did you hear, Mum? Dino Collins is dead.'

Cara had been flinching from that name since she'd been fifteen. She hadn't flinched that night. She'd made coffee while listening to Cathy's every gory detail, and when that call ended – because Cathy had been known to pass on incorrect information – Cara had placed a call to Chris Marino, a Melbourne barrister, who'd never been guilty of passing on incorrect information – or not outside of a courtroom. Chris had first-hand details. The woman who Collins had attacked in her garden had been one of his junior solicitors.

JENNY HOOPER

Jenny's foot touched the brake as a whirlwind, raised in a bone-dry paddock, found the heat of the bitumen to its liking and came dancing down its centre, towards her car. She clung to the wheel as that swirling cloud of red dust and debris hit.

'I just washed my car this morning,' she complained, to the dust or to her passengers. She had three today and a boot full of their shopping. Twice this week she'd driven to Willama. It got her out of the house. She couldn't stand its silence since Trudy had taken the boys and gone back to Nick. And God alone knew why. She'd been getting her life straightened out. She'd been looking well, and happy for the first time in three years.

'You fool of a girl,' Jenny had said to her. Shouldn't have, but when you can see a mistake being made, it's hard to bite your tongue and turn away. She and Jim had raised a trouble-free teenager, a sensible, reliable nursing sister, until she'd come into money and gone overseas for a twelve-month holiday. She'd married that bludger over there and stayed away with him for damn near ten years, and may have been wandering the world still if he hadn't got her pregnant.

Stop thinking about her. Think about your new fridge. She'd looked at a big fridge–freezer today, a twin door, one side a freezer and the other a fridge. She had a brochure in her handbag with its measurements, in centimetres. She couldn't visualise centimetres, but she had a dressmaking tape at home with inches on one side and centimetres on the other. It would tell her if she had space enough for that fridge, and if she did, she'd phone that store today and order it.

'I didn't know until Mum told me today that Trudy had gone back to her husband,' Donna Palmer said. Jenny had two Palmers in her car, Jessica in the front passenger seat and her daughter, Donna, in the rear. She'd been married twice, but since leaving the last one Donna had gone back to using her maiden name. 'I heard she had a new bloke in Willama,' she said.

'You didn't hear that from me,' Jessica said.

'I didn't say I did. I heard it from someone though.'

It was a fact, though Jenny didn't admit it. At Christmas time Trudy had spoken to Georgie about a divorce and gaining sole custody of the twins. She'd spoken of a Graham too, a para-medic. Jenny hadn't met him, but he'd phoned twice to speak to Trudy, and you can glean a lot of information from one-sided phone calls.

'You must miss those boys like hell,' Donna said.

Miss them? Jenny ached for them. She spent half of her nights planning to drive down to Croydon and kidnap them, and the other half planning to phone their mother and roar the tripe out of her. She was no brainless teenager controlled by hormones. She was an over-qualified nursing sister – with a ball-and-chain pretty boy dragging her down.

'What happened to change her mind, like?'

'How's your tooth?' Jenny asked. Donna's aching tooth had kept her mouth shut on the trip down. Her jaw anesthetised, the problem tooth extracted, she'd been making up for time lost since getting into the car in the Woolworths car park.

'Numb,' Donna said. 'Someone at the op-shop told me about Trudy's bloke and I can't remember who it was. Someone who'd know.'

If there was gossip to be heard and passed on, the op-shop was the ideal forum, and Donna spent most of her days there behind its counter.

Jenny glanced to her right, where a farmer and his tractor were readying a wide paddock for a crop. Scattered storms had been forecast. The sky was clear and there was a hot wind blowing from the west. It was partying on that newly turned soil, flinging clouds of dust at the road. Officially, summer ended in February. In this part of Victoria, no one paid a lot of heed to calendars. Summer ended when it ended – and had been known to continue into April.

Flat land, flat and dry and ugly, its only relief the grey of distant gums. The forest began at the Mission Bridge.

'Kangaroos,' Jessica warned.

There was a mob of them to the right, well off the road, but Jenny slowed her speed anyway. She and Jim had a serious run-in with a big red roo one night. It wrote off their Holden, or the insurance company called it a write-off. Poor old Itchy-foot – Archibald Gerald Foote – had been killed by a kangaroo, and on this stretch of road.

'What happened to make her change her mind?' Donna asked.

'She doesn't want to talk about Trudy,' Jessica said. 'Learn to take a hint, Donna.'

'I'm interested, that's all.'

The third passenger, Alice Dobson, who'd spent her day at the hospital with her dying mother, hadn't said a word since they'd picked her up out the front of the old folks' home.

'Marilyn Willis,' Donna said. 'That's who told me! She works down there as a domestic. She said that Trudy's new bloke was a male nurse or something. She said she'd seen them having coffee together, that he'd reached across the table and taken her hand.'

The road curved into the long approach to Mission Bridge and Jenny touched the brake to get her speed down. That bridge had a sixty-kilometre speed sign. She usually obeyed speed signs.

'I can remember the old ones talking about building this bridge back when we were kids,' Jessica said. 'I must have been thirty before they got around to doing it.'

Like everything else, the plans for that bridge had been put aside when the Great Depression hit, then shelved when war broke out. It had taken Bob Menzies to shake the dust off the blueprints and get it built.

'It opened to traffic in '52,' Jenny said. She remembered that year well – because of the school bus. The new bridge and the sealing of an old road out to the Aboriginal mission had given Woody Creek kids access to higher education – and given Jenny access to a doctor. She'd ridden the school bus down to Willama with Donny on her lap and schoolkids staring at him. She'd gone to the bank too –

Shook her head, shaking the memory of that day away. She'd had her hair cut today, and every time she had it cut, it showed more grey. She'd looked at bottles of hair dye at the supermarket, thinking a colour might lift her mood. It would take a bucket full of dye to lift it. Those boys and Trudy had been her life – and Jim's.

He'd begged Trudy not to go. He'd begged her to leave her boys with them for a few weeks, and to give herself time alone with Nick. He'd never been a begging man.

Jenny hadn't begged. She had a bad tongue when she let it loose. She'd said too much, and most of what she'd said hadn't been complimentary to Nick.

Just couldn't believe it. It came out of the blue. They'd been eating dinner.

'I'm taking two weeks of my holidays,' Trudy said. 'We're going down to Croydon.'

'You're not taking the boys,' Jenny said.

'They're my sons and Nick's, Mum. Of course I'm taking them.'

They might have carried his genes, but he'd played no part in raising them. Jenny had raised them. She'd been at their birth. He hadn't seen those boys until they were a month old, and he wouldn't have seen them then if his parents hadn't driven him up to Woody Creek expecting to take Trudy and her babies back with them. She'd been in no state to go anywhere. She'd been a depressed mess, determined to breastfeed two babies when she hadn't had milk enough to feed one. They'd spent their first month of life exercising their lungs. Nick's mother could screech louder, but her menfolk had decided to leave well enough alone.

Baby bottles and formula had silenced the boys, a six-year-old Commodore stopped Trudy's howling. She'd owed a fortune on her credit card. Jim would have paid it, but the hospital had been advertising for nursing staff. Since they'd been three months old, those boys had been Jenny's. She'd pushed them around town in their twin stroller, had strapped them into twin car seats, had loved and adored them – and lost them.

Jim missed them. He had a habit of crawling into a black hole when his world turned bad. For a week Jenny had considered joining him in that hole, but they'd run out of toilet paper. People can't survive without toilet paper and Woody Creek had no super-market since the last owners had gone bankrupt.

The Mission Bridge behind her, she kept her speed down until she was by the old Aboriginal mission. All bar its church was gone, a church with no windows. Someone had built a service station-cum-general store beside it. A few families still lived out here.

After the mission, the road moved away from the forest. It was straight and wide enough to encourage speed. Wandering minds encouraged speed, and Jenny's mind was wandering when she heard the siren. It flinched her mind back to the present, flinched her foot off the accelerator.

'Someone tell me it's an ambulance,' she said.

'It looks like that new cop,' Donna said.

JOY DETTMAN

Jenny braked, pulled off to a shoulder of the road and wound her window down. Hot air outside – and him, full of hot air.

He was the sandy-headed, pinch-faced coot of a man she'd seen around Woody Creek for a couple of months and never once had seen him smile. Woody Creek wasn't the optimum posting for constables with city-born brides.

'Sorry,' Jenny said. She'd been speeding. No gain in denying it.

'Licence,' he said.

She found it amongst her many cards. The photograph on it wasn't awful. Her date of birth emblazoned on it was. Granny used to say that if you didn't count the numbers, the numbers didn't count. Driving licences counted every year. She didn't look at it often. He looked at it then looked at her before handing it back.

'Her husband's not well,' Jessica said. 'She had to leave him home by himself.' Sob stories went down well in some quarters. This one didn't. Pinch-face wrote her a ticket.

The figure he wrote widened Jenny's eyes. Age hadn't stolen their blue. They had a patch of today's sky in them with a touch of angry ocean. She loathed fines, loathed money spent and nothing to show for it. Only once before had she been pulled over for speeding and that had been years ago, when the fine was a lot less.

The figure silenced Donna – or Alice Dobson silenced her by suggesting they split it four ways. She was a pensioner. All three of Jenny's passengers were pensioners. Woody Creek was that sort of town. School leavers who wanted to work left town. Those who didn't signed up for the dole. There was work to be had in Willama, if you owned a reliable car. Donna could have got work in an office – had she owned a car.

The dashboard clock showed five o'clock when Jenny offloaded her passengers and their shopping. It was five-ten when she turned into Hooper Street. She'd told Jim she'd be home by four-thirty.

Someone had been here. She'd closed the big gate when she'd left. It was open. She's back, Jenny thought, her eyes scanning for Trudy's navy-blue Commodore. It wasn't in the driveway or on the lawn. Had she parked down the back, Lila would have been down there. She was waiting in the driveway for her lady.

They had a big old shed-cum-garage, too full of junk to park in, and even if there had been space, the effort required to open and close its sagging timber doors would have been reason enough not to park under cover. Jenny parked down the back, beside Jim's ramp, easier for him to get in and out of the car; also easier when she'd had two little boys and their stroller to lift in and out. These last three years she'd worn a curving track between an overgrown liquid amber and a crepe myrtle, then across the east side lawn to the house.

No little boys to unload today but five supermarket bags, one containing three loaves of crusty bread, two she'd freeze. When she bought her new fridge–freezer she'd have room to freeze a dozen loaves. She couldn't live without her crusty bread.

The car locked, her hands loaded with shopping bags, she walked up the ramp to the back veranda. Twelve months ago, a local handyman had built that ramp so Jim could get his electric buggy up and down. He needed two hip replacements but refused to go near a hospital. He had his reasons, which Trudy refused to understand.

'You're a stubborn old man,' she'd said to him.

'He's been a damn good father to you,' Jenny told her.

No key necessary. The security door was hanging open and the main door unlocked. She stepped into the kitchen. 'In or out,' she said to Lila. Lila chose out, and Jenny walked to the table to dump her load.

'I'm home,' she called. 'Everything that could go wrong, went wrong today, then that pinch-faced cop gave me a ticket.'

No reply. He needed two hearing aids along with two new hips – and he'd reached the age of sleeping where he sat.

THAT THURSDAY

*F*or three years Trudy's life had been in a holding pattern, like a plane circling a fog-shrouded airfield, unable to land but with too little fuel left in her tank to fly to another airfield. For those three years, she'd lived with her parents, and Nick had nothing in common with them. She'd never expected him to stay in Woody Creek. She hadn't expected to stay in Woody Creek. She would have been down here when the boys were three months old if his maternal grandmother hadn't died. He'd flown over to Greece to represent his branch of the family – and he'd stayed there until the boys were eighteen months old, until his parents moved into their new house, built by old Nicholas for his retirement. He hadn't lived to enjoy it. Jenny found his death notice in the *Herald Sun*, a column full of words praising the life of Nicholas Papadimopolous. He had one son, four daughters, a beloved wife and relatives by the score. His daughter-in-law received no mention but her boys' names had been listed amongst his grandchildren.

You weren't supposed to think ill of the dead. Three times Trudy had met her father-in-law and all three meetings had been unpleasant. Buying a black frock for his funeral would have been hypocrisy.

Then, two days after the funeral, Nick had turned up in Woody Creek, in his father's Range Rover. He hadn't come to the house. He'd booked into a cabin behind the hotel and phoned her. They needed to talk, he'd said.

She'd needed to speak to him. At Christmas time she'd asked Georgie to begin the business of divorce. For three years Nick had been living as a single man, and when she'd knocked on that cabin door, she'd been convinced that he wouldn't argue about making their separation permanent. She'd had the words ready. 'It's for the best,' she'd say. 'I can never be a part of your family. I've made a new life for myself up here.'

She hadn't said those words. He'd held her, kissed her. First love is hard to kill, and the older you are when it hits, the harder it dies. She'd been passionately, madly in love with him the first time they'd slept together, in Venice. Her visit to his motel cabin had ended in bed.

Couldn't face her parents, so she hadn't. She'd showered at the cabin then gone to work. Had missed out on the Range Rover drama, had missed meeting his oldest sister and her husband and son and his mate.

They'd knocked on Jenny's door. She'd thought they'd come to take the twins and refused to unlock the security door. They'd wanted the Range Rover. His father had willed it to his first-born grandson. He'd left Nick nothing.

The phone calls began then. Nick had said that he was living with his mother, who wasn't handling the loss of old Nicholas. He'd phoned Trudy at night, at her work, begging her to move down to Croydon.

Then she missed her period, and it couldn't be. She didn't want another baby. But he'd kept on phoning. He'd been working, he'd said, driving one of his brother-in-law's taxis.

'You won't need to work, Trude. You'll be able to stay home with the boys and Mum. I want to know my sons,' he'd said. 'I love you. I'm nothing without you.' He'd had nothing when she'd married him, which hadn't mattered, not then.

Couldn't tell Jenny she was pregnant. Couldn't get an abortion in Willama. She'd been stressed out of her brain when her father cancelled an appointment she'd made for him months before.

'You're a stubborn old man,' she'd said. 'You'll both be in nursing homes twelve months from now.'

Her father would be. He couldn't get from the kitchen table to the back door without his walking frame. He needed Jenny's help to get in and out of the shower, and when Trudy offered to help, they'd shooed her away.

'I'm a trained nurse, Dad.'

'Your mother will help me,' he'd said.

'For how much longer!'

Five days later, sick with the baby, or sick about it, she'd packed up and moved down to Croydon.

'It's a trial, Nick,' she'd said. For her it had been time out, and that's all, time to think about her predicament, or time to find an abortion clinic.

The house was a mansion, furnished with the best that money could buy from Franko Cozzo. Everything in it was new, from the space-age washer–dryer to the bedroom furniture. Nick's father, determined to qualify for a part-pension, had spent money like water, then blown more than fifty-odd thousand on the Range Rover. As a couple he and Tessa may have qualified. As a widow, Tessa's assets disqualified her.

She wasn't well. She swallowed packets of pills, swallowed them haphazardly unless supervised, and she didn't like Trudy's interference – and Nick didn't like supervising.

'You need to diet, Tessa. Diabetes and blood pressure can be controlled with exercise and diet,' Trudy had advised – too often.

Diet was a dirty word. Exercise was for others. Tessa couldn't climb the stairs to the upper floor – which the twins worked out on their first day in Croydon. They ran for the stairs now as soon as boogieman grandma started screeching at them in Greek.

Nick didn't know about the baby. Every morning Trudy woke determined to find an abortion clinic. She'd known where to find one fifteen years ago. She'd driven a friend there and driven her home after it was done. Too long away from Melbourne, everything had changed, the roads, buildings, shopping centres, and her friends had found new friends. One girl she'd been at school with had grandchildren the same age as the twins – and most of the people she used to know now owned or were buying their own homes.

Trudy had owned a house in Kew for a few months. Should never have sold it. Should have put tenants into it, as her father had advised at the time. She could have been living in Kew now, instead of in Tessa's Franko Cozzo display house.

The hospitals hadn't changed. She'd worked at a few, had temped at more before going overseas. Maybe that's what she ought to do, get some temp work and give herself time to make the right decision. She'd been thinking in circles since the day she'd slept with Nick.

And he had bills she'd known nothing about until last week. He'd taken her out for dinner and the restaurant refused his credit card. She'd paid. He'd always been hopeless with cards. If he'd had a ten-thousand-dollar limit, he'd worked on the theory that the bank owed him that ten thousand.

They'd argued on the way home, about money. They'd argued that night in bed until he'd come clean about what he owed. He'd taken out two personal loans and both had accrued interest, and the interest accruing on his bank card was astronomical. What was hers had always been his. The same would apply with his debts.

Shouldn't have come down here. Should have gone through with the divorce.

The phone was ringing downstairs. Tessa took the call. Her only exercise was getting out of her chair to pick up her phone. It was *her* phone, *her* display house. Trudy had no more rights in it than the cleaner who came in once a week.

'Trudy,' Tessa called, which didn't mean that the call was for her, only that whoever was on the line didn't speak Greek.

Trudy walked downstairs to take the call.

She'd been thinking hospital, thinking temp work, and that call was from St Vincent's hospital. Nicholas Papadimopolous had been taken there by ambulance for scans but was ready now to be picked up.

'What happened to him?'

'He was involved in an accident. The scans reveal no injury.'

'Can you put him in a taxi for me, please? I'm here alone with two small boys and his unwell mother,' Trudy said.

Nick wouldn't like it. He would have enjoyed the drama of a frantic wife, mother and sons battling peak-hour traffic to run to his side. Three years ago, Trudy would have run to his side. She'd had her quota of drama today. Tessa had a leakage problem and refused to use the pads her daughters bought for her.

Paying for a taxi from the city to Croydon could be dramatic. Nick wouldn't have the money. She looked at Tessa, aware she stockpiled cash in her bedroom.

'Nick had a minor accident. He's coming home in a taxi. He'll need money to pay the driver,' she said, in Greek.

More drama, lots of drama, before Tessa went to her room and returned with a fifty-dollar note. She didn't hand it to Trudy but placed it on the table beside her phone, then picked up the phone to make a call, squeezing what drama she could from her Nicky's minor accident.

Trudy climbed the stairs, listening to one side of a conversation. She'd spent enough time in Greece to have a good working knowledge of the language. It was Tonia, the eldest daughter, and according to Tessa, Tonia's husband's fault that Nicky had the accident. Tonia was the wife of the taxi owner. She hung up when her mother started screeching blame down the line.

There was still Demi, Cia and Angie to call. They never hung up. Tessa was dialling one of them when a crash from above, followed by a bellow, had Trudy running to her boys.

Jamey was on the floor between the twin beds, Ricky attempting to lift a small bedside chest of drawers off his brother. Trudy lifted it and checked for injury.

'You're not hurt,' she said.

The chest used to hold a top-heavy lamp. She'd got rid of it the day she'd moved in. She'd need to get rid of those drawers too. 'I've told you not to climb on things.'

'It just falled over,' Ricky said.

'Because you opened its drawers and climbed on them,' she said. 'Find a video and I'll play it for you. Daddy is going to be late.'

They looked down towards the boogieman on the phone at the foot of the stairs, then in unison, shook their heads.

'In Mummy and Daddy's room,' she said. Nick had turned the largest of the upstairs bedrooms into his den, a wide bed, desk, laptop, television and video–CD player, conveniently positioned. It wasn't accustomed to playing *Thomas the Tank Engine* but accepted it. She settled the boys on the bed to watch the busy trains, then sat with them, not watching trains but looking down through a window that offered a view of a neighbour's backyard, their clothesline, their back door. She'd been familiar with the elderly mother and daughter and their two fluffy white dogs before introducing herself and the boys over the back fence.

They were a Mrs and Miss Morrison, and the daughter's name was Margaret. The instant she'd heard that name, she'd wondered if she'd been sent by fate to this house, to this court.

Way back, maybe a year before she'd gone overseas, she'd temped at the Frankston hospital where, on one slow night, she'd glanced through old hospital records, seeking the record of her birth. Only one premature baby had been delivered by caesarean section that day, and to nineteen-year-old Miss Margaret Morrison –

Her mind was far away when Tessa screeched up the stairs. Her poor injured Nicky was home, her baby boy.

'You stay here wiff us here, Mummy,' Jamey said when she stood.

'Finish watching your show.'

'It nearly is finish now,' he replied. He'd know. He and his brother had first watched that video at eighteen months.

Nick was standing at the open door, with the taxi driver, unwilling to let his passenger get away before he paid for his ride.

'You look healthy enough,' Trudy greeted him.

'I hurt my back,' he said. 'Have you got any money?'

'How much have you got?' Maybe not the right thing to say to a man with an injured back.

'Fifteen. I need eighty-two.'

She made up the difference with Tessa's fifty and her own twenty.

'Keep the change,' she said to the driver, then closed the door.

THE BREAKING

*J*enny didn't notice that Jim's electric buggy was missing until after she found his note. He'd ridden out to the Monk property, where the new owner, a city chap, was building a house. According to Harry, the builders were setting it on the site of the old Monk mansion. They'd spoken about it yesterday, and about Monk's cellar.

The leftovers of a chicken casserole heating in the oven, potatoes bubbling on the stove, Jenny walked to the window to peer through greenery to the road Jim would have taken. No sign of him. His note said he'd be home by five. It was close to six now. They were still on daylight saving time and there was plenty of light left in the day. He'd probably lost track of the time. She was reaching for his note when the refrigerator hiccupped, shuddered and died.

'You know what I'm planning, you old bugger,' she said. She'd used her dressmaking tape to measure the fridge recess, and unless that tape had been shrunken by the years, the fridge–freezer would fit. She hadn't ordered it. She wanted to discuss it with Jim before making that call. Too late now to call. On Thursdays, the shop closed its doors before six.

She checked the power plug, thinking she may have disturbed it with her measuring. She hadn't. Then she tried the light switch – and not a flicker from the fluorescent tubes.

'Damn and blast electricity companies to hell,' she said. There'd been too many blackouts lately. Most didn't last long but were annoying. She stood, watching those fluorescent tubes, hopeful of a fast fix. It didn't happen, and still cursing electricity companies, she read Jim's note again.

Dear Jen, Gone out to have a look at Monk's place. I believe I have enough battery power to get there and back. If not, you'll know where to find me. Jim XX.

'I told you we'd drive out there tomorrow, you impatient bugger of a man,' she said, then turned the note over to see what was printed on the other side.

Nothing. He'd used a clean sheet of paper.

'Why?'

Her heart knew why. It started racing. For years they'd been writing each other notes on the reverse side of Juliana Conti's draft printouts. They had a pile of used pages on the bottom shelf of the pantry and a larger pile in the library. They used the blank sides for scoring card games, writing shopping lists, as scribble paper for the twins, and when done with them, they'd burn them. Juliana Conti was their secret.

When Jim had picked up his pen today, he'd been aware that what he was about to write wouldn't be burnt.

She was out the door, mobile in one hand, car keys in the other. She was down the ramp, unlocking her car and climbing into it, reversing too fast out the way she'd driven in, praying she was a madwoman and knowing she wasn't, knowing that something had been going on in his head since Mary Grogan's funeral. He hadn't gone to it for Mary Grogan but to hear Jenny sing, and that night he'd told her she could sing *Ave Maria* at his funeral.

A right turn into Hooper Street, right again into Three Pines Road, then on down to the bridge, and no sign of him.

No sign of him on the road out to Monk's big old gates, and those gates closed and padlocked. They stopped her car. They didn't stop her. She walked down to where the curved brickwork ended and a wire fence began, where she spread the wires and climbed between them.

The creek cut in close to the road at this point. She found his old grey cardigan a few steps back from where a high bank fell away to deep water.

*

Eight-fifty, Hooper's corner a pit of darkness when the lights of two vehicles turned into the driveway. For the last hour Jenny had been sitting on her front steps, and Lila, psychic as all dogs are, hadn't left her side since she'd returned to the house. The beam of her torch identified a police car but not the two uniformed men who stepped from it. Harry Hall parked his old ute on the lawn. Her torch lit his face for an instant. It looked grim, so she turned off the light, needing to hide a while longer in the dark.

The dark doesn't silence voices. 'He's gone, Jen,' Harry said.

Of course he'd gone. She'd known that the second she'd turned his note over and seen its blank side, though until she'd seen that cardigan lying in the dust, she'd clung to hope. Nothing inside her now. She was a skin stretched over a black gulch of waste. She'd tried so hard to be enough for him since Trudy and the boys had gone. She hadn't been enough.

'Can we go inside, Mrs Hooper?' one of the officers said.

Whether there is a word in you or not, you have to reply to a direct question. 'No lights,' she said.

There could have been. She had half a packet of candles in her kitchen drawer, had half a dozen pre-used candles in a plastic bag, could have had light in every room. Didn't want light. Wanted the dark to swallow her, to swallow the last seven hours of this day, or for this day never to have happened.

They spoke their words in the dark, just police words, the necessary feeding of information to the newly bereaved. She'd heard it all before on television. They sounded like second-rate actors in a road-safety commercial.

'It appears that he may have been reaching for his fallen cardigan and lost control of his vehicle –'

Very conveniently lost control of it, nice and close to that high bank too. He'd known that land well.

Stay back from that edge, Jen. The clay is unstable there.

And he wouldn't have needed a cardigan today. The temperature had edged up to the mid-thirties. A deep thinker, her Jim, he'd put a lot of thought into his last ride, had put thought into which cardigan might best serve his purpose. That old grey thing was pure wool and heavy enough not to blow away. A forward-thinking chap, her Jim, a problem solver. He'd solve problems before they'd become problems. She'd spent half her life telling him that he'd built mountains out of molehills for the pure pleasure of sweating while climbing them.

No more problems for him to solve. In one easy movement, he'd solved the lot – and abandoned her alone on the desert island of old age.

'He was pinned underwater by his vehicle.'

Stop calling it a vehicle, she thought. It was his *gopher*. The twins used to call it Papa's *go far*. It had gone as far as Jim had needed to go this last year – over to the newsagents to get his daily papers, around to the post office to buy stamps. If he needed to go further, she'd drive him.

She'd nagged him to go a lot further before his hips crippled him. She'd wanted to fly to Greece for Trudy's wedding. He'd posted the happy couple a cheque. Born in this bloody town, raised in it, lived most of his life in it, now he'd be buried in its dirt.

She should have been howling. That's what wives did in road-safety commercials, howled, or collapsed, or both. But she could see Jim's mind ticking over while he'd planned his afternoon. Kids had been lost in that creek for days. A camper drowned at Christmas time and his body hadn't been found for five days. Jim solved that problem with a worn-out cardigan – worn out at the elbows with his leaning on them. She'd darned them twice. She'd been a perfectionist darner. Her work would now be on show in Willama's police station evidence room – and if those officers knew what she was thinking, they'd have her committed.

'Would he have any reason to ride out there today, Mrs Hooper?'

She knew a few reasons. She'd been itemising reasons since sitting down on the steps. 'No,' she said.

'The house they're building,' Harry said. 'We talked about where they were putting it. His father owned that land years ago.'

A lifetime ago. When Jenny had been seventeen and Jim twenty-one, when Monk's old mansion had been standing. It had a huge cellar beneath it. Jimmy was conceived in that cellar.

'Perhaps we should go indoors, Mrs Hooper?'

Mozzies biting? she thought. She wasn't feeling their bites. She wasn't feeling anything. There was nothing inside her to feel with. Lila was aware of the mozzies. She snapped her teeth at their buzzing but didn't move from Jenny's side.

'Have you phoned the girls, Jen?' Harry asked. No space on the steps for him. He'd perched on the edge of the veranda. Old praying mantis Harry, all skinny arms and legs and oversized head – or overgrowth of hair on his head. He'd never liked wasting money in a barber's shop.

She hadn't phoned Trudy since she'd left. Their parting hadn't been amicable. Jim had phoned her. This morning he'd written to her. He'd left the envelope on the hallstand, a cheque enclosed – his apology perhaps for being a stubborn old man. Jenny had felt the paperclip when she'd picked up the envelope to post it. He'd always used paperclips to hold cheques.

It was still in her handbag too. She'd forgotten about it. By the time she'd dropped Alice off at the hospital, she'd been rushing to get to her hair appointment. Then the bank had held her up for half an hour while she'd waited for someone capable of hitting the right computer keys to roll over an investment she'd been rolling over for years. Then the refrigerator, then the supermarket, and then Alice to be picked up.

'Do you have your daughters' numbers handy, Mrs Hooper?'

She had Georgie's. Like its owner, Georgie's phone number had remained unchanged by the years. She reeled it off. Trudy's number was keyed into her mobile, and where it might be located was anybody's guess. In the car maybe. Beside the creek where she'd dialled triple zero.

And what was the hurry anyway? Jim would still be dead in the morning.

Dead. Gone. Passed away. Demised. Lost, but mainly gone . . .

'Trudy Papadimopolous,' Harry said. 'She lives with her mother-in-law in Croydon. Their number should be easy enough to find.'

Their name wasn't easy enough to write. The constable couldn't spell it. The twins couldn't say it. They could say Hooper.

They wouldn't remember their Papa Hooper. They were barely three years old.

Did you think about that, you fool of a man? Did you think about me, about anything other than marking the spot for your searchers? she thought. Better for Trudy if I don't mention that old cardigan. Better for Katie too. She loved her Papa, and would believe in an accidental drowning. Jim had never been a swimmer. He'd told Katie once that his mother hadn't allowed him near water deeper than what was in his bathtub; that his father had attempted to teach him to swim by tossing him into the middle of the creek one day. The loss of one foot and half of his shin in a Jap prisoner-of-war camp had given him a good reason to stay out of the water.

'Your husband had relatives, Mrs Hooper?'

'Two sisters. Both dead,' she said.

He had a son in England. Give them Jimmy's name, she thought. She didn't know his phone number but could give them a possible address. He might send a condolence card, she thought, then shook her head, shook Jimmy away and found a name for them.

'He had a cousin in Balwyn. Ian Hooper,' she said. 'He was alive a couple of years ago.'

'I believe you have a note, Mrs Hooper.'

She had a note addressed to her but written for them, and she sighed and pushed herself to her feet, knowing she had to get this over with, had to get them gone. She sighed again, then took her first step up and into what comes later.

There was no later. There were the raw edges of nothing. She led the way into the house with her torch, led them through the entrance hall into a passage and through to the kitchen. They followed her. Lila followed them.

By torchlight she found that bag of used candles. Harry, never without a box of matches in his pocket, without the makings of a cigarette with his matches, lit the first candle then looked for a place to stand it. No candlesticks in Jenny's kitchen but a cupboard full of jars, big ones and small. Glass jars had been a precious commodity once. Old habits don't die easily. She opened a cupboard packed full of jars and chose half a dozen of the smallest – the Vegemite, mustard, crushed ginger jars – and while the police officers waited, she dribbled melted wax into one after the other, then stood candle stubs upright in hot wax.

A soft, kind light, that of flickering candle flames, though never good to read by. She read Jim's note one final time by candlelight then handed it to an officer to become evidence of accidental death.

My clever Jim.

He would have left her a personal note somewhere, written on the back of a Juliana page, to be read then burnt. He would have hidden it in one of her favourite books, or under her pillow. Somewhere in this house she'd find his last letter.

He'd left one inside a bankbook the morning they'd packed up their room in Sydney, before he'd gone off to war; hid it in a bankbook then buried the book down the bottom of her case.

She hadn't found it for months. Still had it. Still had every letter he'd written to her during the war. He used to write beautiful letters – when he'd been an undamaged boy.

Six stubs of candle flickering, the short and the tall. Grouped together, they looked like the candles in a Catholic church. She moved the two tallest to the table where at twelve-thirty today, Jim had been sitting, a mug of tea in one hand, a slice of fruitcake in the other. She'd kissed his wiry white hair, told him she'd be back by four-thirty. 'Be careful,' she'd said, and she'd gone on her way. He would have finished his cake, written his note – notes – found his cardigan and gone.

Trudy's fault for leaving and taking those boys. And my fault, she thought. She'd let him edit a draft of *We'll Meet Again*. It wasn't their story but it was set during their young years, and in some places she knew she'd cut too close to the bone. He'd used his red pen liberally on the first eighteen pages, then put the pen down to read.

'It's good,' he'd said when he finished it. 'Publish it when I'm dead, Jen.'

She'd never publish it now.

Georgie would. It was in Jenny's will that her computers and discs would go to Georgie. A final Juliana Conti, published post-humously, might keep a roof over Trudy and the twins' heads. Nick wouldn't.

The uniformed men were at her now for the name of a friend they could call to sit with her until her girls arrived.

'I'm fine,' she said.

'I'll stick around,' Harry said. He'd been 'sticking around' for most of Jenny's life, more brother than friend.

He stoked the stove when the officers left. He opened the refrigerator, removed a cask of red wine from the top shelf, found and filled a glass. 'Get that into you, Jen.'

'I'd rather drink fly-spray,' she said.

He wasn't a wine drinker. He took the glass to the sink, emptied it, rinsed it.

'All things pass, Jen,' he said. 'I know it doesn't feel like it right now, but it gets easier. After I lost Elsie, I used to go to bed at night telling myself that all things pass and wake up still saying it in the morning. Then one day I started believing that it could have been so.'

'He's broken something inside me,' she said. 'Some nerve that's supposed to feel can't. I feel hollow.'

'Eat something.'

His words reminded her about the chicken casserole. She opened the oven. The dish and chicken it contained looked black. A tea towel protecting her hand she removed the dinner that never was and placed it on the sink. She lifted the lid of the potato saucepan, one of her near new saucepans. Its contents were black but black potatoes might soak off. That casserole dish wasn't worth soaking. She tossed it into her kitchen bin.

Lila sniffed it. She'd missed out on her dinner tonight. There were cans of dog food in the pantry and an electric can opener on the bench, and when it didn't work, she slammed open her cutlery drawer and tossed things around, looking for an opener that would work. Had to gouge the can's solidified contents into Lila's bowl. Harry made tea, then sat and removed the makings of a smoke from his pocket.

How many times had she watched him open that old tin with a coin, remove his cigarette papers, place one on his lower lip so both hands were free to pinch out strands of tobacco, to shape then roll those strands in fine paper. A lick, then behold, one of Harry's ultra-slim cigarettes.

'I suppose I should change the girls' sheets,' she said. 'Georgie's haven't been changed since she was up here at Christmas time.'

'I sleep in mine until Vonnie starts hounding me for them,' Harry said.

'Dust mites in the bed feed on our skin particles, according to the six o'clock news.'

'Just another one of their fear campaigns,' Harry said. 'I remember a time when the biggest danger we had to face in bed was bedbugs.'

'And unwanted pregnancies,' Jenny said. 'Roll me a smoke, Harry.' He rose and tossed his smoke into the stove.

'I didn't mean for you to do that,' Jenny said.

'I didn't need it,' he said. 'It's just a habit.'

'People died a lot happier from smoke-related diseases than they do from diabetes and obesity.'

'You're in no danger of that. When did you last eat?'

'I'm not hungry. Roll me a smoke then go home, if you don't want to watch me light it,' she said. 'And take Lila with you.'

'You don't want that.'

'I don't want a lot of things,' she said. 'I don't want Trudy trying to drive herself and the boys up here tonight, and I don't want him in this house. It's a case of which one I don't want more, I suppose.'

Lila licked her bowl clean and returned to Jenny's side, to plead her case with her eyes. She would have appreciated a bite of Nick. On the few occasions they'd faced off, he'd been lucky to get inside with his jeans intact – not that Jenny was concerned about his designer jeans, but he'd be carrying one of her boys tonight. She cared about them. They hadn't taken Jimmy's place in her heart but had carved out their own space there.

THE WIDOW HOOPER

*T*hat west wind, grown stronger in the night, had the chimneys wailing for Jim when Jenny woke before dawn, woke to that sledgehammer blow of knowledge that he wasn't in bed, that never again would he be beside her in bed. Unable to handle that knowledge in the dark, she reached to turn on the bedside lamp. The switch clicked. The globe offered no light.

'Bloody electricity company. Bloody trees.' In Woody Creek, trees had a bad habit of flinging their branches at power lines. Her ice-creams would be melting, chocolate coated she'd bought for Jim. The meat she'd bought for him yesterday wouldn't have had time to freeze. The girls and their men might eat it tonight, or Lila would.

She'd placed a torch under Jim's pillow when she'd got into bed last night. It was still there. She turned it on, then lay on her back, allowed its circle of light to play over the high ceiling, down deep blue drapes, across the fireplace.

There was a lot wrong with the design of this house, its many fireplaces the worst of it. It had six. In the days when ladies had sat on their backsides with their embroidery, ringing bells for maids to bring more wood, six open fires may have burned from summer's end to spring in Vern Hooper's house. Jenny, the last Mrs Hooper, cook, laundry maid and wood carrier since she'd moved in, had sealed four of the chimneys with newspaper and cardboard cartons, then hidden her work with fabric-covered masonite screens. Only the sitting room and kitchen chimneys hadn't quit the smoking habit. All six wailed.

Her moving circle of light disturbed a spider, a hairy huntsman snoozing in the corner near the door. With too many trees growing too close to the house, they had frequent eight-legged visitors. This one ran from that narrow light beam towards her dressing gown, hung last night with Jim's behind that door. The spider moved her from her bed. She snatched her gown before he reached the door, then, checking that his mate hadn't spent the night in her slippers, she picked them up, opened the door and walked through to the entrance hall, a large place of wasted space, furnished with a hallstand and a scattering of photographs above dark wooden panelling. Her gown on, slippers on her feet, torch lighting her way, she crept through the hall to the kitchen.

Her sister, Sissy, had coveted this house and its bathrooms. Jenny had never wanted to live in it. She'd argued with Jim for two months before agreeing to move back to Woody Creek. A couple with one baby hadn't needed two bathrooms or six bedrooms. A couple with one baby had needed a modern, three-bedroom home in Ringwood.

He'd promised to modernise the kitchen, and had, forty years ago. It was a large room with not an inch of wasted space in it. A warm room, the only warm room in the house in winter, because of its slow-combustion stove. She'd stoked it last night before going to bed.

Georgie, Paul and Katie had arrived an hour before the others. They lived in Greensborough and knew a faster back way out of the city. Katie's eyes had been red rimmed and swollen with weeping. Thank God she'd been asleep before the others arrived.

'It's my fault,' Trudy must have said a dozen times, and how could Jenny deny that. She had. A dozen times last night she'd denied it. A dozen times she'd told the lie of the accident, the lie of the house being built out there, the lie of the dropped cardigan. Didn't want this day. Couldn't take it.

The kitchen chimney had a whistling wail that harmonised with the haunting howl of a big, old oak tree, planted too close to the western veranda. One of its branches provided the rhythm, tapping against the guttering.

How many times had she paid to have that limb cut back? She used to nag Jim to have the tree removed, to have a few of them removed. He'd liked trees, or liked the privacy they'd offered. No gum trees grew on Hooper's corner. Gums were killer trees, Jim said. He could name a dozen men felled by the forest they'd worked in.

Jenny's first husband, Ray King, had died when a log stack rolled and he'd been standing in the wrong place. A fallen branch had crippled Ray's father. Big men both, bred to labour in the timber industry.

The harvesting of the forest that surrounded Woody Creek had built this town. Sawmills had screamed their way through Jenny's childhood, five in town, two more in the bush. All gone now, and without them, Woody Creek was dying.

One of the twins coughed. Jenny turned in their direction, not eager for a repeat of last night. They'd slept their way home and hadn't been ready for bed when they'd arrived. It had taken an hour to settle them.

They looked like their father but had Trudy's eyes. Nick was a good-looking man. In their wedding photographs, he'd looked like a long-haired young Greek god. He was her junior by a few years, a detail Trudy failed to pass on when they'd married.

'He'll stray,' Jenny had said when those photographs arrived.

'We raised a sensible girl,' Jim said. 'She knows what she's doing.'

She'd stayed away too long, had been five months pregnant when she'd come home. Nick had seemed pleasant enough, until Trudy returned the hire car. He'd wanted to drive it back to Melbourne, to spend a few days with his parents.

'We'll catch the bus down,' Trudy said.

'When?'

'Give me this time, Nick. I need to catch my breath for a while.'

Two days later he'd helped himself to Jenny's car. She'd drive anyone anywhere, but never, never loaned her little car – which she'd told him in no uncertain manner when he brought it back. He'd caught the bus to Melbourne the next day. He hadn't gone home. He'd phoned Trudy from Darwin.

That was when she and Jim had found out who he was. He'd helped himself to Trudy's bank card. She'd cancelled it. That's when they'd found out that she had no medical insurance, and no money in the bank.

There were embers in the firebox and wood on the hearth. Jenny opened the flue wide before feeding the embers a rolled-up newspaper and then wood. Several times a day she cursed that stove's greed for fuel, but her kettle was boiling, and with the firebox open there was light enough in the kitchen for her to turn off the torch.

She smelt the wax from last night's candles. They'd done a brave job and were lined up now on the sink like a battalion of burnt-out soldiers. A few had fallen. Three replacement troops had been sent in late to take their place. They still stood tall. She struck a match and sent them into battle again. The fallen and the jars they were in were given a burial in her kitchen bin.

It needed emptying. It always needed emptying. There was too much waste these days. Granny hadn't owned a kitchen bin or any bin. Waste not, want not, she used to say.

The fly-spray wine she'd placed beside the bin last night had been moved to the bench. Someone had helped themselves to it. Georgie's Paul drank red wine. She returned it to the fridge, then removed the loaded supermarket bag she'd used as a bin liner and tied its handles. The back door unlocked, she stepped out into the first day of no Jim, a grey and blustery day, but light enough out there for her to see where she was walking.

The green council bin lived between the outdoor laundry and the wood heap. She dumped the bag then picked up an armful of wood. Lila's bed was in the laundry, an empty bed this morning. She'd be better off with Harry for a day or two. She liked him. He took her out to the forest and urged her to chase rabbits. She wasn't allowed to chase cats or bark at possums at home.

Jenny placed the wood down on the hearth, brushed the residue from her dressing gown's sleeve, closed the door, then selected a large chunk to feed to the fire god. Her mind was on Lila, when from the corner of her eye she saw Jim walk by the kitchen window. For an instant, the barest flicker of an instant, she thought last night had been a nightmare.

It was a long enough instant to drive a splinter deep beneath her ring fingernail.

The pain immediate and excruciating, she forgot she had a house full of sleepers, forgot she was a widow, and she cursed that wood stove to hell. Smoke gushing down instead of up the chimney, that lump of wood jammed half in and half out, pain, anger and loss meeting head on, she kicked the wood and damn near made a minor accident major. Almost had to grab the chimney to stop her fall, but the wood went in, so she kicked the firebox shut – and lost its light.

Glasses on the bench where she'd left them last night, she put them on. Torch on the table, she turned it on, then stood, studying that splinter. It was big and had gone in deep. No part of it protruded that she could get a grip on.

The finger in her mouth, she moved to the window to look for that figure. She'd seen someone walk by, someone tall and wearing dark clothing. Paul wasn't tall. Nick was shorter than Trudy – and Jim had never worn black.

His sister had, Lorna. With Jim dead, had she come out of her grave to take her morning constitutional around the verandas?

She used to. Every morning she'd march around and around the verandas, a grown woman when Jenny had been a girl. They used to spy on Miss Hooper, Jenny and her friends. They'd hide behind the rose hedge and count how many times she'd walked that square of wide verandas.

Scissors, tweezers, Jenny thought, and her slipper-clad feet whispering on carpet, she walked down the hallway to the bathroom to fetch her pointy-nosed tweezers. If she cut that nail back hard, the tweezers might get a grip on wood.

Jim's showering chair was in the shower recess where she'd left it after he'd washed yesterday. She was standing, staring at it when Georgie crept in behind her.

'What are you doing rattling about at this time of day?' Georgie asked.

'Were you outside a minute ago?' Georgie was tall and she wore little that wasn't black.

'I was asleep until a minute ago. What's doing?'

'I rammed a log of wood under my fingernail. Can you reach my pointy-nosed tweezers? They'll be in the top, right-hand corner of the cabinet.'

Georgie took the torch and saw what Jenny would have needed to feel for. Armed then, they walked through to the library, where Jim's magnifying glass lived in the top drawer of an elderly roll-top desk.

'You don't do things by half measures, mate,' Georgie said, examining the splinter under glass.

'Do what you have to. It's killing me.'

Scissors from the sewing machine's drawer, good light now coming though the library's eastern bay window and a pincushion full of needles on the sewing machine's bench top. Georgie operated at the window. When scissors and tweezers failed, she dug for the splinter with a needle until Jenny called it quits.

'Trudy might be able to do it,' Georgie said.

'Let her sleep,' Jenny said, and they walked through to the kitchen where Georgie found a frying pan and placed it onto the stove.

She was about to add butter when Jenny offered her a bowl of dripping, saved from bacon and roast lamb. Granny had always saved her dripping, back before animal fat killed. It was living that killed – or not wanting to live.

Twice in her life, Georgie had come within a whisker of dying, once by fire, once by knife. She wasn't afraid of animal fat. A good dollop added to the now hot pan, she reached for a packet of sliced bread.

Taller by half a head than Jenny, sixteen years her junior, her eyes green, her hair – hanging long this morning – still that dark copper red. She'd never looked like Jenny's daughter, except a little around the mouth and chin. She knew what Jenny was thinking before she thought it.

'Armadale?' she said. 'Remember frying your homemade bread? Jimmy wanted to use it as a football.'

'It bounced,' Jenny said. It had been edible when fried in pure white pig's lard. In those distant days you could buy blocks of lard for a few pennies from any butcher shop. Lard had kept a lot of kids alive during the Great Depression. It had kept Jenny and her kids alive in Armadale in the late forties, when they'd lived with Ray. He'd been a worker. They hadn't seen a penny of his wages – and if she hadn't behaved herself, he hadn't fed her or her kids – or he'd brought home tripe and livers he'd known she'd refuse to cook.

They were discussing the burying of those livers and tripe when they heard tiny footsteps running. Jenny opened the door to her dark-headed cherubs in their identical *Thomas the Tank Engine* pyjamas.

'Shush, you two, or you'll wake Mummy,' she whispered, cuddling both, one handed, the other held high until they settled sufficiently for her to show them her splinter. They had to kiss it better. She had to lie about their kisses making it much better.

'If you sit quietly, Georgie will make you a surprise breakfast.'

'An some cup-a-teas?' Jamey said.

'Wiff some litta bit a sugar, Nanny,' Ricky said.

They ate fried bread spread thick with homemade apricot jam. They drank their cup-a-teas, half milk, half tea with sugar enough to sweeten. Trudy didn't approve of tea, sugar, fried bread or jam, but who, other than the experts who wrote their myriad books on child raising, claimed that a Nanny surprise breakfast was bad for little boys?

Beautiful beings, they had no resemblance to the Macdonald clan, other than their duplication. Every generation of Macdonald had produced a set or two of identical twins. Georgie knew of their Macdonald connection. Trudy didn't. Trudy knew that Jenny and Jim had adopted her but had never been told the details of her birth. Harry Hall and his family knew. They never mentioned what they knew – because of Jim. He'd preferred to deny Trudy's Macdonald connection.

'Where's Papa?' Jamey asked.

'Sleeping,' Jenny lied.

'When him waked up, we can wide him's go far,' he said.

Papa's gopher was stuck in the mud, in the creek behind Monk's. Papa was sleeping in a cold cruel place Jenny refused to think about.

'We'll see,' she said.

Little boys ask too many questions. She left Georgie to find replies while she went to the bathroom to move Jim's showering chair before Trudy or Katie saw it. Move it to where? The library was close. No one went in there. It was Jenny's workroom, her sewing machines and computers lived in the library.

She placed the plastic chair beside her original dining table, extended to hold three computers, two elderly desktop models and her laptop – and the hard copy of *We'll Meet Again*. She'd been working her way through it, transferring her pencilled changes to the file yesterday morning. She closed the doors on it today and went to her bedroom to dress.

Block-out lined drapes and tall trees kept that room dark in the mornings. She opened the drapes a crack and peered out. The news of Jim's drowning would be doing the rounds out there. They'd be discussing him on street corners, in the newsagency, over fences. She loathed the thought of him being today's news.

'Did you think about that, you fool of a man?' she asked his wardrobe.

They had his and her wardrobes. Like most of the rooms, the master bedroom was oversized. She opened her wardrobe to look for widow's weeds. She owned five pairs of black slacks, a black suit, black sweaters, black shirts. She removed a pair of slacks from their hanger, looked at a lightweight black sweater with three-quarter sleeves.

She wasn't a widow. She was an abandoned wife, and the abandoned wife chose to wear blue.

Opened his wardrobe then. A tidy man, her Jim, trained to be tidy by a dominating sister. His shirts hung on hangers, his shoes were set side by side . . .

A male voice in the kitchen turned her head. Not Paul's voice. She heard the scuttle of little feet up the passage. The boys didn't know Daddy. They wanted Mummy. A moment later fingers tapped high on her bedroom door. Georgie opened it and caught Jenny holding Jim's prosthesis, a hollow skin-toned shin, a black sock and a shoe still on its foot.

'He took it off,' Jenny said, offering it as evidence. 'I helped him put it on after he showered yesterday. He took it off, Georgie, then he rode his gopher out there and drowned himself.'

'Put it away, Jen.'

'He wanted to make bloody certain, didn't he? He took it off!'

'It was an accident, and keep your voice down. He's in the kitchen, looking for painkillers. He ran into a tram yesterday and hurt his back.'

As if Jenny cared about his back. 'Here's your proof that it was no accident,' she said, pushing her proof at Georgie. 'He came in here, took his leg off and hid it in his wardrobe where I wasn't likely to see it.'

Georgie took the prosthesis and placed it on the bed. Jenny followed it.

'I should have known. When we came home from Mary Grogan's funeral, he told me I could sing *Ave Maria* at his service.' She was nursing the prosthesis, polishing the toe of the shoe with her hand. 'I told him I would if he'd recite *Daffodils* at mine, and he smiled. I hadn't seen him smile since Trudy took the boys, but he was planning this then.'

'Put it away, Jen.'

'He took that rotten old grey cardigan with him to mark the spot. That's how they found him so fast,' Jenny said.

The twins were at her door, wanting in, demanding in, demanding Papa and go-far rides. They couldn't reach the doorknob, and a finger to her lips, Georgie returned to the door to lean her weight against it, just in case they worked out that if one stood on the other, they'd gain enough height.

Trudy retrieved them. 'Nanny's sleeping,' she said. 'Come away from there.'

'Her is not *thleeping*,' one argued, and behind that door, Georgie flinched. Margot, her sister, hadn't been able to say an *s* to save her life.

'They need reminding. That's all,' Jenny said as their noise abated.

No lock on that door, or no key to turn in the lock, Georgie moved a bedroom chair against it. It was weighty enough to slow an intruder. She walked to the window then and drew the drapes wide.

She was sixty plus to those who counted. Her hair may have shown a trace of silver between hairdressing appointments, but few got close enough to Georgie to see her roots. She could thank Charlie White's old barn of a grocery store for her unlined complexion. For twenty years she'd worked behind his counter, protected from the harsh rays of Woody Creek's sun. Life had changed for her the night she'd been dragged out of the burning house bare minutes before the roof fell on her bed. Harry couldn't get to Margot. She'd died in that fire.

With the drapes open, the wide window of Jenny's bedroom offered a panoramic view of the front lawn, the trees, the hedge of rosebushes that perfumed this town in spring. A few were still blooming. A few would continue to bloom until they were pruned in June and July. Like a park, Hooper's half-acre, well shaded in summer, russet and gold when autumn came, but cold and grey in winter when the last of the leaves fell.

Winter only two months away, with its brutal frosts and pea-soup fogs.

That window offered a view of the rusty corrugated-iron fence behind the hotel. Peppercorn trees used to grow there. They'd been removed to make way for six prefab motel cabins. There was an evergreen *Vacancy* sign on display on the corner of Hooper Street and Three Pines Road. It had a *No* in front of the *Vacancy*. Had it been switched on it might have been red. It hadn't yet been switched on.

Had those cabins been built two years earlier, that sign might have caught the eyes of a few weary travellers, when to get from Willama to Nettleton, traffic had driven through the centre of town. City engineers and their massive machinery placed the final nail into Woody Creek's coffin. They'd gouged a connecting road from where old Joe Flanagan's property ended to where McPherson's began, giving traffic a direct pathway through.

They'd put up signs, one pointing left to *Town Centre*, one pointing right to *Caravan Park*. During the holiday seasons, cars hauling boats or caravans turned right. The town prospered little from holiday-makers. The caravan park opened its own kiosk during the holiday seasons.

Jenny's mind was far away when Georgie took the prosthesis again. This time she placed it out of reach, on top of Jim's wardrobe.

'Take this for what it's worth, Jen, but whatever it is that you're thinking, I'd keep it to myself. Insurance companies don't pay up on suicides.'

'He had insurance policies for both of us,' Jenny said, and she was at the door, moving that chair. Georgie followed her down to the library, to the roll-top desk. Jim's black concertina file was in its bottom drawer.

Jenny hit her finger while removing the file. The pain didn't stop her search. She found the policies filed under *Insurance*, found Jim's will, filed under *Will*. If he'd written her a personal note, given his mindset at the time, placing that note into one of those envelopes would have seemed logical to him. She knew he'd left her a note somewhere. He hadn't been the world's greatest talker but give him a pen and paper and he'd fill a dozen pages.

She opened the two policies. No note in either envelope but she found what she was looking for in with his will, a folded, hand-written page. It wasn't addressed to *Dear Jen*. He'd left instructions for his executors, information on investments.

And the name and phone number of a Willama funeral director.

Her mouth open, her eyes disbelieving, she ripped the page in half and pitched the pieces at the window.

'I stuck by him through thick and thin, and he could go and do a thing like that to me,' she said, and she was gone, out the side door she slammed behind her. Its glass shuddered in the frame.

THE HOOPERS

*G*eorgie picked up both halves of the page. She saw the funeral director's name, then read the rest while sticky taping the pieces together. Jim had organised his own funeral, had prepaid to be buried beside his parents in the Hooper plot.

She'd known for years that he'd named her and Jenny his joint executors. They'd need those details, but like Jenny, she couldn't believe the funeral instructions. Vern Hooper and his daughters had dogged Georgie's childhood. They'd hounded Jenny until they'd got what they'd wanted, Vern's grandson, Jimmy.

She'd been seven, Jimmy six when they'd lost him. She could remember that morning. They'd had a killer influenza, Granny, Jenny and the rest of them, and Jimmy wouldn't wake up. Lorna Hooper had arrived in her car. She'd picked him up and driven him away so the hospital and doctors could make him better. Lorna hadn't taken him to the Willama hospital. They'd never seen Jimmy again.

She could remember the day Vern Hooper died. She'd been twelve, still young enough to believe in miracles. For weeks she'd believed that Jimmy's father would bring him home.

She'd been eighteen the year Jenny met up again with Jim Hooper, in Melbourne. She'd written to Georgie. *Jimmy isn't with his father. He's never been with his father. Jim signed him over to his sister Margaret . . .*

Eighteen is old enough to form very strong opinions. Having grown up loathing the Hooper name, Georgie had loathed Jim Hooper. Then she'd met him, and seen a glow in Jenny she'd forgotten, heard the laughter she'd forgotten. Whoever, whatever Jim Hooper was or wasn't, he'd made Jenny happy – and Jenny hadn't blamed him. She'd said that he wouldn't have known what he'd been signing when he'd relinquished Jimmy. She'd said that for years after the war, his family had kept him locked away in private hospitals where he'd been stuffed with pills, zapped with electricity, prodded and poked by enough doctors to put him off the medical profession for life.

Georgie didn't doubt that he'd taken his own life, and maybe she respected him for it. This last year it had become obvious that his future would be in a nursing home. He'd struggled to stand – and he'd been wearing Jenny down. At Christmas time, Trudy had spoken about Jenny.

'She won't let me help her with him. I feel so useless, Georgie.'

Right or wrong, Georgie believed that Trudy had gone back to Nick so she wasn't forced to watch her father's disintegration.

Hothouse raised, Georgie thought. Overprotected by two parents who'd believed she was Jesus Christ in female form. Raised in this beautiful old house, given an education. Georgie had envied her at times.

As a tiny kid, she'd envied Jimmy's studio photograph of his toothy daddy, envied his rich grandfather who'd bought him toys. For a time, she'd envied Margot who'd had no photograph of her father – and hadn't needed a photograph. The Macdonald twins had lived in Woody Creek. She'd learnt early to pity Margot.

Only thirty-nine when she'd died, and Georgie should have died with her. For some reason she had been allowed to live. It had taken her a long time to come to terms with that.

For most of Jenny's life, she'd been attempting to get out of Woody Creek. Until the fire, Georgie had never tried to.

It was too easy. She'd got into her ute one day, wearing borrowed clothing, borrowed sandals, and she'd driven away, driven north until she'd run out of north and had to turn to the west. She'd continued driving until she'd found a reason to turn back.

Raelene, Ray King's daughter, had petrol-bombed the house. It, or Granny's ghost, had turned on her. She'd died beneath the roof of the old kitchen. Dino Collins, her bastard boyfriend, hadn't died. He'd been arrested. Georgie was in Perth when she'd learnt that he was playing possum in a psychiatric hospital. That was the day she'd decided to come home and gain the qualifications to hang him.

She'd spent five years at university. She'd got her piece of paper then ended up a general dogsbody with a group of solicitors who'd made a name for themselves defending murderers, not prosecuting. She'd been in her forties. The jobs she'd wanted had gone to the bright young men. Not that it had mattered by that stage of her life. She'd been with Paul.

They'd married a few months before Katie was born. The name on her office door said *Georgina Dunn*. She didn't defend murderers. She wrote good contracts, wrote good wills, did a lot of dogsbody work, was used on occasions when one of the big guns needed a female on his team. She would need to call her office. She had an appointment at ten. 'My stepfather died,' she'd say. Jim had never been her stepfather but it sounded better than 'my mother's second husband'. She'd referred to Ray King as her stepfather – for twelve months – then stopped referring to him.

Katie's bedroom door was closed. She opened it a crack, enough to peer into the dark room. Katie was asleep. With luck she'd sleep until midday. The door closed silently, she walked down to the back bedroom she shared with Paul.

He was awake but still clinging to his pillow. 'What's going on out there?' he asked, nodding in the direction of noise.

'They're in the kitchen,' Georgie said. 'Nick's moaning about his back and hitting Jim's pills.' She offered Paul the envelopes and the taped-up page, then his glasses. 'He's organised and paid for his own funeral, in the Hooper plot. Jenny read it and ran.'

Paul sat up and put his glasses on. What little hair remained on his scalp looked much as it had when he'd gone to bed – grey. She'd liked his eyes the first time she'd met him. He had brown cow eyes. A reliable and patient man, Paul Dunn. He'd needed patience to run Georgie down. She opened the drapes, asked him to put the envelopes into her handbag when he was done with them and to keep an ear tuned in for Katie. Then she closed his door and walked back to the glass door and out into the wind.

Trees blowing, her hair slapping her face, she held it back while scanning the garden for movement. No sign of Jenny. She wouldn't have gone far, not this morning. The shed's back door was closed but never locked. She walked across the lawn to it while branches overhead swayed and groaned.

Found her, perched on an upturned oil drum, beside a motor mower, her finger in her mouth.

'We're going down to the hospital. They'll anesthetise that finger and have your splinter out in a second.'

'It will grow out,' Jenny said.

'If your finger doesn't fall off in the meantime. There are things we need to get started on, Jen.'

'He's already finished them. He made bloody certain he wouldn't end up buried with me, didn't he?'

'You're not dead yet.'

'I wish I was. I can't do it, Georgie. None of it. I can't.'

'You can do what you have to, mate. On your feet.'

'Mum!' Trudy called from the back veranda. 'Mum. Are you out there?'

'Keep her away from me or I'll end up telling her it was her fault for going back to her toy boy.'

'You're all talk and no action, Jen – and we're going to Willama. Stay here and I'll ask her to move her car.'

'Don't! She'll want to drive me. She said last night that she wanted to say goodbye to her father. I'm not going there with her.'

'You don't have to. Stay here. I'll be two minutes.'

'No,' Jenny said, and she stood. 'Get my handbag. It's in my bedroom. Use the glass door.'

'Your car is as blocked in as mine.'

'I'll get it out,' Jenny said.

She'd done it before, had driven around driveway blockages a couple of times. She'd driven around a truck twelve months ago when that chap had been here building the ramp for Jim's wheels. It meant reversing over a garden bed, making a tight three-point turn on the front lawn, but she'd squeezed out before and would do it again.

She did, five minutes later. They got away unseen, except by Paul. He watched the manoeuvre from the front veranda.

Driving was freedom, the drive away from that town was always preferable to the drive home. She didn't speed, didn't speak until the Mission Bridge.

'I think of what they did to that little girl every time I cross this bridge,' she said.

'They're dead, Jen. She's alive.'

'Probably brain damaged.'

'They wouldn't have released her from hospital so soon had she suffered any permanent damage.'

They spoke then of Cara and that night, spoke of old Joe Flanagan, long dead, and Lila Flanagan, Jenny's dog's namesake. They were both bitches.

Jenny parked in front of the hospital and handed her keys to Georgie. 'Do what you have to while I'm in there,' she said. Jim's prosthesis had travelled down on the back seat, in a supermarket bag. He'd look intact when Trudy drove down to say goodbye.

The original hospital building had been standing for a hundred and twenty years. It said so on a plaque beside the old entrance.

It had been extended, the old wards gutted and made new, then extended again. It sprawled now, to the west, to the south, but that old entrance had remained intact.

*

A boy doctor shook his head at Jenny's splinter, then told her to remove her rings, two diamond rings and a plain gold wedding band. They slid off easily and were zipped safely into her handbag before she offered her hand again.

He didn't know she was an abandoned wife, and for the time it took to anesthetise her finger, to mutilate her nail and remove that log of wood, she was just another silly old woman who'd been staring at ghosts instead of watching what she'd been doing. She told him about her wood stove. He told her to buy herself an electric model.

'I had boiling water for a cup of tea this morning while the rest of Woody Creek went without,' she said. 'We had a blackout last night.'

He swabbed and bandaged her finger, asked what she'd eaten with her cup of tea.

'You wouldn't approve,' she said, and he pointed to a set of scales.

'I'm nine stone,' she said.

'If you make eight, I'll eat my hat. Scales,' he said.

He didn't need to eat his hat. 'I weigh more when I'm wearing my rings,' she said.

He smiled and checked her blood pressure, listened to her lungs, asked if she was a smoker – and she was pleased Harry hadn't rolled her a smoke last night.

'Everyone of my age used to be a smoker,' she said. 'Can you hear something going on in there?'

'A pair of lungs that sound healthier than they ought to. Keep that finger out of water,' he said, then smiled and dismissed her.

Georgie was waiting to drive her around to the funeral parlour.

A big business, death. Those requiring funerals had to form a queue – or to take what they could get. Jenny and Georgie took ten-thirty on Monday morning, then had to find words for the death notices the undertaker would place in the *Willama Gazette* and the *Herald Sun*.

'Loved husband of Jennifer, father of Trudy –' Georgie said.

'And Jimmy,' Jenny said.

'James?' the undertaker asked.

'Jimmy,' Jenny said.

'Deceased?'

'No.'

Georgie's eyes wanted to say 'yes'. He'd never come back to find them. If he'd been alive, he would have come back.

'Adored Grandpa of Katie, Jamey and Ricky,' Jenny said. And that was it; written down it didn't look enough, though. Jim wouldn't want to be remembered as the father-in-law of Nick, and who else was there?

'You can add, "Only son of Vern and Johanna Hooper, deceased. Brother of Lorna and Margaret, also deceased",' Jenny said, then she got out of that place and left it to Georgie to finish up.

They had an appointment with Jim's solicitor at midday, and with half an hour to kill, they had a coffee. Watched their watches, watched the wind lift an elderly woman's skirt high. It didn't lift her clinging petticoat.

'Can you still buy petticoats?' Jenny asked.

'In specialist shops maybe,' Georgie said.

'I've never thrown mine away. I've never thrown anything away.'

'Waste not, want not,' Georgie said.

The solicitor offered further proof of suicide, proof too that Jim had started planning his escape well before Trudy moved out. Last November he'd transferred ownership of the old Hooper house into joint names and done the same with his investments and shares. Jenny had to sit though that fifteen-minute appointment and keep her mouth closed about what she thought she knew. Georgie had told her to.

She talked when they were back in the car, talked about that cold-hearted house. 'I'll burn that bloody place to the ground,' she said, then remembered that burning was the wrong thing to say to Georgie, so changed the subject to milk, to bread and ham for sandwiches.

Entering the supermarket was like walking into an oasis of normality. They separated there so they could grab what they needed fast. Easter not far away, there were displays of colourful eggs, of gold-wrapped chocolate bunnies. They slowed Jenny's feet. Every year she'd bought chocolate eggs or bunnies for everyone. Jim had only ever bought one egg, the biggest he could find. They'd spent weeks eating chocolate egg while sitting side by side on the couch, watching their favourite television shows. She bought no chocolate bunnies or eggs but picked up a dozen Easter buns. The living still needed something to eat with their cups of tea. She bought more butter, because what was an Easter bun without plenty of butter?

Half of her hand still numb, she sat in the passenger seat on the drive home, nursing Georgie's handbag. They were crossing the Mission Bridge when her bag vibrated.

'It'll be Katie,' Georgie said. 'Tell her we won't be long.'

Georgie's phone was modern, but Jenny picked out a brief reply and sent it.

We're twenty minutes away.

At Christmas time, Katie had been a young woman. She'd been a weeping child last night. Fourteen is neither one thing nor the other. Jenny remembered being fourteen. She'd been a young woman the night she'd competed with city singers in a radio talent quest and walked away with the third prize. At fourteen, she'd been an innocent child who hadn't understood the possible repercussions of rape. Fifteen when Margot was born, by sixteen she'd been the town pariah, but far more knowledgeable. Despised that town and had to go back there, had to do and say the right things.

And couldn't. Not yet.

They were approaching Hooper Street when she asked Georgie to drop her off on Teddy Hall's corner. Harry lived in a bungalow behind his middle son's house, and whether Lila took a piece out of Nick's leg or not, she was coming home. Katie had been one of Lila's pack since puppyhood, the twins her first litter, and today, Jenny needed her.

A mind reader that dog, she'd known her lady was coming. She was waiting at the gate. A mood reader too, she didn't greet her lady with her usual wriggles and licks, her 'Where have you been?' yips. One sniff of her bandaged finger and Lila knew where she'd been.

Jenny had to explain her finger to Harry. She blamed Lorna Hooper's ghost for the splinter. Told him that Lorna's targeting of her wedding finger had been a statement on Jim's marriage to the town trollop. Then told him that Jim wanted to be buried with his family.

'In the Hooper plot?'

'Fenced in with them,' Jenny said. She would have said more if Vonnie, Harry's daughter-in-law, hadn't joined them at the gate.

'We were so shocked,' Vonnie said, then in the same breath asked when the funeral was likely to be.

'Monday. Ten-thirty,' Jenny said, as she might offer the date of a dental appointment. She turned away, walked away then, Lila at her heels.

'She seems to be taking it all right,' Vonnie said.

Harry didn't comment. He watched Jenny and Lila walk to the Hooper Street corner where they didn't turn and disappear but turned back. He thought she had forgotten to tell him something, so waited at the gate. She didn't look his way but walked on towards the railway crossing.

'She never puts that dog on a lead,' Vonnie said.

'Smart dogs don't need leads,' Harry said. 'I wouldn't mind getting a pup. Paddy Watson's bitch whelped seven they say.'

'He charges a fortune for them, and they dig and poop everywhere,' Vonnie said. 'Where's she going now?'

'Walking her dog, Von,' he said. The walkers now gone from his view, he returned to what he'd been doing, pulling weeds from his vegie plot.

CHINA LADIES

*I*t had started, the visitors with their cakes and condolences and flowers. She'd seen a bouquet making its way in through her small gate, and in no mood yet to play the widow, Jenny had turned back and walked towards the town centre, or what used to be a thriving town centre, dissected by railway lines.

There were two crossings, Blunt's, so named for Blunt's Drapery on the corner, and Charlie's crossing to the west of town, named for old Charlie White's grocery store. Both buildings had lived a few lives since their owners died. Blunt's, was now a residence, Charlie's an opportunity shop. Jenny and Lila used Blunt's crossing that morning then continued to South Street where they turned right.

She'd spent her childhood in South Street, in a railway house built next door to the station; her playground had been the park, directly opposite the station yard. It used to have swings, a merry-go-round, a bandstand. The old swings and merry-go-round, decreed dangerous by some do-gooder, had been replaced by a slippery slide and monkey-bars, very dangerous when preschoolers played unsupervised there. She waved her fingers at two climbing Macdonalds – or Macdonald offspring, thickset, short-necked, snowy blond heads. They looked like Margot. Lila eyed them but she remained at her lady's heels as they walked through the park that led to Park Street. The football oval was on its far side.

No footballs being kicked there today, no cricket balls being hit for six, a school day today. A pack of Duffys were looking for spoil up the far end. They raised Lila's hackles, and Jenny's, so they took the diagonal track across dead grass and dust, giving the Duffy pack a wide berth.

They lived nearby, on their great-grandfather's acre, out Cemetery Road, a junkyard of rusting vehicles and crumbling caravans, lean-to sheds and the remains of a house. The cemetery was between their acre and the oval, and Jenny went no further than its small gate.

She knew that field of the dead well, and not looking to her left or her right, she made a beeline for the Hoopers' wrought-iron fenced plot, needing to curse it and every Hooper in it before Jim joined them on Monday.

Couldn't believe he'd want to join them. In life he'd had nothing to do with his family. It may have cost less. There'd been a vacant space beside his mother's stone forever.

Only six when he'd lost her. He'd never forgotten her. The day he'd gone with Trudy to search Lorna's house for the old Hooper documents, he'd returned home with his mother's collection of fine china ladies. Lorna had left her all to Trudy, house, furniture and twenty-odd thousand dollars. Jim claimed his mother's china ladies and these past weeks he'd sat handling one of them.

Jimmy was six when the Hoopers stole him. Did he sit remembering his mother? Jenny hadn't owned any fine china ladies. In 1947 she'd owned little more than the clothes on her back.

Mourners would be lined up around that fence on Monday. It was rusting. A decent kick might have done it some damage. She considered that kick, but the anaesthetic beginning to wear off, her throbbing finger suggested she shouldn't. She didn't need a throbbing toe.

'You won,' she told Vern Hooper's polished stone. 'I hope you're rotting in hell.'

You won't raise my grandson a bastard in this town, girlie –

Could still hear his voice. Could still see his sagging mouth spitting those words across Granny's kitchen table.

Jimmy's hands, his double-jointed thumbs had marked him a Hooper at birth. She'd kept him and his hands hidden for months. Had to take him into town to start his injections and Margaret Hooper saw him. That's when the war over Jimmy began.

They'd come on a Sunday morning, Vern and his daughters.

I'll take him off your hands and raise him decent, he'd said.

Not that day. Jenny had snatched her beautiful boy up from his pram and run with him, across the goat paddock to Harry and Elsie's house. The Hoopers hadn't followed her there.

He'd been eight months old the day Vern took out his cheque-book and offered five hundred pounds for her signature on his piece of paper. Five hundred was a fortune back when the basic wage had been thirty bob a week. She'd shredded his paper and told him where he could shove it and his chequebook.

It's your prerogative, girlie. Take my money now or let the courts decide that you're not fit to raise dogs.

She'd had to run further than Harry and Elsie's house that time. She'd taken a ten-month-old baby by train to Sydney. Jim had a week's leave from the army. He'd wanted them to marry. She'd been eighteen, and in 1942, eighteen-year-old girls had required their parents' permission to marry. She'd worn his ring. For two years she'd waited in Sydney for the army to be done with him. She'd called herself Mrs Hooper, had worked as Jenny Hooper.

She'd sung with a band of elderly gentlemen, sung at parties, weddings, dances, and on Friday nights she'd sung at a servicemen's club for tips.

Should have put her age up and married him before he'd been sent overseas. She would have been the one informed by the war department. Vern Hooper had been informed when Jim was reported missing in action. He'd informed Granny, who'd informed Jenny, but missing hadn't meant dead, not when she'd been nineteen.

Jimmy was three years old before she brought him home. She was twenty, plenty old enough by then to believe the Hoopers' lies. An hour after she'd stepped inside Granny's door, Vern and his daughters had been knocking on it. She'd asked them if there'd been any news of Jim.

Dead, that old bastard had said. *You need to do the right thing now by his boy. He'll inherit everything I've got when I'm gone. He'll get every penny Jim's mother left to him.*

As if she'd give Jim's son away. He was all she'd had left of a love affair that might have begun when she was four years old.

When the war ended, for a time she'd dreamed that Jim had been found somewhere, then Norman, her father, died. The night of his funeral, Granny told her that Norman hadn't been her father, not by blood, that she'd been born to a Juliana Conti, an Italian woman. Too much to swallow. It wouldn't go down. Then Ray King wanting to marry her – and who else would marry a girl who'd given birth to three illegitimate children?

She hadn't loved Ray. She'd pitied him. She'd been honest with him too. She'd told him that she'd never have another baby. He'd said he wanted her, not babies. He'd had a house in Armadale. He'd had a job. She'd married him to give her kids a name, to get them out of Woody Creek, and to put distance between Jimmy and Vern Hooper.

For six months being Mrs King had seemed possible, then Maisy Macdonald told her that Jim had been carried alive from a Japanese prisoner-of-war camp. Thereafter, sleeping with Ray had seemed like adultery. Twice he'd got her pregnant. Vroni Andrews, a neighbour, had aborted Ray's babies.

That was how Vern Hooper won. The second abortion landed Jenny in hospital and the police became involved. Somehow Vern Hooper had got his hands on the details of that abortion and threatened to plaster those details on the front page of every news-paper in Australia.

Murder of the innocent, Granny used to say of abortion. She hadn't known what Jenny had done, twice, and could never be allowed to know. The Hoopers had blackmailed Jenny into signing Jimmy over to Jim and had she known of his condition at the time, she wouldn't have done it. He'd signed his own papers. Margaret Hooper and her husband had adopted Jimmy.

And Lila knew. She commented on that rusting fence with pee.

*

Trudy was discussing a Margaret Morrison when Jenny walked into the kitchen. The power was on, Nick was sprawled on Jenny's easy chair, taking care of his back. The others sat around the table.

'Where have you been?' Trudy asked.

'Just walking. Who is Margaret Morrison?'

'A neighbour,' Trudy said, with a barely perceptible wink in Georgie's direction. 'I thought she might have been one of your father's family?'

Something was bubbling hard in a saucepan. Wood stoves have no knobs to adjust. Jenny knew where to place that saucepan so its contents would simmer.

'Trude thinks she's her birth mother,' Nick said.

Jenny glanced at her son-in-law. 'Lila's home,' she warned him, then turned to Paul, who asked if she had any pasta. It was excuse enough to step into the pantry where she hid her face a moment from Trudy's eyes. She'd have to be told about Margot, but not today.

There was little method to her pantry. Most feared to enter it, but she could quickly put her hand on what was required. She picked up an unopened packet of spaghetti and one that was half full. Paul would be feeding eight tonight.

They were over the shock of Jim's death. The boys were on the floor renewing their acquaintance with their bucket of colouring pencils and Nanny's never-ending supply of scribble paper.

'Where's Katie?'

'She went looking for you,' Georgie said. 'Sit down, Jen.'

Two easy chairs, side by side near the door to the hallway, a matching pair. She looked at Jim's. He'd never sat on her chair. She'd never sat on his – and had no intention of sitting beside Nick anyway.

'Something I have to do,' she said, then left them to discuss birth mothers and pasta while she collected Jim's china ladies. On the walk home from the cemetery she'd decided to bury them with him, but remembered that Katie had always loved them.

Two by two, she took them down to the library, only a library in name because of its two walls of built-in bookshelves. They stored more than books, and she stood scanning them for a carton large enough to hold Jim's ladies. There were boxes aplenty but none large enough. She turned to a tower of cartons, stacked like bricks beside the window wall. One of them would do the job. They were full of free copies of Juliana Conti novels; a few of the cartons had never been opened. The reprints. She'd ripped her way into the others, needing to see the finished item, to hold it – then to sit down and read it.

She found what she was looking for on the floor, pushed beneath her sewing-machine bench. It was full of fabric, off-cuts, dress lengths she'd never got around to making up, fabrics she could barely recall buying. She upended it on the floor, then began wrapping Jim's ladies in off-cuts before burying them carefully in the carton, and cushioning each layer with a dress length. A mass grave, she thought.

There was a roll of duct tape on one of the bookshelves, and memory in the sealing of that carton. If you live too long, every-thing is memory.

Her finger was throbbing, and the young doctor's bandage dusty before she was done. The ceilings of this house rained dust. She stood tall a moment, stretching her back, looking at the bandage and thinking Panadol until she heard Trudy and Nick outside the window and moved quickly out of their view. Her chair was where she'd last sat on it, a new office chair and comfortable. Her legs wanted to sit down, so she sat.

'I said I'd drive you up here. I didn't say I'd stay until Monday.'

'I need my car – and your support, Nick,' Trudy said.

It was her car, registered in her name three years ago. Teddy Hall found it for her, a six-year-old Commodore with only fifty-seven thousand kilometres on the clock. Jim paid for it. It had done a lot of kilometres since, most of them on the road to and from Willama.

'I'll be back in time for the funeral,' he said.

'I need the car tomorrow. I want to take the boys down to say goodbye to Dad.'

'Use your mother's.'

'Their car seats are in mine, Nick!'

'Then take them out of yours!'

'You're not taking it, and if you're in agony now, you'll be in worse agony before you get there.'

The trip to Croydon would take three and a half hours or more. A man with a bad back didn't put himself through that for no good reason. What was his reason? Lila? Maybe. His in-laws, who had little to say to him? His boys' demands?

Some men are born to be fathers. Jimmy was ten months old before Jim met him, but for the week they'd been together in Sydney, he'd never been far from his father's arms. Jenny had believed it was a blood thing, one Hooper recognising another. It had nothing to do with blood. By birth Trudy was Jenny's grand-daughter. She had no blood link to Jim, but from day one, he'd been her adoring Daddy.

Norman may not have been born to the job but he'd done his best, and done it alone for seven years, seven happy years. They'd eaten a lot of fried sausages, boiled a lot of potatoes – and made the best fried cheese sandwiches. From the age of three to ten, Jenny had lived happily with Norman and Sissy. Then Amber came home, and sausages and fried cheese sandwiches and happy went out the window.

Jenny hadn't gone to Amber's funeral. She'd sung at Norman's. She'd sung at many funerals. Her first, when she'd been fourteen, at little Barbie Dobson's. Twenty-two when Norman died. She'd gone straight from the cemetery to the railway house to pack Norman's life away, then to ride his bike home to Granny.

And he'd been there, Archie Foote, Granny's philandering husband, buying eggs.

He'd known Juliana Conti – in the biblical sense, a foreign woman who'd come to Woody Creek on the evening train, given birth to Jenny, then died before telling anyone her name or where she'd come from. Amber, Granny's daughter, delivered of a second dead son the next day, the living infant had been swapped for the dead.

Born a Conti, turned Morrison by default, became Mrs King for all the wrong reasons, then forty years ago she'd become Mrs Hooper. Jim had wanted Trudy, but only if they could legally adopt her. Adopting couples had to be married in those days. They'd used the wedding ring he'd bought for Jenny in Sydney.

Elsie and Harry Hall had named Trudy for Granny. They'd registered her birth. Jenny hadn't expected that tiny baby to live. Cut two months early from Margot's swollen belly, Trudy had spent two months in a city hospital.

Elsie and Harry had planned to raise her. Jenny hadn't, or not until that call came from the hospital. Harry and Elsie couldn't get down to Melbourne to take delivery of their granddaughter until the weekend. Jenny, working in Frankston at the time, had agreed to collect Margot's baby and care for it until they arrived.

She'd never loved Margot. She'd done her duty by her and little more. She'd felt no instant rush of grandmotherly love for that undergrown infant. To this day, she didn't know how, where or when it had happened, only that somewhere on the road between that city hospital and Frankston, as a ewe in the paddock will recognise the scent of its own lamb, she'd recognised Trudy as her own.

She and Jim had changed the Gertrude Maria Hall-Morrison to Trudy Juliana Hooper, and the night her new birth certificate arrived, Jim burnt the original. There'd be a copy of it sealed away in some dusty file. Those files were now being opened to the flood of babies given up for adoption before Gough had made unwed motherhood a viable career choice. Only two times in her life had Trudy mentioned her adoption – when she'd inherited Lorna's house and money she'd said she'd felt like a fraud, then when she'd been carrying the twins, she'd been concerned about possible genetic issues. Sooner or later she'd apply for her birth certificate.

She wouldn't like what she found. She'd known Margot and been afraid of her. She liked Teddy Hall, her blood father.

He was as tall as Harry but had Elsie's colouring. Trudy had inherited his colouring and enough of his tall genes to cancel Margot's stumpy frame. At times, when she cried and clenched her jaw, Jenny saw the shadow of Margot in her face, only a brief shadow.

There wasn't a whisper of Jenny in her, though perhaps a smidgen of Itchy-foot – Archie Foote – had leaked into her character. He'd spent his life travelling the world, never thinking of tomorrow, and like Trudy, had returned to his native shores with little more than his well-travelled luggage.

The voices outside the window had grown louder, and Jenny stilled her mind to listen. The neighbours would be listening. She stood and walked over to hide behind the sheer curtains.

They were at the car, removing the boys' car seats.

'You're a self-obsessed, thoughtless pig of a man, and if you leave today, then don't bother coming back.'

'I said I'd be back for the funeral!'

The phone was ringing in the hall. Paul took the call. 'Jen's resting,' he said. 'Thank you. I'll tell her you called.'

At first sight, Jenny had liked Paul. She'd known she would. Georgie had taken her time in choosing him, taken so much time,

Katie had been lucky to be born. She was a mixture of her parents. She had Paul's eyes and his freckle or two, Georgie's copper hair but Jenny's curls. A perfect mix, Katie Dunn, or to a grandparent's eyes she was perfection – and to Lila's eyes. Her return silenced the arguing pair in the driveway. Nick got into the car, and the way he threw himself into the driver's seat didn't suggest that he had a bad back.

Gone then, and Jenny hoped he didn't return on Monday.

There'd be a crowd at the funeral. She'd have to wear her black suit, have to wriggle into pantihose, wear shoes with heels –

And after the suit and the pantihose and shoes came off, what then? Book myself on a cruise and jump overboard between some place and the next? she thought.

Me and my dog walk together, in cold weather or hot. Me and my dog don't care whether we bloody well live or not, she thought. I probably wouldn't drown. Someone would toss me a lifebelt and I'd grab it with both hands.

She'd taught the twins to swim before they could walk – as she'd taught Georgie, as she'd taught Jimmy.

What would Nick teach his sons?

In their wedding photographs, he'd looked like a beautiful boy, his hair as dark as Trudy's but longer. He was losing it. He wore it short now. Give him a year or two more and he'd be as bald as his father. He had his father's heavy-lidded eyes, very dark, impossible to see behind.

'A law unto himself,' Jim had said.

Hadn't been around when the twins were born. Jenny had been in this room writing when Trudy crept to the door. 'My waters have broken, Mum,' she'd said. 'They're coming.' She'd been at a lot of births. She'd had no fear.

Jenny had feared. All the way to Willama she'd feared that she'd have to pull over and deliver a pair of Macdonalds beside the road, but they'd made it to the hospital. She'd been gowned and masked before Ricky's head of black hair emerged and she'd howled with relief. Every Macdonald ever born had looked like a hairless grub at birth. Jamey arrived minutes later, as dark and with the same amount of hair.

They were out there now with Katie, cupping their hands to the window glass, spying on Nanny, calling to her. She waved to them. They responded by slapping at the window until Katie took them away.

I should be out there enjoying them, Jenny thought, but they'd leave again on Monday.

She'd never wondered what she'd do if she lost those boys. They'd been her own from the instant of their birth. She'd lost them, as she'd lost Jimmy.

Lost.

Wrong word. It was too small to describe the empty agony of loss.

She used to search the crowds of Melbourne for Jimmy, used to search the 'Births, Deaths and Marriages' columns in the *Herald Sun* for James Hooper, James Morrison, James Grenville-Langdon, then two days before Trudy and Nick flew home from London, she'd found her boy when she hadn't been searching. Found him at a television studio.

Georgie and Katie had talked her into playing Juliana Conti on a morning show. They'd bought her a dark brown wig that covered most of her face, bought her a lolly pink suit from an op-shop. Makeup plastered on thick, a pair of dark-framed glasses that blurred the world.

She'd been spaced out, clutching a packet of cigarettes and looking for an exit when Georgie caught her eye with a wave. She'd wanted to introduce her to a tall grey-headed chap.

'Juliana, meet Morrie,' she'd said. 'He's Cara's husband.'

Jenny, who'd spent that last hour in front of cameras with Cara had been running from her, but her husband had offered his hand.

She'd known him the instant she'd shaken his hand. It was Jim's hand. She'd known his little Jimmy boy smile when she'd looked up at his face, then dropped his hand and run from him and the realisation of what he'd done. Until that day she'd had no secrets from Georgie, but how could she tell her that she'd introduced her own brother as Cara's husband? She couldn't.

She'd caught the bus home to Jim, and when she'd arrived back here she couldn't tell him. She'd told her computer. Computers don't accuse.

I've searched for him for fifty years and I find him when I'm not searching, when I can't tell him who I am. I can't tell Georgie. She spent an hour talking to him and she didn't have a clue who he was.

Margaret Hooper and her husband would have changed his family name when they adopted him, but for some reason they allowed him to keep the Morrison. Morrie he calls himself, a shortened version of Morrison . . .

She'd poured her heart out in the dead of night, had got her word count up to thirty thousand. Then Trudy at the door, needing to get to the hospital. She'd closed the *Jimmy* file mid-sentence.

A full stop had been added later, but little more. She'd saved it to disc then deleted the *Jimmy* file from her laptop.

SUNDAY NIGHT

Nine-fifteen and no sign of Nick. Trudy texting, phoning his number, his mother's number, his sisters. They hadn't seen him.

He'd be back. His wife was only one small step away from becoming a wealthy woman. Years ago, Jenny and Jim had made wills, each of them leaving their all to the surviving partner unless they died together, when the lot would go to Trudy. Georgie, always too independent, hadn't needed money, and there'd been no thought of a son-in-law or grandchildren when they'd made those wills.

There was one item Jenny had never intended leaving to Trudy. She could fix that tonight.

Her jewellery box was on her dressing table – her box via Granny, Granny's via Archie Foote, his via Juliana. The first time Jenny had seen it, she'd wondered at the patient hands of its craftsman. He'd inlaid its dark wooden lid with ivory and mother of pearl. Jim, who'd had some knowledge of antiques, believed that box could have had an earlier owner than Juliana.

It contained little of value, other than the brooch. Only once had Jenny worn it, and all day she'd kept grabbing at her lapel, afraid she'd lose it. Her pearl in a cage pendant was kept with the brooch. It wasn't junk but wasn't the original pendant either. Raelene had got away with the original. A Willama jeweller replicated it. It matched the earrings that were never far from her lobes, but the knowledge that Juliana had never worn that pendant devalued it in Jenny's eyes.

Also in the box was a blue glass necklet, which had no value, other than sentimental. Norman had given it to her for her twenty-first birthday. She used to wear it with a blue linen frock. She'd worn Granny's amber necklace the night she'd come third in the radio talent quest – and many times since, when her hair had been gold. Amber didn't match beige–grey hair. Jim's letters from the war years were in the bottom of her jewellery box. They had value, as did three old bankbooks. She glanced at them. They told the story of Vern Hooper's blood money, from 1947 to 1976, when Jim had suggested she invest it in a term deposit. She flipped through the letters, seeking an envelope that was new. He'd known where she'd kept his old army letters. He could have added a new one.

He hadn't.

She'd searched the house this morning for his final letter, had flipped through every one of their favourite books, expecting his note to fall out. She'd found old bookmarks but that was all.

Her handbag was on the floor between the bed and dressing table. She unzipped it, unzipped its inner pocket and removed her diamond rings. She wouldn't wear them again. He'd decided that he'd had enough of her and life, had waited until the coast was clear, then crept away like a thief in the night, never giving a thought as to how she was going to survive without him. She looked at her wedding ring and at the engraving on its inner circle, then dropped it back into the pocket and zipped it in safe. The other two rings she took with her jewellery box to the kitchen.

'See if these will fit your finger,' she said, placing the two rings on the table in front of Trudy, who put her mobile down to look at them.

'They could use a clean,' she said.

'They're yours. You clean them,' Jenny said, and handed the gold filigree bauble to Katie, who placed her playing cards face down on the table to take it.

'I love that,' she said.

'It's yours, darlin',' Jenny said.

'It's too precious, Nanny. I'll lose it.'

'You won't lose it,' Jenny said and Trudy passed the rings back. 'Your dad would want you to have them. Try them on.'

'He bought them for you. My wedding ring is in a drawer, Mum.'

'Then put them in a drawer – or sell them. Your father paid fifteen hundred for one of them and damn near as much for the other, years ago,' Jenny said, as she delved deeper into the box for Juliana's brooch.

It was worth more than fifteen hundred. She held it to the light, watching fire flash from the stones, and as Georgie placed a mug of coffee beside the jewellery box, Jenny handed her the brooch.

In her mind it had always gone to Georgie. She knew its story, had heard as an eight-year-old how that brooch had fallen from Juliana's coat the night Granny washed blood from it in her old wooden wash trough, how for years it had lain in the dirt beneath the trough.

After the Hoopers stole Jimmy, Granny had brought that brooch out to her kitchen and suggested they sell it, that they use the money to chase Vern Hooper through the courts. They'd passed it around the table that night, and when Jenny had handed it to Georgie, she'd known it was too precious to hold and allowed it to lie on her open palm – as she held it now, her eyes flashing that same green fire they'd flashed by lamplight.

It was a golden oval with a ruby the size of a five-cent coin at its centre. The diamonds and rubies surrounding it weren't small. In 1948 it would have been worth enough to pay a top Melbourne barrister, but the Hoopers would have won. Back then, no court in the land would have returned Jimmy into the care of a woman known to have aborted her husband's baby. She would have lost Jimmy, lost Juliana's brooch and Granny's respect, though maybe not her love.

'It's worth a fortune,' Georgie said.

'It's been hiding in the dark for too long. Wear it on your lapel the next time you have to go to court. It will dazzle the magistrate.'

'You'll be sorry later,' Trudy said.

She was sorry about a lot of things. She was sorry she had to go to that church tomorrow, sorry she'd agreed to sing *Ave Maria*, but sorry about giving what she loved to those she loved? Not likely.

Katie was attempting to open a grey leather drawstring pouch, worn grey by the hundred years it had protected Granny's amber beads, its leather drawstring stiffened by those years. She got its knots undone and poured the necklet to the table.

'Were these Juliana's?'

'Granny's,' Georgie said, reaching for the beads. 'Itchy-foot bought it for her somewhere in Africa. There's an insect trapped in one of them.'

'It's near the centre,' Jenny said.

Georgie found it, and Katie and Paul were as enthralled by that prehistoric mozzie as Jenny had been the day Granny showed it to her.

Katie wanted to see the insect under a magnifying glass. She ran to get it. Trudy wanted her mobile to ring.

'He could have had an accident.'

'He could be driving too and can't answer his phone,' Georgie said.

Trudy took her turn with the magnifying glass, then used it to study the lid of the box.

'Remember the day Raelene almost got away with it?' she said. 'I saw her creeping out the glass door with your box under her arm and you took off like the cavalry when I told you.'

'I wore a bruise the size of a football on my thigh for weeks after,' Jenny said. 'She was wearing my new boots, but I got my jewellery box. That's how the lid was chipped.'

It was after ten when Trudy gave up waiting and went to bed. The boys would be up and running early.

'Canasta, Nanny?' Katie asked.

'Why not, darlin'?'

They played then, Jenny and Katie against Georgie and Paul, Georgie wearing Juliana's brooch on her black sweater, Katie wearing her pendant. The rings remained on the table. They remained there until Paul called it quits and he went to bed. Jenny, who didn't want tomorrow to begin, sat there fiddling with the diamond rings Trudy had left behind until Katie fetched Woody Creek's centenary book, a coffee-table book that was kept on a radiogram in the sitting room. There were small photographs of Jim and John McPherson on the back cover, John, the town photographer. He hadn't taken that photograph. He'd taken the one of Granny's house on the book's front cover and every photograph inside it. The mills were in it, the schoolchildren, and child Jenny, child Jim – and bloody Vern Hooper and his daughters.

'I should have married Jim in '42,' Jenny said, and she opened the jewellery box and took out his parcel of love letters.

'You're supposed to tie them with blue ribbons, not old wool,' Katie said.

'It's from an old spinster lady's cardigan,' Jenny said. 'It brings back memories. Everything brings back memories.'

'Have you still got the letter Pa left for you in your bankbook?' Katie knew what Jenny had been searching for in odd places.

'Every letter he wrote to me during the war is in there, darlin'.'

'Wasn't your first husband jealous of you keeping an old boyfriend's love letters?'

'He couldn't read,' Georgie said. 'Go to bed, Katie. It's late.'

'I didn't get up until afternoon. Can I read them one day, Nanny?'

'Ignore her, Jen. She pesters me about Itchy-foot's diaries.'

'She's going to be a historian like her grandpa,' Jenny said, then sorted through the letters for a particular stamp and its postmark. She found the one she needed tonight. 'There's not a thing in any one of your Pa's letters that you couldn't read. He was a gentleman. He wrote this one to me before I went up to Sydney – before the army censors started taking to his letters with black pens.'

There were two pages in the envelope. She glanced at both, then passed them to Katie. 'Read it to me, darlin'. I want to but . . .'

'You're allowed to howl, Jen,' Georgie said. Jenny shook her head but made no reply.

Dear Jen, Katie read.

I sent a telegram to the solicitor demanding that he ignore Pop's instructions. I've written to him too, told him that we're engaged and that we're getting married as soon as I get back down south. He was Mum's solicitor before he was Pop's and he's holding a lot of her money in trust for me. He'll do what I ask.

You, dirt beneath my feet? Moon dust maybe, sprinkling down from a moon far too high above my head for me to ever reach. Think back for a minute, Jen. While you were winning talent quests, having your photograph in newspapers, I was the town drongo, tagging around behind Margaret and Sissy and pleased to have someone to tag around behind. I wouldn't wish on anyone what happened to you, but it put the moon and stars within my reach.

I've been giving a bit of thought to how I might have felt about that photograph of your other kids, and all I can say with any honesty, is that they are half you and they're Jimmy's half-sisters, and they'd probably grow on me – and even if they didn't, I promise I'd do the right thing by them. There's one sure way to put a stop to Pop's plans, so stop putting up barbwire fences and say you'll marry me.

You told me that you'd loved me since you were four years old, since I taught you the right way to eat an ice-cream. Just try for a second to think what that must have been like for me, Jim Hooper, town drongo, hearing that and being able to write it on paper tonight. It makes me a bigger and better man . . .

There was more, but Katie couldn't read it. She put the pages down, hugged Jenny goodnight, then went to bed. Georgie followed her. Jenny had never howled publicly but she was close to doing it.

GREENSBOROUGH

*T*he worst day of Katie's young life over, she was healing now. Sitting in the back seat of the car, her iPod blasting directly into her ear canals, she had her eyes closed.

Many times Georgie had claimed she could do this trip blindfolded. Today Katie played guessing games with herself as to where they were on the road. At the end of each song, she opened her eyes to see how far wrong she'd guessed.

She guessed right with the roadhouse, only because the car slowed then turned right. They always stopped at that same roadhouse for coffee and chips. Back when she'd been in primary school, every school holiday, her parents and grandparents used to meet at that roadhouse, swap her and her case from one car to the other, then turn around and drive home. It was the halfway mark between Woody Creek and Greensborough.

Given optimum conditions, they could do the trip in three hours. They'd left Woody Creek at four-thirty, so should be home by seven-thirty or before. They'd wasted no time at the roadhouse tonight but eaten their chips and drunk takeaway cappuccinos in the car.

They tried to talk Jenny into driving back with them, but she'd kept saying, 'I'm fine,' like a robot with a limited vocabulary. They'd delayed and delayed until they'd had to leave, or they'd be driving home in the dark.

She'd been robotic at the funeral. She'd walked into the church holding tight to Katie's hand, had sat beside her in the front pew, her eyes never leaving that flower-bedecked coffin. She hadn't cried.

She hadn't sung either.

The organist had expected her to sing *Ave Maria.* He'd played the introduction three times before giving up. She'd been going to sing *The Last Rose of Summer* at the graveside and hadn't done that either. She'd stood behind that iron fence until the parson was done with his words. Then she'd thrown a red rose down that gaping hole, taken Katie's hand again and walked away.

They'd been home well ahead of the others, had time to make a pile of salad sandwiches. Trudy and Nick stayed long enough to eat. The twins screamed blue murder when they were carried out to the car. One screaming three-year-old was loud. Two had every dog in the street barking, and Lila. She thought those boys were her pups.

A song started that Katie had loved when she'd loaded it onto her iPod. It was too sad today, so she turned it off then removed her earplugs.

Usually on long trips, she took the opportunity to question her parents, while she had them captive in the car. They were still twenty minutes from home. She had time.

'Was Trudy's nose out of joint because Nanny gave me Pa's ladies?' she asked. The carton, heavy with china, was riding beside her in the back seat, buckled in.

'They'd last five minutes with the twins,' Georgie replied. She was driving. They always swapped drivers at the roadhouse.

'In other words, yes, her nose was out of joint. Is that why she left in a hurry?'

'He wanted to get home to his mother.'

'She's younger than Nanny and we left her up there alone.'

'His mother isn't well. Trudy was about to tell me what was wrong with her when he arrived.' He'd arrived fifteen minutes before the funeral began.

'She looked so old,' Katie said.

'Jenny?'

'Trudy,' Katie said.

'She's just lost her father,' Paul said.

'What changed her mind about divorcing him, Mum?'

'That's none of your business or mine,' Georgie said.

'She couldn't stand him touching her at the funeral. He tried to put his arm around her when that army bugle started playing but she stepped away.'

'She expected him back last night. If I'd expected your father and he hadn't shown up or contacted me, I'd be niggly too.'

'Is that bugle thing played at all ex-servicemen's funerals?'

'It's a last goodbye,' Georgie said.

'Did you see Nanny cry?'

'She used to tell Margot to save her tears for when she was peeling onions, when they might do some good,' Georgie said. 'Granny was the same. She told us half a dozen times that if we cried at her funeral, she'd come back and haunt us.'

'Did you – at her funeral?'

'She's still haunting me,' Georgie said.

'Do you remember Nanny's first husband's funeral?'

'Why?'

'Did she cry at his?'

'No one cried at his,' Georgie said. 'And he hadn't been her husband for years before he died. He lived in a back room with Donny and he paid Jenny to look after his kids.'

'Like she never forgave him for cheating on her with that Florence woman?'

'He did a lot worse than that,' Georgie said.

'What worse?'

'A lot worse, now enough about him.'

It was all she'd get. She knew he'd moved some Florence woman into his house after Jenny left him, that she'd had Raelene and Donny then she'd left him too. She knew he'd taken those kids up to Jenny, that she'd raised them until he'd died. The Florence woman had hired a solicitor then, to get Raelene back. Just scraps of information, collected where she could and not enough about anything. Last night she'd collected a few new scraps, such as that Raelene had been a thief.

'Was Nanny together with Pa as soon as Ray King died?'

'Why would you ask that?'

'I saw his tombstone on our way back to the gate. The date he died is on it. I know when Trudy was born.'

'She was two months premature,' Georgie said as she turned left at the corner that would take them up to their street.

'Actually premature or on-paper premature?'

'She spent the first month of her life in a hospital incubator. She was two months old before she weighed enough to be released,' Georgie said, and she made a right-hand turn into their street.

'If we got a fence, Nanny and Lila could live with us and I wouldn't have to come home from school to an empty house.'

'We'll book you into after-school care again if you like,' Paul said.

'I'm being serious, Dad. An iron fence with spikes on it like the Hoopers have around their tombstones would keep out robbers – and keep Lila in.'

'She's an old dog accustomed to her own big yard. She'd go stir crazy down here,' Georgie said. 'What Jen needs now is time to come to terms with living alone – and without your advice or interference.'

'It felt horrible, driving away and seeing her standing there alone. There's always been the two of them waving from the veranda. She looked . . . shrunken. And the house looked too big.'

Their own house looked like most houses, just bricks and tiles and windows, a little larger than some, a little smaller than others. It was home, and Katie pleased to be there.

*

That house had been home to Paul for three years before Georgie moved in. He'd shared its rent with two mates. They'd had a history, Georgie and those three guys. She'd first met them in Darwin, then again up the top of Western Australia, then in Adelaide, and when the youngest of them had moved up to Sydney, Georgie had taken over his room and his share of the rent.

It had a rented-house garden. The lawns hadn't been mowed in twelve months. She'd mowed them. She'd planted a lemon tree in the centre of the front lawn, an apricot tree near the fence, then a passing bird had sown a fig tree. It was too close to the house but it had liked that position and thrived – and grew bigger and better figs than Granny's fig tree ever had.

Given time, she'd got rid of the back lawn and turned it into a vegie garden. No trees grew there. The neighbours' trees already stole too much of its sunlight.

She nosed her red Mazda in close to the garage door and turned off its motor. They had a double garage, built on the east and north fencelines. Paul's Ford and her old red utility were parked under cover. She was first out most mornings, last home most nights. Her Mazda had spent its six months of life in the open.

They spoke about selling the ute. It only saw daylight when they needed to take a load to the tip or to carry anything that wouldn't fit in her hatchback. But it was a part of her history and she didn't want it sold off like an old horse who'd had his day.

Katie brought the carton of china ladies inside; Paul and Georgie carried the cases. The house unlived in for four nights smelt musty.

They'd dropped everything when that call came through from the police. They'd been out the door in five minutes, mugs left on the sink, phone on the table – a dead flat phone tonight. Georgie put it on its charger, Paul opened the windows, while Katie took her mobile from her pocket and called Jenny. They always phoned to let her know that they'd made it home intact.

It rang half a dozen times then went through to the answering machine.

Neither Jen nor I are available to take your call. Please leave your name and number and we'll get back to you.

Katie cut that call fast, put her mobile on the bench and stepped away from it. 'We should have fixed the answering machine. Why didn't one of us think to fix it for her?'

Georgie phoned the number, and again the ghost of Jim answered her call. She left a brief message.

'Where would she be at this time of night?' Katie asked. 'She never goes out at night.'

'Her world has changed. Her habits will change with it. Have a shower and get your things ready for school,' Paul said.

'Can I phone Harry and ask if she's around there?'

'No,' Georgie said. 'And you can't start worrying every time she doesn't answer her phone either.'

'It sounded like Pa's ghost. We should have changed that message.'

'Send her a text,' Paul said.

Katie picked up her phone as if it were haunted. *We're home, Nanny. Where are you?*

She replied. *I'm booked into the Gold Rush Motel, in Willama. I'm going to see a movie.*

'She's going to see a movie,' Katie relayed. *What movie?* she texted.

Pirates of the Caribbean.

I've seen it. You'll love it.

'Told you so,' Georgie said. 'She's got the resilience of a rubber band.'

THAT HOUSE

Jenny knew the Gold Rush Motel. She and Jessica Palmer had shared a room there one night, before Trudy moved out. They'd gone to the movies. The cinema was only a pedestrian crossing away from the motel office. She was down there tonight, not because of the movie but because the walls of Vern Hooper's house had started breathing, but good, bad or indifferent, movies sometimes stopped her thinking. In Armadale, when she'd been with Ray, she and Jimmy had sat through a lot of bad movies.

At seven-forty, she stopped the traffic at the crossing and walked alone to the cinema, where she bought a solitary ticket and wandered in, to sit alone and feel lonely. She was and would be forever more.

She was thinking cruise ships, thinking she'd need to make a new will before booking her cruise. She was thinking of how she'd approach the subject with Georgie, how she might get Jim's and her own money tied up tight for the grandkids when the movie commercials stopped playing and the show began. It was a bit of nonsensical fantasy but tonight she needed to escape into fantasy.

That movie got rid of two and a half hours, a cup of tea and two motel biscuits in her anonymous room got rid of an hour more, and when she was done with the motel-supplied tea and biscuits she wished she'd thought to bring a toothbrush. She'd brought nothing. She'd fed Lila two eggs, picked up her handbag and run from the Hooper ghosts.

No ghosts in this room, just traffic noise. The new cinema had been built in one of Willama's main streets. She'd brought no nightgown, and at midnight she stripped to her bra and briefs and slid between tight sheets. The mattress was as hard as the hobs of hell, the pillows too high, but she knew no more until daylight. She hadn't slept, as in slept for more than an hour, since Wednesday night.

Phone Harry, she thought. Ask him to take Lila around to his place for a few days, buy a few supplies and stay down here. He liked Lila. She liked him. Teddy had good fences. The motel had provided a toaster along with an electric jug. She could survive here.

Widows weren't supposed to hide in anonymous motel rooms. They were supposed to keep themselves busy taking phone calls, opening condolence cards, writing replies on thank-you cards then wasting stamps on posting those cards to people who lived around the corner.

She sighed, then turned on the jug and dressed in the clothing she'd shed last night.

Paddy Watson, a recent widower, hadn't written thank-you cards. He'd put an advertisement in the *Gazette*. That's what she ought to do.

The Hooper family wish to thank . . .

What Hooper family? They were all dead. Trudy was a Papadimopolous. Jenny might have been a Hooper on her driving licence, might have booked into this motel as Jenny Hooper, but had never been one of them.

Put an ad in for that house while you're about it, she thought. *Hundred-year-old house with six bedrooms and resident ghost, guaranteed to freeze your bum off in winter and fry it in summer.*

Or burn it down, then do a Georgie. After she'd lost everything in that fire, Georgie had taken off around Australia, had kept driving away until she'd been ready to face the reality of what she'd lost.

Couldn't face no Jim waiting at home, not today, not tomorrow or six months from tomorrow.

No more pills to nag about, no more shirts to iron, no more prosthesis to fetch and hold while he pushed his stump into it. It was with him, down that hole.

She hadn't said goodbye to him, hadn't sung one final song for him.

Trudy had kissed him goodbye. Paul drove her and the twins down here. He'd watched her lift the boys up to kiss their Papa goodbye.

'Papa won't wake up, Nanny,' Ricky had said.

'Stop it! Stop it! Stop it!' Jenny demanded, then checked the time. Not much after eight. She didn't have to give up this room until ten.

She opened her handbag to see how much cash she'd brought with her. A big bag, black, frameless soft leather, not heavy when it wasn't loaded. It was always loaded. The brochure for her dream fridge was still in it. She wouldn't be ordering it now. She found her wallet. Plenty of coins in it. Not enough notes to pay for the room. She had their joint-account Visa card and her own savings card. Always carried them. Jim had carried the chequebook. He would have paid by cheque. He'd paid all of the bills by cheque. Had been able to fill his mornings writing cheques and addressing envelopes, sticking on stamps. If she'd been the one who'd died, he would have been at home writing personal thank-you letters to the neighbours then riding his gopher around to the postbox –

He wouldn't have. He couldn't get in and out of bed without her shoulder to lean on. Couldn't get his foot on unless she held it. Couldn't boil water.

Trudy would have signed him into the nursing home behind the hospital –

Like hell she would have. He hadn't been near a hospital since he'd walked out of that last psychiatric place in the mid-fifties.

He'd attempted to talk Trudy out of a nursing career. That was the first time she'd driven in her heels. 'It's what I want to do, Dad.'

My fault, Jenny thought. She'd filled her head with tales of Granny, Woody Creek's midwife-cum-bush nurse for sixty years. Elsie and Harry had named her for Granny, named her Gertrude, but Granny had been Trude or Trudy to her friends.

Jim's letter to Trudy was still in her handbag. She'd picked it up off the hallstand the day of her haircut and forgotten about it. Tuesday now and the envelope was creased. She flattened it, felt that paperclip again and wondered if a cheque was legal tender when the one who'd signed it was dead.

Should have given it to her, she thought, as she stared at the Croydon address. They lived in a court, at Number 14. She hadn't known that – hadn't been interested enough to ask. Apparently Jim had.

It would be legal tender if she added her signature to it, and with that thought in mind, she started easing the creased envelope open, which was easy enough to do with those self-seal things – if you took it slow.

He hadn't written Trudy a goodbye letter. There were two lines of his handwriting on a full sheet of paper.

My dearest Trudy. You were always a wise girl. Please use the enclosed wisely. As always, Love from Dad XX

'Why not add, *I'm off now to drown myself. Have a good life,*' Jenny asked that note. She was composing more when she saw *Fifty Thousand Dollars* written on the cheque – then the figures. *$50,000.*

Those figures got her to her feet. 'You bloody fool of a man!'

He'd written cheques to Trudy before, for birthdays, for Christmas. He'd written one for five thousand as a wedding present, but this was madness. Fifty thousand dollars would have gone close to emptying their joint account.

It would have bought Nick a 4WD. A nine-year-old navy-blue Commodore didn't match his designer jeans and pigskin jacket –

He wasn't getting his 4WD. She didn't add her signature to the cheque, she shredded it. She shredded Jim's note, then shredded the shreds. The motel had provided a bin. She shredded the envelope, apart from the corner with the stamp. With a bit of glue, it would post one of her thank-you cards.

Found a comb in her handbag, the tail end of a lipstick and sunscreen face lotion. It stung if you got it in your eyes. She allowed them to sting while using the lipstick, while wetting and combing her too-short hair. It would grow. It grew too fast. The bag over her shoulder then, she unlocked the door and walked across the car park to the office to pay for her night's lodging with the joint Visa card.

'Fifty thousand dollars!'

She needed milk. Had to open an emergency carton of long-life milk yesterday and been pleased to find it in her pantry. Milk used to be a daily commodity. What she'd opened yesterday might have been in her pantry for six months. Didn't know what the factories added to it to keep it tasting fresh. Like the rest of the human herd, she'd checked its use-by date, opened it, smelt it, then poured it into her tea.

Granny's goats used to supply milk fresh morning and night. With only the old Coolgardie safe to keep it cool, it had been on the turn by the next day, fit for pudding but not much else.

She unlocked her car, got in and started it up. It always started. At the pedestrian crossing she had to give way to a bike rider, a girl with a little boy in a carry-seat, a pretty dark-headed girl who appeared little older than Katie. Her infant might have been the twins' age.

Silly little girl, Jenny thought. Too many of us settle for mother-hood before we've had a chance to grow up and find out who we are. Then before we know it, we've been abandoned on the scrapheap, too old to start again.

She made a left-hand turn out to the street, then drove on down to the business centre of town where she found a park in front of the Commonwealth Bank. A dollar bought her half an hour of time and the bank wasn't open.

The ATM in the bank wall was. She'd never withdrawn from their Visa account, but if Jim had been prepared to buy Nick a 4WD, then why not spend that money? She inserted the card, had to think to remember his PIN, then tried 2113. It worked. Users were warned not to use their dates of birth. Jim had used a portion of hers, in reverse. She asked that machine for a thousand. Didn't need a thousand. It was her finger's response to Nick's 4WD, but the machine didn't argue about it, just went into counting mode, then spat out a pile of fifties.

I've lived to see an amazing world, she thought – or caught glimpses of an amazing world while moving through it like an uncomplaining goat who'd found a safe paddock to graze in. The old goat looked over her shoulder for a robber as she stuffed the notes into her bag. Jim would have stood there counting. When he'd been forced to use Woody Creek's ATM, he'd stood counting. He would have studied the receipt. She glanced at it and was proven right about Nick's fifty thousand. Had she posted that cheque on Thursday, there wouldn't have been enough cash left in that account to pay the motel bill.

'We can't choose who we fall in love with, Mum,' Trudy had said. 'I know his faults, but none of us are without fault.'

They'd tried to raise her faultless. Jim had written huge cheques each term to educate her. They'd done everything right with Trudy, but somewhere along the way they'd got it wrong.

Trudy had never mentioned Nick's name until he'd flown overseas with her and Sophie on what was supposed to be a twelve-month working holiday. Sophie came home. Trudy and Nick didn't.

They'd married in Greece, spent their honeymoon volunteering in Africa with a medical group. For some reason, Jenny had believed that Trudy's new husband had been in the medical profession. He might have been, might have become a dentist had he completed his university course. He'd dropped out midway through his second year.

She crossed over the road at the lights, then walked on, her mind back at that motel. If not for Lila, she could live in motel rooms, no stove to keep burning, only one bill to worry about. She could see all the new movies.

A table of sweaters reduced to half price caught her eye. They were thirty-five per cent wool, long enough, of the fine knit she preferred to wear but not a lot of choice in colour, or not in her size. They had a sickly green, a pinkish red, a greyish beige. She didn't like beige, but she bought the beige. It matched her hair, and if she decided to stay another night, she'd need a change of clothing.

Gave way to a car and caravan at the post-office intersection. Two grey heads in the car, off together on an adventure. Years ago, she'd nagged Jim to buy a caravan and drive off into the sunset with her. He could have. Once Trudy had been safe at school, they could have travelled. She'd nagged him into flying to England in the mid-sixties. When he'd agreed, it had nothing to do with her nagging. John and Amy McPherson talked him into taking the trip.

'Never again,' he'd said before they got there. He'd been too tall for cramped plane seats and in the sixties the trip had taken longer.

They'd seen Paris. They'd rented a unit in London. They'd caught a train to Thames Ditton. Lorna Hooper had given Jim their sister Margaret's address, Jimmy's address. *Langdon Hall, Thames Ditton.*

A taxi driver delivered them to a flat-faced old manor house, and the size of it put Vern Hooper's house to shame. It had a front door built for giants, a lion's head knocker. Jim had knocked. Jenny had hammered that lion's head down, then Amy made them laugh with her suggestion that Lurch, from the *Addams Family* would open the door with his usual, '*You rang*'. The door hadn't opened, and twenty minutes later, their waiting taxi had dropped them back at the station.

A travel agency window drew her mind back to the moment, or an advertised return flight to London for only fourteen hundred and ninety dollars. Jim had probably paid as much or more in the sixties. They were advertising cruises too, one for under a thousand dollars.

Book it, she urged.

But why look at cheap? This morning she had fifty thousand to spend – minus the motel, minus the thousand in her bag. She walked on to the *Gazette* office, where she placed her thank-you advertisement, brief, no hearts, no flowers.

'In Saturday's *Gazette*,' she said. The condolence cards should have stopped arriving by Saturday.

Vickery's estate agency was on the corner, its windows full of houses and properties for sale. There were three photographs of houses for sale in Woody Creek – and the photographs looked better than the houses.

Busy Hands

Space, storage capacity and forty years of standing still had allowed every room in the old Hooper house to suffer the fate of the obese. Jenny walked the rooms that Tuesday afternoon, making lists on the backsides of Juliana Conti printouts. She listed the antiques on one, Lorna's antique dining suite, her hallstand, her massive chest of cedar drawers, her bedroom chair. No one had explained the facts of Trudy's birth to Lorna. She'd died believing her to be her niece and the legitimate granddaughter of the great and powerful Vern, and so believing, had named Trudy her sole beneficiary.

Jim offered to store the better pieces of furniture until Trudy needed them, or so he'd said. He'd wanted them. They'd belonged to his mother before they'd belonged to Vern or Lorna. Jenny hadn't known Jim's mother. She'd known Lorna, and every item Jim had moved in smelt of Lorna. The dining room stunk of her, as did the entrance hall.

The library smelt of machine oil, of dusty books and paper. For years Jenny had conducted a dressmaking business from that room. She'd had a buzzer installed beside the glass door so she didn't need to walk her customers through the house. She listed her big old industrial sewing machine on a second sheet of paper, listed her original dining suite. Its chairs were somewhere. Its table, fully extended, was buried beneath computers and a small printer.

The day Paul and Georgie had set up that first desktop computer, they'd needed multiple power points. The library was the only room with enough. She'd had them installed for her sewing machines, iron and small heater. Still had that original computer she'd once named *God*. Still had her larger, more powerful desktop model. Hadn't used it since buying her laptop, smaller but with a huge memory, which she'd needed for the internet.

Her laptop's lid was open. She'd used it last Thursday morning. She closed it, then turned in a circle to survey the plethora of junk she'd allowed to accumulate in here.

One of the bookshelves had become storage space for shoe boxes full of odds and ends, ice-cream containers full of cottons, cartons of leftover wool. There were piles of magazines, a pile of knitting books – you name it and it was on those shelves.

She'd bought a roll of twenty garbage bags at Woolworths. She ripped off the plastic and pulled one bag free, opened it and began ridding those shelves of junk, and when that bag became too heavy, she tied its load in and ripped off another. She had three full garbage bags and one wall of near empty shelves before she turned to Jim's plastic showering chair. She listed it, and his walking frame and his raised toilet seat. The shop where she'd bought those items secondhand would buy them back. They specialised in second-hand aids for the elderly. Her phone was ringing. She allowed Jim to take the call, as he'd been doing since they'd bought the answering machine, as one by one, she dragged the bags down to lean against Lorna's hallstand.

The phone and its answering machine sat on Lorna's hallstand, where its predecessor had lived, close to where Vern Hooper's old box phone had lived. Its red light was flashing messages. They'd wait. She wasn't in the mood to listen to more condolence calls right now. Too angry, but anger was good. It kept the tears at bay.

Jim took another call when she felt angry enough to empty his wardrobe, where clothing had been allowed to hang long after it passed its use-by date. She sorted as she worked, pitched his new suit at the bed and stuffed an older suit into a garbage bag. A maroon cardigan, hot off her knitting needles last spring, flew towards the bed. Harry would wear it. He was of similar height to Jim and hadn't owned a sweater that fit since Elsie put down her knitting needles. Old shirts in the bag, good shirts on the bed, two more sweaters tossed to the bed. She emptied the wardrobe then climbed onto a chair to haul his case down. Packed it one last time, not for Jim, but for Harry, who'd never been too proud to wear secondhand clothing.

By nightfall, the entrance hall loaded with bulging garbage bags, she played her messages. Jessica had phoned twice last night, and Georgie. The estate agent had left the last message. He'd said he'd be in Woody Creek on other business tomorrow morning and would come by with his camera.

She'd put Vern Hooper's house and its ghosts on the market. She didn't want it, never had wanted it, and doubted that anyone else would. A relatively modern brick home opposite the school had been wearing its *For Sale* sign for six months.

To erase all messages, press erase again, the machine told her, a Yankee voice. She pressed erase again and that red light stopped blinking.

Stood looking at the hallstand she'd seen as a goggle-eyed four-year-old the day she'd first entered Vern Hooper's house, clinging tight to Granny's hand. A dark house then, dark wallpaper, long dark drapes, dark polished wooden floors and dark panelling. They'd lightened it, she and Jim. They'd covered the floorboards with a blue–grey carpet, paid a man to remove every scrap of wallpaper, and had the walls above the panelling painted white. Over a period of years, she'd made new drapes for every window. It had almost become Jenny's house until Jim had moved in

Lorna's furniture. That hallstand looked like her, tall, dominating, immovable – and antique.

There were two antique dealers in Willama. Their numbers would be in the telephone book. She reached for it and stood flipping pages until she found the page she needed. She phoned both dealers. Neither one picked up, but she left messages, only her number and that she had a few antiques they might like to look at. She didn't leave her name.

A pair of antique kerosene lamps decorated the dining-room mantelpiece. They'd belonged to Jim's mother, pretty things with ruby-glass bowls embossed with gold. Their bulbous glass shades were dust collectors – and every time she'd dusted them she'd been afraid she'd drop one, smash one. Had always liked those lamps. She'd chosen the material for the dining-room drapes to match their bowls, a claret velvet. She'd fiddled for a week to get the pelmet hanging as the one she'd copied had hung. It was a dust collector but looked good.

Bring him and his camera in here, she thought. It will impress him.

The agent had shown little interest when she'd mentioned that her property was in Woody Creek. He'd shown more when she'd handed him a photograph of Trudy and the twins sitting on the front veranda.

'I know that house,' he'd said. 'It's a fine example of Victorian architecture.'

Old Victoria had been dead when it was built – built by Jim's mother and her first husband. They'd set it in the centre of two large Woody Creek blocks, planted the garden, then the husband died in an accident at his mill. Vern Hooper married the widow and got to enjoy the fruits of his predecessor's labour – and damn near killed the widow by getting her pregnant with a Hooper. Jim was delivered six weeks early at a city hospital. His mother survived the primitive operation – or she had until he'd been six.

He'd been eight, Jenny four the first time they'd met, both of them motherless. A long and skinny, wide-eyed, big-eared goblin boy, unlike any other boy she'd known. He'd owned picture books, had bought her ice-creams. They'd believed themselves to be cousins of a kind, because Granny and Vern Hooper had been half-cousins.

The first blackout Jenny could remember had been in Vern Hooper's house, back when electricity was new to Woody Creek. She'd been sitting on the floor with Jim, surrounded by his books, when the cabinet wireless stopped singing and the light globe went out.

So much for your electricity, Vern Hooper. Where do you keep your lamps? Granny had said.

He'd lit those ruby-glass lamps, and to a four-year-old, they'd looked like fairy land.

She'd loved Hooper's corner in spring when the rose hedge had been in bloom. She'd loved that corner in autumn when the trees had changed their work-a-day green gowns for ballgowns of red and gold. Hadn't loved that corner in winter. The naked grey trees had looked like ghosts and the rose hedge had been all thorns. Didn't want to be alone here in winter.

Lila was patrolling her fenceline when Jenny went out to bring enough wood inside to last the night. She checked the mailbox. More cards, a phone bill and a dividend. Jim had shares in a dozen different companies – she had shares in a dozen different companies.

'Dinner,' she called to Lila. She was an outdoor dog, but Jenny needed her inside tonight. 'Lila. Come in and get an egg.'

A slave to her stomach, Lila came for the promise of an egg, and once inside, Jenny locked her in then opened a can of dog food that smelt good enough to eat. She spooned it into a bowl, garnished it with an egg, and while Lila wolfed her meal, Jenny opened condolence cards.

She'd received one from Sissy. She'd been born to Amber and Norman, was Jim's age, and Jenny was almost pleased to receive that card – until she read the handwritten words beneath the verse.

May that dear man now find the peace he never found in life.

'He found more peace with me than he would have with you,' Jenny said as she walked to the stove, lifted the largest hotplate and dropped the card in to burn. She hadn't heard from Sissy for God knew how many years, and she couldn't even send a condolence card without adding a barb.

Jim had become engaged to Sissy when war broke out – only because his father wanted him to marry someone with hips broad enough to birth Hoopers, and to keep Jim safe from the war. Sissy's hips had qualified her. He'd joined the army to get out of marrying her.

One envelope contained a phone bill. She'd need to pay the phone company a hundred and twenty dollars, but some mining company would pay two hundred and seventy dollars into the Visa account.

Jim had a special place for his dividends and for his bills. She walked down the hallway to the library to place the dividend into Jim's *Dividend* file, the bill into his *Bill* file, then to stand a while staring at that tower of cartons, the publisher's name plastered all over them. She'd need to cover them before allowing that estate agent in here – or maybe not allow him to enter her junk room.

If the house sold, her old computers would have to go to the tip. Should have gone there years ago, but *God* had been where that tower of cartons began – though not really. Juliana Conti, the writer's true birth, had been at Amy McPherson's roll-top desk.

Could still see Amy sitting at it, her hands, twisted with arthritis, hitting her typewriter keys while Jenny read aloud from scribbled notes. How they'd laughed. They'd laughed until they'd cried some days.

They'd taken the idea for *Sent in Chains* from Jim's *Molly* tome. After he and John had put together that pictorial history for Woody Creek's Centenary, they'd received commissions for other historical projects, one of which had got Jim researching the early history of Molliston, a town east of Willama. Over a period of years, he'd compiled many pages of facts, figures and John's photographs – which may well have had historical significance but failed to catch the eye of a publisher.

Poor Molly, transported to Australia for prostitution, had caught Jenny's imagination, and the day Jim decided to burn his tome she'd smuggled most of its pages down to Amy.

They'd stripped them to bedrock, then together began the game of reconnection, justifying what they'd been doing by convincing each other that Jim would appreciate their work when he had publishers knocking down the door to get at survivor Molly.

The game should have ended when Amy and her laughter died. It would have – if not for a deathbed promise. 'Finish *Molly* and dedicate it to me, Jennifer,' Amy had said. 'Promise me, Jennifer.'

People will promise anything when a loved one is dying, but she'd tried. She'd had a rough beginning, a wobbly middle and an unsatisfactory end when fate stepped in.

Georgie, attacked in her own backyard, had been stitched from throat to shoulder. One of her arms was out of action and she'd been pregnant with Katie. Jenny elected herself for the job of nurse/companion/carer and she'd taken her manuscript with her to Greensborough.

You can read with one arm out of action. Georgie read *Molly*. 'Shades of brilliance, mate,' she'd said. 'Get it onto a computer, delete the Jim bits, give Molly a background and you've got a novel.'

It was Paul who'd scanned those dog-eared pages onto computer discs. He'd been the first to sit Jenny down at a computer. She'd stayed longer than necessary in Greensborough. Leaving Jim home alone with Lorna's furniture hadn't done a lot for his mood, nor had the clean computer printout of *Molly Squire* she'd dropped onto his lap, her name with his on the face page.

He might have read six pages before blacking out *Jim Hooper*. 'It's all yours, Jen,' he'd said.

'What's wrong with it?'

'For one, the family will sue you,' he said, and read no more.

She'd given up, had left her manuscript to gather dust while becoming a grandmother to beautiful Katie.

Georgie hadn't given up on *Molly*. She'd been on maternity leave and looking for something to fill her days. She'd altered every name on the *Molly* file, altered every place, altered the title, then so as not to defile the Hooper name, she'd typed *Juliana Conti* on the face page – then posted a new printout to the publisher who'd printed the Hooper/McPherson children's books, seven of them, big colourful magical books that were still selling today.

The publisher's acceptance of *Sent in Chains* caused Jim's first major breakdown, or his first since their marriage. He'd laboured twelve hours a day, three hundred and sixty-five days of the year on his tome. Jenny had fed his work into a demon computer and turned historical fact into popular fiction. He'd seen her computer addiction as a modern form of demonic possession.

She'd been possessed by something. *Before Her Time* came next, then *The Stray*, then *The Winter Boomerang*, then *The Town*. She'd ripped Woody Creek apart in that one. *My Sister*, her last novel, was her favourite, if not her best seller. She'd had the time of her life writing it, had named a dog in that book Sissy – for obvious reasons.

We'll Meet Again had been a lengthier project, in time, not bulk. She'd stolen time from her boys to write it, had stolen time in the dead of night. It was a dark love story. Her thoughts always became darker at night.

Jim read every word of that one. 'Publish it when I'm dead,' he'd said.

'What's wrong with it?' she'd asked.

'Nothing. It's good,' he'd said, and he'd kissed her.

'Stop!' she said, and Lila looked at her, not understanding her command. 'Not you,' she said, and she reached again into Jim's concertina file – her file now.

Her will was in the *Will* pocket. She read it, then ripped it in half and the halves in half. She glanced at the manila envelope that had spent the last three years beside her will. It contained no list of investments, no instructions for her funeral. It contained a disc and its contents were black.

She put it away then turned to the twins' stroller. She and Jim had chosen the best. They'd bought it the day they'd brought Trudy and the boys home from hospital. It was folded up beside those cartons of books, free copies, supplied by the publisher, no doubt supplied for her to give away to friends. She had two friends still living, Harry and Jessica. Jessica had cataracts and was waiting for surgery. Harry read newspapers.

'Dump them,' she suggested. 'Seal them into your garbage bags and dump the lot.'

Didn't have enough garbage bags left, so went to her linen closet for sheets to shroud them. You can see through some sheets. She covered the sheets with an old bedspread, then taped it down securely with duct tape.

LANGDON HALL

*T*racy didn't look like a businesswoman, didn't dress like a businesswoman, but somewhere beneath that cap of dark curls was a mind capable of running the country. She was well on her way to making Morrie's estate pay for itself.

Cara knew enough about computers to use the internet when necessary. To her daughter, the cyber world was a second home. Tracy had uploaded photographs of the Hall, its ballroom and two of its better bedrooms. She'd uploaded photographs of a stone cottage she advertised as *The Gamekeeper's Lodge, a private hideaway in the woods.* It looked better than it was, with the old stone bridge in the background.

Born and raised in a boarding house, having spent the first fourteen years of her life tripping over lodgers, Cara refused to become involved in Tracy and Morrie's business – other than to keep an eye on the figures at the end of each month. The lodge was paying back what they'd spent on it.

At a pinch it would accommodate three couples, and since promoting the Hall on the internet, they'd been swamped with bookings, from overseas tourists, honeymooners, jaded city dwellers, and others.

Well away from the Hall, hidden behind five acres of old woodlands, they rarely saw or heard from those who weekended in the lodge. This weekend, Tracy had handed its keys to a mob of students, wild things, seeking a parental-free place to party, with a stream outside their front door where they could wash away the megrims of the night before. For two nights, those at the house had heard that pounding jungle-beat today's youth named music, heard the roar of late-night motors, racing in, racing out.

The dogs may have heard more. This morning, when set free to run, the young pair decided to take off towards the woods, so Cara and Morrie followed them.

The cars had disappeared in the night. The cottage was silent.

'They've done a runner,' Morrie said, walking faster across the stretch of grass between woods and stream. Cara followed behind, expecting to find a dead body.

The lodge was empty – not empty, but empty of bodies, alive or dead. A hotplate was glowing red. Morrie turned it off.

'Animals,' Cara said. There were bottles everywhere, cans, takeaway cartons, cigarette butts littering every surface. 'What gives them the right to believe they can walk away from this?'

'Daddy's money.' Morrie picked up a bottle. 'He can afford to supply them with the best,' he said, glancing at the label before tossing it into the bin provided.

'Tracy's prices were supposed to keep out the bad element.'

'They were medical students, the doctors who'll be operating on us, the dentists pulling our teeth a year or two from now,' he said, and he showed her another label before sending that bottle crashing after its mate. That was as close as he came to showing his anger, tossing bottles – and cursing the mobile phone that the business, or Tracy, forced him to carry. It beeped this time. Less fond of its beeps than its rings, he passed it to Cara. She wore prescription lens sunglasses.

How do you feel about a May wedding? Down there? She read the message aloud. No need to say who that text was from. They'd raised two very different daughters.

'What's wrong with October in Scotland?' Morrie asked, so that's what Cara texted in reply.

Three guesses? Elise shot back.

You're pregnant!

We are, and we're delighted it happened so fast. It took Felicity and Steve two years to get pregnant after she went off the pill. Have you got a free Saturday in May?

Cara relayed the news as she read it. Elise and Ian had been living together for eighteen months. They had a wide circle of assorted friends. He was older, an architect and the only offspring of Scottish parents who'd been planning a big Scottish wedding with kilts and bagpipes.

'We're booked solid through May and you've got that German thing in June,' Morrie said.

'That's the first weekend. You said you'd keep the following weekend free – and leave that for the cleaners, Morrie. You pay them enough,' Cara said. He was picking up shards of a broken glass.

'They'll demand danger money. That weekend's free, but we're going to hire a car and drive around Germany while we're over there.'

'We can do that any time,' Cara said, and her fingers got busy.

'I need a holiday,' he moaned.

'She needs to get married.'

We've got nothing booked for the second weekend in June. How far along are you?

Only just. I stopped taking the pill two months ago. June is good. I'll let his mother know.

Does she know that you're pregnant?

Ian told her last night. It was a bittersweet pill but she got it down. She wants grandkids.

They were still texting when Cara followed Morrie up steep stairs to the bedrooms. No bodies up there. The rooms looked well used but not abused. The abuse was downstairs, and they returned to it.

No Smoking signs hung behind every door. They'd been ignored. There were butts in bottles, butts in cans, on the flagstone floor, in the sink.

'Vermin,' Cara said.

Until the mid-nineties this cottage and its neighbours had sheltered only vermin. They'd been planning to demolish them, to sell the land they were on, until the powers that be had stepped in. The three cottages had historical significance. They weren't allowed to remove one hallowed stone.

At the time, Morrie was running the front half of the Hall as a B&B. Paying two local women to cook, serve breakfasts and do the rooms ate most of his profit; insurance swallowed the rest. Cara had urged him to sell the estate for what he could get. His ties to Langdon Hall weren't blood ties, though maybe stronger than blood. He'd been seventeen when his parents brought him here. Old Leticia, widow of the last Henry Langdon, Morrie's paternal aunt by adoption, had owned the Hall, plus eighty acres of land. He spoke often of his first meeting with old Leticia, of his first introduction to the Hall.

The original section, built in the sixteenth century, had been uninhabitable; the front section, erected two hundred years later, was neglected but intact. Leticia had lived in the intact section, on credit, surrounded by her goldmine of land that developers had been drooling to get at.

A complex tale, the Langdons and the Hoopers, interconnected for the last hundred years. During the Hall's reclamation, Morrie had unearthed ancient documents, account books from the sixteen hundreds, a mouldy bible where every birth, death and marriage in the past two hundred years had been recorded.

Vern Hooper's marriage to Lorna Langdon had been recorded; Lorna, older sister of the last Henry Langdon. She'd died in childbirth, in Australia. Her daughter Lorna's birth was recorded on the same date as Lorna, the mother's, death. Leticia and Henry's eight infants' births and deaths were recorded. One little Henry had clung to life for a week, another for two days. The male infants had all been named Henry.

Bernard Grenville's birth hadn't been recorded in that bible. Left motherless as a five-year-old, Leticia, his eldest sister, raised him. Had he possessed a modicum of intelligence, Henry may have adopted him, but Bernard had been an artist, or he'd spent his life splashing paint onto canvas. He might have been twelve years old when Henry chose his bride, Lorna, his Australian-born niece, and his last chance to gain an heir of the Langdon line. Bernard was in his forties and still solely dependent on Henry before he agreed to the match and was promptly shipped to Australia.

Vern Hooper had produced two daughters, neither one a prize. Lorna would have put the fear of God into a heavyweight boxer. Bernard, only a little fellow, had preferred plump Margaret, who wouldn't scare a mouse. At the time, he'd been unaware that she carried not a drop of Langdon blood, that her mother had been Lorna's flighty little nurse maid.

Henry had known. He'd cut Bernard off without a penny. Leticia, a widow for six years when he'd brought his family home, had welcomed her brother. The night they'd arrived, she'd told Morrie that he'd looked like a worthy heir for her Henry. She'd willed the estate to him.

She wouldn't have approved of what he'd done with his inheritance. He'd sold all bar thirty acres of her land. Vern Hooper wouldn't have approved either. Morrie had sold his land and properties, but he'd paid Leticia's debts. The remainder of that money had been spent on bringing Langdon Hall back from the dead, both the front and older rear section. It had taken years – and money.

They'd been in debt, had been sweating over account books the day Tracy walked into the family room unannounced.

'Aren't you supposed to be in Italy?' Cara asked.

'I've left him,' she'd said. 'If he dares to phone, tell him I'm dead.' She was a dancer, had married a dancer. They'd been performing *Romeo and Juliet* in Rome.

Her death lasted for two days. On the third day she rose and walked with them down to those three crumbling cottages.

'So turn them into self-contained accommodation,' she'd said.

'Money,' Morrie said.

'The bank's got plenty. Start with the best of them and work your way down to the worst.'

Still on the subject of overdue bills, she'd unlocked the old ballroom a week later and, pregnant or not, climbed onto an elderly cabinet to wipe cobwebs and dust from the signature on an ancient portrait.

'You're sitting down there like a pair of miserable old Scrooge McDucks when you have this! Borrow on this, on these,' she'd said, wiping more cobwebs.

They had two walls of *these*, all ancient Langdons and their wives or daughters they'd kept locked out of sight because most of their visages were only fit to be locked out of sight. According to Tracy, a few of the artists' signatures had been worthy of display. She'd listed those she could decipher, then she and Morrie spent the evening looking for the artists' names in an old set of encyclopaedias. One signature could have been worth big money.

She'd called Morrie a dinosaur when he showed her the advertisement for his B&B business. She'd sacked one of the local women she'd caught texting in a bathroom instead of cleaning it.

There wasn't a lot of Tracy. She'd been built to dance. She had the elfin face of a dancer. Her formal education had ended abruptly when she'd received an offer from a ballet company at sixteen. Where her dancing had come from, Cara didn't know but her biological mother must have got into a car with a businessman nine months before her birth. As if born to the job, she'd taken charge of the advertising and Morrie's B&B business.

Tony, her husband, took time off for Tristan's birth, and when he flew away two months later, Tracy was pregnant again and threatening to leave him again. There was a bare twelve months between Tristan and Leona, who'd put in her appearance the day work began on the Gamekeeper's Lodge. There'd be no more little accidents. Tracy had her tubes tied.

'Tell her no more student groups, Morrie.'

'The booking was for three couples,' he said. 'They've paid.' He'd been gathering takeaway cartons and flattening them beneath his shoe. He hadn't crushed a fried chicken container; it was half full of banknotes and coins. 'They've emptied their wallets into it,' he said, offering a receipt from a bottle shop.

Cara took it from his hand, glanced at it then at the banknotes. 'Georgie's mouse money,' she said, then wished she hadn't. They'd buried the past, almost. She'd forgotten Georgie. Most of the time she'd forgotten her.

Morrie remembered her hair. He'd seen her on a television screen back in the late seventies, then in '99, he'd seen her in the flesh, in Australia. On the long flight back to the UK, safe in no-man's-land above the chaos of the world, he'd spoken of his sister, but once his feet were back on English soil, he'd put her and Australia away. That was who he was, and Cara loved who he was.

They should have cancelled that tour when their plane had to turn back. Instead they'd waited eight hours at the airport to get onto another flight. For the next two weeks they'd played catch-up.

An early flight from Sydney should have got them to Melbourne in plenty of time for the interview. It hadn't. They were being ushered into the television studio when the past had called Cara's name. She'd turned, and there she was, unchanged in the twenty years since they'd last met. She'd shaken Georgie's hand, introduced Morrie as her husband, then left him to deal with, or not deal with, the fallout.

Georgie hadn't recognised him. She'd told him she was there as Juliana Conti's minder.

'What's mouse money?' he asked.

'Just a memory,' Cara replied, and wished again that she'd kept her mouth shut. But how can you forever keep biting back words? How can you keep killing memories? 'Georgie worked for an old grocer who waged a private war on the taxation department. I came out from school one afternoon and she was waiting at the gate with her overnight bag. She had a shoe box in it, stuffed full of Charlie White's ill-gotten gains.'

'Charlie White?'

'You remember him?'

He shook his head. 'She kept it? The money?'

'He was dead. She'd been cooking his books for years to cover up his pilfering. She said that if she'd handed the money in, she would have ended up in jail. Charlie White,' she repeated the name. 'He was a little, old moth-eaten bloke. Very memorable.'

'Some names ring bells,' he said.

'You would have known him. Georgie said he'd been around all of her life, that he and his wife were friends of your grand-mother.' She picked up a ten-pound note and smelt it. No whiff of mouse, a little fried chicken. 'I met him for five minutes and never forgot him.'

'Too many people have walked through my life,' he said. 'How much mouse money?' he asked, as he kicked a can through the goalposts of the doorframe.

'Thousands,' Cara said, watching the two young dogs chase the can. 'Old money. Pounds, not dollars. Australia was in the process of changing over to decimal currency so we had to get rid of it fast. It would have been in . . . in '67.'

'*We* had to get rid of it?'

'Georgie and me,' Cara said, and smiled at the memory. 'She opened half a dozen bank accounts in different versions of her name. Then for the next twelve months, I did a weekly bank run, paid in the old money, ten pounds at a time. Remember that day you followed me to the racetrack and watched bug-eyed while

I handed over ten-pound notes to place fifty cent bets? You asked me if I was money laundering?'

'Your Mafioso fiancé's drug money,' he said.

'Would it kill you to say his name, just once?'

She'd been engaged for a time to Chris Marino, a Melbourne solicitor. Her friend Cathy hadn't approved. She was the one who'd started the *Mafioso fiancé*.

'If I'd married him instead of you, I'd be living in a beautiful modern house in Doncaster now, instead of cleaning up after pigs. Home,' she said, to Morrie and the dogs. They had three Border Collies, old Rufus patiently waiting at the door, the two young ones, not so patient, were sparring near the stream. They liked water. Liked to share it too. 'Get!' she said, copping a spray. They laughed at her word, barked at it. Only seven months old, they were still foolish pups. Rufus was twelve and ready to go home for his nap.

Those who'd known Cara Norris, the Melbourne primary school teacher, may have looked twice to recognise her. Miss Norris had dressed in suits and heels, had worn her hair functionally short. Mrs Grenville, rarely seen out of jeans and sneakers, wore her hair in a chin-length bob with a long, straight fringe. It covered her brow, covered her eyebrows. She was slim, had been measured at five foot eight before she'd stopped growing.

Morrie was taller. He'd inherited the Hooper hair, now their gunmetal grey. He hadn't inherited their overly large ears and excessive height. His father had been taller. He remembered being taken to a hospital and being told to shake the hand of a long, match-stick man who'd lived there.

He had Jenny's eyes, though his were more grey than blue. He had her nose, her brow.

He'd chosen to forget her.

PANDORA'S BOX

*A*ltering the date of a wedding is fraught with problems. One of Elise's bridesmaids, available in October, would be skiing in New Zealand in June. Leona, the flower girl, would have been closer to four than three by October. The church, too, was a major problem. They could get it in the morning, which meant that the planned evening reception would become a lunch and that created another problem. Cara had already bought an after-five frock for an evening wedding.

There were too many problems for Elise. She booked a flight to Spain and found a marriage celebrant prepared to say the words and get the papers signed at the airport. Cara could have lived with that. Laura, the groom's mother, couldn't. She phoned Cara.

'Talk to that girl,' she said. 'It will kill Ian's grandmother if they're not married in a church.'

Tracy booked the church for an eleven o'clock wedding. She booked the caterers, photographer, waiters, waitresses. All they'd needed was a bride, so on the fourteenth of April, Cara drove into London to take Elise shopping for a wedding gown.

She didn't want a gown or a wedding. She wanted a baby. She didn't want the nausea that came with carrying it. 'We're getting married at the airport, Mum, and I'll be wearing an elastic-waisted tracksuit,' she said.

She'd been a determined two-year-old when they'd brought her home from foster care. She hadn't changed since, but without that determination she may not have survived her first year of life. Her leg had been crippled by abuse when she'd been found abandoned in a park. The day Cara saw her determined little face on the front page of a London newspaper, she knew she'd been destined to raise her.

It had taken a year to get her. It had taken years of operations to repair the damage to her leg. She still walked with a limp, still wore sensible shoes, one heel a little higher than the other, but otherwise, she was a very modern, determined girl – determined to be married by a celebrant.

Cara was as determined. 'Everything is booked. Ian's grand-mother is delaying her funeral to be there, and you'll be there, in a wedding gown.'

It was two o'clock before Elise agreed to hire a gown. It may have carried the odour of dry-cleaning fluid but it had no waist, just in case. She said she didn't care whether the caterers served chicken, fish or rabbit stew at the reception. She wouldn't be eating it. She had no interest in wedding bouquets or in what her solitary bridesmaid wore, but did agree to cancel the marriage celebrant.

Back to the car park by three, another address to find and the London traffic had given Cara a headache. Elise, more familiar with the city, drove to the art restorer's address, where she double parked while Cara ran in to reclaim and pay for what she had no desire to claim or pay for.

There'd been a large gap on the ballroom wall while old Henry Whitworth Langdon's leer was being given more attention than it deserved. His frame's restoration may have been worth the money.

She and the money man manoeuvred Henry sideways into the rear of the car, then Elise gave up the keys to catch a bus back to her unit. Cara drove home, old Henry Whitworth's frame blocking her rear vision all the way.

Tracy was in the courtyard waiting for Henry. Morrie got him out of the back seat, then together they carried him in through the house, up the front stairs and back to his place in the ballroom.

'Did you buy an outfit?' Tracy asked.

'I'll wear my blue linen,' Cara said.

They hung Henry, Morrie up the ladder, Cara holding it steady, Tracy directing, to the left or the right.

'He's straight enough,' Morrie said.

'No doubt straighter than he was in life,' Cara added. His appearance suggested he'd deserved to be hung, though not on a ballroom wall.

'The bottom needs to go a smidgen to the left,' Tracy directed, and patient Morrie adjusted until Tracy said, 'Perfect.'

There wasn't a perfect face amongst the lot of them. The Langdon women were long-nosed and haughty, their males sly-eyed and leering. A few had value. Henry Whitworth Langdon's artist had paintings hung in high places. In Leticia's time that illustrious signature had hung uninsured and forgotten.

Tracy, who'd spent months sorting through curled-up history, had unearthed the receipt for that portrait and been on his paper-trail since. Old Henry Whitworth was the Langdon who'd won, stolen, or wed money enough to build on the front section of the Hall, in 1739. She'd found the name of the architect who'd designed it. He'd designed the ballroom's ceiling to impress, had designed multiple impressive bedrooms for guests, but hadn't concerned himself with their hygiene. Through the years, various renovators had done what they could to rectify the bathroom problem, but not until Morrie went into the B&B business had he realised that guests were prepared to pay more money to spend a night in a manor house if the rooms offered private bathrooms. His renovators stole space enough from the larger rooms for small ensuites, and where there'd been too little space to steal, they'd knocked holes through walls and turned two lesser bedrooms into four full bathrooms. Under Tracy's supervision, the B&B business was now making money.

Her current research into architects who may have been working in the area during old Elizabeth's reign was doomed to failure. The rear section of the Hall, standing since Elizabethan times, had no architectural input. To Cara it appeared to have begun life as a couple of old stone cottages that grew into one, then decided to climb higher. There were three levels to it, the lower level, a rabbit warren of passages leading to where they were required, with steps where no steps were expected, and staircases not far removed from ladders. The second level was smaller. The third, where Morrie and Cara slept, consisted of four rooms, squeezed in beneath the roof.

Robin, a Grenville Langdon by birth, had no interest in the estate. He referred to it as a money-guzzling fire hazard. Since his marriage, he'd spent more time in Australia than at home. Nine years old when they'd moved to the UK, he'd been too old to change his core allegiance, he said.

Tracy's research into the Langdon history had sparked Robin's interest in his Australian forebears. He'd tracked the Norris family back to the sixteenth century. He knew the port the original James Richard Hooper had sailed from and the name of the boat he'd sailed on. He'd delved into more recent Hooper history, had details on Lorna's murder. He and the girls had been raised on tales of Lorna, the family witch – the reason Morrie's parents left Australia.

Cara had met her once, on the day of Margaret's funeral – and one meeting had been enough. She'd met Jim Hooper, the last James Richard Hooper. She'd been sitting across Georgie's kitchen table from him the night half of the police in Victoria had been in Woody Creek, searching for Raelene and Dino Collins. They'd broken into Cara's Melbourne home and taken Tracy from her bed. Morrie had questioned her about Jim but not about Jenny. He remembered her, but when Robin asked if he had any recollection of his biological mother's name, Morrie said no.

He had good reason to forget her. When he was a six-year-old boy, she'd sold him to his grandfather for two thousand pounds, and to this day he carried his bill of sale in his wallet. He'd shown it to Cara twenty-odd years ago. 'What with inflation, who knows how much I'm worth today. Want to put in a bid?' he'd said.

It was a legal document, couched in legal jargon, signed, witnessed and dated. Morrie could quote both pages. Cara could quote the opening sentence.

I, Jennifer Carolyn Morrison-King, without coercion, and being aware that it is in the best interests of my son, James Hooper Morrison, do hereby relinquish my parental rights to his father, James Richard Hooper . . .

Her signature was on it, twice. He knew his mother's name.

Years ago, Cara had suggested he have his bill of sale framed before it disintegrated, that he hang it on the family-room wall. Its folds had begun their erosion. As with most of life's problems, time wears them away to dust, and eventually they blow away.

He and Tracy were studying the cleaned-up Henry Whitworth Langdon and discussing the painting next to it, a woman who may have been the wife with money. The artist had put a lot of work into her jewels. They'd found no receipt for that one and no record of her artist. Tracy called her Regina, the wife of Henry Whitworth Langdon, when she led her tour groups through the front section of the Hall. She never showed them through the rear section. It was family only there. Cara and the children went missing on tour-group days, or hid in the family room from peering eyes.

The ladder folded, they carried it downstairs and out through the front door, where Morrie lifted it to his shoulder to take it back to where it belonged. Their garage had housed a coach and horses in another era. Like the house, it had received its renovations, and today housed two modern vehicles and a ride-on mower. Morrie rode it. They had acres of lawn to mow.

In Leticia's day, there'd been no lawn and only nature's garden. She'd been in her eighties when newly divorced Cara had come here to spend one night. She'd stayed for three months. If not for Myrtle and Robert, her parents, and Robin, she may have stayed forever. She'd seen the Hall at its worst, had become lost in its maze of passages – had stepped over fallen ceilings too – and never been happier in her life.

She entered the house today via the dog's door, or the door with the doggy entrance cut into it. They had their own room, but preferred the family room – long, low-beamed, in another lifetime it may have been a dairy. Today it had a modern kitchen at one end, Cara's desk at the other, and between kitchen and desk the family lived, ate and watched television. Not one Langdon disgraced its walls. Photographs of the children and the dogs graced its one long wall.

As an infant Cara had wanted a black and white puppy. Myrtle and Robert bought her a fine fluffy dog with a key in its tummy. She'd named him Bowser. He'd barked, wagged his tail and nodded his head until she'd wound his key once too often. A silent Bowser then, he'd guarded her bed until he'd gone mangy and semi-bald with loving.

Aged thirteen when they'd moved from Sydney to Traralgon. Thirteen too old to cling to worn-out toys, Bowser had been disposed of.

She'd been a mother, a foster mother to Tracy, when Robert and the children presented her with a wriggling black and white puppy that required no key. Of course, his name had to be Bowser. Raelene King and Dino Collins murdered him the night they stole Tracy.

There'd been no more dogs, or not until she'd moved her family to the UK. She'd had a few since. Old Rufus celebrated his twelfth birthday before she'd bought the pups. He'd spent the last six months evading them. She found him today under her desk, when she sat at her computer.

Half a dozen emails came through, two from Cathy. She read a few lines of the first before printing both, to read at her leisure.

Cathy's emails were long-winded. She'd been contacted about the new date for the wedding.

She and Gerry had flown over for Robin's conventional wedding, and for Tracy's unconventional woodland nuptials. Her groom had worn the white. Tracy had clad herself in a gown of filmy green and pinned flowers in her hair. She'd looked like a woodland nymph, had climbed trees and perched on branches, playing hide and seek with the photographer. No reception, no speeches for Tracy. She'd wanted a picnic on the lawns.

Cathy hadn't approved. She'd said they'd have beautiful children if they survived long enough to reproduce. They'd produced a pair of dark-headed, dark-eyed pixie children who adored their father, who flew in and out like a migrating bird.

One of the emails was from Cara's agent. She'd included half a dozen brief sentences, in German, with translations and phonetic pronunciations. She printed it and was practising when Morrie came in.

'*Guten Morgen. Ich bin . . . glücklich . . . dass ich mit dir sprechen kann.*'

'It's dinner time,' Morrie replied.

'*Vielen Dank . . . für dein Wilkomm,*' she said.

'Do you know what you're saying?'

'My readers will. According to Hillary, they'll appreciate any halting attempt I make to speak their tongue,' she said, then offered him Cathy's pages.

Cara's latest book was selling well in Germany, just a boy-meets-girl, set before, during and after the war, an English girl, a German boy, with a large, braying mother who looked a lot like Laura, Elise's soon-to-be mother-in-law.

She was a mare of a woman . . .

'You told her we'd arrive home from Germany on the eleventh? She says she's changed her booking to arrive on the eleventh,' he said.

'She'll decorate the church,' Cara said.

She'd decorated the Ballarat church with big white bows and flowers and blue cardboard love birds the day of Cara and Morrie's second marriage. They'd been in Australia for Robert's funeral and made the mistake of asking Cathy to be their witness at a civil ceremony. She was eight months pregnant and unable to travel, so she'd said, and like the fools they were, they'd allowed her to talk them into a marriage celebrant in her back garden. She'd railroaded them into hired and borrowed outfits and a wedding in her church.

'This time it's going to stick,' she'd said. A control freak, an organiser, Cathy, given little more than a week's notice, she'd managed to round up a crowd, her friends and relatives, a teacher or two, half of Cara's multitudinous Sydney cousins.

If anyone present knows just cause why this couple should not be joined in holy matrimony, let them speak now or forever hold their peace.

Just cause had dissolved their first marriage. Just cause had kept them apart for eight years. No one present in that church to stand up and protest. So it was done.

Pandora's Box, Robert had named Woody Creek. He'd called Jenny Pandora. How many times had he warned Cara not to open that box? In her youth, she'd heeded few warnings. At fifteen he'd warned her to stay away from Dino Collins – and for fifteen years she'd paid for ignoring that advice. He'd warned her to wait for a month or two when she'd broken her engagement to Chris Marino to marry Morrie. She hadn't waited. Their first marriage had been a few words spoken at his dying mother's bedside.

Not a day for happiness, but she'd been so happy. After years of their pen and paper romance, he'd finally been at her side and would be at her side forever. She'd been so happy she'd started telling secrets in their bridal bed.

Neither bride nor groom slept in that bed. Morrie had picked up his case and car keys and left her howling on the bathroom floor. She'd caught a taxi home to her dogbox unit, unaware that night that their lovemaking would result in Robin.

Had never expected him to be born alive. Had refused to look at him and demanded the papers be brought to her bed so she might sign him away. Myrtle and Robert took out a court order to prevent her giving their grandson up for adoption.

Crazy, desperate, out-of-her-mind months she'd spent in Melbourne, while in Sydney, Myrtle and Robert played grandmas and grandpas. They'd named Robin, had baptised him, adored him. He'd been eight months old before fate forced Cara back to Sydney. For two years she fought against loving Morrie's son, but he'd bewitched her.

Her eight-hour marriage had been wiped from the record books before she'd told Morrie he had a son, and in the same breath, told him to stay away from him.

Then Myrtle died, too soon, too fast and so easily, in her sleep, Robert at her side.

It broke him. Overnight Cara inherited responsibility for her three-year-old son, her father and his mortgage. She'd been at breaking point the day she'd agreed to foster Raelene King's baby, a tiny, mop-headed mite, sentenced at birth to a lifetime of that vicious slut.

'If she goes into the welfare system, I'll never get her back,' Raelene said that day at the prison. 'I'll get a single mother's pension if I've got a kid with me when they let me out of this place.'

A wild plan, hatched in the dead of a crazy night by a frantic woman, but that plan had included retirement from teaching, no crèche bills for Robin, full-time supervision for Robert, plus time to write the great Australian novel. If, while achieving those four prime objectives she could take something of monetary value away from Raelene, wasn't that a bonus?

Someone should have seen that she was unfit to foster an infant. Someone should have said no. No one had seen or said no.

The day she'd brought Tracy home, she'd expected tantrums from Robin. But he'd been enamoured by his baby sister. She'd expected Tracy's wail to drive Robert over the edge. Tracy hadn't wailed. She'd chuckled, and, given time, Robert had started smiling at her chuckles.

Love a baby born to Raelene? Cara had been unaware that she felt more than responsibility for her charge – until that vicious slut was set free and given supervised access to her daughter.

Supervision hadn't gone down well. Tracy was four years old the night Raelene and Dino Collins gained unsupervised access. He had no parental claim on that little girl, no interest in her. He'd taken the opportunity to take his revenge. At fifteen, Cara had broken his nose and knocked out one of his front teeth with the spine of *Mansfield Park*. He'd murdered Bowser, had cut a circle of glass from Tracy's bedroom window, drugged her, sealed her in a cardboard carton and driven her up to Woody Creek, where he and her slut of a mother had dumped that carton beside a farm fence.

Until the day she died, Cara wouldn't forget that night. She'd driven late to Woody Creek, to Georgie. She'd been sitting with her when a neighbour came bellowing up to the back door. His dogs had found Tracy. 'She's breathing.'

They'd run, Cara and Georgie, hand in hand beneath a star-filled country sky, the farmer bellowing his news as he'd led the way through wire fences, around trees, his dogs barking at their heels.

So much noise. Sirens. Police. Dogs. So much light and move-ment. At some stage Cara had released Georgie's hand to hold Tracy's. At some stage she'd stopped seeing Georgie and only seen Tracy. In the ambulance she'd held her tiny hand. She'd held it on the plane that flew them through that star-filled night to the lights of Melbourne. She'd held it later in a room where tubes and machines and nursing staff kept Tracy alive.

Dawn was creeping over the city, early trams grinding their weary way by when Robin materialised at her elbow. He'd brought Bunny Long Ears, Tracy's bedtime friend.

'How did you get here?' she'd asked.

'The man who you said owns our toy car drove me.'

She'd known that Morrie was in Australia, that he'd flown over to take possession of his elderly MG. To this day, she had no idea what had been in her mind when she'd released Tracy's hand and walked out to the corridor.

Night staff leaving, day staff arriving, that transitional time at a hospital when death is on the prowl. And there he was, waiting to drive their son home. She hadn't seen him in five years. He'd looked older, but so tall and strong and alive.

Perhaps she'd meant to tell him again to stay away from their son. Perhaps she'd known she had too little strength to keep fighting death away from that hospital bed alone. She didn't know why she'd done it, but she'd held out her hand to him and told him she didn't want to wait alone.

He hadn't left her side thereafter, not that day, not the next. He and Robin were with her when Tracy opened her eyes.

Tracy had studied them for a moment, studied the strange room, then asked, 'Why is that man wiff you for, Mummy?'

'Because he's our father,' Robin said.

Right or wrong he'd been their father since.

TROUBLE

*L*oss, guilt, the day-to-day demands of her mother-in-law and the boys had allowed the heat of March to become the rain of April. It was the rain and the blacked-out days of Easter on the magnetised calendar that held Tessa's list of medications to the refrigerator's door that told Trudy she was eight weeks pregnant. Hadn't done anything about that baby she didn't want but was imprisoned by it, and by nausea, lethargy – and no car. Nick spent his days running free. She resented his freedom.

The boys were going stir crazy. Accustomed to half an acre to run wild on, to prickly fences they knew to stay away from, to tall gates and their canine babysitter, they whined about their imprisonment, demanded, screamed and stamped their feet to go home.

She'd explained death to them. They'd kissed their sleeping Papa goodbye but this morning while she'd slept, they'd got her mobile and spoken to him.

'He waked up now, Mummy. Now we can go home, Mummy.'

Jenny had taught them how to use her mobile, how to make her big phone ring. They'd made it ring many times this morning, enough times to waste almost fifteen dollars. Trudy prepaid for her Telstra connection and she needed it. It was her contact with the world outside of this overheated prison. She had to break out of it, had to get to a Telstra shop and sign up to a plan.

In Woody Creek, prepaying had been easy. She'd done it over the phone, paid with her bank card. Three days ago, she'd cut that card into many pieces and thrown the pieces at Nick. Before the boys, she'd never denied him her card. She had money, saved since the boys' birth, and he wasn't getting one cent of it to waste on his scamming solicitor.

'We want you to go home, Mummy.'

'Go outside,' she said.

They wouldn't, not unless she went with them. They wouldn't go downstairs unless she was with them. Tessa was a nasty old woman – and she had more wrong with her than diabetes and high blood pressure. She'd spoken English the day Trudy met her at the airport. She'd screeched English in Woody Creek. She screeched in Greek now.

'You come outside too.'

Children learn from those they live with. They'd learnt to demand in Tessa's house.

'Go and find a video,' she said. They had half a dozen in their room. Had watched most of them too many times. Videos silenced them for a time. She needed silence. Needed to think.

Needed to see a doctor too.

'Mummy. Mummy.'

They found *Pinocchio*. She took the video and walked down to Nick's room, no longer her room. She hadn't slept with him since the funeral. At home the boys had shared a large cot. They had single beds in Croydon but wouldn't go to bed unless they were tucked in tight together. She slept in the other bed.

Everything was *since the funeral*, as if a dark line had been drawn across the calendar that day, as if she'd been a person on one side of that line and a pregnant someone one else on the other side. Her breasts were sore. She couldn't eat. Her hair looked lifeless and her bones ached from dawn to dark.

Still hadn't told Nick. Hadn't told anyone.

'Trudy,' Tessa screeched. When she called her by name it usually meant another catastrophe, usually a bathroom catastrophe, sometimes a kitchen catastrophe. She'd put food in the microwave yesterday and instead of hitting 2.25, she'd hit 22.50.

'You stay here wiff us,' Jamey said.

'I won't be long.' She might be, depending on today's catastrophe.

'The law,' Tessa said in Greek as she pushed the landline phone at her. The law was anyone who didn't speak Greek. Bills came from *the law*.

Trudy took the phone from Tessa's hand. 'Good afternoon,' she said.

'It's me, Trude,' Georgie said. 'Jen just called. She's been trying to phone you.'

'How is she?'

'She said your mobile isn't working and Tessa keeps hanging up on her. The boys left her half a dozen messages about no car and no shops and no outside.'

'Tell her we're fine. Nick's been using the car.'

'He's working?'

Working on a fraudulent insurance claim. 'Sort of,' Trudy said.

'What's wrong with your mobile?'

'It's prepaid – was prepaid.' Trudy explained her boys' calls to their Papa, Tessa was at her elbow, wanting to know what the law wanted.

'I'll be a minute,' Trudy said, in Greek.

'What's with her?' Georgie asked.

'I've got a fair idea,' Trudy said. She'd needed that call, needed to spill her load to a sympathetic ear. Georgie might know Nick's cousin's solicitor, and she'd definitely know something about Margaret Morrison. She dodged around Tessa and escaped upstairs with her phone, Tessa screeching behind her.

She didn't return to the boys and *Pinocchio*. She went to the bathroom and closed the door to muffle Tessa's screech and *Pinocchio*.

'Are you there?'

'Still here,' Georgie said.

'I think Tessa's got early stage Alzheimer's. There's something more wrong with her than losing her husband,' Trudy said.

'What does her doctor say?'

'She hasn't seen him for a while,' Trudy said, then changed the subject. 'What do you know about my birth mother, Georgie?' That question created a silence. 'I've got it into my head that I was sent down here by fate to find her living over my back fence.'

'Life doesn't happen like that, Trude,' Georgie said.

'It happens all the time like that.'

'I'll go as far as to say that your Margaret Morrison isn't who you think she is.'

'How do you know?'

'I do, and as I said in Woody Creek, you need to speak to Jen about this, not me.'

'It's the wrong time, Georgie. What do you know?'

At the other end of the line, Georgie rattled papers, sighed then said, 'Your birth mother has been dead for twenty-odd years. I know this for a fact – and that's all I'm saying on the subject – apart from why the sudden interest?'

'It's like Dad took Trudy Hooper with him and I don't know who I am,' Trudy said. There were tears in her voice. She took a moment, took time to breathe. 'My new driver's licence came yesterday. I've never changed it to my married name and it looks fraudulent. Was she a relative of Mum's father?'

'You're related to me and Jen by blood, and I'm at work. I'll have to go –'

'Before you do, I was going to ask you about a solicitor Nick is using to sue his brother-in-law's insurance company –'

Tessa must have made it halfway up those stairs. Georgie heard her. 'Get her to a doctor,' she said.

'Tonia tried to, Nick's oldest sister. Tessa bit her. If she'd had her own teeth it would have been worse. Her false teeth ended up on the floor.'

'Call the CATTS ambulance,' Georgie said. 'I'll get Katie to put some money on your mobile. She prepays hers online. And give Jen a call. She's selling stuff hand over fist up there. She sold Lorna's dining suite and is talking about selling Amy's silver cutlery set.'

'Dad loved that suite.'

'It smelt of Lorna – according to Jenny. She reckons Lorna's ghost is walking the verandas looking for a way in. Thinks if she gets rid of her furniture Lorna might follow it. Call her tonight,' Georgie said.

Then she was gone and Trudy joined her boys to watch the end of *Pinocchio*.

On Thursday night, the night before Good Friday, Georgie phoned again. She'd received a text from Jenny. Trudy had received an identical text.

House sold. Got a good price. Sixty-day settlement. The buyer's choice. Bad timing for me. Am currently at cinema. Have to turn off mobile. Talk tomorrow.

SOLD

*J*enny had been railroaded into agreeing to that sixty-day settlement. It had happened too fast. Everything. She hadn't expected
the house to sell. The first couple to look at it bought it.

It started at three o'clock last Saturday. She should never have
picked up the phone. It was the agent wanting to show the house
to a retired city couple, only up from Melbourne for the weekend.
They'd been looking at houses in Willama but seen nothing that
appealed. They were cash buyers, he'd said, had sold their house in
the city and were desperate to buy up this way before their settlement date – a Pat and Mike Bertram, a professional couple who
should have had more sense than to go looking for a house in
this town.

She'd done her best to talk them out of buying. She'd told
them that Woody Creek had been dying since the supermarket
went bankrupt.

They'd already known that. Their eldest son owned a business
in Willama.

They'd wanted a large block. Jenny had a large block. They'd
wanted a house with character and at least five bedrooms. Vern

Hooper's house had a nasty character and six bedrooms. They'd made an offer for it that evening. Jenny had refused it, and not because they'd offered thirty thousand less than the advertised price. She'd still been considering arson, had been putting herself to sleep at night by considering possible ways of burning a house to the ground but still collecting the insurance.

She couldn't empty it. She knew that much. She'd sold Lorna's suite, the antique bedroom chair, Amy's cutlery, Jim's invalid aids. She'd sold the twins' stroller, a bedroom suite and outdoor furniture. She'd delivered boot loads to the tip and opportunity shop, but every item she sold, dumped or donated was more proof of the impossibility of getting rid of forty years' accumulation.

Her refusal of the offer hadn't killed Pat and Mike's interest. On Monday morning, they'd knocked on her door and asked to take a second look. She'd let them in, then warned them that Lorna's hallstand was immovable, that it went with the house. Two antique dealers had praised it but neither one had wanted it – and it was that bloody hallstand that sealed the deal. Pat wanted it.

The necessary documents had been rushed through by their solicitor and at three-thirty today, Jenny had signed away Vern Hooper's house, conditional on it passing a building inspection. She'd walked out of the solicitor's office in a daze, had walked around to the motel and got their last room. Willama was a Mecca for tourists, and with the school holidays beginning today, the motels and caravan parks would have been booked out by tomorrow.

She sat alone in the cinema, her mobile turned off, not because the screen had told her to, but because she didn't need her girls' replies, not tonight. Try as she might, she couldn't concentrate on the movie, which may or may not have warranted her concentration. She was thinking dates, thinking numbers, thinking twenty-eight from sixty equals thirty-two. She was thinking cruise, thinking of that thank-you advertisement.

She'd put the house on the market because Vickery's real estate agency was next door to the *Gazette* office, then on her way back to her car, she'd called into the travel agency, Jim's fifty-thousand-dollar cheque still playing on her mind.

A bad movie followed by a bad bed, Jenny vacated the room early. She'd shopped yesterday. No supermarkets opened on Good Friday. She'd bought long-life milk. Miniature motel refrigerators weren't designed to hold bottles of milk. Their freezers weren't designed to hold three chocolate-coated Magnums. She'd taken one with her to the cinema.

Drove home on automatic pilot, didn't see the road, the roos or the bridge, and no Lila to greet her at the gate. She'd spent the night with Harry. He'd said he'd bring her home at ten and take a look at what was in the shed. Jenny didn't know what was in it. Before unlocking the house, she moved a crate against the garage doors, climbed onto it, dragged down two large bolts that kept those doors closed, then swung them open. One swung. She had to lift and drag the other over the concrete. Stood then, surveying the chaos of that shed – a workbench buried beneath a clutter of tools and dusty bottles and half-full cans of paint. Every wall was hung with power cords, pieces of hose, chains and tools no one had used since Jesus was a lad. There were rotting hessian bags hanging from nails driven into wall studs, coils of fencing wire in the rafters – and redback spiders everywhere. Jenny didn't like redbacks and moving a motor mower disturbed two. She took her shopping inside, dumped it on the table, then reached beneath the sink for her can of insect spray, its label suggesting it would kill spiders. Thus armed, she returned to the shed.

Norman's toolbox, unmoved from its corner in forty years, was woven in by dusty webs. John McPherson's toolbox, a more recent resident, lay open beside his wood router, where he'd left it the day before he'd died. His antique photographic equipment leaned close by and was redback riddled. She drowned a few with spray, dosed a few more on a lawnmower. There were three mowers in this shed. One of them used to start, or five years ago it had. She used to start it until a retired chap knocked on her door looking for work.

Thereafter, she'd paid him to mow. She sprayed all four corners of the shed, sprayed the bench and beneath the bench, sprayed until she ran out of Mortein. Maybe there'd been enough in that can to make a few redbacks drowsy – or angry.

Harry knew about the sale. She'd told him yesterday when she'd dropped Lila off. He'd been shocked. Jenny was still in shock. Vern Hooper would probably rise up from his grave tonight to walk with Lorna.

She tossed the empty spray can into her green bin then stood staring at the house. Pat and Mike Bertram had been concerned about white ants. Their building inspector wouldn't find any – or in the nineties, when they'd had the house restumped, it was termite free.

Her mobile was flat. It spent half of its life flat and the other half plugged into its charger. She needed a new mobile, or a new battery, but no one made new batteries for four-year-old mobiles.

The girls would have replied to last night's text. They'd probably left messages on her answering machine. She didn't need to play those messages to know their varied responses. Katie would be pleased. She'd have Jenny's future living arrangements worked out by now. Georgie would be non-committal. Trudy would blow a gasket.

She was unpacking supermarket bags when the beeps started coming through. They didn't interrupt her task. She'd bought a packet of four Magnums from the supermarket. The three she'd squeezed into the motel's freezer were soft and misshapen. They'd harden up.

Her freezer was half full of meat she'd bought for Jim. She looked at a roast. He'd liked roasts. He'd liked chops and steak. Lila would appreciate a slab of steak she'd bought to make Jim a stew. He'd loved her steak and onion stews. She placed the steak on the sink to thaw, placed a tray of sausages beside it. She liked sausages. They always reminded her of Norman.

The stove was dead. The kitchen saw no sun until the afternoon and this morning it needed the stove's warmth.

'I won't miss hauling in wood,' she said, and glanced at her fingernail. It was growing but looked more deformed than the rest. She wouldn't miss paying for loads of wood either, which she'd need to do again after Easter. She got the stove burning with kindling and junk mail and was on her way out to the wood heap when she diverted to the laundry, a flat-roofed shed, overgrown with wisteria, pretty when it bloomed, but by mid-April, a rampant weed poking its feelers between the weatherboards, attempting to get at the junk stored on ancient shelves – ancient junk most of it.

'When did I last use starch?' she asked a dusty box full of it. Couldn't remember when.

Mike and Pat hadn't been impressed with the outdoor laundry; it hadn't killed their interest. 'Rustic,' Pat said. They'd wanted character. They'd got plenty of that. They'd never used a wood stove. Would probably toss it. Would probably install central heating after their first winter here. They hadn't been impressed by Jim's ramp, which was an eyesore. 'Easy enough to get rid of,' the agent said.

She gathered an armload of wood and when she dropped it on the hearth, she wondered how many tons she'd carried in her lifetime. She added two chunks to the stove, added a bunch of Juliana's draft printouts then closed the firebox and wondered how many thousands of those pages she'd burnt. She'd burnt Jim's stockpiled cheque butts and taxation returns that went back to '79. He'd kept everything. As had she.

Pat and Mike had loved the garden. They wouldn't when the leaves fell. They weren't fond of rosebushes but might change their minds about roses if they allowed the hedge to bloom before bringing in a bulldozer to get rid of their thorns.

That's life, Jenny thought, the thorns and the beauty. You can't have one without the other. Her path was thorny at the moment, but it might bud up and bloom again. She was standing at the window looking at the hedge and the road behind it, remembering that final day of Jim, when she'd stood here watching that road for him to come riding home and eat his leftover chicken casserole and mashed potatoes. There were a few electric buggies in Woody Creek, but she'd always recognised Jim's from a distance. There'd been so much length in him he'd looked like an adult riding a kid's tricycle.

Her mobile was on the bench to her right. Sooner or later she'd have to read her messages. Texts had become her preferred means of contact recently, but she stood staring at the phone for minutes before picking it up

Katie's message was brief. *GR8 stuff Nanny but don't you dare sell Amy's desk.* Georgie's was as brief. *The original dark horse. What's the story, mate?* Donna Palmer's was typical. *I told Mum when I recognised your phone number in that* Gazette *ad that you were up to something over there.*

Trudy had left two messages on the answering machine and in the second of them she sounded as if she were crying. A Helen Anderson had left her name and number twice. She was interested in buying the dining suite from the library. For two weeks Jenny's advertisements had been running in the *Gazette's* 'For Sale' column.

She'd listed the boys' cot. Its emptiness haunted her. She'd listed the big television, bought so recently by Jim. Trudy's bedroom suite was listed. They'd bought it for her twenty-first birthday, which made it over twenty years old. It looked new.

The dining table didn't. As a twelve-year-old, Raelene had started gouging her name into its surface. They'd caught her but not before she'd gouged the line for the *R.* Polish disguised it. It didn't remove it.

Jenny returned Helen Anderson's call. She told her about that gouge. 'Apart from that, it's in good condition.' Or it had been before she'd buried it beneath computers.

'We'll come now,' Helen said. 'We're at Bungala. We're interested in the easy chairs and television too – if they're still available.'

There was a dirt road direct from Bungala to Woody Creek, or a less direct but sealed route through Willama, and when the phone was down, Jenny walked through to the library to make the dining-room suite available. She'd need to clear the table and round up the chairs.

Her two desktop computers would have to go. She unlocked the glass door, propped it wide, then returned to the library to untangle electrical cords, but found it easier to pull out plugs and worry about the tangle later. She freed her laptop and moved it onto Amy's desk. The desktop models weren't as easy to move, but she did it piece by piece. The monitors were heavy, but she got both out to the veranda. One of the towers was heavy. She was making space for her old printer on Amy's desk when she changed her mind about it and carried it out to add to the pile. She untangled her laptop's cord but took the others out in their tangle. Harry would take them to the tip.

The table hadn't smelt polish in ten years. Its extensions concerned her. They'd been extended and weighted down by computers for so long that she had difficulty sliding one of them in, but it went in and she hurried off to locate and dust the chairs. She'd told Helen they were upholstered in a smoky blue fabric and were comfortable. They were. She'd loved that suite the day she'd chosen it – and had she been in the market for furniture today, she would have bought it again.

She gave the table top a quick polish, gave the empty bookshelves a wipe over with the polishing cloth, then turned her attention to the easy chairs. They'd lived in the kitchen for the best part of forty years, were well worn but had worn well. Furniture used to be made to last. She smelt Jim's chair; he'd sat for so long on it, the scent of him had permeated the fabric, but it had to go. Everything had to go. She was removing a stain on its seat with carpet cleaner when she heard a motor that didn't sound like Harry's ute. It would be Helen Anderson, who must have taken the back road.

Lila not fond of strangers, Jenny went out the side door to save her visitor but changed her mind when she saw Trudy's Commodore in the drive. If he was in the driving seat, Lila was welcome to his leg. She stood, expecting him to get out. Trudy got out of the driving seat. She didn't look Jenny's way, or not until the boys were free and running, when Jenny ran to greet them and was almost knocked down by her boys.

Then blown away by Trudy. 'You can't do this, Mum, and I'm not allowing you to.'

'You can't park there either,' Jenny said. 'Harry's coming around to take that lot to the tip for me.' The boys were into *that lot*. They recognised Nanny's computers that they'd never been allowed to touch.

'Why is your fings out here for?' Ricky asked.

'They're too old,' Jenny said. 'Move your car onto the lawn, please, Tru. I need the driveway clear.'

'What the hell were you thinking about? This is my home.'

'Move your car first and argue second,' Jenny said.

Trudy walked back to her car and Jenny took the boys through to the kitchen, where she found their plastic cup-a-tea mugs with the bunnies on their sides. She was making tea when Trudy came in ready for war.

'To go and do a thing like that without telling me or Georgie. Your behaviour is irrational, Mum. It's been irrational since Dad died. You're cancelling that sale and speaking to a professional.'

'I've been speaking to professionals all week,' Jenny said. She had. Mike was a retired accountant, Pat a retired schoolteacher, add to them the solicitor, plus the agent, and that added up to an overdose of professionals. 'Tea or coffee?' she asked.

'Have you signed anything?'

Jenny made tea for four and placed the mugs on the table. She opened her biscuit tin. The boys liked an oatmeal biscuit with their cup-a-teas. Trudy wasn't interested in tea or biscuits.

'You've lost more weight. Sit down and eat something,' Jenny said.

'Have you signed anything?'

'Signed, sealed and witnessed – and will deliver in sixty days.'

'When did you sign it?'

'Yesterday, when they paid their deposit – conditional on white ants.'

'There's a cooling-down period.'

'I'm not hot so you'd better start praying for white ants. Sit down and eat. Your clothes are hanging off you.' Her jeans were. Jenny had known them when they'd been skin tight.

'Where is the white ants, Nanny?' Ricky asked.

'I haven't got any,' Jenny said. Trudy was standing, so Jenny drank her tea standing. 'You must have left early,' she said.

'I'm not here to discuss my timetable. You can't do this, Mum. You need time to come to terms with your loss before making any major life-changing decisions. Any professional will tell you the same. It's been three weeks. You're running blind.'

'Where is Papa?' Ricky asked.

'He took a rowboat to heaven, darlin' – and if I'm running blind, you're running yourself ragged down there while he sits on his arse. Drink your tea.'

'I – don't – want – tea! I want my home!'

Jenny's sigh was a moan. She didn't need this, not today. She didn't need a daughter telling her what she could or couldn't do either. 'You left home a long time ago, darlin', and just when we thought you were back, you did it again. It's a house. You, your father and those boys were my home and I would have lived happily in a tent with them and you. I can't live here, not alone, so stop fussing and sit down.'

The boys weren't accustomed to Mummy being told to stop fussing and sit down. They stared but didn't interrupt.

'Where are you going to live?'

'In motels,' Jenny said.

'Can you hear how irrational that sounds? What about Lila, or will you have her put down?'

'That's an irrational question,' Jenny said. 'And what's so irrational about not wanting to wake up dead one day in this town – and have you wanting to bury me in with the bloody Hoopers?'

'Stop your swearing.'

'Then change the subject or I'll do more of it.'

The boys changed the subject to a Nanny *samich*. It wasn't lunch-time; they settled for a misshapen chocolate-coated Magnum, and were dripping ice-cream and shedding chocolate when Harry and Lila crept up on them. Lila cleaned up their drips and chocolate and Trudy stopped arguing to greet Harry.

He wasn't alone. Lenny, his eldest son, owned a trailer and a 4WD capable of towing it fully loaded. He'd backed it up close to the shed and was waiting out there, so Jenny went out to tell him what to load.

Two men with a supervisor and small boys saying, 'Pitch it,' can achieve a lot in an hour. They pitched two lawn mowers. The third, relatively modern, was worth money, according to Lenny, as was the wood router. Jenny brushed dust and drowsy redbacks from both with a hair broom while the men cleared the bench. Tools used by John the day before he died were returned to his toolbox. The timber he'd been shaping, they leant beside his router. He'd helped fill Vern Hooper's house for a few years after Amy died. Like Harry, John McPherson had been more than a friend.

Lenny climbed a ladder once they'd cleared enough space to stand a ladder. He dragged rolls of wire down from the rafters, dragged down angle iron, timber – and a portrait of Jim's great-grandfather.

'I used to wonder what happened to that,' Jenny said. 'Pitch it.'

'*Pichit*,' the twins chorused, and old James Richard Hooper with his white rat moustache and his great-granddaughter's cockroach eyes was gone. The computers were the last to be loaded, and before Lenny vacated the drive, a new Commodore towing a horse float was waiting to back in.

There were four in that car, mum, dad and a young couple just starting out together. They bought Jenny's original dining suite and the easy chairs from the kitchen. They bought the big television but didn't have enough money on them for the cabinet it sat on. Jenny didn't want it. She couldn't move the thing to clean behind it.

'Consider it your wedding present,' she said, 'if you help me clear out what's in it.'

It was packed solid with videos, Jim's, Jenny's and the boys', who were pleased to see their old friends. Helen looked at the one Jim had labelled *Juliana Conti* and Jenny reached fast for it.

'Mum and I love her books,' Helen said. 'Is she on it?'

'My husband taped her one and only interview,' Jenny said.

It took two men to carry that cabinet down to the horse float. It took two men to carry the television and the table. The women carried the chairs, and when they drove away, the marks of what was missing were visible. There was vacuuming to be done then, and a video player to connect to the small kitchen television, but working side by side, Jenny and Trudy connected it then played *Juliana Conti*. The boys would have preferred *Beauty and the Beast*, but they sat down to watch the lady in pink.

'Dad played this the day we came home from London,' Trudy said.

'You laughed.'

She wasn't laughing today, but she'd stopped nagging. Jenny watched the screen with one eye while making salad sandwiches. That pink suit, that wig, that day was etched deep into her memory. She'd had an unscratchable itch beneath the wig, and the skirt of the suit had been too short. The shoes were her own. She still had them. Never wore them now but hadn't been able to throw them away.

'Everything seemed possible the day we arrived home,' Trudy said when the tape was rewinding.

'*Winter Boomerang* had just been released and was selling like hot biscuits. It was a happy day.'

'What made you do it?'

'Not the house again –'

'I meant the video. That interview.'

'Georgie, Katie, stupidity – God knows.'

'Who was Margaret Morrison, Mum?'

'Margaret?' Jenny asked. 'I never knew any Margaret Morrison.'

'My birth mother. Georgie's told me that she was some form of relative,' Trudy said as Jenny slid the tape back into its cardboard sheath. 'She told me she was dead. That she'd died twenty years ago.'

'Papa got dead,' Jamey said.

They looked at him, but his words failed to divert Trudy. 'What do you know about her, Mum?'

'Not a lot. She was nineteen, unmarried, didn't want to raise you.' *We're all dealt a hand of cards at birth, and good, bad or indifferent we have to play the game out to the end*, that woman in pink had said to a camera, and for lack of better, Jenny used her words. 'You were dealt a poor hand at birth, darlin'. You were lucky to make it through the first week, but you ended up with the best hand at the table, with the best father in the world and a mother who did the best she could. That's all you need to know.'

'How was she related to you?'

Tell her, Jenny thought, then shook that thought away. Today she couldn't take the fallout. Trudy's mobile saved her. It was Nick. She needed privacy to speak to him so took the phone outside. It was a long call. All but one sandwich had been cleared away before she returned, and Jenny was dicing the stewing steak she'd taken from the freezer for Lila. The boys and Trudy liked her steak and onion stews.

There was no further mention of Margaret Morrison and little interest in the sandwich. Trudy used to like her food. When she'd been carrying the twins she'd put on too much weight.

And her mobile rang again. 'Get a job and buy your own,' she said to the caller. 'No . . . I said no, Nick.' And she hung up.

He wouldn't leave her alone. She was on the phone when they ate their dinner. She was on the phone again when Jenny tucked the boys into the cot they'd shared since babyhood. They asked her to put the side up, perhaps liking the security of being locked in, or perhaps because they enjoyed climbing over it.

Trudy was in bed by nine, her mobile left charging on the bench. It rang twice, rang out twice, then started beeping, continuously beeping – and at eleven, temptation got the better of Jenny.

Answer me, you fucking bitch.

She dropped the mobile and stepped back from it, washed her hands of it, then wanted to wipe her fingerprints from it – or wipe that text – or read his previous texts. Instead, she went to bed. It was one-fifteen before that mobile stopped beeping.

*

The boys were out early. Their breakfasts used the last of her fresh milk and a good dash of long-life, which didn't taste quite right in tea.

Trudy ate a few bites of dry toast, drank her tea black.

'The caravan kiosk will be open this morning. They'll have fresh milk,' Jenny said. 'Take the boys for a drive out there and get some bread too.'

'I'm out of petrol,' Trudy said.

'Teddy's service station will be open.'

'I left in a hurry. I've got about five dollars in my purse.'

The boys had left messages about no money, no car, nowhere to play and a boogieman lady who talked funny because all her teeth fell out. Trudy was reading her messages, or flipping through them, Jenny watching her face for a reaction. There was none.

'There's money on the television,' she said – a wad of it from yesterday's sales.

'I've got money, just not with me.'

Jenny picked up two fifties and placed them on the table. 'Get bananas too, if they've got any, and a couple of tomatoes.'

Jenny vacuumed the library while they were away. It was starting to look bare. Amy's desk would remain until the end, as would the office chair. That tower of Juliana cartons was a problem, but a shrouded problem. She was adding more duct tape to its shroud when the phone rang. It could have been Nick. It could have been a buyer. She walked down to answer it. It was a chap from Willama, interested in the cot.

'It's not available right now. If you leave your number, I'll get back to you when it is.' She was pencilling his number on paper beneath *cot* when she heard a car drive in. Trudy's old motor had a distinctive sound. She hung up and opened the front door.

There was a silver–blue van in her drive. It looked new. She stepped outside to see if she recognised its driver. Recognised the passenger, as did Lila.

'Trudy isn't here,' Jenny called.

'Where has she taken them?'

'I don't know.' Her lie may have got rid of him had Trudy not driven up Three Pines Road at that moment. She didn't notice the sliver–blue vehicle until she started her turn into driveway. She came no further, and as she backed out, Jenny thanked the old coot in the clouds – thanked him too soon. The Commodore parked in the street, Trudy freed the boys and they came running in through the small gate.

'Get back in that car,' Nick said. 'We're going home.'

Trudy kept coming, a shopping bag in each hand. 'The situation down there is impossible –'

'You live in the best fucking house in the street –'

'Then go home and live in it.'

'Get back in that fucking car, I said.'

'Go inside,' Trudy said to the boys. 'Run.'

One dodged him. He got Ricky. He carried him, screaming and kicking, to the back door of the alien vehicle and flung him in. Then he got in to hold Ricky there.

'Go,' Nick said to the driver. 'Go!'

It was a replay of another day. Jenny could see it, could hear the gears of Lorna Hooper's old green Ford grinding as she'd turned that big car around, Jimmy in the back seat that day.

There'd be no replay. That silver–blue vehicle would have to reverse over Trudy to get out to the street. She'd tossed her shopping on the lawn and was behind the vehicle, pounding its shiny new paintwork with her fists.

'Back up,' Nick yelled. 'She'll move.'

Maybe she would. Jenny had allowed Lorna to kidnap Jimmy. She'd stood half clad in the yard, watching that big old Ford hit every pothole in the rutted track, Granny's gate wide open and too far away.

Noise in a yard that had previously been quiet, and the noise makers not watching her, Jenny ran between trees and shrubs to the gate. Slammed it, adding its shuddering crash to the noise. Old, heavy metal and wire with a latch that couldn't be trusted. They'd always chained it and looped a padlock through the chain when they'd left the house unattended. The rear of the van was close before she clipped the padlock, Trudy backing up behind it.

'They're not going anywhere,' Jenny said to her. The key to that padlock was on her key ring and her keys were inside. 'Call the constable.'

Nick didn't like that word. He was out before Trudy's mobile was out of her pocket, then the driver got out. He looked like one of Nick's relatives, though one Jenny hadn't met.

'I'm not involved,' he said.

Lila didn't believe him. Perhaps he smelt of Nick. She ran at him, showing her teeth and not in a smile.

A neighbour on the east side came out to stare; his wife stood at her open front door.

The driver's door of the vehicle was open, and Ricky was over the seat, out and running, while Nick twisted Trudy's arm up her back until she dropped her phone. It didn't smash. It landed on the lawn.

Jenny didn't hear the vehicle pull in behind her. She felt its hot breath and turned, expecting to face more of that bastard's relatives. Saw a dusty farm utility nosing in close to the gate and recognised its driver. It was young Paddy Watson.

A big chap, young Paddy Watson, toughened since boyhood by farm labour. Nick Papadimopolous and his relative weren't big. They knew they'd been beaten, and the world silenced. Trudy knew Paddy, and embarrassed, she ran from him, Nick behind her.

'Everything jake here, Mrs Hooper?' Paddy asked.

No reply necessary. Shopping spread on the lawn, yellow bananas, white milk, brown bread, red tomatoes, and one tomato squashed in the melee. It might seed Pat and Mike's front garden next spring.

'I'm not involved,' the driver repeated. 'I gave him a lift up here, that's all. If you open the gate, I'll go.'

'What do you reckon, Mrs Hooper?' Paddy asked.

'No key,' Jenny said.

'He said he needed to talk to his wife –' the driver said.

The neighbours closed their front door. The woman would be on the phone to her cronies. Jenny picked up Trudy's phone. It was working. She didn't know Pinch-face's number and didn't need him now. She had young Paddy.

'If I'd known what he had in mind, I wouldn't have driven him,' the driver said.

Trudy's purse had been in her shopping bag. It had spilled coins – and her car keys. She still had a key to the padlock on her key ring.

'Let him out, Paddy,' she said.

She unlocked the gate. Opened it while Paddy moved his vehicle, then stepped out to the street to watch the van back out and take off fast up Hooper Street.

'I hear you've got a wood router you might be interested in selling, Mrs Hooper,' Paddy said, finally getting to the reason why he was there.

'I've got a lot I'm interested in selling,' she said as she walked back to the lawn to pick up coins then the shopping bag. Paddy came to help pick up the scattered shopping and drop it into Trudy's green bag while they spoke of John McPherson's wood router.

'I don't know if it still goes, Paddy. It hasn't been turned on since he died.'

The front lawn now safe, the twins came from the west side of the house as Jenny picked up a ten-dollar note that had blown under an azalea bush. She folded it and tucked it beneath her bra strap as she placed the shopping on her front veranda.

The door was open. She could hear Trudy and Nick arguing inside but turned her back on that house and led the way to the shed where she pointed out the solo power point and the coiled extension lead John used to use. Paddy did the rest while Jenny, her boys and Lila watched.

He got the router working. He knew how to use it. They watched him put it through its paces, watched him make sawdust fly and watched him turn it off.

'She's a good one,' he said.

'John used to make toys for kids with it,' Jenny said. *Used to*. Everything was *used to*. Trudy *used to* be happily married and roaming around Europe with her handsome husband. Jenny *used to* tell those who asked after her that Trudy was footloose and fancy free. She *used to* envy Trudy a husband who'd enjoyed travelling.

'Have you got a price on it, Mrs Hooper?'

'I haven't advertised it, Paddy. Take it and bless you for coming when you did.'

He wrote her a cheque. She didn't need it, didn't look at it, just folded it and slid it in beside the ten-dollar note.

'An old fencing-wire strainer,' he said, handling an oddity Jenny hadn't been able to name.

No one had strained fencing wire on this property. Vern Hooper may have used it when he'd owned his farm. Paddy's grandfather still owned his farm.

'Give it to your grandfather. There's an old crowbar in the corner. Take it too, if it's any use to you. I can't lift it. Take those shovels if you can use them. What's left in here when I move out will end up at the tip,' she said.

He backed his ute in then to load the router and wire strainer, he squashed a few red-backs beneath his working boot when he reached for a massive pair of multigrips he might be able to use. He took what he named a good post-hole digging shovel and the long iron crowbar, picking it up as if it were a toothpick. He took two rolls of fencing wire, then stood there patting Lila while glancing from time to time towards the house.

There weren't many Lila allowed to pat her. Maybe she'd picked up the scent of her siblings on Paddy's working trousers. His father had trained two of her litter mates to round up his sheep.

'Just thinking, Mrs Hooper. Those blokes setting up their museum would like to have a poke around in here. Want me to have a word to them for you?'

'Have a word with anyone, Paddy. I'm thinking of hanging a *Help Yourself* sign on my fence,' she said.

'Don't go doing that. You'll end up with every Duffy in a fifty-k radius helping himself to more than what's in your shed.' He nodded towards the house. 'Anything you want me to do about . . .'

'She has to do it, Paddy. No one can do it for her. We're going for a walk, aren't we, darlins?' she said to her boys.

They followed the ute out to Hooper Street. He turned towards Three Pines Road so they followed him to it. He turned right. They turned left and walked by the hotel. No sign of that silver–blue van, so they walked on down to the takeaway shop, to the smell of fish and chips. Her boys had become addicted to hot chips and potato cakes at a young age. She had ten dollars so ordered ten dollars' worth of chips and potato cakes, and when the money and the hot parcel changed hands, they walked east to Harry's bungalow. He'd have the very necessary tomato sauce.

They picnicked with him, elbow to elbow around his tiny table, sharing their food with him and Lila. Happy little boys who didn't understand about listening to a football match on a radio. They sat quietly, taking turns to cut pictures from Harry's supermarket junk-mail with Jenny's nail scissors.

Jenny and Harry spoke adult short-hand while listening to that game until the siren hooted its end. Jim used to watch or listen to football matches – if Collingwood had been playing.

Daylight saving had ended. A fine warm day had become cool evening before Jenny walked the twins home. Trudy's car was still parked in the street. He was behind its wheel, Trudy met the returning walkers near the gate.

'Did you find my car keys?'

'I'm not giving them to you.'

'We're going home, Mum,' she said.

'You don't have to do this,' Jenny said. 'Please don't do this, Tru.'

'Look on the bright side,' Trudy said. 'You can sell their cot. Sell my bed too. Sell everything.'

'Please don't do this, my darlin' girl.'

'Where are my keys?'

They were tucked into one of Jenny's bra-cups. She took them out and dropped them. Trudy picked them up then turned to her boys. 'In the car,' she said. 'Be quick about it.'

Jenny kissed little hands that still smelt of potato cakes and of all things good. She kissed two worried faces, got a grip on Lila's collar, then walked alone through the gate. She didn't look back. No gain in looking back. No gain in begging. Jim had begged and two and a half weeks later he'd died of a broken heart.

People can choose to die of broken hearts or decide they have no heart to break. Heartless is less painful.

No White Ants

*P*at and Mick's building inspector declared Vern Hooper's house termite free the day Jenny sold Trudy's bedroom furniture. She sold the sitting-room suite to a couple from Willama who also needed a washing machine. April was running short of days when her industrial sewing machine sold.

She signed her new will before April ended. She'd told Georgie that she wanted her money to be placed into a trust account for Katie and the boys, for Trudy to receive a monthly allowance for the boys' upkeep only, and that if anything happened to Trudy before the boys were twenty-one, Nick wouldn't get his hands on one cent of her money unless he could produce receipts relating to the boys' upkeep.

She'd signed it at home, in the presence of Georgie, one of her associates and his secretary. Georgie's firm had offices in Sydney and Melbourne; she'd been the complimentary woman on a few big defence teams, had flown up and back many times. She was driving a big-name barrister that day who had been warned by his doctor not to fly. Jenny fed them lunch in her kitchen, then they got back into a luxurious limo to continue their drive.

Donna and Jessica Palmer had been helpful. She'd put them to work in the kitchen, emptying cupboards. Most of what they'd packed had gone with them, to the op-shop. She could have used their help in the library but couldn't take them in there. Donna would have that shroud off the Juliana books in ten seconds flat.

They were too many. She couldn't donate them or dump them. Every carton she unloaded at the tip, sealed or not, old Bert, the tip man, opened.

Books start life as trees. The night after she signed her will, she'd decided to do a Hitler and burn the books – save money on firewood – and before hitting her pillow, she'd stoked the stove with two copies of *The Winter Boomerang* and two of *The Town*.

They hadn't burnt well. She'd woken to a cold kitchen, a dead stove and four badly singed books, which took all day to burn, one at a time.

Hadn't heard from Trudy. She'd gone over to the dark side. That's what happened in some families. Jim had denied his family – in life. He was with them now and she hadn't been near the cemetery since the day of the funeral.

Idle hands are the devil's tools, Granny used to say. *Never put off till tomorrow what you don't want to do today.*

She had to get an ad in the *Gazette* today, a shorter list of items for sale, no suggested prices. *No genuine offer refused*, she'd add to this one. She was running out of time. Didn't have to hand over the keys until the eighteenth of June, but would be flying away on the fourteenth of May.

The day after the funeral, half out of her mind and mad as hell at Jim for that fifty-thousand-dollar cheque, she'd walked into a travel agency to blow his fifty thousand on a world cruise – and jump overboard before the boat completed its circle.

She hadn't booked a world cruise. The agent had shown her a cruise of the Greek islands. The water would be warmer there, she'd thought, and she'd never heard of white pointers eating Greeks. It hadn't cost fifty thousand, so she'd upgraded her flights to business class, paid for top-of-the-range travel insurance, paid the deposit with the Visa card, then driven home and forgotten about it – until the itinerary arrived and a bill for the balance of her cruise.

She could have cancelled it. Might have got back a little of her deposit. Had thought about cancelling it, but she'd read that itinerary then written a cheque for the balance.

May was five days old when she wrote a final cheque for the woodman, then a larger cheque for the lawnmower man. She paid him in advance to come in weekly while she was away. He had a vac-blower that made short work of fallen leaves. They were falling.

On the fifth of May she wrote her hairdresser a cheque for a trim and dye job, went to the bank to collect her new bank card, guaranteed by that bank to access any overseas ATM, then drove out to the Willama tip with a load, just to check it out.

It was more businesslike than Woody Creek's. It had a uniformed man in a small office who took her money, told her where to unload and left her to do it. She got rid of a boot-load of plastic pots and a few pot plants. She'd get rid of Juliana's cartons there tomorrow.

That evening she'd removed the shroud and was sealing the first carton into a garbage bag when the phone rang. She thought *buyer* and ran. It was Georgie. The case won or lost, she was back in Greensborough.

'Heard from Trudy?' Georgie asked.

'No.'

'She's back at work, doing the nightshift at Box Hill.'

'Who's looking after the boys?'

'They might keep Nick at home,' Georgie said.

'They might not too.'

'What have you been doing? You're panting,' Georgie said.

'I ran from the library. I'm dumping those cartons in Willama tomorrow.'

'Filled Woody Creek's, eh?'

'Old Bert opens them. The publisher's name and mine is all over them,' Jenny said.

'Kill that thought,' Georgie said.

'The Willama tip is impersonal. No one sees what you dump,' Jenny argued.

'You're not dumping those books, Jen.'

'Then what do I do with them?'

'I'll give them garage space. We'll bring the ute up at the weekend.'

'I'll need any space you've got in your garage for the stuff I want to keep.'

'We'll find space. We'll be up on Saturday –'

'No. Make it the following weekend and I'll drive back behind you. I'm going to tell Trudy about Margot – and I've got something to tell you too.'

'I'm here.'

'You'll try to talk me out of it.'

'What?'

'I'm booked on a cruise, leaving on the fifteenth.'

It was much more than a cruise, but *cruise* was enough for Georgie to swallow over the phone. Without giving her space to ask, 'Where to?' Jenny added, 'That's why I've been in such a hell of a hurry to get things done. I won't get back until the sixteenth of June and I hand over the keys on the eighteenth.'

'The sixteenth of June? You're going for a month?'

'Twenty-eight days – plus the time flying.'

*

They came on Saturday, the tenth of May. They loaded Amy's desk, then the cartons. They loaded the ruby-glass lamps into Jenny's car with two large cases and one that was smaller, brand new and already packed for her cruise. It had wheels and a handle that turned it into a trolley. The laptop, zipped into its bag, went into the Toyota's boot, with Jim's concertina file and Jenny's near new set of saucepans. The jewellery box rode on her front passenger seat with her handbag.

Lila knew what was happening before Harry arrived on foot. Her tail was down, her eyes pitiful. She knew that worse was about to happen when Jenny clipped on her lead then gave her house keys to Harry, just in case she didn't get back by the eighteenth, D-day, delivery day.

No comfort is ever given or received from long goodbyes, so with a final rub of that red coat, a final kiss on a hanging head, Jenny got into her car and reversed down the side of the house, across the lawn to the concrete driveway, then out to Hooper Street to where the old red ute was near pawing at the earth to be on its way.

Jenny followed it, made a right-hand turn into Three Pines Road, then right again onto the highway. She passed what used to be Joe Flanagan's land where the road straightened out and the ute showed that it had a few miles left in it. Its speedo would be showing sixty miles an hour. Jenny's was showing a hundred ks, the legal limit on this road.

A long drive ahead of her, but the ute leading the way, she relaxed and allowed her mind to write a denouement to the story of her life.

She drove that familiar road, the sum-total of her life in her car and in the vehicle ahead. She didn't look back. Having set those wheels in motion the morning after her husband's funeral, the wheels had turned, gaining momentum as they raced headlong downhill towards her final day.

PART TWO

HOUSE OF HORRORS

*T*hose who'd grown with Melbourne's traffic had no fear of it. Five days a week Georgie joined the slow-moving stream of cars into the city, where she spent her days on the twenty-third floor of the skyscraper office building where Marino and Associates leased one floor.

On Monday, Jenny spent the day alone at Greensborough, a street directory open on the family-room table. She was a confident driver. If she could find a route that would take her direct from Greensborough to Croydon, she'd have her car handy should she need to make a quick getaway. There was no direct route, only kilometres of roads and multiple turns, so on Tuesday she rode into the city with Georgie to catch a tram. She knew trams. They'd altered little since the forties and their routes hadn't altered at all.

The trains had. They now went underground, but she knew where to catch a tram that would take her to the Richmond station where she could catch a train to Croydon that didn't go underground.

Tram tickets had altered. Back in the forties she'd handed a coin to a conductor and he'd handed her a paper ticket. Tickets had to be prepaid now and verified when you boarded. She'd phoned Trudy, who'd spoken about her job, about Nick's job, then, before hanging up, she'd invited Jenny to stay the night in Croydon.

'We've got two empty bedrooms,' she'd said. 'The boys miss you,' she'd said.

Georgie had urged her to go. She'd offered to meet them at a restaurant in Doncaster and drive Jenny back to Greensborough.

Facing Nick would be difficult, but he'd be at work all day. She wouldn't need to see much of him.

Croydon was on the Box Hill–Ringwood line. In the fifties, Jenny had known those stations well. Jim used to live and work in Ringwood, and Florence Dawson, Raelene's natural mother, had lived at Box Hill. For months, every second weekend, she'd catch a train from Frankston to the city, catch another to Box Hill, drop Raelene off with Florence and her stepfather, then return to the station and ride the train out to Jim.

That section of the line looked much as it ever had to Box Hill, then it changed. Jenny remembered those lines passing through farmland and orchards. She remembered cows grazing on green grass. The cows and grass had succumbed to the city's greed for land. Today, to her left and right she saw only the creeping plague of houses.

Every small town close to Melbourne had been swallowed up by the city. Lilydale had. Frankston had. She'd stayed at a guesthouse in Frankston before the war, had worked at that same guesthouse in the fifties when that town had still been a beachside resort. Raelene had been with her in Frankston. She'd loved the beach.

Then Margot and her trouble had joined them, and Frankston had turned bad.

Trains were more efficient than trams. She was at Croydon too early. Trudy had told her to give her a call from the station and she'd pick her up – but not at eight-thirty, and barely eight-thirty, so Jenny went in search of a bus. She'd Googled Croydon's bus timetables and bus routes and two were waiting. The first driver she asked was going her way. He was an Australian. He understood the map Katie had printed out for her, a cross marking Tessa's court, so she sat close to him until he told her they were at her stop.

'Have a good day,' he said.

'You too,' Jenny said, but thought it highly unlikely. Last night's weather reporter had forecast intermittent showers, and before Jenny turned left into Tessa's court, that reporter was proven right. The sky started spitting at her.

Number fourteen was an off-white monolith with a marble tiled, columned porch that looked down its European nose at its more common neighbours. But it had a common doorbell – an *Avon calling* ding-dong. It dinged and donged as the sky stopped spitting and started to rain down. She stayed dry beneath the porch, where she leant harder on the button. Someone inside must have heard its *Avon* song. No one opened the door.

The garage was open. Trudy's car wasn't in it. She could have popped out to get something, and so thinking, Jenny made a break for the garage where she reached into her bag for her mobile and sent a text. No reply from Trudy.

The garage was so new its cement floor was still clean. She walked down to the back wall, to a door she expected to be locked. It opened and a blast of heat slapped her in the face.

Tessa had central heating. How many times had Jenny threatened to have central heating installed?

She'd met Trudy's mother-in-law twice, when the twins were a month old and again when they'd been eighteen months. She was in the kitchen, standing in front of Jenny's dream fridge–freezer, both doors open.

'Good morning,' Jenny said. 'I rang your bell.'

Tessa took a large ice-cream container from the middle shelf before turning to face the burglar.

'You're looking well,' Jenny lied. She was twice the woman she'd been eighteen months ago, her hair was uncombed and her face looked like bread dough someone had forgotten to bake. 'Is Trudy about?'

For her question, she received a spurt of Greek followed by a screeched 'Trudy!' Then, the ice-cream container shoved back into the refrigerator, Tessa waddled into a passage, both refrigerator doors left open.

She's gone to get Trudy, Jenny thought, and took the opportunity to study the interior of her dream fridge–freezer before closing its doors.

No Tessa. No Trudy, but water running overhead, a television playing nearby. Jenny waited – in her dream kitchen – with its black granite bench tops and white cupboard doors.

Who wouldn't want to live here?

No sound of Trudy or Nick, but she heard the boys giggling overhead, so walked through the kitchen–dining room to a staircase. Tessa wasn't fetching Trudy. She was sitting on a couch, watching a television commercial for exercise equipment.

There was something wrong with that woman. Deciding not to disturb her, Jenny followed the sound of giggling and splashing water. She found them, water running full blast into a bathtub, pyjama-clad boys leaning over its edge, making sheets of toilet paper float.

'Turn that tap off,' she said. They didn't turn it off. They tackled her around the knees, and apart from their pyjamas they were barely recognisable. They'd been shorn, their cherub faces stolen with their hair. She kissed two spiky heads, turned off the tap, scooped up the toilet paper, wadded by its attempt to get down the plughole. She mopped water from the floor with a towel, then asked about Mummy.

'Thleeping,' Ricky said.

'*Ssss*,' Jenny said. '*Ssss*, like a snake.'

'*Ssss*-leeping,' he said.

'Good boy.'

She could have cured Margot's lisp, had she been interested enough, early enough. They led the way to Mummy, down a passage to an open door where Trudy was asleep in one of two single beds, asleep with one eye open.

'You're here already,' she said, rolling fast to her feet.

'I got a lift into the city with Georgie. She drives in early. A bus was waiting at the Croydon station.'

'You're wet,' she said, noticing the boys' pyjamas. 'What have you been doing?'

There were dark smudges beneath her eyes. They'd been there in Woody Creek, but today one smudge was darker than the other.

'What happened to your eye?'

'It's nothing,' Trudy said and turned away.

'Daddy went *whoooosh*, and her felled over,' Ricky said, with actions.

'And Mummy cried,' Jamey said.

'They're talking rubbish,' Trudy said. She'd opened a built-in robe, her back to them until she found matching tracksuits. Jenny looked at her face when she turned but said no more, or no more about that dark smudge. She mentioned the open garage door, no car in the garage.

'I told you he was working,' Trudy said. 'They do gardens. Incidentally, I have to work tonight.'

'You said you had tonight and tomorrow night off.'

'I've got tomorrow night. There's a throat virus going around.'

They got the boys dressed, got shoes and socks onto tiny feet. They spoke about tomorrow night, about the throat virus, about the kitchen. Then Jenny told Trudy to go back to bed, told her she'd look after the boys.

They took her on a guided tour of the upper floor, showed her Daddy's bedroom and his television, his video and CD player.

There are ways of gaining information from three-year-olds if you ask the right questions. 'Did Daddy give you some breakfast before he went to work?'

'No,' Ricky said.

'Because he went when he went whoosh, not now.'

'Why did he go whoosh?'

'Because . . . because . . . videos,' Jamey said.

'And Mummy said, "Go",' Ricky said.

'Where does Daddy work?'

'Wiff a man, so he can get some money.'

'He can't get any now, because . . . videos.'

'What videos?

Two shorn heads shaken, and more interested in breakfast, they led the way downstairs. They crept by Tessa, still seated on her couch, a very fine couch, the television now playing a morning panel show. Once past that doorway, they skedaddled into the kitchen to show Jenny where the bowls were, where the Weet-Bix and Cornflakes lived. She found a banana and milk, found honey, and added it liberally to sliced banana and Cornflakes, and when she put the milk away, she looked at what was in the ice-cream container – packets and more packets and bottles of pills. She recognised the names of a few, recognised bottled medications lined up on a door shelf, a laxative, an antacid, a brown bottle she didn't know, and when she lifted it to read its label, Ricky said, 'We don't want some now, Nanny.'

'Is that your medicine?'

'When we go to bed. Not now time,' Ricky said.

It was an over-the-counter thing, an antihistamine, for children. *Do not exceed recommended dosage*, the instructions said. *May cause drowsiness.*

Trudy was drugging those boys so she could work – or he was drugging them. Their bowls emptied fast, they wanted to show her outside. She returned the bottle to its shelf and unlocked a glass door. It opened onto a roofed and paved barbeque area, where six padded outdoor chairs were set around a long glass-topped table.

They ran to a barbeque, a gas bottle beneath it.

'It coming, Nanny.'

The driver, an Asian man, spoke English, but badly. He may have said he was going to Eastland. That's where he delivered them, to a city within a city and all new to Jenny. It wasn't to the boys. Daddy had paid a lady there to cut their hair and her shop was near a shop that sold dinosaurs.

They bought two plastic dinosaurs, and colouring pencils and a book to colour. They bought a big, colourful ball and were toting two plastic shopping bags when their noses led them to a food court, where you could buy everything from sushi to a roast dinner. They ordered potato cakes and chips, then helped themselves to a tomato sauce bottle on the counter.

Eating lunch at Eastland. XX. The boys made the kisses then sent the message flying to Mummy's phone.

They sent another one from the supermarket at two. *Anything you need us to pick up for you?*

Still no reply. Maybe she was helping herself to the boy's medicine – or to Tessa's sleeping pills.

They bought a small packet of Jenny's brand of teabags, bought cheese, dry biscuits, bananas and two chocolate Kinder Surprises because good boys had always deserved a Kinder Surprise. They'd been so good it hurt. It was Jenny's best day since . . . since a very long time ago . . . or it was until her mobile beeped a reply.

Where have you taken the twins?

Read your messages. We're at Eastland.

You were not given permission to take them out of the house.

It came from Trudy's mobile but her finger hadn't picked out that message.

Had I known your number I would have texted you directly to find out how long you might be away this morning.

Stay where you are. I'll pick them up.

You weren't so concerned about their welfare when you left the garage and laundry doors unlocked. A murderer could have walked in. The boys are fine. We'll be home when we get there.

No beeped reply to that. They were eating more chips and sharing a hamburger before the next beeps came through, this time from Trudy.

He panicked when he got home and they were missing. Are you on your way?

We're having afternoon tea. You can tell him from me that he won't need to drug them tonight. They'll sleep like logs.

She hit *send* before censoring that message. As with the postal service, once a letter is dropped into the mailbox, you can't retrieve it. Shouldn't have mentioned the drugging, but that's what that bottle was for. Those boys didn't have an allergy between them.

She didn't take them home. She lifted them into a supermarket trolley to give their legs a rest, then they went window shopping. She'd done a lot of window shopping with Jimmy, in Sydney and in Melbourne. She'd taken him with her to ladies' rooms before catching the train or tram home. She took the boys into a ladies' room at Eastland where she washed all evidence of junk food, tomato sauce and Kinder Surprise chocolate from their faces, hands and parkas. She spoke to a woman who told her that she was on her way back to where the buses pulled in. They followed that woman and her shopping trolley. It was after four-forty when she walked the boys that last block home and be it weariness or apprehension, they'd grown silent.

Nick responded to the doorbell's *ding-dong*.

'Nanny's buyed us dinosaurs,' Ricky said.

'An' a big giant ball,' Jamey said. It was in the bag with the dinosaurs, with the colouring pencils, books and Kinder Surprise toys, and while retrieving their dinosaurs the ball got away to bounce merrily towards the stairs.

'Go up and let your mother know that you're alive. She's been frantic,' Nick said, his 'frantic' added for the benefit of their abductor.

'Tell Daddy how you sent kisses to Mummy.'

'We send six kisses. One two free, an' one two free,' Jamey said.

'And we made it go,' Ricky added.

'You were not given permission to take the boys away from the house,' Nick said.

'I was given all the permission I'll ever need three years ago when my daughter screamed them out of her. As I recall, you were missing at the time. Excuse me, Nick.'

He allowed her inside. He closed the door to keep the heat in, and when he turned, he tripped over a squatting twin, still eager to show Daddy his dinosaur.

Daddy snatched the tyrannosaurus and threw it at the front door.

'You broked him,' Ricky said.

Plastic is indestructible. Little boys aren't. 'Take them up and show Mummy,' Jenny said. Mummy now standing at the top of the stairs, keeping her mouth shut, looking like an abused Alice in Wonderland.

Three years ago, Georgie had put her finger on the Trudy–Nick problem. 'She was hothouse raised, Jen. Hothouse plants don't do well when planted out into rocky ground.'

This place was rocky ground in disguise.

'He lost them last week at Eastland,' the wilting hothouse plant said.

'Put that down to lack of experience,' Jenny said.

She followed the boys up the stairs, walking away from confrontation, as she always walked away from confrontation – when she could, but women didn't lock their gates on little tin gods, or turn their backs and walk away. Jenny was in his castle where he was Jesus Christ. He caught her arm.

'I have ultimate authority in this house. In future, you will ask my permission before you take my sons anywhere.'

'Unlike your wife, I have ultimate authority on who puts their hands on me,' she said, then shaking his hand off, she continued up.

'From what I've heard, you weren't always so fussy,' he said.

Since when have you been so fussy, Jen?

A sick wash of memory stilled her feet, knife in the gut memory. She'd been the town pariah at seventeen when she'd dared to show her face at the town hall, when *Gone with the Wind* had been playing. Town pariahs are open season for bastards.

Bobby Vevers had put his hand on her in the park beside the town hall, where she'd been hiding her shameful face during intermission. She'd turned the other cheek that night. She'd run from him. She'd been running from him and his ilk for half of her life, running or hiding.

She was a step above Nick when she did what she should have done at seventeen. Every ounce of strength she possessed she put into the swing of her arm. Heard the satisfying smash as her palm connected with his cheek. Didn't feel it, or not at the instant of impact.

He felt it. And unexpected, if not for the handrail, she may have felled him.

It shocked him, shocked his wife, but interested his sons. They'd seen Daddy go whoosh and now they'd seen Nanny do it. Wide-eyed, they waited for what came next.

Leaving came next, putting space between her and that bastard came next. Her hand was tingling, old words playing in her mind as she stepped by him.

Sixpence a ride and a discount for two —
You're an infectious disease —
You're not fit to raise dogs —
I'll have you in court, you hot-pants little slut —

She'd hit out at the lot of them, and connected. Her one regret was she hadn't been higher up the stairs, that the handrail had been close enough for him to grab. Wished he'd gone head over heels from top to bottom. Wished he'd broken his neck. He was all of them, every male who'd ever put her down, every bastard who'd ever put his hands on her.

Trudy's fault. She'd given him the ammunition, had probably laughed with him in bed while telling tales of her mother's colourful past.

Should never have phoned her. Should have known better than to come here today. She'd wanted to see the boys. She'd wanted to tell Trudy about Margot.

She opened the front door, stepped out, then slammed it behind her, and the hand she'd hit with shaking, she dug in her bag for her mobile. If Katie hadn't keyed the number of a taxi company into it, she would have had to walk back to that bus stop, in the rain.

There was a voice on the line when Trudy opened the door enough to look out. Jenny ignored her while giving the stranger the address.

'You're not leaving like this, Mum?' Trudy said.

'I'm leaving, and if you had half a brain in your head, you'd leave with me.' She stepped out to the rain then. The woman on the line had said they'd send the first available car, which could be in five minutes or twenty. The rain wasn't heavy.

'We're having dinner with Georgie tomorrow night,' Trudy said.

The rain smelt clean, and cleansed by it, Jenny turned to face that fool of a girl. 'How dare you?'

'How dare I what, Mum?' That voice, that patient nursing sister voice she used when dealing with the elderly.

'Tell him about my life?'

'He's my husband –'

'He's a parasite that's attached itself to your back and tapped into your blood stream. When he sucks you dry, he'll fall off and attach himself to someone else – and he'll ruin those boys before he sucks you dry. Leave the bastard.'

'I can't.'

'Because you love him – or you love living in that bloody house of horrors.'

'You sold my home.'

'As far as I can recall, until you needed someone to raise those boys, in twenty-odd years you might have spent two dozen nights beneath its roof.'

'You had your Georgie. All of my life you've had your Georgie – and your Jimmy – and you spent half of my childhood worrying about Raelene. I don't know why you bothered to adopt me.'

Sibling jealousy Jenny understood. She used to be jealous of Sissy. She half turned. It was the opening she needed to tell that fool of a girl that she was her granddaughter. Not the right time or place, so she walked on, wondering if the boys would remember her. If their dinosaurs and rubber ball survived their bastard of a father, they might remember their day out at Eastland.

They'd remember Tessa's screech. That open front door was letting cold clean air inside. Trudy closed it.

Jenny walked three house blocks to a tall brick fence that had a gum tree overhanging it. There was shelter there and the clean scent of wet eucalypt, the scent of home, of Granny's home. She reached up to a cluster of leaves and stole one, crushed it and held it to her nose until a taxi turned into the court, when she stepped out to the rain to wave it to her side.

'Greensborough,' she said.

The driver, an Indian or Arab, knew Melbourne's freeways. Peak-hour traffic had choked the outbound lanes but not a lot was inbound. They made good time to Greensborough. She tipped the driver five dollars for his efficiency and for his silence.

Paul and Katie were cooking dinner. Georgie was still out on those roads.

'We thought you were staying the night,' Katie said.

'I hit him,' Jenny said. They didn't ask who she'd hit. They knew what had happened the last time she'd seen Nick in Woody Creek. 'Tell Georgie to cancel that restaurant booking,' she said, then walked through the house to the guest room.

LUGGAGE

A crowded room, Georgie's guest room. They'd squeezed Amy's desk into a corner, placed Jenny's near-new office chair beside the bed. Her big cases were beside it, the new case on top of them and a small, aqua-blue case on top of it.

Katie had bought the aqua blue at a local garage sale. It was small enough to travel as cabin luggage but too small for a twenty-eight-day tour. Her coat off, shoes off, Jenny sat on the bed, staring at aqua blue but thinking of that slap.

Raised by Norman, the original pacifist, little Jenny Morrison hadn't known how to hit back, or not until Amber came home. After seven years of being alone with his girls, Norman had employed Amber to housekeep and he'd given her Jenny's room. Sharing a bed with Sissy and her BO had taught little Jenny how to pull hair.

She had fire in her blood. Vern Hooper had raised that fire on a few occasions. She'd cursed him to hell and would have liked to brain him with the wood axe. Then Ray King. She'd been a fool to marry him and for eighteen months had kept turning the other cheek – until the night he'd smashed her face to pulp. She'd armed herself with a tomahawk. Had he come near her again, she would have killed him. Her mother's hot Italian blood was in her.

In Itchy-foot's diaries he had described Juliana Conti as a fighting, clawing tigress protecting the cub in her belly. She'd died before she'd had the chance to mother her cub. Tonight Jenny knew that environment didn't have a chance against genetics. She'd hit that swine of a man – and enjoyed it.

And she had to stop thinking about it. Had to force her mind to Thursday, to the flight, to the cruise, to the long jump she'd planned to take between one Greek island and the next. She wasn't going to jump. She was going to tour Juliana's land after the Greek island cruise. For years she'd wanted to see Italy. Trudy had spent a lot of time in Greece and a little in Italy. She'd been everywhere – and she was jealous of Georgie who'd been working like a slave since she'd turned fourteen, who'd been raised fatherless in what most would classify now as a hovel. Trudy had had the best of everything. She'd been Jenny's adored final chance to do something right.

Hadn't given her enough of something. Should have given her Jim's cheque, Jenny thought as she continued to stare at that aqua case Katie had presented to her on Sunday. It might have been big enough for the Greek island cruise. Then Rome, Pompeii, Venice – and Switzerland too. Then London.

Jimmy lived forty miles from London, or he had forty years ago.

She shook her head to shake him away – as she'd been shaking him away since the twins had been born, when she'd promised Jim that she'd forget him. Most of the time she'd kept that promise, but Jim was dead and all promises ended at the grave – and she'd never forgotten Jimmy nor ever would.

The past was eating her alive tonight, Ray, Raelene, Bobby Vevers, Vern Hooper. All dead, along with most of those she'd loved, Granny, Elsie, Amy. Granny had seen the world. Amy had seen a bit of it. Elsie had seen Woody Creek.

I'm going to see the Sistine Chapel, to see bodies turned to stone, she thought. She stood then and reached for the aqua case, bought with Katie's own pocket money. It was inches smaller than the one she'd packed for the tour, but how could she tell Katie it was too small?

She'd be flying into summer. She wouldn't need the sweaters she'd packed. One cardigan maybe. If she took only items that didn't crush, she might squeeze enough into that case. She lifted her tour case to the bed and opened it, then placed the aqua blue at its side. The blue looked happier than the brown. She'd packed three frocks. She rarely wore frocks. One would do. She chose the lightest, a frock of muted blues she'd bought to wear to Donna Palmer's daughter's wedding. It was uncrushable, would roll into nothing. She removed a pair of lightweight beige slacks, was digging for uncrushable tops in one of her large cases when she uncovered the rubber-banded pages of *We'll Meet Again*.

She'd almost burnt that manuscript. Jim's red pen edit of page one had stopped her. He'd put his red pen aside on page eighteen. She knew why. On page eighteen her poorly disguised lovers had become Jen and Jim – with different names.

She sat with her cases on the bed, reading that old love story. She was on page five, still seeing red when Georgie knocked then entered.

'Did you flatten him, mate?'

'He grabbed the stair rail, or I might have.'

'What did he do to you?'

'Trudy had a bruise beneath her eye. "Daddy went whoosh and Mummy fell down and cried." The twins saw it. They saw me go whoosh too. I wish they hadn't.'

Georgie didn't reply but stood looking at the loaded bed while Jenny slid the rubber bands back onto her pages.

'That's the new one you were working on?'

'It's the draft Jim read. There's a later draft in my laptop I never got around to printing,' Jenny said.

Georgie changed her mind about reaching for the pages. She moonlighted as Juliana Conti's agent and editor – without the red pen.

'Much later?'

'I'd just about called it finished.'

Laptop zipped into its bag, which was leaning beside Amy's desk, Georgie unzipped it and took out the laptop and cord.

'What did you name the file?'

'*Time*,' Jenny said.

Minutes later, the pages of *Time* were being spat out, hot and fast, from Georgie's laser printer. It spat three hundred and forty pages before it was done.

There was better light and seating in the family room. Three readers sat until eleven, reading those pages – until Katie started reading over Jenny's shoulder, too impatient to wait for what came next.

'Go to bed. You've got school tomorrow,' Georgie said.

'You've got work,' Katie said.

'I have,' Georgie said. 'I'm taking this with me and posting it, Jen.'

'It's Jim before the Japs stole who he was, Georgie. He was . . . was a beautiful boy.'

'It's the girl he fell in love with too. It's going tomorrow, Jen. Now we're all going to bed.'

She sounded like Granny. *Close that book and go to bed . . . and don't even think about taking that lamp into your bedroom. One lick of flame and this place will go up like matchwood.*

Jenny gave up her pages. She knew how that tale ended. She'd altered little of her meeting with the older Jim at the station, of her mad run to get to him before his train came in and stole him away. She'd deleted Raelene. In the novel, she'd never lost Jimmy. He'd been the one holding her hand, running to his daddy, a happily ever after ending for everyone.

Life doesn't end happily ever after. Life turns to ashes, as had Granny's old house. She'd been right about open flames and cigarettes and kerosene lamps. Her old house had burnt like matchwood.

Jenny went to her room but didn't go to bed. She packed and repacked that aqua case until the house settled, when she crept into the study to retrieve her laptop. There was a power point beside Amy's desk. She plugged it in, moved her office chair into place, then turned on the computer.

And her friend of many sleepless nights woke up to greet her. She didn't reopen the *Time* file but created a new file she named *Parasite*. She was going to write Trudy and Croydon and the parasitic growth out of her head.

*

If there'd been roosters in Greensborough, they would have been crowing before she moved the cases and crawled into Georgie's guest-room bed. It raised crazy dreams. She dreamt that Jimmy was a drug lord, dreamt that Raelene had arrived home with that aqua case full of tiny babies, dreamt of Juliana too. She was wearing a burka but Jenny knew her because of the brooch she'd pinned above her visor. She may have dreamed longer had her mobile not woken her at eleven.

It was Trudy. *I hope we are still having dinner tonight. We need to clear the air.*

Jenny didn't reply. Couldn't. Each time she thought about her she saw that bruise beneath her eye – or heard her laughing with Nick in bed. Her mobile needed charging. Had forgotten about it last night. She didn't charge it but showered, dressed, turned on her laptop, then made tea and toast she shared with her keyboard.

She added Raelene to the *Parasite* file. Nick's eyes had always reminded her of Raelene's.

I've seen apes with more humanity in their eyes . . .

She wrote of Raelene's infancy, of the seven-year-old who'd sat down on the station platform and screamed the day Jenny ran to Jim. That was the day she'd made her choice. She'd allowed that brat to sit and scream while she'd kept on running, then a month or so later, without a fight, without the need of a courtroom or judge, she'd handed Raelene back to her natural mother. She'd been a brat at seven but controllable. Five years later, Florence Dawson had washed her hands of an out-of-control twelve-year-old and given her back to Jenny.

She'd tried, Jim had tried. Raelene hadn't liked the competition of a little sister. She hadn't liked school. She'd liked the Duffy pack. Trudy was going on twelve when they'd sent her to a city ladies' college, to protect her from Raelene.

Shouldn't have sent her away. Should have allowed her to learn about the ugly side of life.

Two o'clock when Jenny came up for air and a cup of tea and to charge her mobile.

Georgie had texted. Trudy, having received no reply from Jenny had contacted her about their dinner tonight.

Cancel it. I'm not going, Jenny replied.

You were going to tell her about Margot.

It will do more harm now than good.

I'll tell her next time she asks, but it would be better coming from you, Georgie texted.

Trudy had known Margot. She'd been told of Margot's connection to the Macdonalds, a rape connection, pack rape, when the Macdonald twins had been eighteen and Jenny fourteen. Jenny had to tell her the truth to combat the lies Raelene scraped up from Woody Creek's gutters.

Raelene had spent a lot of time wallowing in gutters. She'd been on drugs at sixteen and selling herself to feed her habit. At twenty-one, she'd been responsible for the death of an elderly woman. Hadn't been charged with murder or manslaughter. A judge sentenced her to twelve months for robbery with violence. It wasn't Raelene's fault that the old woman died. All she'd wanted was the handbag. If that frail old lady had given it up, Raelene wouldn't have had to knock her down to get it, and her victim wouldn't have spent the final month of her life in a hospital bed.

Raelene, pregnant when they'd locked her up, gave birth in jail. Until the night of the fire, Jenny had assumed that her baby had been fathered by Dino Collins – and whether it had or hadn't, it wouldn't have made a scrap of difference. She wouldn't have given it a home. One Raelene in a lifetime was one too many.

That baby's parentage had been important to Cara. She'd demanded blood tests before agreeing to foster it. Tracy, she'd named it, or Raelene had named it. Cara had cared about that baby – as Jenny had once cared about its mother.

They'd heard about the kidnap on the news before Cara had arrived that night in Woody Creek, or heard that a four-year-old infant had been stolen from her bed in the night.

It was Cara who'd told them that Tracy was Raelene's daughter. Cara who'd told them that Dino Collins had been involved, that he'd left his calling card, a circle of glass, cut from a window.

Raelene hadn't taken her daughter to love, to mother, but to murder her.

Police swarming in Woody Creek that night, road blocks on every road, on every dusty track leading in or out of that town. They'd got Collins on the Mission Bridge. He'd been driving Raelene's car but neither she nor Tracy had been in it.

Eleven o'clock when a police sergeant drove down to the old house to tell Cara that Collins was in hospital, under guard. He'd been relaying his news over a coffee when Joe Flanagan, who'd shared a boundary fence with Granny's land, came bellowing up through the orchard. He and his dogs had found the little girl, sealed into a cardboard carton and left to die beside his fence.

The police hadn't found Raelene. They'd searched Granny's land, Joe Flanagan's, and the bush beside the creek.

A dark place, Granny's fifteen acres – a big old shed, two houses, chicken pens and trees to hide in. Raelene had hidden somewhere until dawn when she'd made her final attack. She'd firebombed the house where Georgie and Margot were sleeping and with its dying breath, the house had turned on her and got her. She'd been twenty-six.

Those who were paid to know such things said that Margot would have died from smoke inhalation before she'd felt the flames of that inferno. Harry and two constables broke a window and dragged Georgie out. The old kitchen roof fell in on Raelene.

Trudy, eighteen at that time, had been old enough to be told the truth. Jenny had wanted to bring her home for Margot's funeral. Jim wouldn't agree to it.

She'd been hothouse raised, but by Jim, not Jenny. To his last days, she'd been his little girl. He hadn't allowed her to build up immunity to parasitic life forms.

Katie crept in at four, when she came home from school, to read the words pouring from Jenny's fingers, and too deeply immersed in that other world, she was unaware of her onlooker until Katie moved nearer.

'It's unfit for general exhibition, darlin',' Jenny said, and closed the lid.

'It's about Raelene.'

'Some of it is.'

She didn't open it again. Paul came in at five. He poured two glasses of wine then asked Katie what she wanted to eat. 'Mum and Jen are going out for dinner.'

'I told her to cancel,' Jenny said.

THE RESTAURANT

*P*rimed with a glass of wine at five, topped up with a second at six, Jenny saw little on the drive to Doncaster. Her mind a morass of things she wanted to say, things she had to say, things she mustn't say, she sat staring at the traffic ahead and seeing nothing.

They found a park close to the door, recognised Trudy's Commodore two spaces away. She was punctual and was sitting alone in the near-empty restaurant. Georgie greeted her. Jenny took her jacket off, hung it over the back of her chair and was searching for something to say when the drinks waiter arrived. She found something to say to him.

'A bottle of sparkling wine, and three glasses.'

'I'm not drinking,' Trudy said.

'Not from your top shelf,' Georgie added. She could afford top shelf but didn't flaunt the fact.

Direct opposites, Trudy and Georgie, they were of similar height but that was as far as similarity went.

'We need to discuss yesterday, Mum. I know that Nick went overboard, but he worries about the boys,' Trudy began.

'I'm more worried about your eye,' Jenny said.

'If you're going to start on that, I'll leave.'

'If you're going to mention him, I'll leave,' Jenny said, and she took her nail scissors from her bag to trim back her deformed nail. She was snipping her other nails when the waiter brought a bottle and three glasses to their table and stayed on to fill them.

'Could I have some water?' Trudy said.

'Please,' Jenny added. She tasted the wine then asked, 'What's wrong with your mother-in-law?'

'Her memory is going. That's another reason I wanted to speak to you. Nick's taking her home to Greece for a holiday in June. I was going to ask you yesterday if you'd like to move in with me and the boys while they're away.'

'I won't be here,' Jenny said.

'When's your settlement date?'

'Eighteenth of June,' Georgie said. 'When are they leaving for Greece?'

'The tenth. Tessa has sisters over there she hasn't seen in almost fifty years. They'll be away for three weeks.'

'I'll bet you a pound to a penny he doesn't bring her back,' Jenny said.

Trudy sighed and looked for the man with her water. He wasn't coming, so she turned again to Jenny and spoke with the tone she used when dealing with obstreperous patients, the tone she'd used on Jim when he'd refused her help.

'Would you like to explain what would make you say a thing like that?'

'I only saw her for five minutes and I'd leave her at a lost dogs' home,' Jenny replied.

'Jen's booked herself on a tour,' Georgie said.

'Where are you going?'

'I'm having a taste of Europe –'

'For twenty-eight days,' Georgie said. 'I've already told her it will kill her.'

'It's for seniors. They won't expect us to climb the Jungfrau – or whatever mountain they've got down the bottom corner of Switzerland.'

'You're not capable of doing a month-long tour,' Trudy said.

'You don't know what I'm capable of.'

'The flight will kill you,' Trudy said.

'Not unless the plane's hijacked. I upgraded to business class. More leg room, free wine, private television,' Jenny said, and she emptied her glass and refilled it from the bottle. 'I'll be able to watch all the new movies . . .'

'Make her cancel it, Georgie.'

'I've tried,' Georgie said.

'She's trying to kill herself and go to Dad.'

'He's in with the Hoopers,' Jenny said. 'And if either of you put me in with him, I'll haunt you until your dying day – and nobody is cancelling anything. I've never been on a cruise.' She sipped. 'Or anywhere else. We spend a week in Italy. I've always wanted to see where Juliana came from.' She turned to Georgie. 'And I'm going to find Jimmy while I'm over there. We have three days in London before we fly home.'

'He'd dead, Jen,' Georgie said.

'He's not.'

'He's not in your Thames Ditton either,' Trudy said. 'When Nick and I went down there we asked about a James Langdon, a Jimmy Hooper and a Jim Morrison. No one had heard of any of them.'

Because he wasn't any of them. He wasn't James, Jimmy or Jim, Hooper, Morrison or Langdon. Margaret Hooper had married Bernard Grenville. Jimmy would have taken his adoptive father's name when they'd adopted him, as Trudy had taken Jim's.

Juliana, meet Morrie. He's Cara's husband, Georgie had said that day at the television studio. Had Trudy asked after a Morrison Grenville, someone would have known him. The night of the fire, the police had called Cara Mrs Grenville.

Georgie's eyes were boring a pathway into Jenny's wandering mind, and tonight she mustn't read what was going on in there. She'd introduced Jenny to Cara's husband, not to Jimmy. For the best part of an hour Georgie had been with him, spoken to him and hadn't recognised him.

It had taken Jenny ten seconds –

'You've got your father's eyes,' Jenny said, lifting her too-narrow wine glass to her brow to protect her neurons from Georgie's penetrating gaze, then changed the subject. 'Oh, by the way, Tru, the next time you're pillow-talking to your parasite, you might mention that I've never been sorry for one day I spent with Laurie Morgan.'

He'd fathered Georgie, and she knew it, had always known it. 'Stop it, Jen,' Georgie warned.

'It's true. He might have helped himself to what he wanted, but he went about it in a more honest way than . . . than one who shall remain nameless.'

'If you're going to keep bitching about Nick then I'll go,' Trudy said.

'I'll go,' Jenny said. She'd seen an arrow with a ladies' room symbol when she'd hung her jacket. The wine she'd drunk at Georgie's was going through her.

Only one cubicle. She used it, washed her hands in a tiny washroom then studied her face in the mirror. Jimmy hadn't recognised the dark-wigged Juliana. He wouldn't recognise that face in the mirror either. She looked like a pale-faced old woman with champagne-blonde hair.

Cara would recognise her – and no doubt had at the television studio. She'd known the Juliana Conti story, had raised her eyebrows when the host introduced them, and several times Jenny had caught her staring.

Morrie Grenville. Morrie would have been an abbreviation of Morrison. Would he have clung to Jenny's maiden name if he'd wanted to forget her? Thames Ditton was only forty miles from London. Trains went there, and according to the bio in Cara's latest novel, she still lived there.

Ms Langhall lives with her partner in a five-hundred-year-old manor house forty miles from London.

Georgie had bought a copy of Cara's latest novel. The bio hadn't altered. And if that wasn't proof enough, then her pseudonym was. Why choose to write as C.J. Langhall if she didn't have some connection to Langdon Hall?

Jenny combed her hair, added a little lipstick, polished her glasses with toilet paper, delaying her return to that table. Trudy had disguised the bruise with foundation but makeup on a face unaccustomed to it only made what it disguised more obvious.

We can't choose who we fall in love with, Mum.

Cara and Jimmy hadn't chosen.

What manipulative hand of fate had been behind the meeting of a Melbourne schoolteacher and the heir to a crumbling English estate? Somewhere, somehow, they'd met and fallen in love.

Jenny had never *fallen* in love. She'd grown into it. She'd licked ice-creams with Jim, watched mesmerised while he'd turned the pages of his magical books, full of colourful pictures of elves and fairies perched on spotted mushrooms or hiding amid blossom in trees. She'd tailed bull ants with him too, poked sticks into their holes and run away laughing when they'd come out fighting. She'd discussed the world in general with Jim, and when his father and the rest of the town had treated her like the plague, Jim hadn't. He'd driven down to Granny's with his favourite books so she might read them, had sat late playing cards for pennies. How could she have not loved him?

She'd sung for him that night in Monk's cellar, because he'd wanted to hear how her voice sounded underground. Then he'd kissed her, just a sweet young boy kiss, but it had melted that hard lump of lead she'd had inside her since she'd been fourteen.

They'd made love on a camp stretcher. Five nights they'd made love on that stretcher and from one of those nights had come

Jimmy, Jenny's one baby conceived in love. Loved him before his birth, loved him at birth, because she'd loved his father.

A thousand times she'd told herself to forget her beautiful boy. Not while there was breath in her body would she forget him – and whether he remembered her or not, she was going to find him while that tour was in London.

The girls were discussing estate agents when she returned to the table. 'Tonia brought him in to give her a valuation.'

'You've put her house of horrors on the market?' Jenny asked.

'Not yet. The girls hope to move her into a nursing home when they get back from Greece.'

'That's why your . . .' Jenny started, then washed the remainder of the sentence away with wine.

'Why my what?' Trudy asked.

Why your father drowned himself – because you mentioned nursing homes to him, Jenny thought. She didn't say it. She lied. 'I must be drunk. I've forgotten what I was going to say.' She sipped a little more wine. The bottle was empty. She'd have to make this glass last. 'So,' she said. 'So. We are all here to discuss your birth mother? Drink your wine and decide if you want to know or not.'

'Of course I want to know.'

'It's no fairytale –'

'Stop prevaricating, Mum. Who was she?'

'Margot,' Jenny said.

That name wounded Trudy, but only for an instant. 'You forget that I've seen the hospital records. Her name was Margaret Morrison.'

'The hospital got it wrong. Your original birth certificate didn't. Your father burnt it.' She looked her in the eyes and saw only the bruise, and she reached for her glass. 'Elsie and Harry registered your birth. Teddy Hall's name was on it in the place that said *father*.'

'Take her home,' Trudy said.

'It's a fact, Trude,' Georgie said.

'She told me I was born at the Frankston hospital.'

'You were. I was working at Vroni Andrews' guesthouse and living behind it with Raelene. Georgie and her friend drove Margot down to me. She was with me for two months, with me and Raelene – and if you can imagine hell on earth, those two months were it,' Jenny said, but Trudy was on her feet.

She started towards the entrance, then turned and walked to the ladies' room.

'I shouldn't have told her like that.'

'You're right about that, mate. You're right about being drunk too,' Georgie said and refixed a pin holding her hair high.

'It could have been worse. I almost told her that Jim drowned himself because she'd mentioned a nursing home.'

'Watch your tongue.'

'No one said it was going to be easy.'

'Nor will be wandering around Europe for a month. You've got top travel insurance. It's not too late to pull the plug.'

They were discussing travel insurance when Trudy came back to the table, pale faced, jaw clenched. She looked like a skeletal Margot. 'You could have told me all of this on the phone,' she said to Georgie.

'It wasn't my business to, Trude.'

'Ted wouldn't have gone within a hundred metres of that crazy bitch.' Trudy liked Teddy Hall. She used to call him Uncle.

'He slept with her for seven years,' Georgie said. 'Before and after you were born.'

'She was repulsive, toothless –'

'She had teeth when he slept with her,' Jenny or the wine said.

'Does he know?'

'He would have married her. She refused to admit to sleeping with him –'

'Blamed her bloated stomach on indigestion and attacked anyone who attempted to tell her otherwise,' Jenny added.

'She was stark raving mad. You left me down there with Nan one day and she came across the paddock screaming.' Trudy stood, her hands gripping the back of her chair, looking from one to the other, wanting one or the other of them to take back what had been said.

'I thought about allowing you to keep on believing in your Margaret Morrison –' Jenny began.

'Teddy Hall is my father?'

'Jim was your father,' Jenny corrected. 'Teddy and Margot signed papers releasing you.' She reached for Trudy's untouched glass of wine. Trudy snatched it and drank it standing.

'We should have let you grow up knowing the truth,' Jenny said.

'Knowing that I was born to a mad woman, you mean?'

'There was nothing wrong with her mind. She was just as mad as hell that she never grew big enough to take what she believed was rightfully hers,' Georgie said.

'Everything,' Jenny added. 'You name it and she wanted it, be it the last biscuit in the tin or the first apricot of the season.'

'She could hold her breath until she turned blue in the face,' Georgie said.

'Elsie used to panic and give in to her, and make her kids give in to her.'

'So did Jimmy,' Georgie said.

'She tried her breath-holding at the hospital after you were born. They transferred her to a city hospital, with a psychiatric ward, but gave up trying to cure her after a month or so and released her to me – with half a dozen bottles of pills. I would have flushed the lot down the loo but Elsie took her home and fed those bloody pills to her.'

'They were the end of her – or Teddy breaking up with her was the end,' Georgie said. 'She attacked Maisy with a broomstick the night Teddy and Vonnie announced their engagement. An ambulance took her down to the Bendigo mad . . . psychiatric hospital.'

'And you tell me she wasn't mad,' Trudy said.

'Only as mad as hell that she had to sleep alone,' Jenny said.

Trudy sat, her chin low, Jenny watching her, hoping that the storm was over. It wasn't.

'Oh, my God,' she said, looking up. 'She's the reason I had twins. The Macdonalds.'

'You had them because old Mother Nature knew she was running out of time –'

'Then Georgie should have had triplets – and if Margot was my mother, Bernie Macdonald is my grandfather.'

'None of the Macdonalds knew that you weren't born to Jim and me –'

'Their ignorance doesn't alter my blood lines, does it?' Trudy said, and she was on her feet again and walking to the ladies' room.

On Trudy's recommendation they'd ordered garlic prawns. Their meals arrived before she returned to the table. She looked no happier as she sat and pushed her meal away. 'You kept it from me because Teddy is part Aborigine. You didn't want me to know I had black blood. Nick's right. You're a nest of racists.'

'Nick doesn't know his arse from his elbow and if you mention his name again, I'll mention that bruise again. Eat your prawns,' Jenny said.

'Admit that what I said is true,' Trudy demanded. 'You didn't want me to know that I had Aboriginal blood. Dad never accepted Nick because he was Greek.'

'He found him unacceptable,' Jenny said around a prawn. 'And more so when he found out that he'd gone through the two hundred and twenty-odd thousand dollars you got from Lorna.'

'Jen,' Georgie warned.

'Don't bother "Jenning" me. You know where that money went as well as I do – on his bloody designer jeans and pigskin jacket . . . and God only knows what else. And she knows as well as you that Elsie was more sister to Jim than his ugly bloody sisters who conned him into signing Jimmy away when he was in no fit mental state to sign anything.' She pointed to Trudy with a prawn tail.

'You were his chance to undo what he'd done, his second chance at fatherhood, and he worshipped the ground you walked on. He didn't want to share you with Teddy Hall, and not because of Elsie's black blood but because of his Hooper possessive streak – and as for that blood-sucking louse you brought into the family, Jim wouldn't have given a damn if he'd been black, white or a bloody green Martian, but you brought home a bludging, grab-all, wife-abusing bastard, who treated him like a geriatric fool.'

'You have no idea of the life he led before he met me –'

'What? A poverty-stricken pretty boy gigolo, flogging his wares to old ladies?'

'You've got an evil mouth, Mum.'

'And butter wouldn't melt in yours, would it? Oh, except when you're spooning drugs into three-year-old boys so you can go to work to pay for your parasitic pimp's Greek holiday.'

Heat rising from that table, a drinks waiter came to cool it with his fake smile.

'A glass of sparkling wine,' Jenny said, pushing her empty glass towards him.

'She's had enough,' Trudy said, and waved him away.

'Make that a bottle,' Jenny said. 'I'm not driving.'

'One glass,' Georgie said, and he went away.

'You were probably drunk the night Margot went into labour –' Trudy accused.

'It was afternoon and she didn't go into labour,' Jenny snapped. 'She relieved her indigestion with a vegetable knife, stabbed herself in the belly to let the air out, and if the blade of that knife had been half an inch longer, you wouldn't be sitting here tonight accusing me of Christ knows what.'

The legs of Trudy's chair squealed back from the table. 'Why bring me here to tell me that? What did you gain by telling me that, Mum?'

'I'm only here for the wine,' Jenny said. 'As for gain. It's you who gained. You found out that you're my blood and Georgie's,

Katie's and Harry's, that you've got aunties and uncles and cousins coming out of your ears. And I'll guarantee that the least of them cares more about you and your boys than that poncing pimp you allow to knock you around. Incidentally, is he on drugs?'

'How dare you –'

'You've got an audience, ladies,' Georgie warned.

Jenny glanced over her shoulder. With umpteen chairs to fill, a foursome was being seated at the table behind her chair. She lowered her voice when she turned back to Trudy. 'I'll bet you ten cents to ten dollars that he's on something. He's got Raelene's dead-snake eyes.'

Georgie changed the subject. 'There're millions of people living in London, Jen. How do you plan on finding Jimmy in three days?'

Jenny didn't want the subject changed but she turned to Georgie. 'I know where he lives.'

'Because of what Lorna Hooper told you forty years ago?' Trudy asked.

'He's still there. Her mother was a Langdon. Margaret Hooper's husband was connected to them. Lorna told Jim that they would have inherited that estate and that Jimmy would after them.'

'You didn't find him when you flew over there when I was six years old – and left me home alone for weeks.'

'I left you with your grandparents –'

'We didn't find him when we were over there – because he's not over there to find,' Trudy said.

'He's probably dead, Jen. He would have come back to find us if he'd still been alive.'

'He's not dead, and I'll find him.'

'Let's say you do. Let's say you knock on his door and a second Vern Hooper opens it. They raised him, Jen. God knows who they turned him into.'

'I dreamt he was a drug lord,' Jenny said. 'I don't care if he is. It's not about him. I need him to hear the truth from my mouth before I die.'

'He won't want your truth any more than I do,' Trudy said, disinterested in that shadow child Jimmy, long gone before she'd been born, but there, always there. He was an out-of-focus photograph hung on the wall in the entrance hall, a tiny boy in a sailor suit, a wide-eyed toddler seated on a young Jenny's lap.

Georgie had known that shadow boy. She'd run from Ray with him, had ridden the train home to Granny with him, then a few days later, he'd gone.

'What if you find out that he's been dead for forty years and you're stuck over there, thousands of miles from home, Jen?'

'What home, Georgie? Until March I had a home, then with one God-almighty stroke of his pen, that old sod in the clouds wiped out the lot. I've got Lila, but she's ten years old. If I make it back, if I hand over my keys, in a year or two I'll have to face losing her. So what home?'

'Us,' Georgie said.

'I've asked you to stay with me and the boys –'

'I heard you. I also heard myself begging you to leave the boys with me when you went back to that bastard. I heard your father begging you, pleading with you not to go back to him. Twice in my life I've heard Jim beg, that day and the day you told him you wanted to become a nurse.' She stood then, close to tears, but determined not to cry in a restaurant. Walked away, her chin high, walked again to the toilets.

A group of five was being seated when she returned. She sat and kept her mouth closed while the girls discussed solicitors, bad backs, insurance claims and wives who earned too much money for their husbands to qualify for Centrelink handouts. She kept her mouth closed until the waiter came with one glass of wine. Georgie got to it first. She drank an inch before passing it to Jenny's reaching hand.

'Let's say the search turns belly up, Jen,' Georgie said, harking back to her former subject.

'I catch my plane home, drink wine all the way and watch movies – and it's not going to turn belly up. For six years he was my little shadow, and for some reason he kept my na–' She caught her tongue, altered *name* to *memory*, but her halting alteration raised Georgie's eyebrows, so Jenny downed an inch of wine. 'How much have you forgotten about Ray and Armadale?'

'He scarred me for life,' she said.

He hadn't, or not physically. His daughter and her boyfriend had, though few saw Georgie's scars, the internal or external. Clever feathering with a pencil concealed her missing centimetre of eyebrow, missing since the night Raelene died. She'd fought Georgie earlier with a shifting spanner. She'd opened up a deep gash in her eyebrow.

Dino Collins had scarred Georgie from throat to shoulder with a box cutter. She'd been in her back garden, turning over the earth with a shovel, when he crept up behind her. He'd started that fight. Georgie and her shovel finished it.

She looked beautiful tonight; she'd dressed in her usual black, a high-necked sweater and a scarf of muted greens, oranges and blues, and her mass of hair pinned lose and high. Her eyes, freed of their reading and driving glasses, were magnificent.

Poor Margot, Jenny thought. Poor Trudy. She wore more colour than Georgie but looked colourless beside her in a gloomy green shirt, a bulky grey cardigan and baggy jeans.

'He'll remember the rhubarb,' Georgie said. 'He used to love your rhubarb pies.'

'I've never grown it as well before or since Armadale,' Jenny said. 'It was Ray's livers.'

'What are you talking about now?' Trudy asked.

Georgie explained. 'Meat was rationed during and after the war. Ray used to bring home hessian bags full of roadkill and empty the lot onto the kitchen table, sheep heads, livers, tripe. We buried half of what he brought home in the garden, then had to hammer in stakes so we'd remember where not to dig.'

'Jimmy will remember those stakes,' Jenny said. 'You and he used to use two of them as your goalposts – when you played football.'

186

'What's wrong with lambs fry and bacon?' Trudy asked.

'Ray didn't bring home the bacon,' Jenny said.

Georgie laughed. She had an infectious laugh, as had Granny.
It eased the tension at their table.

Exporting Live Sheep

'*K*eep your passport zipped into that inside pocket at all
times. At *all* times, Jen. Never allow it out of your sight,'
Georgie instructed.

Katie had nagged her into buying a new camera, a small digital
thing she could carry in her handbag. She'd done her best to talk
her into a new mobile. Jenny knew her old phone well and learning
to use one new piece of technology was enough for a stressed-out
mind to process. She'd bought a new wallet, red and instantly
visible when she unzipped the top compartment of her handbag.
Her new bank card was red. She'd tested it. It worked in Australia
and had been doubly guaranteed by bank staff to access ATMs
in any country on her itinerary. She had cash in her wallet, Australian
and a handful of alien notes procured for her by Georgie.

Behind the front side zipper, she'd packed Panadol and aspros,
lipstick, a comb, a new tube of sunscreen, face cream and a tiny
green nylon pouch that unzipped into a shopping bag – just in
case she needed it. Her aqua case was bloated. An hour ago, she'd
squeezed her laptop into it. So involved now with her *Parasite* file,
she hadn't been able to walk away from it.

Her nail scissors had to stay in Greensborough, as did Norman's pearl-handled pocket knife, which she loathed giving up. Since finding it the day she'd helped pack up the railway house, she'd carried his pocket knife in her every handbag.

'How will I peel an apple?'

'With your teeth,' Georgie said. 'Sharp objects are not allowed, Jen. They'll X-ray your handbag, find your father's knife and confiscate it. Do you want to lose it?'

She didn't. She gave it up.

Seven hours, then six. Five hours, four, then three.

'Ready?'

She wasn't ready. She was a danger magnet and shouldn't have been doing this to the three hundred-odd other passengers. Lightning would strike an engine, or they'd run into a flock of birds, or hijackers would pull out guns and shoot the pilots –

'Where did you put my sunglasses?'

'The sun's gone down, Nanny.'

'I don't want to see anything,' Jenny said. 'Which pocket did I put them in?'

Katie found them, in the rear zip pocket.

'You can still pull the plug, mate,' Georgie said.

'I'm going. I'll see the Sistine Chapel.'

They became a pair of dictators during that evening drive to Tullamarine.

'Don't allow your handbag off your shoulder when you're out of your hotel rooms,' Georgie warned.

'Don't leave your chargers plugged in when you pack up your rooms,' Katie said.

'Check every bathroom before you leave it, Jen.'

'And under your bed, Nanny, and keep your mobile charged! I don't know why you won't buy a new one.'

'It works if I charge it every night. Where do I keep the copy of my new will, Georgie?'

'You're not taking the shuttle to the hereafter. You're having a holiday.'

'Tell me where it is.'

'In your black concertina file, in the bottom drawer of Amy's desk, in the slot marked *Will*.'

'Keep in touch with Harry and Lila – and Trudy.'

'We've said a dozen times that we will. Text us the second you land,' Katie said. 'And don't worry about the time difference.'

'What did Google say the time difference would be?' Jenny asked.

'That we're about half a day ahead of you wherever you are, and don't worry about it.'

'Where did I put that list of emergency numbers?'

'It's in with your passport,' Georgie said.

'The first day you don't text us, I'll open your will and see if I'm getting Amy's desk, so every day, Nanny. Cross your heart and hope to die.'

Then all of her time was gone, or her time with her girls. From here on she'd have to do it alone. She hugged them. They offered final instructions she was no longer processing, but she found her camera, and as she backed away from her pair of redheads, she focused it on their worried faces.

Click. Her first holiday photograph – or three. It clicked twice more, accidentally.

'We want pictures of where you've been, not of us,' Katie said. 'Text us the second you land, Nanny, and every single day after. Love you heaps.'

'Love you more,' Jenny said.

At the security gate, a woman in uniform told Jenny to take her shoes off, and when she didn't jump to do it, the woman pulled rank.

'There's nothing in them but my feet,' she said, but took them off. They were X-rayed with her handbag and aqua-blue case, then given back. She had to lean on her case handle to put her shoes back on, and the case fell over.

Panic, blind, out of her mind, heart-racing panic. She was in a world outside of her own solar system and half of the world appeared to be there. She didn't know where to go, until a nicer woman in uniform pointed the way. She followed Jews wearing black hats, was tailed by a bearded suicide bomber, and she wanted to go home.

All so different from when she'd flown with Jim and the McPhersons. Excitement, laughter that day; she'd been off to find Jimmy. Now her legs felt weak, her top-heavy case kept threatening to tip over, but she found the right gate number, found a seat and damn near fell into it. Sat then, sat clutching the handle of her case until the other travellers, as if at some given signal, started forming a queue. She stood and joined their queue.

Passport, boarding pass, then herded into a makeshift corridor that wobbled as she boarded that oversized jam tin, boarded it with the enthusiasm of a sheep being exported to have its throat cut.

Found her seat number, a window seat. Katie's choice, not Jenny's. A businessman stowed her bloated case in an overhead locker. She'd lifted cartons of books, had carried computer monitors out to the veranda, had loaded and unloaded garbage bags by the score from her boot, but had no strength to lift that case. Had no strength in her hands to buckle herself in. She wasn't thinking of Jim, Trudy, the boys or Lila. She was thinking about travel insurance, of making a run for the exit – until a woman sat beside her and blocked her in.

Katie had flown to Queensland, she'd flown to Perth. She'd told Jenny how the lights of Melbourne had looked like fairy land from the plane's window. Jenny saw no fairy land. She sat, eyes closed, until the frantic roar of that flying jam tin dragged her away from Mother Earth, and up, up, up – within striking distance of the vengeful old bugger in the clouds, who'd been out to get her since birth.

The woman seated beside her ordered a drink, so Jenny followed suit. The woman swallowed two pills with hers, so Jenny swallowed two Panadol pills with sparkling wine. The woman was asleep before an attendant showed Jenny how to find movies on her private television. She watched three before Singapore.

Her itinerary told her the flight went via Singapore. It hadn't told her that all passengers would be herded off while the plane refuelled, that they'd have to take their cabin luggage with them, or that the luggage would pass through X-ray machines that were not Australian.

Katie had picked up that case for three dollars at a neighbour's garage sale. It was in good condition. Why had its previous owner decided to get rid of it? He'd been into drug smuggling, that's why. Jenny was thinking drug smuggling when she queued to get out of Singapore. She wasn't fated to take three hundred people down with her when a bolt of lightning hit. Instead, she was going to be shot at dawn for drug smuggling when the Singaporean X-ray machines picked up her case's false bottom or its handle packed with cocaine. She took her shoes off, so they wouldn't make the metal detector beep and draw the attention of officious officials – they looked officious, but the one who returned her shoes smiled.

Never had a sheep under sentence of death pushed harder to get back into its truck.

GONE

*K*atie knew how many hours it took to fly to America. Her friend's grandmother had been there recently. She knew that the flight from London took an entire day. Athens was closer than London. How much closer in flying hours, she didn't know. She'd expected a text from Singapore while the plane was refuelling. Jenny hadn't texted, but twenty-four hours after they'd driven home from the airport, Trudy texted to see if they'd heard anything.

'Something's happened, Mum,' Katie said.

'Her mobile is flat. She'll charge it by morning.'

No beeping from beneath her pillow that night, no text to read at breakfast time. No planes hijacked either, or blown from the sky. The television played until ten when they had to take the Mazda to a body shop for an insurance assessor to look at its dent. Someone had rear-ended Georgie.

They were backing out, in convoy, when Trudy drove in. The twins were with her. Nick wasn't, and she looked as if she'd been howling. The twins unbuckled themselves and were out and running for the Toyota, parked on the front lawn.

'Where's Nanny?' one asked.

'She's gone for a holiday,' Katie said – or she was in hospital in Greece or Singapore with a blood clot on the brain.

You can't cancel appointments with insurance assessors. You can't allow a woman who shouldn't have been behind the wheel of a car to get back behind it either. Katie, elected babysitter/caretaker, unlocked the house and took the visitors inside while Georgie parked the Commodore in the street.

Then her parents were gone and Katie was stuck with a depressed woman and wild twins. She herded them out of the lounge room. Pa's china ladies lived in there. She closed the door then asked Trudy if she'd like a cup of tea.

'Just water,' Trudy said.

The twins wanted tea. They got cordial and a biscuit.

She'd known them since they were babies, had spent most of her school holidays with them. With their heads shorn, they didn't look like the twins she'd known, or behave like them – and she couldn't tell them apart. Jenny used to part their hair on different sides so she knew at a glance.

She'd seen a bit of Trudy in Woody Creek, but she'd usually been coming or going to work. She'd never called her Aunty Trudy, and how could anyone actually be expected to say *Aunty Trudy*. Those words didn't fit together – which, as it had turned out, was just as well. Trudy wasn't an aunty but a cousin.

'If you don't mind, Katie, I'll lie down for a minute on Mum's bed,' cousin Trude said. 'I worked last night.'

Katie didn't mind at all. Finding something to talk to her about had never been easy.

The twins minded. They wanted to see Nanny's bedroom.

'Sit,' Katie said, and when the door was closed, she resorted to bribery. There was a packet of chocolate buds in the fridge, cooking chocolate, but they weren't fussy.

'Why did Nanny go for . . . for holiday?'

'She's in Greece. You know about Greece.'

'Daddy's will go too,' one of them said.

'Good,' Katie said.

'Papa did go too?'

'No.'

'Where did him go?'

It wasn't up to her to explain death to three-year-olds, so she fed them more chocolate buds and thought of that funeral and how it had changed everyone and everything.

While Pa had been alive, nothing had ever changed. It was like he'd been the keeper of un-change. Then he died, and an earthquake had changed the landscape. He'd been the keeper of a key to a sealed room Katie had always known was there, but for fourteen years hadn't been allowed to enter. Its door was open now and the answer to every question she'd ever asked was behind it.

Such as Jimmy. She used to believe he'd been 'lost' because in the old days unmarried girls hadn't been allowed to keep their babies. It had nothing to do with that. Last night, her mother had told her all about how his aunty had stolen him, and how she hadn't even been charged with kidnap.

'Who cut your hair?'

'A lady.'

'Did Mummy or Daddy pay the lady some money?'

'Daddy did.'

'Which one are you?'

'Jamey.'

She fetched a marking pen then and marked their hands with *J* and *R* – and gave them their first reading lesson, with that marking pen on the shopping list. They took her mind off blood clots and her mobile. She checked it from time to time, just in case she hadn't heard its beep. She heard it when her father texted.

Still waiting for assessor. All okay there?

GR8, Katie replied.

Jenny used to say that training little boys was much the same as training pups. You rewarded obedience and yelled when they disobeyed, which was all very well when their mother was out of hearing range. Trudy didn't yell. She reasoned, and three-year-olds weren't reasonable. They wanted to go outside and they couldn't.

'We haven't got a fence, so you have to stay inside. Do you want a video?'

They wanted a video.

She had a box of them in her wardrobe and chose *The Secret Garden*. They might have preferred a cartoon but she used to love *The Secret Garden*, and as she had to watch it with them, they could put up with one that she could tolerate.

It was midday before Paul's car drove in. He let Georgie out then went to the football. On Saturdays he usually went to the football with one or both of his brothers. Georgie had never been to a match. Katie had, but preferred not to. She turned the video off. The twins offered no protest.

They were eating a sandwich and drinking tomato soup from mugs when Trudy came out. She ate the twins' crusts, stole a few sips of their soup, then spoke about why she was here.

'I left him in bed,' she said. 'We were going to drive up to Woody Creek so I could talk to Teddy.'

'His back still troubling him?' Georgie asked.

'No. His cousin phoned while I was at work last night. He needed Nick to work today,' Trudy said, and she started howling.

Katie hit the *play* button and sat down again to watch the video. Eventually, the boys came to sit with her.

'I need to speak to him, Georgie.' Trudy howled, and Katie listened with one ear. She learned that she was talking about Teddy Hall, not Nick, though talking to Teddy was a serious waste of time. Katie had never heard him do much more than grunt. His wife talked, Harry talked – Lila was with Harry.

'We could drive up there and stay at one of the hotel's cabins,' Katie said to her mother.

'I'm working tonight,' Trudy said. 'We were going to leave early and get back before dark.'

She looked so old and colourless. Her hair, which could look nice, was pulled back hard from her face today and twisted into a topknot, and she was wearing a baggy grey tracksuit, one that gathered in at the ankles, which looked seriously atrocious. She had interesting eyes, deep set and dark, but more sunken than deep set today – and red rimmed.

'How about Wednesday?' Georgie said.

'I'm going,' Katie said.

'You've got school.'

'I want to see Lila.'

Katie discovered, when the boys asked her to take them to the bathroom, that the marking pen's *J* and *R* refused to wash off, which was why the pen was called a marking pen. It would wear off, but if it didn't before next Wednesday, then that was to the good. Trudy agreed to Wednesday, as long as they were back in time for her to go to work.

It was four o'clock before the Commodore left for Croydon. Cooking chocolate to be wiped up then, biscuit crumbs to be swept up, old video to be wound back and put away before Georgie started looking for something for dinner.

'Was Jimmy as wild as them, Mum?'

'He was their age when Jenny brought him home from Sydney. I remember him being too scared of me and Margot to leave Jenny's side.'

'Will she find him?'

'If he's alive, I don't think he wants to be found,' Georgie said. 'She wrote to him years ago. He didn't reply.'

'Did you write to him?'

'No.'

'Why not?'

'I was seven the last time I saw him.'

'How come his aunty wasn't arrested for stealing him?'

'He was sick. He needed to be in hospital and she drove a car. We thought she'd taken him to Willama. Jenny was taken to hospital the next day, with pneumonia. She was down there for weeks. I thought they were together, that she'd bring Jimmy home when she came. She didn't.'

'Didn't you visit them – while they were down there?'

'It was a different world back then. The train didn't go there and only the rich owned cars. We weren't rich. Maisy Macdonald drove Jenny home. She wasn't herself. Not for years. I nagged her about Jimmy and finally Granny told me that he'd gone to live with his father. That's what we believed until Jen met up again with Jim ten years later and he told her he'd signed Jimmy over to his family.'

'Why would he do something like that?'

'A lot of soldiers never got over the war. He spent years in hospitals.'

'I tried to interview him once for a school thing, about Anzac Day. All he said was that boys not much older than me had been used as cannon fodder by fat old men sitting safe in their city offices.'

'That's more than I've heard him say about it,' Georgie said, and she looked at her mobile, like Katie, willing Jenny to text. She'd boarded her plane forty hours ago.

'Trudy was going to divorce Nick at Christmas time. Why did she go back to him, Mum?'

'She wanted the boys to know their father.'

'If he'd really wanted to know them he wouldn't have had their hair cut off. I didn't know which one was which today.'

'They're having a power struggle at the moment,' Georgie said. 'When Trudy had her money, she had the power. I used to think that she had it all, but she looked a wreck today.'

She turned on the television and they caught the headlines. No planes had crashed. Another suicide bomber had blown himself up for Allah, though not in Greece.

'Believing that your religion will reward you with a first-class ticket to paradise and a dozen or so virgins if you kill people sounds more like devil worship than god stuff – and not very rewarding for girls that stay virgins,' Katie said. Georgie raised her eyebrows, and the one with the gap went higher than the other. 'I've sat through enough sex education classes to know what they think they're going to do with their virgins.'

Paul's football team lost, which wasn't news. If they'd won, he would have texted Katie the second the siren went off. Both mobiles were on the table. Neither one had beeped or buzzed.

'The tour guide who was supposed to meet her plane mightn't have turned up – or his tour company went bankrupt, like that one that stranded all of those people in Bali,' Katie said.

There were a million things that could have gone wrong. Katie's friend's grandmother's legs had looked like an elephant's legs after she flew home from America, and everyone knew about blood clots that could go to the brain or lungs, or somewhere.

When Georgie's mobile vibrated, they pounced on it.

No name. A strange number, but the text was from Jenny.

Jen here. I'm using Daren, a Canadian chap's mobile. Mine was dead flat when I got here. I had to buy an adaptor to plug it in and it still won't pick up a signal. Daren is looking at its innards for me. May have to buy a new phone after all. No need to reply.

Two mobiles beeped at nine o'clock. *Phone back in business. Am in a twin cabin with a big German woman, Johanna somebody. She's not happy. Neither am I. I expected my own cabin. Beautiful boat.*

'Don't mention Trudy,' Georgie warned as Katie's fingers got busy.

'Can I tell her we're visiting Lila on Wednesday?'

'No. She'll know why.'

'What can I tell her then?'

She found plenty to say. They texted back and forth for an hour, just silly talk, bits and pieces about boats and the Mazda and the time in Greece and in Australia, just talk.

TEDDY HALL

On Wednesday they were in Woody Creek by ten-thirty, and when Jenny's Toyota pulled up at Teddy Hall's front gate, Lila went out of her doggie mind expecting Jenny to step out from behind the driving wheel. She could take or leave Georgie, as Georgie could take or leave Lila. She sniffed Trudy's jeans, looked for her pups, then greeted Katie in her usual way. Since puppyhood, she'd been allowed to jump up on Katie for a cuddle.

Teddy Hall didn't yip with delight when he saw Trudy. He was working with tools beneath a car he had high on a hoist. And when Trudy walked the narrow track between tyres and tools to his side, he offered a wry smile and his hand, black with grease and carbon.

'Vonnie was expecting you for lunch. I'll be done here in an hour or so.' And that was that. He returned to what he'd been doing.

They spoke to Harry, to Vonnie for half an hour, then Teddy came in, shedding his overalls on the way. They waited while he washed his hands, then Katie walked back to the car. She'd brought a bunch of flowers to put on her grandfather's grave.

'I'm taking Lila for a walk, Mum.'

'Hang on. I'll come with you,' Georgie said. She'd done her bit. Trudy could do the rest alone.

They took the route Jenny had taken, over Blunt's crossing, through the park, across the oval. They found that wrought-iron fence with its spiked top, then Georgie walked on alone while Katie placed her flowers, and Lila sniffed that fence and commented on it as dogs are apt to do.

She saved no pee for Margot's grave. Georgie was waiting for them beside a tall angel with spread wings. The words had been carved into the stone where her feet should have been. *MARGOT MACDONALD MORRISON 11.4.39–20.12.77. LOVED DAUGHTER OF JENNIFER AND BERNARD: GRANDDAUGHTER OF MAISY. R.I.P.*

'Why is his name even allowed to be on that, Mum?'

'He paid for it. Jen calls it his guilt stone,' Georgie said, and she walked on down a gravelled pathway to Granny's moss-covered stone owl, perched on a mossy stone post.

'Who paid for that?'

'Jenny. She ordered it the day her first husband died.' Georgie never said Ray King's name, or not if she could avoid saying it. 'We had two funerals that week.'

'Why an owl?'

'She was a wise lady – and she liked the barn owls that nested in our old shed. They fed their babies on mice. We'd better get back and save Teddy, I suppose.' Georgie had grown up with him. She knew that Trudy wouldn't get from him what she'd come looking for.

They stopped at a small grey stone with no name and no space for a name. There was space enough for *J.C. LEFT THIS LIFE 31.12.23.* Cut poorly into that stone, it had all but worn away. One day soon, even with imagination, no one would be able to read it. A handkerchief with those same initials embroidered in its corner still lived down the bottom of Jenny's jewellery box, J.C.'s brooch was kept in Georgie's top drawer, with Itchy-foot's diaries. That stone didn't need a name for Juliana to be remembered.

'Nanny said once that she hadn't known her mother's name until she was twenty-two. Was it in Itchy-foot's diaries?'

'The diaries weren't posted to Jenny until after he died. He told Granny her name and gave her that photograph, with the brooch on her hat.'

'Can I please read the bits he wrote about Juliana?'

'When you're thirty.'

'You said before that I could read them when I'm eighteen.'

'Not those bits.'

'I'll bet they're no worse than a lot of stuff I've read. How old were you when you read them?'

'Old enough.'

They walked on then. Lila wanted to go home to Jenny. Her car was in Woody Creek. She couldn't have been far away, and when they reached Teddy's corner, she made a break for Hooper Street. Katie called her, had to call her twice before she obeyed, unwillingly.

They ate ham salad for lunch, in Vonnie's kitchen. The conversation centred on Jenny's trip, on her empty house, and on the Duffy pack.

'They know the house is empty,' Teddy said. 'The copper caught two of the younger kids poking around behind her shed.'

'Kids won't get into the house,' Trudy said. 'Dad had security screens installed on every window to keep Raelene out.'

They left for home at one-thirty, Trudy in the back seat. She'd done her talking and was ready now to sleep, and was by the time they reached their roadhouse. They didn't stop for a coffee and chips, didn't want to wake her.

She woke up when they turned into the driveway. She used the toilet, didn't want a coffee, thanked them for driving her up there, then got into her Commodore and was gone, home to the twins she'd left with one of her sisters-in-law.

'She expected more,' Georgie said. Those with expectations of Teddy Hall were doomed to disappointment – unless he was working on their car. He was nearing retirement age but still the best mechanic in a sixty-kilometre radius.

'Was he in love with Margot, Mum?'

'He would have married her – and God help Trudy if he had.'

'He wouldn't have said that to Trudy, would he?'

'Who knows what he might have said?'

*

Jenny's texts kept coming, usually at night. They'd believed she'd be travelling with Australians. She was one of nine Australians. There were two New Zealanders, half a dozen Americans, Daren, the Canadian, a couple from Ireland, two Dutch women, Johanna, the German roommate, Gus, Daren's Albanian roommate, and enough more to make her group of seniors up to forty-four – though that number shrank to forty-two before the cruise ended. One European woman was taken from the boat to a Greek hospital. Her husband went with her.

They didn't hear from Trudy. Harry phoned. Lila, having seen Jenny's car, having been fed an egg by Katie, decided to move back home. She jumped Teddy's fence.

'I had to bring her home on a lead,' Harry said. 'And she's off her food tonight.'

'Don't let her die, Harry,' Georgie said.

'I'm wondering if it might be better to leave her there. She can sniff out a Duffy at a hundred paces.'

'Do what you think best,' Georgie said, and when the phone was down, she warned Katie not to pass on that bit of news to Jenny.

'Did you know Norman and Amber, Mum?'

'I saw Norman two or three times. I heard a lot about Amber but never saw her.'

'What about Nanny's sister?'

'I heard a lot about her too,' Georgie said. She was proofreading a contract, centimetres thick, which might stop one party being sued by another party. As a ten-year-old Katie had crossed *solicitor* off her list of career choices.

'What was Norman like?'

'A sad old man who rode a bike. He rode down one night with a gold-wrapped present for Jenny's birthday – that blue pendant and earring set she's still got. She called him Daddy and Jimmy thought it was hilarious that Jenny had a daddy.'

'She must have loved him or she wouldn't have kept it, or his pocket knife. How old was Jimmy then?'

'Three or four,' Georgie said, then grabbed for her vibrating mobile.

Breakfasting with Dutch women and Daren. He's discussing Gus, the Albanian. Apparently he snores. Johanna hasn't complained about my snoring, but this morning she complained about the noise my laptop's keys make.

You can't write a lot in a text. Katie wasn't allowed to write the truth about Lila who was pining. She couldn't tell her that Paul had missed out on his football match so he could drive up with them and take Lila to a vet. They didn't have to. Lila ate half a dozen eggs for Katie, then topped up on chips and potato cakes. Katie told Jenny about the eggs and potato cakes, but not why they'd driven up there. She told her that they'd taken Lila around to sniff through the house, and while they were there, robbed the freezer. Lila loved raw meat.

MEMORIES

*A*t nine-fifty on the final day of May, Cara climbed the stairs to her bedroom. The children were with their carer. Morrie and Tracy had forty-five conference guests to keep them busy. Next week was spoken for, but today was her own.

Her case was waiting open to be packed for Germany. She'd have four full-on days over there, would see four cities then fly home, meet Cathy and Gerry at the airport, and thereafter Cathy would control her time.

She'd need dressed-up casual in Germany, and dressy for one evening gig. She was tossing garments onto the bed when a small and battered brown case caught her eye. It held the only memories she allowed herself to bring to the UK. Her first diary and half a dozen more, old letters and notebooks, just bits and pieces of the life she'd left behind. She had time today, so lifted it down, blew dust from its lid, then opened its elderly catches.

The docket book letter was on top, umpteen pages of *Charlie White Grocery* on one side and Georgie's print on the other. Cara had stapled them together. A shiny staple once, it was rusty now. She read the first page, then placed it on the open lid and picked up her diary from 1958. It used to have a tiny key, lost a long time ago. She'd forced its lock, also long ago. Nothing written in it that she'd needed to lock away, not many pages of it filled. She'd never been a reliable keeper of journals.

Itchy-foot had filled thirteen diaries. Once upon a time, she and Georgie had planned to hole up in a motel room, midway between Melbourne and Woody Creek, where Georgie would read an early draft of *Angel at My Door* while Cara read Itchy-foot's diaries. It never happened. His diaries would have been turned to ash as everything else in that dilapidated old house had been turned to ash.

Flame can kill or it can cleanse. The burning of Georgie's house had cleansed the world of Raelene and freed Tracy for adoption. Her only living relative, Raelene's mother, located by Chris Marino, had wanted nothing to do with any child born to her daughter. Chris' office handled the adoption.

Fire had freed Georgie. When they'd seen her in Melbourne, she'd told Morrie that she lived at Greensborough.

How many times had Cara attempted to talk her into moving to Melbourne and sharing a unit? 'Margot,' Georgie used to say. To Cara, Margot had been a reason to leave, not to stay. Be it love, pity or perhaps the early loss of her brother, Georgie had lived on in that house with Margot.

I should have written to her after the fire, Cara thought. Or sent a card or flowers. Something. There'd been too much happening in her own life at the time. She'd been back with Morrie too, and had known she'd had to cut her ties to Georgie – not quite cut. *Rusty*, her first novel, had been accepted for publication and she'd patterned its redheaded heroine on Georgie. The girl in the photograph on its cover had Georgie's copper hair. Had almost posted her a copy. She'd autographed one, *For Georgie, my inspiration, Love from Cara*, then changed her mind about posting it. A clean break had seemed the better way to go.

She'd posted an autographed copy to Chris Marino. *In appreciation of your support*, she'd written – and had to hold her pen back from adding, *I told you so.* During their relationship, Chris had strongly discouraged her hopeless pursuit of publication. He'd wanted a wife to manage his home, to bear his children. He'd found one. She'd given him seven babies.

All so long ago.

She picked up her 1959 diary, which may have contained something of interest had she not ripped three months of pages out. Could remember shredding them, flushing them down the toilet. Dino Collins, her first boyfriend's name, had been all over those pages.

So many diaries she'd started, full of good intentions. Her good intentions had lasted for a few months in 1966, its pages full of Morrie. In '67, Georgie and Morrie shared several pages and at the back, three pages of the diary were filled with Georgie's convoluted non-relatives. Robin would have loved to get his hands on '67.

Could remember the night she'd filled those rear pages and where she'd been at the time – seated on the kitchen bench of her dogbox unit, beside her phone. No cord-free phones in those days.

'How do Elsie and Harry fit into the family picture?' she'd asked.

'They don't, or not blood family. Other than Jenny, Margot, Trudy and a father I've never met, I've got no blood relatives,' Georgie said.

Elsie Hall. Part Aborigine, raised since the age of twelve as the daughter of Granny (Gertrude Maria Foote). Elsie married Harry Hall.

Laurence George Morgan. Father of Georgie. Address unknown.

Edward Hall (Teddy). Middle son of Harry and Elsie, owns Woody Creek garage.

Trudy. Daughter of Jenny and Jim Hooper.

Raelene King, daughter of Florence Dawson and Raymond King, born during the years Ray and Jenny lived separately.

Itchy-foot (Archibald Gerald Foote) married to Gertrude Maria.

Amber, daughter of Archibald and Gertrude, married Norman Morrison, adoptive parents of Jenny.

Juliana Conti, blood mother of Jenny, died in childbirth. Italian, married, but had an affair with Itchy-foot which resulted in Jenny.

Those notes would make a novel, she thought. She was bookless at the moment. *A Case Full of Memories*, she thought. It sounded like a title. While she was thinking about the book idea, the phone beside the bed rang.

'Are you and Dad free tomorrow? I've found something Dad might be interested to read.'

Cara closed the case. She and Robin had a telepathic link and she didn't want him gaining access to her secrets.

'We've got a crowd here and at the lodge today. Dad and Tracy will be tied up with them until lunchtime tomorrow.'

'No worries,' he said. 'We'll make it next weekend.'

'We'll be in Germany. We leave on Thursday night. We could drive in earlier – if it's important.'

'It's interesting, not important,' he said. 'I'll see you at the wedding. Have you got the bride under control?'

'More or less,' Cara said. 'She's still refusing to drive down on Friday. Will you and Sally be staying the night?'

'No can do. We'll drive down early on Saturday.'

'I'll put Cathy and Gerry in your room, if you're certain you won't need it.'

'It's a definite. I'm on call on Sunday. When do they arrive?'

'The day we get back from Germany. Cathy said they'll wait at the airport until our plane gets in then drive down with us.'

'It will be good to hear Aussie accents again,' he said.

'Six weeks of them? Bite your tongue.'

'What about Pete and Kay?'

Pete was Cara's favourite cousin. She hadn't seen him for three years, and they weren't planning to stay. They'd rented a unit in London. He'd spent several years in London. Kay hadn't and she'd said she wanted to see what he'd got up to during his years away.

'They're flying in on the Friday,' Cara said. 'They'll get themselves down here. We'll have them for three days. We've got Laura and Tom down our end of the house too. We've run out of B&B rooms. There are Scots booked in all over town.'

'I thought you'd put Laura in the regency room.'

'Ian's ninety-odd-year-old grandmother is in it. She can't do stairs.'

They spoke of the book tour, the cities Cara would see, not that she'd see much of them.

'Take it easy,' he said and signed off.

He and Sally rarely spent a night at the Hall. Several times Cara had suggested that their too serious Richard might benefit from time spent with his adventurous cousins. He was a head taller than Tristan, not quite a year older, but as unimpressed by the Hall as his father, who'd been unimpressed the day he'd arrived. He'd spent his first week sniffing for smoke and leaving doors open so they could make a quick getaway.

He'd seen the news broadcasts of the fire that killed Margot and Raelene. He'd seen photographs of what remained of Georgie's house and refused to sleep in an upstairs bedroom. Morrie had turned a morning room into a bedroom for him, because of its access to open space. As boy and man he'd slept in that room.

Tracy should have been the one with the phobias, but born fearless, she'd loved Morrie's house at first sight, had called it her princess castle and spent her first week here exploring her castle – and getting lost.

Cara's mind wandering in the past, she found herself staring at a lone page of a letter with no beginning and no end but written in Georgie's block print.

. . . was nineteen. She used to say he looked like the Angel Gabriel, had the heart of a devil and a voice that could charm the knickers off a nun.

Cara didn't need a name to know who could *charm the knickers off a nun* and she read on, seeking more of Itchy-foot.

She found Ray King.

She said once that she'd married Ray to get Jimmy away from the Hoopers. For a while we thought we had a stepfather. We took his name at school. I liked the sound of Georgina King, but a couple of years later she left him. The Hoopers were like a wolf pack, tracking their injured prey. That's when they got Jimmy.

There was more but only news of the town – and Charlie White.

When Charlie was alive he wouldn't give a starving Duffy a handful of flour, but since his death, he's become the town philanthropist. He willed his shop . . .

He'd willed his shop to Georgie, his shop and an old house. Cara wanted more of that letter. There was no more of it. She upended the case in her search for the other pages; she looked in old envelopes. In one she found a letter that mentioned a man. There'd been very few in Georgie's life.

He was a cop, and a good bloke. I was eighteen at the time. I didn't know who I was and he didn't hang around long enough for me to find out.

Honest to a fault, Georgie. Ask her a question and she'd look you in the eye and reply – as had Jenny – and Cara could have done with less of her honesty.

ROME

The city is old and looks worn out but in every direction I point my camera, I'm trapping history. I should have learnt how to delete the poor shots. I was trying to get a shot of a gorgeous old fountain yesterday but most of what I got was tourists' heads. They're everywhere and they've got no manners.

Look for a rubbish bin symbol, Katie replied. *Scroll to the photo you want to get rid of and put it in the bin.*

You can scroll when I get home.

The tour was relentless, as were the crowds, the queues, the heat. Even during the worst of Woody Creek's summers there'd been shade to be found. Rome had no shade. Rome had blazing sun and too many stairs. Rome was wearing Jenny down. She may have been half-Italian by birth but she'd been Woody Creek raised, and Woody Creek was dead flat.

Their tour guide, a man in his early forties, spoke English with a European accent, spoke Albanian to Gus, Italian to the bus driver, German to Johanna, and when you caught him between languages, he looked bored. His herd ranged in age from sixty-odd to eighty-three, and as with any group, cliques had formed. On the cruise two Australian couples and the Irish had cohered. Brian and Freda, also Australians, mixed with the Americans. Canada wasn't a part of the USA. Canadian Daren had gathered a bunch of leftover women – Jenny, because he'd fixed her mobile, and two Dutch women, Eva and Bertha. He and Bertha had been everywhere. They did the talking, Jenny and Eva tagged along behind them.

Albanian Gus walked and sat and ate alone, or those who made the mistake of sitting with him didn't repeat the exercise. He appeared to have packed two shirts, both polyester, and if he'd washed either of them since joining the tour, Jenny would eat her hat – a white cotton thing she'd bought in Greece. Gus had a perspiration problem, which may have saved Jenny's life the day they toured the Vatican. They'd been packed into the Sistine Chapel like Granny had packed her peach halves into preserving jars, but even in the chapel, Gus' polyester shirt created a space.

He was a short, round man, a bare inch taller than Jenny. They'd seen little – other than that much heralded ceiling. Gus had stopped to aim his camera upwards, so Jenny had stopped behind him and followed suit. She'd taken half a dozen good shots of the ceiling with not one tourist head in them.

She'd texted her girls about little Gus. She'd texted about the New Zealand couple she envied. The man was eighty-three, Jim's age. She'd envied Bertha's huge case, or on the cruise she'd envied it. She'd had an outfit for every occasion. Jenny had packed one frock. Johanna's uniform, day or night, was half-mast trousers, cotton shirts, boat-style sandals and a white cap. By Rome, Jenny was becoming accustomed to Johanna's abrasive manner – and her sleeping habits. She went to bed at nine. As soon as she cleared the bathroom, Jenny set up her office in there, the toilet lid her chair, her laptop on her lap. If you're desperate to write, you'll do it anywhere.

She'd given Nick a sex change on the cruise. From day one, his heavy-lidded eyes had reminded her of Raelene's. A lot of Raelene had crept into her *Parasite* file and, initially, she'd made her Nick's sister. It hadn't worked, so she'd turned the two into one, and named her Charlene. Charlene had given Jenny's fingers the freedom to fly – and a more complex character.

Trudy, the hothouse plant, was in it, as Ruby, Charlene's abused mother. Jenny had filled a lot of pages on the cruise where she'd been able to set up her laptop on a table, to sit on a chair. Not many pages had been filled in Rome. Worn out by the heat and the daily grind, she'd been ready for bed at nine, which meant that she woke too early.

Granny used to say that the early hours of the morning were the best of a day. They weren't in Rome. She couldn't get a cup of tea unless she phoned down for room-service, which she couldn't do or she'd wake Johanna. The dining room didn't open for breakfast until seven, and Daren, also an early riser, was usually waiting for the doors to open and ready to start in again about poor little Gus.

Jenny dodged him on her last morning in Rome, waited until his back was turned, then made a break for the front door.

The sky already threatening to burn, she found shade against a wall and texted her girls. Couldn't text in her room. Their beeping replies woke Johanna, and a disturbed Johanna was a step up from abrasive.

Off this morning to see where men were slaughtered for the entertainment of Rome's upstanding citizens. Wonder if our antecedents were the entertained or the entertainment?

There was always a delay before her girls replied. She didn't mind that delay. For a time she was with them in Australia.

Katie's texts were newsy. Georgie kept hers brief. Trudy didn't reply this morning. Jenny waited, waited until seven-thirty, not eager for another dose of Daren and Bertha, but her need for a cup of tea got the better of her.

Bertha had dressed for another day at Queen Lizzie's garden party. Daren, who reminded Jenny of a bull terrier, was yapping. Eva's mouth was kept busy by a heaped plate of bacon, eggs, sausages and tomatoes when Jenny carried two cups of tea and two croissants to their table.

They weren't her type of people – if she had a type. She pitied Eva, brought along as handmaiden to Bertha. Jenny ate and ran, and still no text from Trudy. She worried about her, worried about the boys while she packed her laptop into her case and then knelt on it to close the zipper. Cases had to be in the corridor by eight-thirty. The luggage would travel with them today, on a bus. They'd move on from Rome after they saw the Coliseum.

Queued at nine to board the bus. Queued to get off. Queued to get into the Coliseum, where they climbed aged stone steps. She took too many photographs, a few might be worth keeping. When they were done with their climbing, they weren't done. The sun now burning down, they were expected to climb a hill behind the Coliseum to see something of interest.

Johanna, born of a mountain goat and a bison, led the herd. Rotund little Gus, born of a hornless sheep, brought up the rear. Jenny started the walk close to the guide but gave up to sit on a rock and consider what her life may have been had Juliana cuckolded her banker husband and given birth in Italy. She probably wouldn't have had a life. She probably would have expired in infancy.

'*Only mad dogs and Englishmen go out in the midday sun*,' she sang quietly as Gus panted by.

He had half a dozen words of English but sang more. '*Da Japanee don ta care to. Da Chinee would no dare to*,' he sang, then smiling, tapped his chest. 'Mad dog one, eh.'

Jenny tapped her hat and showed two fingers. 'Mad dog two,' she said and returned his smile, and not the fake smile she flashed for others. Stood then and tailed him and his BO up to where the herd had stopped.

They hadn't reached their promised magnificent view of the ruins because the male half of the New Zealand couple had fallen. He was sitting where he fell, one of the European women examining his wrist.

It looked broken to Jenny, who didn't stop to stare. There was water nearby, water that appeared to be gushing out of the rocks. She needed it.

Had she been able to read her mother's language, she may have learnt that the spring had been blessed by some thirsting saint. It was chilled, and in a world of blistering heat, chilled spring water bubbling out of rocks deserved sainthood. She drank from it, swallowed Italian bugs, filled her water bottle with chilled Italian bugs, filled her hat then placed it full on her head.

Albanian Gus' hat was made of straw. It leaked like a sieve when he attempted to follow her lead, so she helped him out with her bottle of water, poured it over his hat and shoulders, then went back for a refill while Bertha tut-tutted.

And bloody Daren asked Gus if he'd like a bar of soap. Gus didn't understand, but a few who did sniggered.

And bloody Johanna smiled, and bison or not, Jenny wanted to hit her – until she realised that Johanna wasn't smiling at Daren's humour. She walked to the water, placed her Johanna-sized camera down, filled her cap with water and placed it full on her head.

'You can use the good camera?' she asked Daren, offering her old Canon.

He couldn't, but the guide could. He photographed three dripping ruins against the backdrop of the ruins of old Rome, and before a pair of paramedics arrived to take the New Zealand chap and his wife away, the guide trapped similar photographs on Jenny and Gus' cameras.

Only forty heads to count when they boarded the bus for Pompeii. The air conditioner blasting cool air, Daren providing the entertainment. He'd found a seat opposite the guide and was demanding to be moved into the New Zealand couple's empty room. The guide's microphone was turned on. Every ear and hearing aid on the bus heard him.

He was still at it that evening but didn't get the New Zealanders' room, and at breakfast time he smelt of alcohol.

Jenny and her camera were both suffering from an overload of the incredible before the bus moved the remaining forty on. Johanna carried spare rolls of film for her camera, and when one roll was full, she popped it out and inserted a new one. Jenny's fool of a camera had a memory card, a tiny thing she'd watched Katie insert. By Pompeii, she was becoming concerned about her memory card running out of memory.

She was concerned about her beige slacks too. They kept sliding down. She needed elastic to run through their waistband but had seen no shop that might sell it – and needles and thread.

They boarded another plane that evening. Bertha flew business class, as did a second honeymooning couple of Americans. The tour price had included economy flights and, on the flight to Venice, Jenny wished she hadn't upgraded. She had undiluted Bertha all the way.

They misplaced little Gus at the airport. Daren looked happy for the twenty minutes it took the guide to locate his missing sheep.

Another bus. Another queue, and the Venice Jenny had read about didn't have buses, or roads or massed greenery. She photographed the road and the greenery through the bus window. The bus took them to water, where they were herded off the land bus and onto a water bus. She hitched up her slacks, found a seat beside Gus and breathed through her mouth, not her nose – as she'd learnt to do during Sissy's early teen years – before Amber introduced her to underarm deodorants.

Gus' camera was the same brand as Jenny's, as new but a slightly larger model. They were comparing their cameras, she attempting to ask him about memory cards, when they heard sirens. She stood to see a road. Saw only water and buildings with water lapping at their doorsteps. As their water bus moved to the side of the canal, Jenny and Gus found a space at the railing in time to click at two speedboats going by, their sirens wailing. They were crewed by helmeted firemen.

She got one perfect shot of the Venetian police boat following the firemen. Somehow she managed to frame it against a bridge.

It was a keeper, and an accident. Most of her better photographs had been accidents. The lights were on in Venice. She'd caught their reflections in the water.

She trapped more of Venice before their craft got to where it was going. She clicked at a gondolier in a striped t-shirt. He was singing a love song to his passenger while standing, poling his upturned-nosed craft down the canal. She trapped multicoloured buildings, flowers blooming in pots on narrow pavements, a boat parked at a watery front door. As the water bus docked, she exchanged her camera for her mobile, and uncaring of what the time might be in Melbourne, she texted all three girls.

I'm in Venice and it's magic land.

No replies. Her girls would be sleeping.

The guide and another man helped her to dry land, or to a pavement. There was no land. There was water, buildings, pavements, an outdoor restaurant where the diners sat bare millimetres from water. Jenny photographed the diners and the black-clad waiters until the tour guide shepherded her with his flock into another hotel foyer, where they queued for another key-card.

No key-card tonight. The guide handed her a key, an actual key that turned in an actual lock, its large room number and a red tassel attached to it. No chance of misplacing it in her crowded handbag, and in the foyer of that pink hotel, Jenny fell head over heels in love with Venice.

CATASTROPHE

*T*rudy wasn't in love. She'd told Nick this morning that he'd need to cancel his holiday plans, that his mother was incapable of flying. She told him to take Tessa to her doctor, that her mind was going. She told him to speak to his sisters about selling the house, that Tessa needed to be in care.

He'd walked away from her.

'Your sons are afraid of her. I'm afraid of her,' she'd said, then played her trump card. 'I'm pregnant, Nick.'

'Who is the lucky father?' he asked, and continued out to the garage. She hadn't slept with him since her father's funeral.

'You can't take the car today. I've booked it in for a service. It needs an oil change and new wipers.'

He didn't care about oil or windscreen-wipers. He didn't care about her or the boys. He might have cared about his mother. He liked her house. He liked her money. She'd paid their fares to Greece. When her mind was clear, Tessa spoke of Greece and her sisters. Trudy had heard her speaking to one of them on the phone two nights ago and she'd sounded normal. She wasn't. Tonia and Angie knew it and they saw less of her than Trudy saw. She'd forget that she'd eaten breakfast, forget that she'd taken her pills, forget that Trudy was her Nicky's wife.

Jenny could have been right about his plan to leave her with her sisters in Greece, out of sight, out of mind. He had power of attorney.

He could no longer get at her money. Tonia had seen to that. Her father had made her executor of his will. Her father had left instructions that the bulk of his money be placed in a trust account, accessible only to the girls. It paid the bills, paid Tessa a monthly allowance. He must have known that Tessa had been losing her mind when he'd died. He must have known his son too.

Nick took the car and left the garage door open.

Cold out there. Melbourne's winter had struck with a vengeance. Trudy closed the big door then returned to the kitchen where she listened for Tessa. Some mornings she slept late.

The boys never slept late. They were upstairs, and needing sleep, she offered them a video.

They didn't want a video. Their ears as attuned to Tessa as her own, they knew she wasn't in her kitchen, which meant they could play outside. She got their parkas, got her own, and took them out to the patio so they could kick their ball, climb, do what little boys do.

They were still out there when they heard Tessa, rattling around in the kitchen.

'Stay here. I'll be back in a minute,' she said and went in to dole out pills and cereal, high blood-pressure pills with Tessa's breakfast and a Valium, and she was almost out of Valium. It kept her calm – or calmer.

'Sit down, Tessa.'

Tessa didn't sit. She wanted her Nicky.

'He had to go out. Take your pills.' Mobile beeping in her parka pocket, Tessa standing at the fridge. 'You don't need anything in there. Sit down, take your pills and eat your breakfast, Tessa.'

She wanted her laxative. If she didn't explode every morning before breakfast, the world might end. Trudy poured a dose of the laxative into a measuring glass and placed it beside the cereal before reading the message.

It was from Angie, Nick's youngest sister.

I can't raise Nick. Is he with you there?

He went out, Trudy replied.

Has he cancelled Greece?

No.

Do you know where he is?

No.

You need to make him cancel.

Was that worth answering?

Angie and Tonia had killed Nick's dream of a big insurance payout for his back. They'd trapped him on video, twice. He hadn't spoken to either of them since.

A text had come from Jenny in the night. *I'm in Venice and it's magic land.*

Trudy didn't reply to it either. Venice had been her downfall. She'd argued with Sophie there. They'd been friends since their early days at high school, but in Venice Sophie changed her ticket and flew home.

'Three's a crowd,' Nick had said.

He'd told Trudy he'd loved her in Venice. She'd slept with him for the first time in that city.

'Don't be taken in by his pretty face,' Sophie had said. He was her cousin. He had multiple cousins.

Sophie had introduced them, at Kew. They'd been painting Lorna Hooper's kitchen when Nick and Sophie's brother had arrived with a hired trailer. They'd stopped painting to load tons of newspapers and assorted junk. The boys had gone, and Trudy hadn't expected to see Nick again.

He'd been a beautiful-looking boy, but just a boy, still at university. He'd come back alone and knew how to use a paintbrush, so they'd put him to work. He'd been painting the lounge-room ceiling when the agent came to value Lorna's house.

Should never have sold it. Her father had told her to rent it out until she'd needed it. It was Nick who'd encouraged her to sell.

She'd paid Sophie's fare to Greece. She had a grandmother still living there and relatives willing to give them beds.

Sophie's relatives were Nick's. He'd decided to go with them.

'What about your uni?' Sophie said.

'I'll take a year off,' he'd said.

His mother paid for his flight. She hadn't given him spending money, but Trudy had so much from the sale of that house that for the first year her account had seemed like a 'forever ham'. Cut a slice from it and it grew back. They'd had a brilliant twelve months – until Venice.

She read Jenny's message again and couldn't think of a reply – and her battery was near flat.

Her charger was on the kitchen bench. She plugged it in, looked through the window where her boys were kicking goals. Tessa's cereal had become soggy. Her pills were still waiting. She was still demanding Nicky.

'He's at work.' He helped out a cousin and was paid enough to spend on his back. She and the boys didn't see a cent of what he earned. She turned on the jug, reached for coffee mugs. Tessa didn't want *bloody Australian coffee.* She preferred Greek coffee, grounds boiled on the stove.

'Go for your life,' Trudy said in English, and she went outside to her boys. She was tired. She was always tired. She'd reached the stage of exhaustion where the body takes over and snatches sleep where it can, and within seconds of sitting on a cold padded chair, her chin dropped.

On some level she may have heard the smash of china, the thump, but the boys' ball was hitting against the fence, so she slept on.

'Her felled over, Mummy,' Jamey said. He was standing on the outdoor table, looking in through the window.

She stood to lift him down. 'That table is made out of glass. Glass breaks, and when it does, it cuts very deep,' she said, then, opening the sliding door, she stepped from wintery chill into summer heat.

No Tessa in the kitchen, or Trudy didn't see her immediately.

She was on the floor in front of the sink, on her stomach, her legs asprawl, her dressing gown showing more than was fit to be seen by little boys. They'd followed her inside. Tessa's upper thighs and backside had more meat on them than a side of beef.

'Outside,' she said. Then, 'Can you get up, Tessa?'

No screeched reply. Not a grunt, and Tessa wasn't all that was on the floor. There was spilled stew and shards of china everywhere. 'Get outside,' Trudy said. 'And don't climb on that table.'

They'd backed away, but the boogieman was silent. They didn't back far.

'Tessa!' The dressing gown pulled down to cover her bare backside, Trudy reached for a side-of-beef arm. 'Tessa!'

There was no response. Nothing. She got down to her knees then to feel for a pulse on the wrist, almost hoping she didn't find one. A fast death would be better for her and her family than the slow deterioration she'd been witnessing since March, when she'd diagnosed early stage Alzheimer's. Tonia and Angie agreed with her diagnosis, Nick and the other two girls refused to see it.

There was a weak pulse at Tessa's throat and Trudy stood, stew on one knee of her tracksuit. Not a priority, not at the moment. She reached over her mother-in-law to get her mobile.

'I told you to stay back,' she said to Jamey. 'There's stew every-where.' It had been in the fridge the last time she'd seen it, in a casserole dish, ready to place in the oven for tonight's dinner. It was on the floor, on the white cupboard doors, on the refrigerator's twin doors.

She dialled triple zero and wiped her knee with the kitchen sponge while waiting for a voice at the other end.

'Ambulance,' she said. 'Possible heart attack or stroke.' Waited then, and the smell of spilt stew raised the urge to vomit – as did the smell of boiling coffee grounds. She turned off the hotplate, knowing she should have been over the morning sickness by now – and the knowing made it worse. There was something wrong with this baby.

Finally, a voice prepared to listen. Trudy knew the patient's history, her date of birth, was able to give the medical names of the patient's many medications. She didn't mention early stage Alzheimer's, did mention the patient's excessive weight.

'The ambulance is on –' the voice began then died.

Trudy looked at the phone. It was plugged in. It was also dead. Her eyes followed the cord back to the power point. Too much on her mind. Nick, car, boys, baby, windscreen-wipers, work – and that lingering nausea; she hadn't turned on the power. Stepped in stew to reach it, wondered if she should dial triple zero again. It would take a while to trickle enough charge into it, and the ambulance was on its way, so she squatted to feel again for that weak pulse.

'Did her go to sleep like Papa?' Ricky asked.

'She slipped in the stew and so will you,' Trudy said. 'Go outside and play with your ball.'

Slipped and hit her head? No blood. Had a stroke and dropped the stew? Her heart had given up the battle? One way or another, she was down and out – and Trudy didn't care. She didn't. She should have. It was her job to care, but this morning she cared more about that stew.

There was a full roll of paper towels on the bench. She reached for it, ripped off half a dozen sheets and used them to wipe her knee then the soles of her shoes. She checked the soles of the boys' shoes then began wiping her way back to Tessa. When that bunch of paper towels would wipe no more, she ripped off a second bunch.

Scooped up carrot rings and shards of broken china, pitched what she'd scooped into the sink. She'd used most of that roll of paper towels before the doorbell sang its song, and did what she could to cover Tessa's thighs before opening the door.

Two men, one built to handle this morning's job. She led them through to the kitchen, then took the boys into Tessa's sitting room. They would have preferred to watch the live drama than a midday show with commercials.

'Find something,' she said and handed Ricky the remote.

Tessa's landline was near the stairs. She'd have to phone Nick, or Tonia. She'd be at work. All four girls worked, as had their father. Nick hadn't inherited the work gene.

'Stop supplying a crutch and let him fall over,' Tonia had said two days ago.

'He's got no intention of taking that miserable old bitch to Greece. It was a con to get her to pay for his holiday,' Angie had said, a fourth daughter, a disappointment. She claimed that her parents had hated her since infancy – for being born without the required male equipment.

Trudy used to see herself as the mother of three little girls. This one could be a girl. A scan would tell her. A scan would tell her if it was developing as it should. At times she was petrified that it wasn't.

Nature set women up. It got their hormones raging when they were most likely to conceive. She knew to the hour this one's conception, to the half hour.

She hadn't seen Nick in months the day he'd turned up in Woody Creek in his father's Range Rover. She'd told Jenny to lock the doors, then walked over to the hotel to speak to him.

They hadn't lived together as husband and wife in three years. The twins hadn't known him. Divorce had seemed the only way to go.

'My father died,' he'd said when he opened the cabin door.

'We saw his death notice,' Trudy had said, then raised the subject of divorce. 'It will be simple. Any money I've got, I've saved since we separated.'

'We have two sons,' he'd said.

'You've had minimal contact with them, Nick. You've paid nothing towards their support – and knowing your work record it's unlikely that you'll ever support them. I'd want sole custody, which won't mean that you can't see them if you want to.'

It had gone to script until she was about to leave for work, when he'd put his arms around her and howled on her shoulder. He was the only man she'd ever known to cry. Of course, she'd held him. Of course, she'd comforted him. She'd walked him to the bed, sat him down and sat with him, soothing, talking, explaining how little boys needed stability; how the life they'd lived before the boys hadn't been reality.

'Some of it was fun, but life has become very real since the boys were born.'

He'd been the first man she'd slept with, the only man. That day in the cabin he hadn't forced himself on her, not entirely. She'd tried to fight him off, initially. A woman of forty was at her sexual peak, so she'd read somewhere. She'd been celibate for three years.

*

The paramedics, having moved Tessa onto a trolley, had exposed more spilt stew and one of them stepped in it. She reached again for the paper towels, wiped up a footprint, another carrot ring, while answering their questions.

They'd masked Tessa, wired her up to a machine. Her breakfast and pills still on the table, Trudy swept four pills into her hand. The boys had given up on midday television to stand in the doorway watching the paramedics at work.

'Papadimopolous,' Trudy said, then spelt *Papadimopolous.* Spelt it again while looking at the multicoloured pills. Tessa wouldn't be taking them. She tossed them into the sink, then walked over to her boys to stand between them, brushing their twin spiky heads with her hands.

They'd had thick, dark hair, with Nick's slight curl. He was losing his. His father's head had resembled a billiard ball – with wrinkles. Nick knew what was in store for himself so took his sons out to Eastland and got rid of their hair.

Mirror, mirror on the wall, who's the prettiest boy of all.

She continued brushing spikes until one small hand caught hers to still it. She kissed that warm little hand and wondered if Tessa died today, would the twins remember more than the paramedics and their trolley?

They remembered Papa's go far. Had photographs of them and Papa riding in circles on the front lawn, and a bad shot of Jenny lifting Ricky down.

'Don't you point that thing at me,' Jenny had said to her.

I'll have some news to text to Venice, Trudy thought, when the trolley was wheeled out. She had stew footprints on the carpet too, but when the front door was closed the spray cleaner removed the stew.

'Run up to your room and get a video. We'll play it on Tessa's television.'

She mopped the kitchen to the music from *The Lion King*, her boys content to sit through that one again and again. She mopped the cupboard doors, the refrigerator, the tiled floor, and when the kitchen smelt clean, when her mobile had enough charge, she phoned Nick.

He didn't pick up. She left a message, and seconds later he called back. He was vetting his calls. Who didn't he want to hear from?

'What happened to her?' he asked, and she told the condensed tale of her day.

'Let your sisters know.'

'I'm not phoning the bitches. You've got their numbers.'

They were all bitches, Tonia because she was married to the brother-in-law who owned the taxis, and because she and Angie had trapped him on video, loading crates into the back of his cousin's vehicle. Once not enough evidence for Tonia, she'd got him again at Bunnings, loading the boot of the Commodore.

'They're your sisters. It would be better coming from you – and cancel your flights. If you do it today, you'll get a part of the money back.'

He hung up.

She didn't phone his sisters. She sat on the couch, closed her eyes and was dead to the world when *The Lion King* ended.

'Is Daddy home?'

'No.'

She called him again. He didn't call back. She called Tonia, who was unaware of today's catastrophe, and not pleased to have been kept in the dark for so long.

'Nick knew. It was his place to call you,' Trudy said and ended the call. She'd slept for almost two hours and felt worse for it. She needed eight solid hours of dark, silent sleep, in her own bed. And her bed was gone, her home, her father – and her mother gone to Venice.

Been there, done that, Trudy thought, and she took the boys out to the family room where she served them cereal for lunch. They liked cereal. She didn't phone the hospital, didn't reply to Jenny's text, instead she found a kids' show on the ABC. The twins weren't fussy.

Nick came home at five to change the channel to a pack of bunched-up cyclists, pushing uphill, as interesting to little boys as watching the front lawn grow.

'What's wrong with your mother?' Trudy asked.

'What did they tell you?'

'Nothing.'

'Have you called the hospital?' he asked.

'I called Tonia. Where have you been all day?'

He looked at her briefly, before turning the volume higher, and in that moment perhaps she saw what Jenny had seen in his eyes. Snake eyes, she'd called them. In Venice, Trudy had described them as dreamy.

He had an obvious bald spot on the back of his crown. She'd paid for an expensive hair treatment in London. It hadn't worked.

The boys had gone upstairs to play dinosaurs. She went out to the kitchen to take a container from the freezer. Just soup. She placed it in the microwave, selected *defrost*, then while it hummed, she walked through to the laundry to get a load of washing started.

His pigskin jacket, bought in London, for the equivalent of five hundred Australian dollars, was on the machine. Someone else hung up Nick's clothing. Tonight she tossed it on the floor and heard the jangle of car keys. There was more than her car keys in its pocket. He'd bought a new mobile a few months ago. He liked the best, the best mobile, the best brand-name jeans and sneakers. She looked at her parka, hung on a hook behind the door. It was as light as a feather and warm as toast but she left it hanging, and as the microwave beeped, she slid her arms into pigskin, then opened the door to the garage.

Cold out there, his jacket was cold – and restricting, but she hit the remote-control button and the big door opened. He must have heard it, or heard her car start up. He could move fast when he wanted to.

'I need that car,' he called. She selected reverse. 'I need to see Mum tonight.'

'You've had all afternoon to see her. Feed your sons.'

He opened the door on the driver's side, but her foot was on the accelerator and she bore down. Forced to decide between getting the car keys and being crushed against the garage brick-work, he released the door. It slammed against bricks as she roared too fast out to the court, where she rammed the stick into *drive*. The door swinging wide, she drove out of the court before stopping to close it. Had to slam it three times before it closed. Too early to go to work, not clothed for work, and she'd left her boys alone to absorb his anger. She didn't turn back, but out of habit, drove towards the place where she was still Sister Hooper.

'Don't trust him, Trude,' Sophie had warned.

She'd trusted him. She'd trusted him to use a condom and had to marry him because he hadn't. Shouldn't have. Should have bought a ticket home. Her mother wouldn't have cared if her grandchild was born in or out of wedlock. Her father would have. There'd been no grandchild, not that time. She'd lost it at eleven weeks.

And Nick had been relieved. 'A kid is the last thing we need,' he'd said.

A *kid*. A *thing*. It had been a little girl to Trudy. She'd mourned that little girl for months.

They'd been happy in France. They'd been in Spain when she'd told him that they'd need to move to the UK so she could get work. They'd killed their forever ham. Every slice she'd cut from it in Spain had made it smaller.

He'd worked for a month in Manchester. She'd worked there for twelve months, then moved on again. They'd seen the northern lights in Norway then flown back to Greece. Plenty of relatives in Greece with spare beds and food in the fridge but little money. She'd become concerned about money.

Had got work in Greece, caring for the aged, and been desperate to get him out of that country. He'd been in with a bad mob of cousins. She'd applied for and secured work in Scotland. A cold place, Scotland. He didn't like the cold. They'd argued the night before she'd left. That was the first time he'd hit her. She caught her plane, and for five months she'd been alone and at peace.

He'd turned up when summer came. She'd been sharing a tiny unit and refused to open the door.

He'd found work as a barman and kept coming back. Her roommate moved on and Nick had moved himself in. She'd got herself a prescription for the pill.

When her period had been late, she'd blamed the pill, blamed it for her sore breasts, blamed it until she'd felt that flutter of butterfly wings. A scan exposed the two tiny beings inside her.

She hadn't told Nick. She'd given notice at the hospital and booked her flight home. Should have crept away like a thief in the night, but that had never been her way. She'd told him. He'd told his parents. They'd paid his fare home, and on the same plane.

Trudy met them at the airport. Tessa was overweight, her English was poor, but otherwise she'd seemed . . . normal. Old Nick, an alpha male, Trudy's relationship with her father-in-law hadn't begun well. In his native tongue, he'd offered his opinion of her, so in the same tongue, she'd explained that the *skinny old Australian bitch* had hired a car, that she would be driving it home to her parents in the country, but that Nick was more than welcome to drive home with his parents.

'Lovely meeting you,' she'd said, then left them standing, Tessa's arms wrapped around her prodigal son's neck.

He'd shaken her off to follow Trudy and her bank card. His parents followed him. His father was loud while she'd waited to pick up the keys to the hire car. His mother howled because Nick was going with his *skinny old Australian bitch*.

He'd expected to drive the hire car and got into the driver's seat.

'My name is on the insurance. They have my bank card details. Out, please.'

'You let her talk shit to you?' the alpha male said.

Nick rode in the passenger seat to Woody Creek and he'd laughed at her town. She'd been pleased to see it until she'd seen the age of her father. She'd left a grey-headed man and returned to a white-headed cripple. Nick saw only the cripple and Jenny's car, and her car keys on the kitchen bench. The hire car returned to Willama, they'd been home for less than a week when he helped himself to Jenny's keys and disappeared for two days and a night.

It was never a good idea to get on the wrong side of Jenny. She'd aged in years but her tongue still had a bite.

Women didn't speak to Nick as she'd spoken to him that day. He'd caught the bus home the next morning – to resume his university course, he'd said.

His father offered him labouring work at a building site. Nick didn't soil his hands with labour. His brother-in-law offered him a job driving a taxi. His mother gave him money, and he disappeared.

The twins were a month old the day his parents drove him to Woody Creek to collect his wife and sons.

First love doesn't die easily. You can tell yourself it's dead, but hope lingers, as do the memories of the good times. There had been good times. His parents had driven him to Woody Creek a second time, then he'd driven up alone.

She'd been late to work that day and had been aware that she may regret sleeping with him. Had missed out on the drama of the Range Rover.

Nick's relatives had arrived in Woody Creek – Nick's nephew, his brother-in-law, Tonia and the nephew's mate. Jenny spoke to them through a locked security door, certain they'd come to take the twins. All they'd wanted was the Range Rover Nick's father had willed to his grandson.

Before her period had been seriously overdue, Trudy had known she was pregnant. Unable to admit it to Jenny she'd decided to get rid of it, to drive down to Georgie – but she couldn't tell her either. Georgie had prepared the divorce papers.

Then there was that cancelled appointment with a visiting hip-replacement specialist. Her father had needed that operation. Jenny knew he'd needed it but had allowed him to cancel.

The loss of that appointment had become a vent for Trudy's self-directed anger.

'You're a stubborn, selfish old man,' she'd said, and when Jenny leapt to his defence, she'd turned on her. 'He'll have both of you in a nursing home inside of twelve months.'

That's what she'd said, and more, too much more. She hadn't mentioned her pregnancy. Hadn't mentioned abortion.

Fate, or God, or whatever name you gave it, made her decision. Nick had been working. He told her that he needed her in his life, that he wanted to know his sons.

It was an out, and that was all it was. It was a bed for her and the boys. It was time, space in which to decide whether to have that baby or not – and if she slept with him in Croydon, she could admit to being pregnant.

'We'll come down for a week,' she'd said.

Hadn't told him to use a condom, nor had she looked for an abortion clinic. Hadn't gone home at the end of that week. He'd been making good money. The house was incredible. Then she'd met Margaret Morrison.

Tessa had screeched Greek at the boys, but they hadn't spent a lot of time in her display house. Trudy had taken them to visit her old friends. She'd phoned Sophie. They'd met for coffee.

'I thought you'd woken up to him,' Sophie said.

'He wants to know his sons. He's working,' Trudy said.

'I'll give him a month,' Sophie said.

He'd run into a tram. Then that late-night call. Her father was dead. She'd told him she was sorry – when it had been too late.

Rain now whipping her windscreen, she turned on her wipers. One scratched more than wiped, and she sat forward. If she'd dropped the car off at the garage today, that wiper would have been replaced. She'd lost today – as she'd lost most of her days since her father's death. Not lost, just thrown them away, on him, on Tessa.

Papadimopolous. How many times had she repeated that name today, over the phone, to the paramedics? No one could spell it. Her boys couldn't say it – and she didn't want them to learn how to say it. They could say Hooper. James and Richard Hooper. That's who they were.

She made a right-hand turn off the highway, then drove on towards the hospital. She found a park, backed into it, and the wipers stilled. Rain thundering down, she sat imagining what her life may have been had she flown home with Sophie, had she not sold Lorna Hooper's house.

Georgie and Paul owned their own house. Two years ago, they'd put their excess funds into a rental unit in Prahran. She had nothing. Had no purse tonight, no driver's licence, no money, and she was wearing a stained tracksuit beneath his pigskin jacket. She had his mobile and reached into the pocket.

She read her last text to him and his reply. She read Angie's three texts. He hadn't replied to his sister. There was a text from a number, no name. *Did you get the money?*

He'd replied to it. *I'll have it by the tenth. Stay cool.*

What money? She'd paid his cocaine supplier eight hundred dollars in Greece – after he'd threatened to take it out of Nick's hide.

Who did he owe money to?

There was a simple way to find out. She called that unnamed number.

'What's up now, babe?' a female voice replied.

DAWN IN VENICE

Jim was with her. He wasn't using his walking frame, but walking tall behind the guide as they were led through rooms of multi-coloured snakes. It was a factory where they made snakeskin handbags, and in her dream Jim bought one. She tried to stop him. It was too expensive. She couldn't read its price tag but there were four figures, confused as all that was written was confused in Jenny's dreams.

The bag was small. She opened it, wondering how she'd squeeze the contents of her old bag into it, and he tossed her old bag into the canal. Her passport was in it, her ticket home, her mobile, the photograph of her and Jimmy she'd carried for fifty years. Everything she was was in that bag. 'Turn around,' she screamed. 'We have to go back!' And he laughed at her. The canal was too narrow to turn around.

She woke with his laughter ringing in her ears and she hit her damaged fingernail while reaching for her bag. Every nerve in that finger screamed, but her bag was where she always left it, on the floor, with her shoes, beside her bed. She held it to her racing heart as she turned towards Johanna's bed. Apparently her dream had been silent. The hump of Johanna hadn't moved.

Her mobile, along with too much more, was in that bag. She slid the top zipper and, without needing to remove the phone, she could see the time. Too early yet to get out of bed, so she lay down again, the handbag under the quilt.

Jim used to tell her that she'd carried her life in her handbags. He'd been her life until he'd thrown himself into the creek. Was it any wonder he'd thrown her bag away in dream? She drew a breath and held it for the count of ten then did it twice more. She'd lived without him before. From the age of nineteen to thirty-five she'd lived without him – and she would again.

Look what I've seen, she thought. She had a camera in that bag full of the places she'd seen, and tomorrow she'd see Switzerland. She'd find Jimmy too. There were trains to Thames Ditton. She'd get herself down there and this time he'd be at home.

Her glasses were on the bedside table. She reached for them and put them on to reread yesterday's messages, their glow shielded by her bag. Like little letters, texts, they could be enjoyed again and again.

She'd sent a few to Katie yesterday.

I feel like the bunny in the Duracell battery advertisement, the one powered by batteries from the two-dollar shop. Jenny bunny is slowing down while Johanna bunny, powered by Duracell batteries, keeps powering on.

She had nothing in common with her roommate, other than their recent widowhood, but since the day of the water-filled hats they'd been communicating. She now knew that Johanna had two daughters and three sons. Johanna knew that Jenny had two daughters and a son living near London.

By the light of her mobile she found the photograph of her and Jimmy, a professional study, taken in Sydney. John McPherson had made three copies of the original. She'd had one laminated so it wouldn't wear away in her handbag. Jimmy was almost two years old when that photograph was taken. She'd been nineteen.

Had meant to get a family shot when they'd lived in Armadale, when he'd been a little schoolboy, but professional photographs had cost money and she'd been struggling to feed her kids. By the time she'd been making her own money, she hadn't had the time.

She had an out-of-focus shot of Jimmy at fourteen and one of him blowing out ten candles on a birthday cake. Jim's cousin took those shots – and Jenny hated that cousin because he'd been allowed to watch her son grow.

'They've raised a fine boy,' he'd said that day.

They, Margaret Hooper and her husband. *They* may have loved him. *They* had educated him.

At the television studio when Georgie introduced Juliana Conti to a grey-headed stranger, he'd sounded like an educated Englishman. Jenny, gasping for a cigarette, hadn't looked twice at the stranger until he'd offered his hand, Jim's hand. She'd known him by that hand before she'd seen his little boy Jimmy smile.

One more week. Her two-dollar-shop batteries would get her to London.

She closed her bag, placed it beneath her pillow, then eased herself out of bed, and in the near dark, felt her way along the walls to the bathroom door. It was open. She closed it behind her before seeking the light switch. Its cleansing flood of white light washed the last of that dream away. A hot shower and a head wash would recharge her batteries.

Every hotel on the tour had provided their guests with shampoo, and whether the entire contents of those small bottles was used or not, they were replaced daily. She wished they'd been as liberal with teabags. At any time, day or night, she'd been able to get her cup of tea on the cruise.

Nick and his parents had coloured her view of Greece, but their problem was genetic. The Greeks in Greece had been a smiling, friendly race. She'd expected to feel that she'd come home when they'd landed in Italy. She hadn't, but she'd walked her mother's land – or climbed it.

Too many shampoo suds queuing to go down the plughole, Jenny watched them and wondered again how Venice got rid of its waste. As a ten-year-old in John Curry's classroom she'd first heard about this city built in water. From time to time she'd seen glimpses of Venice in movies and photographs but had never expected to walk its pavements.

When that *Taste of Europe* tour came up on the travel agent's computer, she'd seen the words 'Cruise the Greek islands' and seen the price. 'That will do,' she'd said. Then the itinerary arrived, and the places she'd see had blown her mind.

She'd seen bodies turned to stone in Pompeii, learnt that Venice had been built on islands in the middle of an impenetrable swamp, built by rich merchants who'd hidden there with their loot when the hordes of marauding barbarians came. That city, built as a secure marketplace for merchants, had evolved into a marketplace for hordes of tourists. Yesterday, when they'd boarded a ferry, she'd felt like an old cow amid a seething herd of wildebeest, determined to cross crocodile-infested water.

The shower turned off, she reached for a towel, also provided clean each day, whether used or not. She used them, wrapped her hair in one, wrapped herself in another then rinsed out her night-gown and removed the excess water from it with a towel. Draped over the shower rail, the gown would be dry by tonight.

Her hair had grown a little, but that was to the good. Her grey roots may have grown through, but she had enough of the champagne blonde for the roots not to show.

Granny used to colour her hair. She used to swap a few dozen eggs with old Charlie White for bottles of nut-brown dye. Grey hair is aging, she used to say. If we look old, we feel old. Jenny had paid more than a few dozen eggs for her dye job, but the minute she'd seen it, she'd been pleased with the colour.

Back in the bedroom, the drapes still drawn, a gap of morning light was entering, so she crept to the window to open that gap a little more. Johanna didn't move, and on bare feet, Jenny crept to her bed for her bag.

Her itinerary, no longer crisp, promised her a pleasant walk this morning to the Doges Palace, a free afternoon and then an evening walk to the opera. She'd never been to an opera, had watched a few on the ABC, but here she was in Venice attending a Venetian opera.

Yesterday hadn't been an easy day. They'd caught the ferry to an island to watch glass blowers at work in a factory that looked as if it hadn't changed in a thousand years – and she'd done what she'd promised not to do, bought a souvenir.

Her watch told her she had an hour yet to wait for a cup of tea. Room service was only a phone call away but on her first morning in Rome when she'd made that call, she'd woken Johanna. Any odd noise woke Johanna. One eye on her, Jenny wound a window wide. She'd lubricated its hinge with some form of face cream, also provided by the hotel. Whether it was good for skin or not she didn't know, but the window wound wide silently, and she popped her head and shoulders out and looked down on a city that appeared to have been newly roused from a five-hundred-year sleep.

The birds had discovered it. There were hundreds of them, large, white, wheeling, calling, but not a tourist in sight. She looked at Johanna again, afraid the birds would wake her. Still no movement from that hump.

Her itinerary placed back into her bag, she removed her camera, wanting to trap this city, as it should have been. She loved birds. As a kid she'd stood on the bridge with Norman while he'd named every bird they'd seen. She couldn't name these birds, larger relatives of the gull, perhaps.

A garbage barge broke into that peaceful scene. She watched it dock, aware that she was about to learn what happened to the rubbish of this waterlogged city. She photographed a barge man as he tied his craft to a pole blackened by age. She caught a group of birds swooping close to his head. That was a good shot, as was her shot of a Venetian labourer, pushing a small cart loaded with bags of refuse.

What breed of mankind had conceived of such a city? she thought. The tour guide was informative. He had his spiels down pat. He hadn't mentioned how those merchants had managed to barge in enough stone and cement to build this city of bridges and grand cathedrals, or how they'd managed to find foundations in a swamp.

As the garbage barge moved away, Jenny lined up a shot of an outdoor restaurant. It had been packed the night she'd arrived in Venice but deserted this morning, its chairs resting, upended. It was a lonely shot, a perfect cover for an end of the world scenario. Maybe she'd have time to write it.

The hotel room was overwhelmingly Venetian, ornate wall-paper, gold and white lacquered furniture and a window with a view of the Grand Canal. She and Johanna had been lucky with room allocation, perhaps because they never complained. Tour guides had power. Daren complained. Poor little inoffensive–not so inoffensive Gus suffered the worst rooms because of his roommate's complaints. Bertha complained. Eva suffered.

Jenny tiptoed to her laptop, set up on a white lacquered desk beside a power point. Its light had turned green, which meant it was fully charged. She had time to write, had a desk to write at in Venice but wrote in the bathroom.

She'd taken her laptop down to a table in the dining room, but had been invaded by the Dutch, or Daren, or all three. Bathrooms were safe, if not as comfortable.

She glanced at her watch, then silently unplugged the computer and crept with it to the bathroom where she opened her *Tour* file, which needed updating.

9 June
Hit an ATM last night, in an alleyway so narrow, those who
live in it could almost reach out a hand and shake their opposite

neighbour's hand. Used my card, the guide at my elbow. Venetian ATMs are not like our own. Last night's was black and stuck in a blank wall, no bank in sight, or nothing I recognised as a bank. I expected it to eat my card, but it spat out money. Tickets to operas are not cheap and an added extra. Daren complained. What's new?

Manpower means powered by man in Venice. No trucks, horses, donkeys or goats. Men push small carts, necessarily small to get through those alleys. We walked down so many alleys last night I almost asked our guide if he was getting kick-backs from various governmental bodies. Every senior he doesn't send home is one less pension to pay, one less bed required in a nursing home.

We left the New Zealand couple in Rome (husband with broken wrist). They were flown home yesterday. The Irish couple had to go home to bury a parent the day we arrived in Venice.

I don't know how Eva tolerates her patron – patron because Bertha paid for her tour – and I doubt that there is one amongst us Bertha hasn't told, in the strictest confidence. She told me on the second night of the cruise. It's been interesting, watching the dynamics alter. The business-class American couple, on their second honeymoon, still share a room but now sit at separate tables. Daren, so eager to befriend everyone that first night, has become too friendly with alcohol. He stinks of it.

Johanna can down a glass of beer like a man. She's almost as tall as Lorna Hooper, but big with it, not fat, or not excessively. 'That abrasive woman,' Bertha calls her.

She was abrasive on the first night of the cruise. One wrong word and I wouldn't have needed to jump overboard. She would have tossed me over. I spent my days on the boat dodging her and feeling sorry for Daren. Now I dodge him and feel sorry for Gus, who, apart from his sweaty shirts is a lovely little bloke.

Lila got into my head yesterday. We saw an old busker making bad accordion music, a red dog at his feet. Gus and I gave his owner a handful of coins for his dog, not his music. Gus left his dog with a neighbour and his wife in care. She's in a wheelchair. We communicate now with signs.

I found out last night why that final place on this tour came up on the Willama travel agent's computer. Johanna told me that her children had booked the tour months ago, for their father's eightieth birthday. He died five days before Jim. The kids cancelled his ticket but refused to cancel Johanna's, which would have been around the time I booked. I'm over here because her husband died – not that I told her so. She asked me when I booked. 'Six months ago,' I lied.

Jenny took a breather, to straighten her back. Toilet seats would never take the place of her cushioned office chair, and the laptop felt warm. She stood, placed it on the seat and thought of Vern Hooper's bathrooms. She had a choice of two at home, and both would take what was in this room three times over –

With one God-almighty stroke of a biro, I signed those bathrooms away, she thought. Would I have done the same thing today? Maybe not. I can't live in Melbourne. Buy a modern one-bedroom unit in Willama, maybe.

She squatted to close the file, to close the program, then close the computer. The dining-room doors would be opening soon. She returned the laptop to the desk to cool down before it had to be packed.

There was a bubble-wrapped parcel on the desk, a glass unicorn, a perfect object that would probably lose its horn or tail when she packed it. She could take a photograph of it looking perfect, so she unwrapped it and brought it to the window, where she stood it on its four dainty hooves.

It was barely eight inches long, including its horn and tail. She'd been foolish to spend so much on it – though Jim would have paid its marked price – as he'd paid the marked price for her nightmare snakeskin handbag, which was why that nightmare had been so real. When she'd admired a ridiculously expensive pair of shoes one day in a city store, he'd wanted her to buy them. She'd learned not to window shop when he'd been at her side, or what windows to shop in. She'd dragged him into that travel agency more than once to admire travel brochures. He hadn't taken that bait.

He would have loved Venice. He would have loved the old glass factory. Its entrance fee had been included in the tour price, though she would have paid it three times over, would have sat gladly all day watching those artists turn red-hot molten blobs into magical creatures. The show had ended too soon and her group was herded out to make way for the next herd.

They'd been guided down an ancient passageway to a heavy door Jenny had expected to lead back into an alley. It opened into a showroom, filled floor to ceiling with glass of every size, shape and colour. It took her breath away – as it was meant to.

Half a dozen crocodile salesmen and women waiting there to feed on tourists, she'd kept her distance from them and the glass until the unicorn caught her interest. She'd been studying it, wondering how its maker had added the golden flecks to his flowing tail and curled horn when a crocodile approached, picked up the unicorn and offered it to her.

'I'm too far from home,' she'd said. Too far, and if she happened to get home, it would only be to hand over her keys – and the price of that tiny thing was ridiculous. She'd turned away to find the exit, her mind back with boy Jim.

He'd introduced her to unicorns. He'd come to the station one day to show her a book Margaret had bought for him. She could still see his long fingers turning those perfect pages, still hear him explaining why the white horse had a horn in the centre of his head. 'He's a unicorn,' he'd said. 'A magical horse who can grant wishes.'

Fifteen years later, she'd been in Sydney, Jim missing in action, and she'd found an identical copy of that book at a street stall. It had been like a message from him, telling her he was alive. She'd bought it, for him and for herself, not for Jimmy, who would have preferred a book about cars. Still had that book, packed safe in a carton in Georgie's garage. If she'd believed she could get that unicorn home intact, she might have paid the asking price.

The salesman followed her with it, and he dropped his price. She spoke to him near the exit, explained she was from Australia, was midway through a tour and had no space in her luggage for souvenirs. She'd thanked him then walked out to the pavement.

He knew his job. He'd dropped his price again.

We all have our price. She'd paid it and walked away from that factory with her bubble-wrapped unicorn in her green nylon shopping bag.

She photographed it three times that morning, from different angles, then rewrapped it and placed it with her laptop, which would have enough charge left in it to share breakfast with her, and again she unzipped her green pouch shopping bag.

No Daren, no Dutch waiting at the dining-room door. For half an hour she drank tea, ate croissants and typed in peace, in comfort until a message beeped through from Trudy.

Tessa on life support. She was supposed to fly tomorrow.

*

You can see one too many grand old palaces. You can also have too much company, and on her final day in Venice, Jenny begged off the tour to spend some time with her *Parasite* file. Its word length crept up to thirty thousand before Johanna returned. 'Canada will fly home in the morning. They have changed his flight,' she said.

'Daren?' Jenny asked. Johanna spoke English well enough and, like Jenny, had been introduced that first night to their fellow travellers. She'd never troubled herself with names. She'd named Bertha 'The Dutch'.

She'd been shopping. She placed a bulging supermarket bag on her bed. 'He is making argument now because he must pay extra money.'

'I'll pay it,' Jenny said, stretching her aching bones while watching what emerged from that supermarket bag – apples, tomatoes, a circle of cheese, a loaf of crusty bread. And butter, and a knife to cut the loaf and to spread the butter.

'You found a supermarket!' she said.

'Venetians also must eat,' Johanna said. 'There was no peace today. There will be no peace down there.' Dinner was prepaid tonight, in the dining room. 'You will eat with me.' It was more statement than question, but for a slice of that loaf, a wedge of that cheese, Jenny would have sold her soul to the devil. She closed her file, closed her laptop and they ate at the desk, their plates ripped from the supermarket bag, their serviettes, a spare toilet roll. They hacked rough slices from the loaf, took turns with the knife to spread butter, to slice tomatoes, to peel then cut the apple in half, and when they were done, Jenny used the knife to trim her mutilated ring fingernail while Johanna watched, frowning.

'I rammed a splinter of wood under it the day after my husband died. I thought I saw him walk by the window.'

'Every day I see my William in his garden. I am here because he is there,' she said and shrugged broad shoulders.

'I sold my house three weeks after Jim died.'

'You book also for him?' Johanna asked.

One lie always led to another, so she told the truth. 'He refused to travel,' Jenny said. 'I nagged him for years.'

They shared the last of the cheese with wine and beer from the mini-bar, small bottles, expensive, which raised the question of 'Canada's' mini-bar bill.

Johanna's case, small enough to travel as cabin luggage, contained no frock. She changed her half-mast trousers, removed her cap. Her grey crew-cut didn't require a comb. She didn't change her bulky sandals. Jenny changed into her one frock, changed her shoes. She'd squeezed in a pair of lightweight soft-soled things that did double service as slippers. They looked better with that frock than her solid walking shoes.

A pleasant evening stroll to the opera, the itinerary said. Johanna strode up front, Gus huffed and puffed at the rear, Jenny stuck close to the guide. There were stairs to climb but a handrail to cling to. Then more steps to climb down and no handrail, but once seated, she was transfixed.

The tenor sounded like Itchy-foot. She hadn't raised Juliana's ghost in Italy. She'd raised Itchy-foot's. He'd sung that tenor's song at the Hawthorn Town Hall and if she closed her eyes she was back there and twenty-three again.

She'd sung with him later that night and when the audience had demanded an encore, he'd drawn her back on stage and they'd sung *Ave Maria*. They hadn't rehearsed it but had taken their bows to thunderous applause.

Always take your bows, Jennifer.

As a girl he'd called her Jennifer. She might have been ten years old the first time she'd seen him, when to her he'd been another old tramp who'd wandered into Woody Creek and stayed for a while. She was twenty-two when Granny told her that her philandering husband was Jenny's biological father.

She hadn't touched him until that night when he'd taken her hand to lead her back onto the stage. Granny had never trusted him – nor had Jenny, but if she'd run from Armadale to him instead of running home to Granny, she wouldn't have lost Jimmy.

That philandering sod I married, Granny used to say if forced to mention Archie Foote. *That philandering sod had a voice that could charm the natives out of the jungle.*

He would have been in his late seventies or early eighties when Jenny had known him. He'd got her work, singing at a sleazy jazz club, but he'd looked after her there and that club had paid her well. He'd sung at that club and as soon as he'd opened his throat his age had become irrelevant. She'd felt no daughterly love for him but had loved his voice.

Granny was nineteen, he twenty-three when they'd married. They'd remained married until his death, but spent all but seven years apart.

That philandering sod was directed early into doctoring – expected to follow in his father's footsteps. He came alive on stage but never gave a damn about doctoring, Granny once said.

He'd never mentioned Granny but had spoken often of life. 'We each get one chance at it, Jennifer. We are each an accident, born of lust, each allocated a certain number of years before we die like weeds in the great garden of life. Don't waste your allocated years as I wasted mine.'

She'd wasted her allocated years. She'd wasted her voice, would have wasted her writing if not for Georgie. 'If you don't sign this,' the contract for *Sent in Chains*, 'I swear to God I'll write on your tombstone, *Herein lies Jennifer Morrison Hooper, who could have been.*'

Most of her life had been behind her the day she'd sold her first novel. It lit a fire in her belly but wiped Jim out for more than a year. She'd hidden from his dark mood, hidden in her library, the doors closed, her fingers busy. He'd lost a lot of his years in that dark place. Maybe he'd known it was coming for him again the day he rode out to Monk's – maybe he'd known a nursing home was coming to get him.

That's what I should do, Jenny thought, buy myself into one of those places behind the hospital. Some of those units have space for a car.

But not for a dog. Didn't know what she was going to do.

The timing of this tour had been so bad, but in so many ways had been perfect. She was exhausted but felt better in her head for it and could think ahead again.

MISSING

Tessa had a brain haemorrhage and has no brain function. The doctors and the girls want to turn off the machines and let her go but Nick has power of attorney.

He won't agree to it? Jenny replied fast.

He wasn't around to agree or disagree.

There was no more baby. There'd be no more work, not for six or eight weeks. Trudy had a metal plate in her ankle, a cracked rib, one eye was closed and her face was bruised and swollen from brow to ear.

She'd been concussed when she'd told a policewoman that it was her fault. 'I took his passport,' she'd said. She wasn't concussed now, and Angie had already got the true story out of the twins – and got more out of a cousin. Nick had never intended to take his mother to Greece. He'd booked the second flight for a Danielle Simpson, who along with Nick was missing.

A third of all marriages end in the divorce court. Danielle's would. She had four children – two at school, a boy the same age as the twins and a girl of nineteen months.

They hadn't flown to Greece. Trudy had put a stop to that. She'd burnt Nick's passport on the barbeque, poured methylated spirits over it, struck a match and lit it, then stood watching it burn.

Three days later she'd been in hospital, in the same hospital as Tessa. All four of Nick's sisters had popped in to see her. Angie had taken a week of her holidays to care for the twins. Tonia owned the largest house and had only one adult son. She'd told Trudy where she'd be staying when the hospital released her. She'd told her that she wasn't returning to Tessa's house. Tonia had picked her up from the hospital this morning and on the trip to Glen Waverly, told her about Nick and Danielle.

'He was out of his brain the last time I spoke to him. Is he on anything?' Tonia had asked.

He'd been out of his brain when he couldn't find his passport, as had Trudy since she'd called that number on his mobile. The female voice that replied would have been Danielle. She wasn't the first of Nick's women. She wouldn't be the last.

She'd driven home that night and told Nick that she knew where he'd been spending his days, told him to cancel his flight or she and the boys would go.

'Where to?' He'd laughed.

He'd taken the car – so she'd burnt his passport. Then she'd chosen the wrong time, the wrong place to tell him that he may as well stop looking for it. The boys had been beside her. They'd seen everything. She could remember what had happened. She could remember thinking, baby, remember Ricky's eyes. To her dying day she'd remember his eyes.

She must have hit her head on a step or against the stair rail. She remembered no more until she woke in a hospital bed.

If not for her boys she might have bled to death. If Nick had thought to close the garage door they couldn't have got out. They had, had run screaming to the next-door neighbour that, 'Daddy made Mummy dead.'

She'd been concussed, had lost the baby, lost a lot of blood, but wasn't dead. The boys had seen the blood, and the neighbour and her husband had. They'd called an ambulance. Another neighbour knew Tonia. She'd called her.

If not for that blood staining the carpet at the foot of the stairs, Nick might have got away with mortgaging his mother's house. Tonia and her husband had been there trying to clean the carpet when a bank manager phoned and asked to speak to Mrs Tessa Papadimopolous. He'd required a few more details before he could process her loan.

They'd forgotten about the stain and phoned the police. Trudy's poor old navy-blue Commodore, its driver's side door warped by its collision with a brick wall, its windscreen-wiper scratching, was now on the police list of stolen vehicles.

Sister Hooper had seen abused women brought into casualty. She'd known how to deal with them. She knew now how those victims felt. Sore, every muscle hurting, every movement painful but still wanting to hide their husband's abuse from the world.

Had to face it. Had to face the police and Nick's sisters. Didn't have to face Georgie. Couldn't face Georgie.

'Don't contact my sister or mother,' she'd said.

'You're a fool if you can't see what he is,' Jenny had said the day Trudy packed her car and buckled the boys into their seats. 'Your father and I knew what he was the day we met him. At least leave the boys with us.'

She'd been Nick's fool for years. She'd had two hundred and twenty-eight thousand dollars in the bank when she'd flown with him and Sophie to Greece. He'd snorted a lot of that money up his nose, had encouraged her to try it once. Only once.

'Is he on drugs?' Jenny had asked.

'Is he on something? Tonia had asked.

He could have been. She'd been too busy to notice, or too tired, or too pregnant.

No more baby – and she wasn't mourning its loss. That pregnancy had caused this mess and now it was gone and she hadn't killed it. He'd killed it.

Thank God for Tonia – and Angie too. She'd brought the boys around to visit Mummy, so they could see for themselves that she hadn't got dead like Papa.

'Daddy's a bad man,' Jamey said. He didn't attempt to kiss her face better.

THE UNVEILING

*B*usiness-class passengers were loaded before those flying economy. The tour had travelled by bus to Switzerland and as Jenny boarded the plane that would fly them out, she looked at the cloud-shrouded mountains and wondered how the plane was going to miss hitting one of them.

Bertha hadn't paid for Jenny's company but was seated beside her, and the only time she closed her mouth during the hours to London was when she swallowed. She had time to rip most on the tour to shreds and attempted three times to draw Jenny into a bitching session about that abrasive German woman – who Jenny had grown fond of.

They'd gone supermarket shopping in Lucerne, had bought elastic, cotton, a packet of needles and a picnic lunch fit for a king. They'd eaten on a street bench and discussed Melbourne's trams and kangaroos and a train that travelled from coast to coast across thousands of miles of desert. Johanna liked trains, if they provided single rooms. They'd exchanged mobile numbers, email addresses. Today Jenny's beige slacks stayed up and, before they'd vacated their room, Johanna offered to smuggle one needle into London.

The wheels hit hard as the plane landed, but it pulled up and everyone stood up to retrieve their luggage. Jenny hauled down Bertha's vanity case, which was almost as big if not as heavy as her own aqua case. Then, on Bertha's heels, she queued to get off that plane. She queued behind her to get through Customs, which should have been easy. She spoke the language, had an Australian passport. Bertha, who had a Dutch passport, was waved through. Jenny's held up that queue, or an officious fifty-year-old female held up Jenny.

'Your business?' she asked.

Flight attendants handed out declarations to be filled in and signed before planes landed. Since leaving Australia, at the question asking *Reason for travelling?* Jenny had been writing *50/50 business/ holiday*, for taxation purposes. Apparently, elderly women weren't supposed to travel for business.

'Researching Europe,' Jenny replied.

'Occupation?'

'Writer,' Jenny said quietly.

'Published?' The woman wasn't quiet and in that queue at Heathrow, Bertha's ears flapping, Jenny let the cat out of the bag.

'Six adult books and I co-authored seven children's books,' she said, looking the woman in the eye, her hand reaching to claim her passport. She, Jim and the McPhersons had created those seven beautiful children's books, and Jim proud of every one.

'What's your business in the UK?'

Finding Jimmy. Facing Cara – if she could raise the nerve to catch a train alone to Thames Ditton.

'I've got an appointment with an English writer – Langhall.'

Her interrogator may have recognised that name. She returned the passport, and the prisoner at the dock snatched it and made a break for freedom, her bloated aqua case running on one wheel behind her, Bertha on her heels.

'That is why you travel with the computer,' she said, and the aqua case tilted then tipped over.

Jenny righted it, knowing she'd smashed her unicorn. Right then, it didn't matter. She got her case back onto its wheels and continued on to the exit. Bertha's large case travelled separately. She remained indoors.

Cold air and passive smoke greeted Jenny, and that scent of smoke in the cold air raised an old need. If she'd had any English money in her wallet she would have bought a smoke and a light. She'd meant to find an ATM while she was inside, but she wasn't going back inside to find one. Bertha would be spreading her news around the carousel.

Not that it mattered. Not any more.

It had mattered to Jim. She'd turned his *Molly Squire* into popular fiction. It had mattered so much to Jim, he'd crawled into his black hole and pulled down the lid for fourteen months, during which time, Georgie had posted off a second novel by Juliana Conti.

Jenny was standing alone, sucking in passive smoke when Johanna came with her big camera bag and small case.

'The Langhall is in my city,' she said.

'Hamburg? When?'

'My daughter is pay to eat dinner with her.' Johanna shrugged. 'In her email, she said. You are . . . your books are translate, Jenny?'

'No.'

'What are you writing?'

'Australian fiction.'

Others were coming, a few were staring. The Dutch came, Bertha unencumbered, Eva pushing a loaded trolley, and Jenny backed in closer to the smokers. Bertha was allergic to passive smoke. Johanna wasn't. She moved with her. Three smokers now congregated there, a fourth ripping her way into a duty-free carton and about to join them.

'How long you have . . . quit?' Johanna asked.

'Almost four years.'

'I am fifteen. It calls me still.'

They stood sucking their fill until the guide came to gather his shrunken herd. Then, like obedient old cows at milking time, Jenny and Johanna joined the outer perimeter. He'd lost six – and

Daren, who'd remain at the airport to catch his flight home. The rest of them might last another three days – easy days, according to the itinerary.

Thursday today, and Cara in Hamburg. At the Melbourne interview she'd said she'd be visiting four states in ten days, attending dinners and book signings from Brisbane to Perth. She'd do the same in Germany and Jimmy would be with her.

Worn ragged by Bertha, deflated by Johanna's news, Jenny sat alone behind the bus driver. Johanna sat alone. Gus sat alone. Not Eva. She was a captive of her patron's mouth.

Jenny turned her mobile on, praying it would find an English signal. It did, but not immediately, and it needed charging. She hoped that one of her adaptors would fit into English plugs. There was a text from Trudy. Nick wasn't in Greece. Tessa was still being kept alive by machines.

She'd looked like an accident waiting to happen the day Jenny had seen her at Croydon.

I'm staying with Tonia, Trudy had written. Georgie would have given her a bed. *We've booked the boys into a nearby crèche. They love it.*

Something more than Tessa's brain haemorrhage had gone on over there.

Trudy wasn't working. That crèche would cost big money for two. She hadn't mentioned the fees.

They'd allowed her to grow to adulthood believing that money grew on trees, that a shake of the home branch would cause enough leaves to fall at her feet – Jim had. He'd had no respect for money. Since his death, Jenny had shown as little respect. She'd need to pull in her horns when she got home or she'd end up a bag lady – or a busker, singing on some street corner for coins, Lila at her feet.

How much longer will I have her? She was an old lady in dog years, but her mother had made seventeen.

How many more years do I have?

Ms Juliana Conti, author of six . . . Seven, maybe eight novels, if that final plane got her home, if she lived long enough to complete

Parasite . . . Ms Juliana Conti, author of eight novels, died last night in a Willama nursing home.

The traffic heavy, the bus trip into London was slow, but at last they arrived at their final hotel, where they queued one final time while two desk clerks processed them, where one final time, the guide handed out key-cards, Jenny's promising admittance to Room 312. She tailed Johanna's sandalled heels into a lift, tailed them up a series of corridors to 312 and into another anonymous room, much like the Gold Rush Motel's rooms, but without the welcoming teabags and electric jug. It had a small bar fridge, full of temptations, a price list, a room-service folder and a television that spoke English. Jenny wanted tea but settled for a small bottle of wine. Johanna removed its lid, then helped herself to a can of beer, which she took with her to the bathroom.

Tired tonight, Jenny took her bottle to a lone easy chair where she sat, sipping bubbly wine and staring at a quiz show. Someone knocked. The hotel staff delivered the cases. They'd leave them outside the door if she didn't open it. Didn't care much if she lost that case or not, but cared about her laptop and unicorn, so got to her feet, dragged both cases into the room, then sat down again with her bottle.

The game show ended and the English newsreader told her nothing of interest. She eyed England's Prime Minister and royal Charlie and was damn near nodding off, the half-full bottle in her hand, when she heard beeps from her handbag.

Trudy again. *Where are you now?*

London, and they didn't want to let me in. Any word on Tessa?

Tonia got a court order to turn off her life support.

Where's Nick?

Missing.

What do you mean missing?

It would be Friday morning in Australia, very early Friday morning. *Are you back at work?* Jenny texted.

No. Enjoy London. Just touching bases. Xx. The end. That's what Trudy's kisses meant.

Johanna's cap was off. She was ready to go. The herd would be gathering in the foyer for a pleasant evening stroll to an English pub where they could test the local beer and pub fare. It wasn't one of the prepaid dinners and Jenny had no English money to pay for local beer and pub fare.

'You've got rechargeable batteries,' Jenny said. 'I need some – and an ATM.' She emptied the bottle, warm wine now.

'I have their money and we are late,' Johanna said.

The stroll wasn't pleasant. The night was cold and the pub dark and small. Johanna fronted up to the bar. Jenny found a chair where she could rest her back against the wall and continue her texting, though not to Trudy.

What's going on in Croydon?

They're selling Tessa's house. Trudy's in Glen Waverly with her sister-in-law, Georgie replied.

Something has gone on over there. Nick's gone missing.

She was waiting for a reply when Australian Freda and Brian came to the table with pots of beer.

'Do you mind?' Freda asked.

Jenny had barely received a nod out of either of them in three weeks. She put her phone away and looked for Johanna, who may not appreciate their company, but what do you do? There were four chairs at the table and the pub was crowded.

'Go for your life,' she said.

It became clear then what had brought them to that table. 'Brian and I have read everything you've written,' Freda said as she removed a bunch of pages from her handbag. It wasn't her itinerary. The pages were too crisp. She unfolded computer print-outs and one had a photograph of bewigged Juliana Conti on it.

'Bugger,' Jenny said. You can't alter a fake smile. Since that first day in Greece, Jenny had done a lot of fake smiling.

'When we were introduced on the boat, I said to Brian that I knew you from somewhere,' Freda said. 'It wasn't until I heard you were meeting that English author that I twigged as to why you looked so familiar. We saw you with C.J. Langhall on a morning show a few years ago. Your hair was dark and longer then.'

What do you say other than 'bugger'? She'd already said that, but bugger gossiping Bertha and bugger officious Customs officers.

Johanna came with two pots of beer, one she placed down in front of Jenny, who never drank beer, didn't like the taste of it. She picked it up, clicked beer mugs then downed an inch of it.

'Bertha told us that you were researching a new book,' Freda said. Jenny sank a second inch. You weren't supposed to mix beer with wine. She was mixing them – which saved a reply, as did her mobile. It was beeping. Jenny replied to it while Johanna studied the computer printouts.

Brian paid for four more pots of English beer and that's when the night became bizarre to Jenny. She heard herself discussing her writing with strangers. It had been her devious little secret. She heard herself admitting to ripping Woody Creek and half of its population apart in *The Town,* as she'd ripped *Lila Jones/Roberts/Freeman/Macdonald/Flanagan/Simpson* apart in *The Winter Boomerang* – and she was still alive and money hungry. She'd probably sue Juliana Conti.

Then Val and Martin, also Australians, stole chairs from somewhere, and the six sat elbow to elbow, eating English fish and chips at a table hard pushed to seat four, while Val spoke of a neighbour who could have been the woman in *The Winter Boomerang.*

'There can't be two of her,' Jenny said.

Brian went to the bar for more beer. Freda found a biro that worked, and with a drunken flourish, Jenny autographed one of the printouts, *For Freda and Brian, regards, Juliana Conti.* Then she autographed the other, *For Val and Martin, regards, Juliana Conti.* And when her mobile beeped again, Jenny replied, *Currently entertaining my fan club and drinking English beer.*

Friday The Thirteenth

She dreamt of Jimmy, but he was Nick and he'd kidnapped the twins and hidden them in a crumbling castle, and he had Norman's tomahawk and was splitting her own head open with it when Johanna woke her.

'You are alive,' she said.

'Am I?' Jenny asked. She didn't attempt to rise from her pillow.

'We are late.'

'I'm not moving.' If she attempted to, she'd leave her head on the pillow.

Johanna was fiddling with her camera. 'It is dead,' she said. Somewhere between the mountains of Switzerland and the London hotel, the shutter of her elderly Canon had jammed open.

'Take mine – and hang that *Do not disturb* sign on the door when you go. Camera's in my bag. On the floor,' with two hundred photographs on its memory card but this morning Jenny didn't care about any of them.

Johanna attempted to pass the bag to her.

'Take it,' Jenny said, 'and find my Panadol. Side pocket.'

Johanna found the Panadol before she found the camera. She popped two pills then fetched a glass of water.

'Three,' Jenny said, and she got them down.

Johanna had the camera. 'You trust me with this?'

'Get one of Buckingham Palace for Katie,' Jenny said. 'Gus will show you how it works.'

That was the last Jenny saw of Friday the thirteenth. At times beeps seeped through the fog of sleep. She didn't rise to see who'd beeped. She was asleep when Johanna returned.

'You are alive?'

She was alive, felt drugged, but her head was back on her shoulders and she sat up to look at the shots Johanna had taken – and every one of them was a keeper.

'Only nine,' Jenny said.

'I was taking more. Your bad smell boyfriend show me how to put the rubbish in the rubbish bin.'

'Show me?' Jenny said. She found a shot of snow-peaked mountains she'd taken through the window of the bus. It was no keeper. Johanna showed her how to get rid of it. They sat then, side by side on the bed, deleting the worst of Jenny's shots.

Hadn't been able to stand the sight of each other on the cruise, had barely spoken a word until the water-filled hats. Had broken bread together in Venice, picnicked in Switzerland while most of the herd rode chairlifts up a mountain. Johanna had got that small needle into London. Then last night, Jenny had a hazy recollection of Johanna holding her upright on the walk home from the pub, Jenny singing, *Show Me the Way to Go Home.*

While she made her way to the bathroom, Johanna phoned down for room service, a large pot of English breakfast tea, a pot of coffee, plenty of full-cream milk, crusty bread, butter, a fruit and cheese platter, and a hamburger with chips.

A shower and head wash revived Jenny and while she was eating, more messages came through. Her girls had grown accustomed to hearing from her in her mornings and their evenings. The world had reversed that day, or it had for Jenny.

Been down to Thames Ditton? Georgie asked.

Tomorrow, Jenny replied. *Today was my day of rest.*

Katie texted the news. *Good news and bad Nanny. Trudy just told Mum she'd been in hospital with a miscarriage. The good news isn't actually good but you'll probably think it is. Nick's gone missing with Trudy's car. She asked if she could borrow your car.*

I'll need it to get home.

Mum's using it until Saturday. She is getting her dent fixed.

The room-service waiter told Jenny where to find the nearest ATM and at seven that night she and Johanna found it. It spat out ten English twenty-pound notes, which Jenny was studying when Johanna noticed a group of youths circling in like a pack of wolves on two old cows cut off from their herd. The old cows turned tail and walked quickly back to the hotel.

They had three nights in London, the first one lost, one near gone. They had Saturday, a free day, followed by a prepaid banquet with King Henry at some nearby castle. Jenny's English twenties would end up in the pocket of a taxi driver. She was going to Thames Ditton, whether Jimmy was there or not. Saturday was all she had left. On Sunday morning the Australian contingent would catch their plane home.

Too well rested, she couldn't sleep that night. She lay on her back, staring at the ceiling, her mind back in Australia, with Lila, with Pat and Mike and the rose hedge she'd asked her gardener to prune while she was away. She had a secondhand dealer arriving on the seventeenth, and what he didn't buy, Lenny Hall and his son would take – or deliver to the op-shop and tip.

'You are sleeping?' Johanna asked.

Like a voice from an earlier year, her own voice asking Granny if she was asleep. They'd shared a bedroom for years. *Just lying here, planning my tomorrow, darlin'*, Granny used to reply – or not reply.

Jenny considered not replying but she was wide awake. 'Just lying here, planning my tomorrow,' she said.

'You will see your son?'

'He hasn't been my son for over fifty years.'

Silence for a minute from the other bed, then. 'You give birth before you marry, eh?'

'It was wartime,' Jenny said.

'We hear much of this, the child searching, the mother searching. There are happy endings.'

'And unhappy. I'm trying to decide if it's worth wasting all of that money on taxis.'

'You are afraid he will . . . reject?'

'More afraid he won't be there – and then yes, you're right. Afraid that if he is there he won't want to see me.'

'You have make contact?'

'I wrote to him years ago. He didn't reply.'

'Perhaps he did not receive your letter.'

'I used to tell myself that, but I know in my bones that he read it and wants nothing to do with me.'

'Our bones are wrong many times, Jenny. With this tour, I know in my bones I will hate every day. I fight with my children when they say they won't cancel. You want to bury me with your father, so shoot me, I am tell to them, and my last-born son say to me, "Either way, you will be very long dead, Mutti."'

'My girls told me they'd be shipping me home in a coffin,' Jenny said. 'I was pretty certain they'd been right when I woke this morning.'

They spoke as friends that night. It had been a long time since Jenny had spoken honestly to a friend.

JIMMY

'*L*angdon Hall, Thames Ditton,' Jenny told the taxi driver. He didn't ask for details. She had no details to give him. She had the laminated photograph of her and Jimmy in her hand, and it was trembling. She felt nauseous with hope but knew in her head that hoping was hopeless. He'd be in Germany, and if he wasn't, he wouldn't want to see her. She wasn't sure that she'd survive the disappointment, but she had money enough to get herself back to London. Then one more night and she'd be on her way home.

Most parents believe their children are beautiful, whether they are or not. As a two-year-old, Jimmy had been beautiful.

He'd been ten months old when she'd ridden two trains for two days to get him up to Sydney so he could meet his soldier daddy. Jim had sent money to pay for the tickets. Of course she'd gone, just for a week, she'd told Granny. She'd bought a return ticket.

A too-short week that one. They'd gone to the station to see soldier Jim off to war, and when his train was out of sight, Jenny had walked down to book her luggage through to Melbourne.

'All civilian travel cancelled.'

She could still see that youth's face, still hear his voice, still hear irate would-be passengers' complaints.

'All civilian travel cancelled,' he'd repeated, not giving a damn that Jenny would be stuck in Sydney with a baby, not knowing east from west, not knowing one person other than Myrtle Norris, the plum-in-her-mouth landlady, and a few of the lodgers who'd lived at Myrtle's posh boarding house.

Life happens. Granny used to say it was prewritten in the stars. If Myrtle hadn't offered to babysit Jimmy on Jim's final night in Sydney, he wouldn't have introduced her to his army buddies at that servicemen's club. If he hadn't told them she could sing, his buddies wouldn't have marched her up to the old pianist and told him that she'd wanted to sing *Danny Boy*. She'd sung a dozen songs that night. The army boys had kept calling out their favourites and she'd known every one, and if she hadn't, the pianist had, and he'd had the words to it. He'd asked her if she'd sung professionally and he'd given her his name and work number. *Wilfred Whitehead*, who had worked in some governmental office by day and made music by night.

Life was made up of *Ifs*.

For two years Jenny had sung with little Wilfred and his band of elderly gentlemen, at weddings, parties and dances. She'd sung on Friday nights for tips at the servicemen's club, earning good money doing the one thing she could do.

She'd grown to love plum-in-her-mouth Myrtle, the gentle mother Jenny had never known, the doting grandmother to Jimmy. She'd looked after him on the nights Jenny sang. Then after Jim was reported missing, she'd cared for him by day while Jenny sat at a sewing machine, doing her bit for the war effort by stitching uniforms for the fighting boys.

She'd never believed that Jim was dead, or not until her twentieth birthday.

She sang that night in a blue–green shot taffeta frock she'd spent many hours stitching, fitting then stitching again. She'd loved it and been so proud of her first solo attempt at dressmaking.

They'd ripped it off her, five American sailors. One of them had fathered Cara, in the sand, on a Sydney beach.

Should have got rid of her. A girl at the factory had known where to go to get rid of little mistakes. Until her waist had started thickening, Jenny had continued to sing. She'd sat longer at her sewing machine, those Yankees' leavings crushed behind a tightly laced corset, determined to save every penny so she and Jimmy would be safe during the months when she couldn't work.

Myrtle had noticed the bulge. She'd been forty, timid, barren, God-fearing, but had lied and cheated so she might have her own baby to love. She'd allowed an elderly spinster lodger to believe she'd witnessed Cara's birth.

She'd witnessed the mess of birth on Myrtle's kitchen floor. She'd seen her genteel landlady sitting on bloody newspapers, that bald-headed, mewing Yankee baby in her arms. She'd seen Jenny standing at a distance, wearing high heels and makeup.

I popped in to give Myrt some money for Jimmy's keep and I found her like this, Miss Robbie.

That's how they'd done it. That's how Cara had been registered as the daughter of Myrtle and Robert Norris, and not until three years ago had Jenny regretted what she'd done that night.

She'd taken Jimmy home to Woody Creek when Cara was three weeks old, and every mile she'd placed between herself and that baby had been a good mile. She'd felt little guilt, had told herself that she'd given a part of little Jenny Morrison the chance of a fairytale life. Had never forgotten her or Myrtle, though not in her wildest dreams had she imagined she'd see either one of them again.

Babies become people. People look for answers. On a stormy night in the winter of 1966, Cara Norris, schoolteacher, had stepped down from the Melbourne bus and walked into Charlie White's grocery store where she'd asked after a Jennifer Hooper Morrison.

Georgie was behind the counter. Georgie with her all-seeing, all-knowing eyes had recognised the dark gold of Jenny's hair, her bluer than blue eyes. A strong strain, that of the Foote family.

As Itchy-foot's genes had overridden Juliana's dark Italian genes in Jenny, Jenny's had pushed aside those of five Yankee sailors. There was no doubting that Cara was a close relative to Jenny.

They'd met twice more, before that morning-show interview. Jenny had spent a night with her in the city. Cara had been with them in Woody Creek during the search for her foster daughter.

She'd had a son, older than Tracy. Georgie and Jenny saw him briefly on television, holding Cara's hand while looking back at the cameraman. His hair, his eyes had marked him as Jenny's grandson and she hadn't known his name.

He'd be thirty now and Jenny still didn't know his name. She'd given up her right to know it that night in Sydney when she'd pushed his bald-headed mother into Myrtle Norris' arms.

She was never my daughter. I was a surrogate, that's all, Jenny thought. Surrogates have no claim on the babies they carry. I incubated a baby for barren Myrtle and as soon as I was fit enough to travel, Myrtle paid my fare home.

'How much further?' Jenny asked the taxi driver.

'Not far. We're losing the good weather,' he said, then asked what part of Australia she was from.

'Melbourne,' she said. Her few possessions were in Melbourne.

They were driving down a hedged lane, barely wide enough for one vehicle but somehow two managed to pass. There was a park to her left, wide lawns, big trees, and behind those trees an old building. Not until she recognised the stone gateposts did she realise she'd reached her destination. She'd seen those gateposts in the sixties when she'd come here with Jim and the McPhersons. Hadn't seen the trees, the well-kept lawns, the splashes of colour from garden beds.

Jimmy could have sold the estate. New owners could have planted that garden. Cara's bio could have been as out of date as Juliana's.

Same house. Same flat, stone-faced, unapproachable facade. Same disapproving windows staring at the taxi. Same big door.

At the restaurant, she'd told Georgie and Trudy she'd squat on Jimmy's doorstep until he opened his door. That was then. This was now. She wanted to tell the driver to turn around and take her back to London.

No space to turn around. That tree-lined drive led to a big, old, metal-studded door. She had to get out. Had to at least ask after a Morrison Grenville.

'Could you wait five minutes, please,' she said.

He could if she paid him what she owed, and, her hand shaking, she peeled off three English twenties. Each one was almost equivalent to an Australian fifty and more than plenty.

'Five minutes,' she repeated, then got out, adjusted her frock, put her handbag over her shoulder and walked to the door she remembered well.

Same lion's head knocker. On that distant day with Jim it had made noise enough to wake the dead, but the door hadn't opened. Today, it brought two dogs running, barking at her, twin, pretty-faced, black and white dogs.

'Sit,' she commanded. They sat and laughed at her. She was giving one a pat when an elderly male came from around that same corner. He wasn't Jimmy. He was older and only a little taller than Gus.

'I'm looking for Mr Morrison Grenville,' she said.

'Eh,' he said, cupping a hand to his ear.

She walked closer and raised her voice. 'Would Morrie Grenville be about, please?'

He didn't say 'Germany'. 'Wedding,' he said, then repeated the word before Jenny understood his breed of English. 'They'll no be back at house for a time.'

'Where is the wedding?'

'Church,' he said. His expression asking, *Where else, you damn fool colonial.* He pointed towards rooftops, then meandered back the way he'd come. The dogs followed Jenny to the taxi.

Jimmy wasn't in Germany. He hadn't sold Langdon Hall. He was at a wedding. Fighting her pounding heartbeat for air, she asked the driver to take her into the town and to find her an Anglican church. Myrtle had been Church of England, Vern Hooper a Methodist.

Cars parked nose to tail out the front of an Anglican church, the driver couldn't park, but double parked then offered change from her three twenties.

'Just your company's phone number, please,' she said. Cars stuck behind him, wanting to get by, he handed her a business card then cleared the way.

Alone then, though not alone. A dozen women and a few children were waiting near the front steps of the church to see the bride, Jimmy's daughter? His daughter-in-law? His niece or neighbour? Those women would know. They had a right to be here. Jenny had no right. She was a despoiler, there only to disrupt the lives of her lost children.

What if they didn't know what they'd done? A couple can live together for forty years and not know their partner's secrets. She'd never told Jim about those five Yankee sailors as he'd never mentioned his war or his years in psychiatric clinics. He'd had shock therapy to wipe his memory clean. Jenny had never been able to wipe her memory clean of that night.

I'm not her mother, Jenny thought. If she recognises me, she won't admit it. That day at the television studio she must have known who I was. She'd stared when the host introduced them but chose not to expose their relationship on national television. She wouldn't expose it today.

Jimmy won't recognise me. If I stand behind these women, he won't even see me. I'll take a photograph of him. Others had cameras. She'd be just one more local woman, here to see the bride.

It didn't work out that way. Her unfamiliar face, her frock or her age opened a passage between the grouped women. If not for the wind and her flyaway skirt, she wouldn't have climbed the steps. If not for an elderly usher, who may have believed her to be a late guest, she wouldn't have entered the church. He ushered her through and you can't argue with an elderly Scottish usher, or not in a church doorway and certainly not when a parson is preaching, so on her soft-soled shoes, Jenny crept in, sidled into an empty back pew and sat down.

The front pews weren't empty. The bride and groom had their backs to her. Not so a small, dark-headed pageboy. He'd caught her sneaking in and was staring at her. A dot of a girl in pink had little interest in anything other than the removal of a coronet of flowers, pinned to a mop of dark, spring-coil curls, row upon row of familiar dark curls.

Blue scrap of a hat in the front pew, on the bride's side. Not many hats there. A scattering on the groom's side. One large and grey, and a Queen Mother's pink flowery hat next to it. Jenny's interest returned to that blue hat. It was between two male heads, one was the gunmetal grey of the Hoopers, the exact shade of Jim's before he'd gone white. The other male head was a nest of golden curls. She knew that hair.

She saw half of the bride's face as the groom lifted her veil; saw him when he kissed his new wife. Neither one resembled Jimmy or Cara.

Then the blue hat and the gunmetal grey hair rose. It was them. She couldn't see their faces and she had to get out before they saw hers. The taxi driver's business card still clenched in her hand, her feet readied themselves to make a quick getaway. She knew the marriage service well. It would be over soon. The new couple would sign documents, then Jimmy and Cara would follow the bride and groom down the aisle, the groom's parents behind them.

If I stay where I am, they'll walk close by me, she thought. Once they're out that door, I'll find a back way out. There was always a back way out of a church.

Cara was wearing a tailored, midnight-blue frock. It would make her eyes look more blue. Her curls had gone, as had the gold of her hair. She'd be fifty-nine on the third day of October – and never once in those fifty-nine years had Jenny got through October the third and not thought of Sydney.

Hadn't been allowed to. Donna Palmer had been born on that same day. When she'd taken her first toddling steps, Jenny had known that Yankee baby was walking. When Donna commenced school, Jenny had known that Cara was at school. She'd known her at fourteen, at eighteen – because of Donna Palmer.

She'd built many mental images of Myrtle's daughter, a thick-necked girl, like Hank, or baby-faced like Billy-Bob, or long and lean like Link. She hadn't known the names of the other two rapists. One had a broken Jew's nose. Her every image had been wrong. Given too many choices that night, the seed of Cara had grown from the cells of the victim. She'd grown taller.

Jenny's vision blurring, she blinked behind her dark glasses. This was her one day and Jimmy had turned around. She could see his face. He'd never looked like the Hoopers. He had her brow, her nose and maybe a suggestion of Jim's jaw and mouth.

Pooling tears stole her view of his face, still the face of that beautiful little boy she'd lost, she swiped at the tears as the organist began playing the introduction to *Ave Maria*.

How many times had she sung that song? She'd sung it at weddings and funerals, with Itchy-foot and at Mary Grogan's funeral so recently.

You can sing that one at my funeral, Jim had said. Then he'd ridden his gopher out to Monk's and drowned himself so she hadn't sung for him. The organist had expected her to. He'd repeated the introduction three times before playing on alone.

No second introduction necessary today. No flower-bedecked coffin waiting to be put into Hooper ground. A bride and a groom today – and Itchy-foot's rich tenor voice filling the church.

She could see him, standing behind the organist, the light from a stained-glass window glowing on his golden curls. Granny's angel Gabriel. Not Granny's. Cara's son was the singer, Jenny's nameless grandson. Her voice and Itchy-foot's had always admitted their relationship, and with eyes only for her grandson, she joined her voice with his. Didn't see the bride, groom, Cara or Jimmy walk by her pew. She sang that song to its end, and only then was aware that she'd stood. They would have seen her.

A woman in lilac frills smiled at her. A dark-headed girl stared. Jenny released her grip on the pew and moved across to the far side. Then, one hand within reach of the wall, she walked unsteadily towards the back of the church.

He cut her off at the pass, the angel Gabriel.

'You're Jennifer Morrison King, Dad's biological mother,' he said, and he offered his hand.

'I'm his mother,' Jenny said.

JIMMY'S HOUSE

Should have said she was a tourist who'd stepped inside out of the wind. Should have said she was an escapee from a funny farm. Should have said anything but what she'd said. Uncensored words once spoken can't be erased by a backspace key. Uncensored words once out of the mouth are free to do what damage they will, and in the taxi on the way down here, she'd sworn to do no damage.

There were steps down to the back exit, dark steps. He held her arm and his touch made her eyes leak and he saw their leaking when they walked into the light, into wind, and he released her arm so she could turn her face and wipe away her tears.

'I'm Robin,' he said. His accent was English with overtones of Australia still clinging to his vowels.

'My father loved the robins.' Such silly things we say at such times. She wiped her eyes with a crumpled tissue. She blew her nose. 'He was a birdwatcher,' she said.

Then that dark-headed girl came at a run down the side of the church, the mop-topped flower girl on her hip.

'It's her,' she said.

'Jennifer Morrison King in the flesh,' Robin said. 'Tracy, my sister. She's been helping me search the internet for you.'

Tiny Tracy? Found on that God-awful night, drugged and sealed in a cardboard carton beside Joe Flanagan's fence. Raelene's daughter? That Tracy. She'd been Cara's foster child.

She was offering a free hand. Jenny had the tissue in her right hand so offered the left.

Doctors fear permanent brain damage for tiny Tracy.
Raelene King, natural mother of tiny Tracy was found dead . . .

Nothing natural about Raelene King, but not a lot of her had seeped into her daughter. Her colouring, her height maybe, but not her snake-pit eyes or her accent.

'Our sister Elise, the bride, found your name for us when she was down here two weeks ago. And here you are,' Tracy said.

'I'm with a tour,' Jenny said. The business card, curled and damp, was still in her hand. She had to call that number. She had to go. She'd found Jimmy. He was well. She had to go.

'You're touring our part of the country today?' Robin said.

'They're in London,' Jenny said, and as soon as the words came out of her mouth she wanted to draw them back and lie about a bus full of tourists waiting for her around a corner.

Tracy had more pressing concerns than tours. 'I have to go back to the house and redo a couple of the tables,' she said. 'I can't take Leona. They want her for the photographs.'

'What's happened now?' he asked, as the pink flower girl changed arms.

'Maryanne and Rod had a run-in with a bus five miles out of London. His mother just phoned. They're okay but they won't get down here, nor will two more of Ian's lot. I can't have anyone sitting at half-empty tables. You know that Pete and Kay didn't make it?'

Names flying, like in a novel when the author hits you in the eye with a bunch of names and you don't know if they are important to the plot or not. They gave Jenny a chance to back away and to take her mobile from her bag.

She had a watchdog. Robin moved to her side. 'How did you find us, Jennifer?'

'I didn't know about the wedding. I'm sorry I . . . I disrupted it.'

'It's been disrupted since she told us she was pregnant,' Tracy said. 'It was supposed to be in Scotland in October. Dad and Robbie would have looked good in kilts – and I have to go. They're not going to stand around in this wind for long. What time do you have to rejoin your tour, Jennifer?'

'We've got a banquet tonight,' Jenny said, and why couldn't she think fast enough to lie, to say a picnic lunch?

'Can you spare us an hour?' Robin asked.

'I've got sixty-four guests to seat and when I did the tables last night, I had seventy-two. Come back to the house with me.'

'I'd love to talk to you, Jennifer,' Robin said.

'He's tracking the family history,' Tracy explained as she fixed the flower girl's lopsided coronet. 'You be good for Uncle Robin – and for the man with the camera.' She repositioned a pin holding the coronet, told the infant to stop messing up her curls, then turned to railroad Jenny into her car.

'We found umpteen Jennifer Morrisons but without your parents' Christian names or your date of birth, we didn't have a hope. One hour,' Robin said.

'You look as if you could use a stiff drink,' Tracy said.

'Half an hour,' Robin said.

She'd come here to find Jimmy and been found, and if she didn't sit down, she'd fall down. She allowed herself to be kidnapped by her grandchildren, to be buckled into a small red car.

Saw the bride's veil flying in the wind as they drove out. Saw Cara, her arms folded against the wind. Didn't see Jimmy.

'We knew that you sang. Mum told us you used to entertain the troops during the war, that her mother knew you and Dad when he was a baby. Her parents would have known your name, but they died years ago – whoops!' Tracy said.

They were in that narrow, hedged lane and had almost come to grief with a horse rider. The horse and rider, accustomed to cars, gave way. Then, moments later, Tracy swung her car between those stone gateposts. She didn't park where the taxi had parked, but drove down the side of the house, turned left onto a cobblestoned courtyard and parked inches away from an aged stone wall.

No flat face at the rear of Langdon Hall. It was a series of slate roofs, of diamond-paned windows, of old chimneys.

Ms Langhall lives with her partner in a five-hundred-year-old manor house forty miles from London . . .

In Jimmy's house.

'Your dad won't want me here, darlin'.'

'Don't worry about him!' Tracy said. 'He's a big pussy cat.'

Those black and white dogs came running to renew their acquaintance with the stranger, to sniff at her flying skirt as she stepped from the car.

'Scoot,' Tracy said. They rushed in ahead when Tracy opened a door, then stood barking, blocking the stranger's way. 'Scoot,' Tracy repeated. She took Jenny's hand then and led her through a second doorway, along a passage, up worn stone steps to a longer passage, through a large old room furnished with a full-sized pool table, then through twin doors to a small room, furnished with two large smoky blue leather chairs, a television and walls of inbuilt book-shelves. It reminded Jenny of Vern Hooper's library, or of what that room could have been.

'You're cold, Jennifer,' Tracy said. Perhaps she'd seen her shudder.

'Just Jenny or Jen. No one calls me Jennifer.'

'Jenny suits you. Cup of tea, coffee or something stronger?'

'Wine, darlin'. White.'

'Sit down and put your feet up,' Tracy said, then her high-heels clicked away.

Sunglasses swapped for bifocals and Jenny walked to the better light at the window where she read the taxi company's phone number. She didn't call it but keyed it into her contacts then began a text to Georgie. She'd seen tiny Tracy on the night of the fire and said she'd looked more dead than alive. She'd want to know about her. Jenny had picked out five words before realising she couldn't mention Tracy, or Robin. They were Cara's children, not Jimmy's. Georgie knew Jenny's every secret but would never be told that Morrie Grenville, Cara's husband, was Jimmy. For years, Georgie and Cara had been close friends. Until the fire. She'd waited beside the telephone for a week, expecting Cara to call. Georgie was a strong woman but losing Cara and Margot had almost broken her. She could never know about Cara and Jimmy's marriage.

The words wiped away, Jenny dropped the phone back into her bag, and walked to the window where she stood staring through diamond panes at the gravelled driveway and green lawns, and behind those lawns and trees, to rooftops. She stood staring out at Jimmy's world until clicking heels told her Tracy was returning.

She'd brought white wine, a flat white too dry for Jenny's taste-buds. 'Sit down and relax. I could be a while,' she said and was gone. Jenny didn't sit. She was at the window when an old red MG drove by. She couldn't see its driver but knew that car or its close relative. Cara had driven an elderly red MG. Georgie had ridden in it.

Her mind was full of Georgie and Cara when she heard male footsteps approaching. She turned as Robin entered.

'Were you in that old car?' she asked.

'Dad's owned it since near new. I drove the bride to church in it. She wanted to drive back with me too, but they wouldn't let her,' he said with a smile, then gestured towards one of the chairs. 'It was Elise who found your name on Dad's adoption documents.'

Cara knew her name. She knew her life story, had damn near written it in *Angel at My Door*. Her children knew nothing, but today Robin was planning to rectify that. He had a notebook and pen, and he asked her husband's Christian name.

'I married Jim Hooper in 1959. My first husband died young.'

'You mean Dad's father? James Richard Hooper?'

Jenny nodded and sipped the hard wine. 'We would have married before the war if I'd been old enough.' She sipped a little more. 'Jim died in March,' she said. 'On the twenty-sixth.'

She sat then, or perched, on the edge of a too-deep chair.

'They weren't meant to be sat on but lolled in,' he said. 'Sit back and lift your feet.'

She did as she was bid; he pressed a button and a footrest eased away from its moorings. Then he sat to continue his questions, to ask about old Hooper documents, old photographs. He spoke about the original James Richard Hooper. He knew the date he'd sailed away from England and the name of the ship he'd sailed on.

'He had four wives,' he said.

'He married the last of them when he was well into his seventies,' Jenny said. 'She was thirty-three.'

She told him of Granny then, born Gertrude Maria Hooper, how she and Vernon Hooper had shared a grandfather but not a grandmother. She told him how Hooper babies had a bad habit of killing their mothers in childbirth.

'Sally, my wife, is an authority on that. She's not eager to do it a second time. We have a son we named Richard James. He's the blond pageboy.'

'I have twin grandsons, James and Richard,' Jenny said.

'Vernon had three wives,' he said. 'His first, Lorna Langdon, forged our connection to this relic. She was the older sister of the last Henry Langdon. She died in childbirth but her daughter, also a Lorna, survived.'

'She was cut alive from her dead mother,' Jenny said. 'My grandmother knew Lorna Langdon. She was nine years older than Vern – forty, or close to it, when she died.'

'You're a walking history book,' Robin said.

The Hooper family, a safe topic, no censoring was necessary. Granny and Jim were safe topics. He told her that he'd obtained a copy of Jim's war-service record two weeks ago, that he'd applied for copies of Jim's birth and marriage certificates.

'I would have found you,' he said, and his pen busy again, he double checked the year of her marriage to Jim and the date of her first marriage.

She told him of Jim's half-cousin, Ian Hooper. Georgie had contacted his daughter after Jim's death. She told him how Jim had died, or the accidental drowning version.

'What was his occupation?'

'A farmer before the war.' She shrugged. 'Investor, historian, writer – after the war. He lost a leg in it.'

'Mum writes,' he said.

'What do you do?'

'I'm a surgeon,' he said. 'I'm on call tonight – or from midnight.'

'There's more to genetics than we'll ever know in my lifetime,' she said. 'Your great-grandfather was a doctor – and a singer. You look so much like him – though not in height.'

'I thought that height ran in the Hooper family?'

'It didn't run in the Foote family. Archibald Gerald Foote, physician, was my . . . grandfather. I knew him only as an old man, but he had an incredible voice.'

'F-O-O-T-E?' he spelt as he wrote.

'Archibald Gerald,' Jenny said. 'We sang together. When I was young.'

'I've found no mention of Foote.'

'He married Gertrude Maria Hooper. They separated before Amber . . . my mother was born.' Jenny turned to the window as another car drove by and she wondered how many years had passed since she'd last referred to Amber as her mother – but he didn't need to know Amber's details.

Cara and Jimmy could have been in that car, or in the car following it, or the one behind it. They kept coming, crunching gravel beneath their wheels, and Robin stood.

'I'll have to get up there. I'm master of ceremonies today. You'll stay a while longer, Jennifer?'

'Jenny,' she said. 'I should go.'

'Elise will get away when she can. She wants to meet you.'

'Does your father know I'm here?'

'They both know, Jenny.' He left in a hurry to rejoin the wedding guests.

Jimmy might come – if only to evict her.

She'd told Georgie she'd squat on his front doorstep until he let her in. She'd been led inside via a back door, and when she was alone again, she took her camera from her bag to photograph Jimmy's library and his pool room. She was lining up that old window when she heard the staccato click of heels and the rattle of china. She took the photograph quickly, turned then and put her camera away as Tracy entered with a tray. She'd brought a coffee pot, cups and a plate of hot savoury pastries.

'I deserve this,' she said. The tray placed down on the coffee table, she flopped down on Robin's vacated chair. 'I spent weeks working out harmonious tables. Harmony, I fear, just went out the window.' She removed her shoes. 'If I wasn't so short on inches, I wouldn't punish myself with those,' she said, then poured coffee.

She was a talker, but not of Hoopers. She spoke of the groom's mother. 'That big woman in grey with the big grey hat.' She spoke of kilts and bagpipes and Ian, the groom, Laura's only offspring. She spoke around a savoury pastry. 'Yum,' she said. 'Try one.' She mentioned a Cathy and Gerry, who'd flown over from Australia, a Pete and a Kay who had to cancel. 'Their middle son is in hospital with serious head injuries. A motorbike accident. I loathe motor-bikes. Think I caught it from Mum. She had a crazy boyfriend once who rode one and even today, every time she hears one coming, she flinches.'

She spoke of her children, Tristan and Leona, pageboy and flower girl, then asked about Jenny's children while more cars drove by that window and voices filtered through.

'We have parking down the back. We do a lot of weddings,' she said. 'And conferences, and guided tours. The upkeep on this place is astronomical. Heating, lighting, fixing stuff that breaks down.

I promised Mum and Dad I'd have it paying its way before Tristan started school. He starts next year. There's no actual labour involved, or not for us.' She sipped the coffee. 'Just a case of rallying the right troops, caterers, photographers, marriage celebrants, musicians.' She bit into another pastry. 'Our first wedding was chaos. We ended up giving them a twenty per cent discount.' She stared outside. 'We've got it down to a fine art now – unless the guests start dropping like flies, which they've been doing since last night. We've got two in town with food poisoning. They chose the wrong place to eat on the drive down . . . from Scotland.'

Jenny tried a pastry. She drank her coffee, her mind wandering Jimmy's house, aware he had a room in it capable of seating seventy guests, a kitchen large enough to prepare meals for seventy. No clatter of pots and pans, no rattle of china infiltrated this room. She heard knocking from above.

'That's old Henry,' Tracy said. 'Our resident ghost.'

Her eating done, her coffee cup empty, Tracy retracted her footrest and put on her shoes. 'Don't go anywhere. Robin will be back in a minute and Elise said she'd disown me if I let you get away.'

Alone again, Jenny considered escape. She'd find her way back to those stone steps, then open doors until she found the room where the dogs had led the way in. Her directional instinct had always been good.

Go, she urged.

Jimmy might come – if she gave him time. He was the father of the bride. He couldn't leave his guests.

Make her comfortable in the library, he might have said.

Cara might come. She'd caught a bus to Woody Creek to find Jennifer Hooper Morrison.

Couldn't believe it when Georgie had phoned that night and told her that her past had come looking for her. Couldn't believe what she'd seen standing in Georgie's kitchen. Anyone with eyes would have seen the resemblance. She had, and it had shocked her into silence. She didn't want to see her today – she would be the last person in the world Cara would want to see.

Male footsteps approaching, Robin's. He was carrying two glasses of wine, one red, one white.

'Your choice,' he said offering both. She chose the white and hoped it was fruity.

He spoke of Cathy and Gerry, his mother's Australian friends. 'They're from Ballarat,' he said. 'Where do you live, Jenny?'

Nowhere, or not after the eighteenth. She said Melbourne. Melbourne was a big place.

'We lived there when I was a kid, in Ferntree Gully,' he said. 'We used to play cricket in the street.'

'Your father lived with you?'

'They were separated at the time. We lived with my grandfather. Robert Norris. Did you know him?'

'I met him once.' He'd been Captain Norris in 1942. Jim only a lowly private had almost knocked his hat off saluting him.

Memories. Where does the brain store such detailed images?

'I was nine when they got back together, when we moved over here. I still think of myself as Australian. Sally would move to Sydney tomorrow. She has two sisters over there. I've got cousins, Mum's cousins. At times, I'm tempted, though to date I've settled for digging up dead relatives – speaking of which,' he said. 'You mentioned your father, the birdwatcher. What was his Christian name?'

The interrogation continued, and the note taking. She fed him names. She spoke of growing up in a railway house, with train lines running alongside the back fence. She mentioned Sissy. 'Cecelia Louise,' she said then washed that name from her tongue with wine, and as the hands of her watch moved around its face, the day took on a dreamlike unreality. Thames Ditton and Langdon Hall had been little more than names in the grim tale of her life. Now here she was, sitting at her grandson's side, sipping a fruity white wine. She felt like an actor, dropped onto a movie set and expected to play the role of family matriarch with no script to follow. How that movie would end, she didn't know, only that she'd applied for the role and must play it out to the end – and censor her every word before speaking her next line.

His mobile buzzed. He glanced at it. 'What's the latest we can get you back to your tour, Jenny?'

'The bus leaves for the banquet before six,' she said. Should have censored that line. Should have said it left at four.

'Elise and Ian have to be at the airport at five. You could drive back to London with them.'

Locked into a car with the bride who'd found her name on a document Jenny could quote. Vern Hooper's solicitor had posted her a copy of it.

'I'll get a taxi back,' she said.

And Tracy came, unheard until she appeared in the doorway, the pink-clad flower girl clinging to her hand. She'd got rid of her problematic coronet. Both mother and daughter had got rid of their problematic shoes.

'We've had enough of playing dress-up,' Tracy said. 'Say hello to Jenny.' Like her grandfather, Leona was not interested in the uninvited guest. 'She needed a bathroom and I forget to tell you where to find one,' Tracy said.

'I'm fine, darlin',' Jenny said.

'We both need a nap,' Tracy said, and they were gone.

'Tracy was a dancer until Tristan was on his way,' Robin said. 'She started very young. Her feet were ready to retire. What age were you when you began you singing career, Jenny?'

'It wasn't much of a career,' Jenny said.

'Dad said once that you sang on stage in a musical.'

'I sang on stage from when I was a kid.'

'I was in a school production when I was fifteen, and on the way home after the first night, I got it into my head that Dad was embarrassed because I sang a love song. I told them I wasn't doing the next show. He told me that night that I'd inherited my voice from his natural mother, that he'd seen you in a stage show in Melbourne.'

'*Snow White*,' she said. He hadn't forgotten her. He called himself Morrie so he wouldn't forget her. She coughed, cleared her throat before replying. 'A pantomime. He saw it twice.'

She'd been four months pregnant when the final curtain fell, and in hospital a few days later, police standing over her bed – but no longer pregnant. She would have jumped off the roof of Melbourne's tallest building to get rid of Ray's babies.

'How long was he with you, Jenny?'

'Until he started school.' No censor's pen there. Think before you answer, she warned. Be careful. Be very careful.

'We always knew he'd been adopted by an aunt and her husband. Elise was two years old when she joined our family. I always imagined Dad would have been a similar age. Both of my sisters are adopted. Like Sally, having one near ten pounder was enough to put Mum off of childbearing. I believe that I'm the reason she and Dad separated –'

His mobile vibrated and he glanced at it. 'Apparently, I'm required again,' he said.

'I should go.'

'I know he wants to see you. I can read him like a book. He recognised your voice in the church.' Robin said. 'Can I ask why you didn't marry his father after the war ended?'

'He was taken prisoner by the Japanese. His father . . . believed he'd been killed in action. I waited for him until the war ended and when he didn't come home, I married Raymond King.'

'He made you give up Dad?'

She censored that reply. 'Ray had problems. I left him less than two years later and went home to Granny. That's when I lost your dad. Women had few rights in those days and those who left their husbands had even fewer. Jimmy was the only grandchild Vern Hooper was ever likely to have, and he was determined to raise him and legitimise his birth.'

'Jimmy?' Robin said. 'He was James Morrison –'

'James Hooper Morrison,' Jenny corrected.

'For as long as I've known him, he's been Morrie Grenville. Until two weeks ago, we didn't know that Morrison was your maiden name.'

His mobile buzzed again. 'I'm the entertainment as well as master of ceremonies. Fifteen more minutes,' he said. 'Please.'

Jenny wriggled free of the chair when he left. She walked through to the pool room, where she ran her hand over the green baize surface of the table, smelt the age of a sideboard. It didn't smell of Lorna. She wondered why Langdon Hall hadn't been willed to Lorna. Her mother was raised in these rooms.

A tall, narrow-hipped, bitter-faced woman, Granny had described Lorna Langdon. She'd said that Vern had wed her for her five hundred pounds a year. She'd said, too, that Vern hadn't mourned her passing and that he'd shown no interest in the female baby cut from her. He'd needed a son.

His grandfather, Old James Richard, who'd arrived in Australia with a few pennies in his pocket, had become a moneyed land-owner by the time his grandchildren had been of marriageable age. Determined that they would forge him connections to the upper class, he'd arranged both Vern and Gertrude's marriages. Both failed.

Vern's failure had turned a gentle youth into a man as hard as his grandfather. Granny had never hardened. She'd seen the worst that life could dish up and grown wise enough to dodge its pitfalls.

Had Jimmy grown hard?

When the bride and groom left for the airport he might come. She could wait until three. She turned on her heel and walked back to the library to study the books filling the shelves.

An entire shelf had been given over to C.J. Langhall's novels and with her fingers, Jenny counted them. Twenty-three. She was familiar with half a dozen titles.

Sent in Chains was there, on the shelf below that row of Langhall books. She recognised its spine and her hand darted to claim it.

I'm here, she thought, looking at the cover, at Juliana Conti's name. I'm here. They know. Cara must have recognised me that day at the television studio. Jenny glanced over her shoulder, feeling the ghosts of this place watching her, and quickly she placed the book back into its space. There was a book beside it she'd heard of but hadn't read. She removed it, opened it.

One evening, in the spring of 1936, I was a boy of fourteen . . .

In the spring of 1936, Jenny had been three months away from thirteen and she hadn't doubted that she'd become a famous singer and live happily ever after in Paris.

'You've got the world at your feet, Jennifer,' Norman used to say.

'You'll buy and sell this town before you're done, girlie,' Vern Hooper had once said.

On an evening in the winter of 1938, she'd been a fourteen-year-old schoolgirl and the world had been stolen from beneath her feet –

From what I hear, you weren't always so fussy, Nick had said.

Hadn't been given a chance to be fussy. They'd held her down on old Cecelia Duckworth's tombstone and told her they were sacrificing her for a bit of decent weather.

Did you bring a dagger?

I've got something that will do the job.

One after the other, the Macdonald twins had ripped out her every dream. Macka was long dead. Bernie was still pushing his walking frame around Woody Creek.

Used to play in the cemetery. Used to read the stories on the old tombstones. Hated that place now. Her mind was back there with Jim when a door slammed back against the wall. Expecting an irate Jimmy, an angry Cara, she had to look lower to see the dark-eyed pixie pageboy and tiny Leona. Both barefoot.

The pageboy wasn't shy. 'Why did you come in here for?'

'To read a book,' Jenny said. 'You look very handsome in your suit.'

'I'm a pageboy, and I got *cordigal* on my pants.'

'Mummy will wash it out,' Jenny said.

'She can't, 'cause it's from the hire shop. What's your name?'

'Jenny. I'll bet you're Tristan?' There was no doubting it. Raelene was in his wide pixie mouth.

'Who told you?'

'Your mummy. She said you were four.'

And the second pageboy came, but only as far as the doorway. He was wearing shoes and still neat in his hired white suit. He had the blue eyes but not the golden curls. There was something of goblin boy Jim in Robin's son.

'You're not allowed to come here,' he told his younger cousins.

'We can so too because it's our house,' Tristan said, and he turned again to Jenny. 'You don't know his name.'

'Rumpelstiltskin?' she guessed.

'You're silly.'

'Is it Richard?'

'Why did Mummy tell you everything for?' Tristan asked.

'Did she tell you that I've got a little boy called Richard? We call him Ricky.'

'Why? And you're too old,' Tristan said.

'I'm his grandma.'

'We have to watch the other television,' the neat pageboy said.

'We like this one best.'

'Nana said the family room.'

Nana's word must have been law. They scuttled away to watch television.

All of My Lost Children, Jenny thought. I could write about this day, though its writing might break my heart. And they haven't been lost. I'm the one who was lost. I've spent most of my life lost.

She sat again, adjusted the footrest, then opened the book and forced her eyes to follow the words through that first page. Its content didn't penetrate. Twice she returned to the beginning but gave up when she reached 'intensive study of the Japanese language'. Jim had known the language of a Japanese prison camp. He'd yelled alien words in his sleep, then refused to admit any knowledge of their meaning when she'd questioned him the next day. He'd forgotten too much. He'd closed the book on Jimmy . . . and walked away when she'd opened it.

Wine in the afternoon wasn't a good idea, nor was attempting to read when her eyes wanted to close. She allowed them to close, just for a moment.

She was playing Canasta with Granny and Queen Lizzie, and they'd needed a fourth but couldn't find Jim . . .

'He needs to see her like this.'

'What age would she be?'

Women's voices. Jenny didn't open her eyes.

'She had Dad with her in Sydney. He'll be sixty-two this year. She has to be eighty.'

The muffled beep from Jenny's handbag gave her an excuse to open her eyes.

'We caught you nanny-napping,' Tracy said with a pointing finger. She introduced her sister, Elise, no longer in bridal white but dressed for travelling in jeans, black shirt and sneakers.

'Thank you for singing at my wedding,' that Nordic blonde said, offering her hand. 'You have a beautiful voice, Jenny.'

'You were a beautiful bride,' Jenny said.

They spoke about a honeymoon in Spain, about the heat of Rome, and when they left, Jenny followed them out to the passage where Tracy offered directions to the nearest bathroom. Then they went one way and Jenny went the other.

She found the bathroom, a haven of tiled modernity in a house groaning with old age. She used the facilities then read a text, from Georgie.

Lost your mobile. Battery flat?

Jenny didn't reply. She combed her hair, added a touch of lipstick. The bride was leaving. A few of the guests would make their excuses and go. Jimmy might get away. She didn't dally there but found her way back to the library. Then, mobile in hand, she attempted to find a reply for Georgie.

They'd envisaged terrible futures for tiny, brain-damaged Tracy. They'd seen her existing in a home for retarded children, as Ray's son had existed when Jenny could no longer handle him. They'd seen tiny Tracy as a second Raelene, an addict, selling herself on the streets. She'd been raised by Cara, loved by Cara. She'd grown into a kind and beautiful girl – and Georgie could never know it. And what was she doing, texting at this time of day. It would be midnight in Australia.

Go to bed. I'm at Langdon Hall. Will talk in the morning. I board plane early.

What's he look like?

Couldn't tell her she hadn't spoken to him, that she'd spent most of the afternoon with his son. She didn't lie.

Not as tall as Jim. Same hair, Jim's hands, his smile. Go to bed.

I've been trying to get something finished. Heard from Trudy? Nick still missing. House being sold. She's staying with Tonia. You'll hear more when you get home. Don't miss your plane.

Her mobile back in her bag, bag over her shoulder, Jenny stood at the window, watching the bride and groom pursued down a gravelled driveway. They cast no shadow. The sky was blanketed now by heavy clouds, and the pursuing women in their wedding finery looked cold. No rain yet.

She'd waited for five minutes, waited another five before phoning the taxi company. 'Langdon Hall, Thames Ditton. Returning to London,' she said, then walked to the shelves to replace the book. She was standing, staring at the spine of *Sent in Chains* when she heard the tinkle of children's laughter, then footsteps approaching, many footsteps on bare boards.

And he came, marched under guard through the pool room, Tracy and Robin behind him, their army of chuckling little people leading him by his hands and his coat-tails.

JIMMY

*H*e wasn't smiling. He offered no polite greeting. 'Shall we get this over with as quickly and painlessly as possible?' he said.

She stepped towards him. 'If I could take back . . .'

'I believe you need to leave at four, which leaves us exactly eleven minutes.'

A thousand times Jenny had practised the thousand words she'd say to her boy but his eyes looked cold. He didn't want her words. He didn't want to be here and came no closer than the open double doors.

Tristan wanted to see more. He attempted to walk in but Jimmy caught his shirt-tails and drew him back.

'I used to pull you back from danger by your shirt-tails when you were his size,' Jenny said.

'I would have been little older when you cashed in your investment,' he said.

Robin flinched at his words. Jenny thought of Vern Hooper. His bones may have been rotting in Woody Creek for half a century but she was fighting him still, and not once had she backed away from a fight with Vern Hooper. She'd told him to shove his chequebook up his backside one day. She'd smashed his windscreen with a tree branch.

'Your grandfather's blood money has been an interesting example of what happens when money is too tainted to touch,' she said. 'Through the eighties it was earning eight and a half per cent interest.'

He turned away. She thought he was leaving. A taxi was making its way towards Langdon Hall. She'd told the controller she'd be waiting out front of the building. She wouldn't be. Her legs wouldn't get her out there. Weak, shaking, her batteries were done.

'I'm flying home tomorrow, Jimmy. Is ten minutes out of the rest of your life too much to ask?'

'The name is Morrie,' he said.

'Not on your birth certificate,' she said, and she walked to the chair and sat.

'Or on my bill of sale,' he said, and attempted to clear the way behind him.

Robin's curls made him taller than his father. 'Sit down, Dad.'

'A video would be more beneficial to the children than this. Take them away,' Jimmy said.

Saying *video* in the hearing of a child is like saying *walk* when a dog is listening. They wanted a video.

'*Nemo*,' the pink flower girl said.

'You always want that stupid fish,' Tristan said. Not a murmur from the taller pageboy. He was old enough to understand that something he didn't understand was happening, so he stood close to his father's side, his eyes watchful. He'd have Jim's hands. He had his ears. Jenny was attempting to see his hands when Jimmy stepped into the room and closed both doors on his wardens.

'Richard looks like your father,' Jenny said.

'I'm not here for niceties.'

'I wouldn't worry about that. You're not being nice,' she said, and she picked up her wine glass and wished it full. She drained what remained in it.

But he was here. He was with her. How this meeting would end, she didn't know, only that it would, and today, only that had he wanted to end it, he would have gone with his children.

'He wants to see you,' Robin had said.

So many words she'd planned to say to her beautiful boy, words edited a thousand times on the blackboard of her mind, on the plane, on the boat, in Venice. He wasn't the boy she'd practised those words for. He was a grey-headed, sixty-year-old man.

Someone knocking, then Myrtle's voice, more British than the British. 'Morrie, let me in.'

He moved a little, enough to open one door, a little. 'There's no need for you to be here.'

'You're here.' Then, pushing the door wide, Cara entered. He closed it. 'Jenny,' Cara said. 'You never fail to surprise me.'

'Love your frock,' Jenny said. It was Jenny blue, that deep midnight blue, and cut in an ageless tailored style from heavy fabric.

'I like it,' Cara said.

How many years had passed since they'd spoken? And *love your frock*? Their eyes met and held, each afraid of that old resemblance. Both wore spectacles, very different spectacles, Jenny's hair curled, Cara's was straight and sleek.

'England's climate agrees with you,' Jenny said.

'In many ways,' Cara said. She didn't offer her hand, but took Jimmy's arm, showing a united front against a common enemy. And right or wrong, they looked so right side by side.

'I'm not here to disrupt your lives or to accuse –'

'Your presence is an accusation,' Jimmy said.

'You're my son.'

'A DNA test would prove me your daughter, Jenny. Can you begin to imagine our agony when we realised what we'd done?'

There is no defence against a frontal attack. It was unexpected. 'Surrogacy is a thriving business these days. You're Myrtle's daughter. You sound like her – as Tracy sounds like you.'

And she was out there. 'Open up, someone. My hands are full.'

Cara opened the door and barefoot Tracy entered with a half-full bottle of champagne and two long glasses; one she handed to her father, the second she placed on the table.

'Two of Elise's mates just took your taxi, Jenny,' she said. She filled her father's glass then filled the second. 'Can I get you a glass, Mum?'

'I've had enough,' Cara said.

'I told Aunty Cath you'd taken to your bed with a couple of pills. She's gone up there looking for you.'

'She'll be in here next,' Cara said. 'I'll call you another taxi, Jenny.'

'I'll call my own, thank you,' Jenny said. 'Lovely meeting you, Cara.'

'And you,' Cara lied, and she was gone, Jimmy watching her go. He stayed. Maybe he wanted to be here.

'Grandma Tilly and her sons are doing their best to empty the bottles,' Tracy said, then turning to Jenny, added, 'She's Ian's grandmother, and proud to tell anyone who'll listen that she was ninety-two last birthday.'

Cars crunching gravel again on the driveway, moving out, not in. Jimmy took his glass to the window and his back turned, Tracy offered a wink, mouthed, 'Big pussy cat.' Then in the next breath she told her father how Jenny had grown up in the same town as his Aunty Lorna. 'Sit down for five minutes and compare notes,' she said, then with a second wink, she was gone, the doors closed behind her.

The wine, Jenny's type of wine, would be her third glass since a little after midday. She'd sworn off alcohol yesterday, but English beer had been to blame for her loss of Friday. Sparkling wine was medicinal, and she needed its bubbles, so she sipped and stared at her boy, silhouetted against that old window.

She could steal a photograph of him, standing, his face turned away from her.

Didn't need a photograph. She'd wear the imprint of this meeting on her soul until there were no more days, so she sipped again and thought about the banquet. She'd need to leave soon, but she wouldn't need to dress for tonight's outing. She'd dressed in her best for Jimmy. Ten more minutes, then she'd call the taxi.

She got to her feet, and taking her wine with her, she walked to the window. Didn't stand close to him but was too close for his comfort. He took a step to the side, a step to the left.

Two middle-aged couples were standing out in the wind, discussing the bride or the meal or the weather. Behind them, an elderly man was being helped by a woman into the front passenger seat of a grey vehicle, while a second woman folded, then lifted a walking frame into the car boot. Jenny had done that, many, many times. Was he her husband, father, uncle?

'That must be the final indignity for a man – ending his life dependent on women. Your grandfather ended up dependent on his daughters. But you'd know that,' she said and sipped her wine. 'Your grandmother never lost her independence. Six weeks before she died, she rode her horse into town to order new wallpaper.'

He didn't turn to her, and the time now close to four-fifteen, she reached into her bag for her mobile.

Did she need to attend a fake King Henry banquet at some minor castle where she'd drink more wine? No one would miss her. Johanna might, but she'd been tossing up whether to go. Today would have been her husband's eightieth birthday.

We're all alone, Jenny thought. I'm standing where I've wanted to stand for fifty-odd years. I could reach out and touch my boy – and I've never been more alone in my life.

'Granny used to say that we can't change one second of a day once the sun has gone down on it, that all we can change is our tomorrows. I'm trying to do the impossible, Jimmy, trying to sort out my yesterdays before I run out of tomorrows.'

'Morrie,' he corrected.

'You've no more forgotten little Jimmy Morrison than I. Calling yourself Morrie proves it, or it does to me. When you were two years old you could say James Hooper Morrison.'

'It's the name on my bill of sale,' he said. 'Signed by you in the presence of two witnesses.' He looked at her then. 'It's not every man who knows the true value his mother placed on him in infancy.'

'Two thousand pounds?' she asked then sipped again. 'That was your grandfather's valuation, not mine. Ten million pounds wouldn't have bought you. They stole you from me, kidnapped you. Lorna Hooper walked into Granny's kitchen, picked you up and drove away while I was getting dressed to take you down to the hospital.'

'You and Granny pursued her on horseback no doubt – leading the town posse,' he said, and emptied his glass.

'You were always my clever little boy. You could read and write before you went to school. That sounded smart arsed, not smart. We had the flu. Granny damn near died of it. I ended up in hospital with pneumonia, and while I was near dying of it, your grandfather dug up enough dirt to bury me. He blackmailed me into signing those papers.'

'Kidnap, blackmail, or was it common greed, old woman?'

'Georgie told me they would have turned you into another Vern Hooper and I laughed at her. Not once in all the years since I lost you, my darlin' boy, did I imagine they could turn a part of me into a Hooper.'

'You compliment me,' he said.

She shook her head. 'That was an insult. Your grandfather was a self-serving, self-satisfied, hard-hearted old bastard. He'd stand there with his judgemental face on – just like you're standing there, and like you, he'd find the prisoner at the dock guilty as charged, no trial necessary. Be anything, my beautiful boy, but don't end up like him. He looked me in the eye one day and told me that Jim was dead. I'd married Ray King before I found out that your father had been carried alive out of that Jap prison camp. Damaged or not, I would have married him.'

He'd removed his wallet while she'd been speaking, had taken folded pages from it. She watched his hands, Jim's hands, unfolding his signed and witnessed evidence. When he offered it, she placed her glass on the windowsill and took his evidence. One glance was enough to recognise it as the original.

'I can quote it to you,' she said, and she ripped it in half, ripped the halves in half, and while he stared, she tossed the pieces to the floor and walked over them on her way to those closed doors.

She got one open, and then glanced back for a final look at her boy. He was gathering the pieces of his bill of sale.

'Don't worry about it,' she said. 'My copy is in better condition. I'll post it to you when I get home. You can have it photocopied – or better still, there's a company in Melbourne that will turn it into wallpaper for you. This room could use a feature wall.'

He looked at her, looked her in the eyes. He still had her Jimmy's eyes, more grey than blue. She still loved them. She'd come here to tell him the truth, so from the doorway, she spoke her well-practised words.

'You were burning up with a killer flu, taking convulsions. Lenny Hall rode his bike into town to get someone with a car to drive us down to the hospital. Dear Aunty Lorna came. She carried you out to her car while I was getting dressed to go with you, but she left while I was looking for my shoes. I thought she'd taken you to the hospital. All day I told myself that she'd have the decency to drive down and let me know if you were alive or dead. No one came, so I walked into town and phoned the hospital. You hadn't been admitted. I went to the police. The constable was on my side, until your lying bastard of a grandfather got to him.'

'Bribed him too?'

'I hope that felt good, my darlin' boy. I hope it eased some terrible hurt you've got buried deep behind those eyes.'

Too weary to say more, shaking with weariness, but she had a plane to catch tomorrow and she'd make it through to tomorrow.

'Granny used to say that a man's good name was worth more than gold. I didn't have a good name in that town, but before I signed those papers, your grandfather threatened to blacken what was left of it.'

'Your signature was witnessed.'

'It was, by Ray bloody King and a nursing sister. I was in hospital, in bed, half-dead with pneumonia. I don't remember much about it – only your grandfather's fountain pen dripping black tears onto the hospital sheet, and Ray's, "S-s-s-sign it, J-j-jenny." I aborted his baby in Armadale – two of them. In the forties, abortion was murder. Your grandfather found out about the last one and threatened to use it against me in court –'

'I don't recall a court case,' he said.

'You wouldn't. There was no court case. Your grandfather was worth thousands; I swapped eggs for staples with Charlie White.' She stepped through to the pool room and told her shaking legs they needed to get her only as far as the pool table. They didn't obey, and she sighed and clung to the door. 'I didn't know a lawyer who'd work for eggs and Granny didn't know that I'd aborted Ray's baby. That old bastard threatened to tell her what I'd done before I signed his papers – and those papers gave you to Jim, not to the bloody Hoopers.'

'Before or after you took the two thousand pounds?'

She'd been warned. *What do you do if it turns pear-shaped, Jen?*

What do you do? You walk away, but you fling the last words over your shoulder.

'I'll post you a cheque when that blood money matures, on March twenty-six. It was up to thirty-three thousand the last time I rolled it over,' she said, and she grasped the edge of the pool table and dug in her bag for her mobile, pleased she'd keyed the taxi's number into her contacts.

He was at the door. 'What happened to Ray?'

She didn't look at him. She looked for the number. 'Dead. Sawmill accident.'

'Raelene was his daughter.'

'She's dead too.'

'I remember his stutter,' he said.

'I remember more,' she said. *London Cab.* She had the number. All she had to do was hit the green button. She didn't. 'Ray was the one who gave your grandfather my bankbook. I would have stuffed it down that old bastard's throat before I took one penny of his filthy money. You had your bill of sale, but I've still got my bankbooks, every last one of them, every record of where that blood money has been since December 1947 – and I've never spent one red cent of it.'

She released the table to hit *call*, and her legs faltered.

'Sit down, Jenny,' he said.

She'd done her sitting, had done her waiting. She had to go, had to call that taxi and get herself back to the hotel.

He was at the small table, metering what remained of the champagne into the two glasses. Not enough left in the bottle to fill them.

'He wanted you the first time he saw your Hooper hands. You were five months old. You were eight months old the first time he offered me money to sign you away. Five hundred pounds, a fortune in '42. I told him where to shove his chequebook.'

He sat and he picked up his wine. 'I knew your voice,' he said.

'I forgot where I was. I was supposed to sing *Ave Maria* at your father's funeral and I didn't. I was in a church so I sang it.'

'One of my first memories is your voice. I remember walking a dusty track between tall trees. You were singing. I remember seeing you in a stage show, in Melbourne. I knew you were in it, but you were wearing a long black wig and I didn't know you until you sang.'

She looked up at the ceiling, old plaster, not the smooth ceilings of today. Her eyes were full of weary tears and she needed the assistance of gravity to stop their flow.

'You've seen me more recently in a dark wig and you didn't know me,' she said. 'You shook my hand.'

Granny used to call him her little Doubting Thomas. She used to say that seeing would always be believing with Jimmy. A tear got away as she looked at his doubting face, but she caught it with her finger. 'In '99, in Melbourne,' she said. 'Cara did an interview to promote *A Hand of Cards*.'

Loved his face, had loved it bruised and scratched and misshapen by his birth. Could remember the first time she'd held him to her breast. Had wept that night, wept all over him. She wouldn't today. She cleared her throat, moistened her lips, swallowed, then spoke of their meeting in Melbourne.

'Georgie introduced you to Juliana Conti, the painted lady in her lolly pink suit. It was my hand you shook.'

'You're kidding me!' he said.

That was her Jimmy, unpolluted by Hoopers, and two heavy tears escaped. She flicked both away with a finger.

'I recognised you the second I touched your hand. It was like shaking Jim's hand.'

'Georgie knew who I was?'

'She looked no further than Cara. They were friends for many years. Georgie doesn't know she met you.'

'I knew her,' he said. 'I recognised her hair. I refused to forget Georgie's hair. I had a jam jar full of pennies and when the sun was out, I'd sit on the lawn at Balwyn, hold that jar high, then pour those pennies in a stream into my beach bucket, chanting, "Georgie, Georgie, Georgie".'

Tears rolling too fast to keep flicking away, she lifted her glasses and wiped her eyes with her palms. She wasn't bawling, only leaking water, a flood of water, all the tears of her life that she'd saved up since the day Lorna Hooper had stolen her Jimmy.

'Granny used to say that Georgie's hair was like a shower of new-minted pennies. Do you remember Granny?'

'Her chooks laid baskets full of eggs. Her goats gave buckets of free milk.' He shook his head. 'She wore knitting needles in her hair, and men's trousers, and working boots.'

'She died with her boots on. We buried her in them,' Jenny said.

'A crushed leaf from a lemon tree or a lemon verbena bush was you,' he said. 'I used to sit beside Lorna at the movies, a leaf or two in my pocket. She smelt of mothballs. I watched a lot of movies with a leaf held to my nose – counting gun shots on my fingers.'

'I used to watch late-night cowboy movies, hoping to see the one where the cowboy in the black hat shot the good guy with his seventh bullet. "That's seven, Jenny," you said, and everyone in the theatre laughed,' she said.

'While the hero in the white hat lay dying,' he said, and he smiled that little Jimmy boy smile, and a moan escaped Jenny's throat.

She'd never been a public bawler. That wine would help. Too late now to call a taxi, and she had to sit down, so she made her careful way back to the blue chair and near fell into it.

He passed her wine, and as she took the glass from him, her smallest finger touched his hand and a painful, aching ecstasy travelled up her arm to her heart, jolted it, made it jump in her breast. She didn't drink but gripped the glass to her heart because he'd touched it.

'For years I counted names instead of sheep when I couldn't sleep,' he said. 'Jenny, Georgie, Granny, Elsie, Harry, Margot, Lenny, Joany, Maudy. I forgot most of their faces but not their names.'

'Harry's still alive, and his kids. Elsie died.'

'Mum told me you were dead. She said you'd gone to live with the angels.'

Jenny couldn't reply, but her heartbeat settling down, she moistened her mouth with wine.

'You used to tell me that my father died in the war, but like Jesus, he rose from the dead. For years I believed you'd rise and take me home,' he said.

Tears leaking. The time for tears had passed, but that's who she was, who she'd always been, fighting strong until the emergency was behind her, then as weak as water.

'You took me to a hospital once to visit a man with one leg, one slipper.'

'You knew who he was that day.'

'I remember you saying, "Jim. Jim. Jim". I don't know if I knew him or not, but I did when my grandfather and aunts took me to a different hospital to visit the same man. He had two legs by then, two slippers and crutches. The visit ended badly. I never saw him again.'

'He loved you when you were ten months old. He saw you take your first step.'

'Mum used to say he was shell-shocked.'

Mum. That word hurt, but Jenny had never been *Mum* to any one of her three, just Jenny, always Jenny – and that hurt was only envy that Margaret Hooper had watched him grow.

'When did you marry my father?'

'A year after Ray died. You would have been seventeen.'

'We moved over here when I was seventeen.'

He questioned her then and she replied, and her tears dried. She told him of Margot's daughter, of Trudy's twin boys she'd named James Hooper and Richard Hooper for Jim. She told him of fourteen-year-old Katie. Then she put her mobile away and took her camera from her bag. Flipped by all that she'd seen of the world and showed him the photographs taken of Georgie and Katie at the airport.

No one disturbed them, or not until seven, when Robin came in with his wife, his son and the offer of a lift back to London. Then minutes later, Tracy came with coffee, more savoury pastries and her two bathed and pyjama-clad pixies – and her camera.

'Don't point that thing at me,' Jenny said.

WHEN THE PARTY
IS OVER

*C*ara had woken that morning with a mild headache. She'd swallowed two aspros. The ache had been under control until that female voice joined with Robin's in the church, until she'd seen Morrie's face pale. She hadn't recognised Jenny's voice. Had never heard her sing.

Should never have met her. Should never have gone near Woody Creek. Shouldn't have gone near the library today. Curiosity or some unfulfilled need had sent her there. Shouldn't have said what she'd said.

'You're Myrtle's daughter,' Jenny had said, so easily wiping their history from the record books.

There were no record books to wipe it from. Cara Jeanette's birth certificate stated that she'd been born to Myrtle and Robert Norris on the third day of October 1944, and until she'd turned fifteen, she'd known no different.

She'd seen her difference. Her cousins had been short and dark. They'd had brown eyes and not a curl between them. She'd had blue eyes, yellow curls, and at twelve had been taller than her mother. By the time she'd turned fifteen, she'd stood eye to eye with Robert and most of her male cousins. Five foot eight when she'd stopped growing, not tall, except in the Norris family.

Christmas Day, 1959, when old Gran Norris had spilled the beans. 'Motherless babies were two a penny during the war. Why Myrtle would go and do a thing like that with your father away fighting a war, I don't know,' she'd said.

A thing like that.

Cara had forced a partial truth from her parents by threatening to leave home. They'd told her a pretty story of a young war widow's brief love affair with an American sailor, of a baby she couldn't take home to her dead husband's family. Ten years later Jenny reduced that brief love affair to pack rape. 'There were five of them,' she'd said. 'You can't fight five.'

At the time it had explained how a baby could be left behind in a boarding house like so much war debris. Cara had attempted to follow her surrogate's example after Robin's birth. She'd left him at the Sydney hospital, caught a bus back to Melbourne and returned to work, determined to forget she'd given birth to her half-brother's baby. But she'd returned for Robin. Jenny had never returned to claim her war debris.

'Anyone for tea, coffee?' Cathy asked. She'd taken over the family room. She'd taken over the dogs, the children and grandchildren. That's what she did. At eighteen, she'd taken over Cara's life when fate flung them together in a shared room at teachers' college.

Cara shook her head and wished she hadn't. This morning's headache had become a migraine. She needed a dark room and her migraine pills, needed Morrie's uninvited guest gone and for him to come out here and take charge of his invited guests. Since four o'clock he'd been holed up in the library with the unmentionable one, the forgotten one, the bitch who'd dropped her pups and walked away from them, or so Morrie had said and more than once.

That wasn't the Jenny Cara had known. She knew every detail of her life, had told Morrie every detail. Hadn't told the children – or Cathy.

'Make it coffee – if you want me to stay awake,' Gerry said, and Cara glanced at Cathy's tolerant mate, at two tolerant males, Tom, the groom's father, was seated with Gerry on the couch watching television. Had they been born tolerant or taught tolerance by their wives?

They'd carried a boot load of flowers into the church this morning, then hung around until their wives had done their decorating. Cara hadn't hung around. She'd kept an appointment for a shampoo and blow dry, then had her nails done.

The talon, the claw of the female carnivore, designed to drip gore, Cara thought as she studied her ten perfect, almond-shaped nails. They looked a little like Myrtle's tonight, though she'd been born with her own iron-hard, almond-shaped nails – one of their many differences.

The house would be her own tomorrow. Laura and Tom had the keys to Ian and Elise's London flat, and an hour ago Tom had invited Cathy and Gerry to join them there. How long would they stay there? Cara hoped long. The newlyweds would be away for ten days. The tolerant male halves of that unlikely foursome would make it through six months on a desert island and be well mannered and smiling when their rescuers arrived. Cathy and Laura could be hard pushed to make it through a day.

They were discussing the refugee situation and not discussing it quietly when Robin came in to say a final goodbye. He'd started leaving an hour ago.

'See you in Australia, Aunty Cath.'

'We've got spare beds – or we mightn't have if you're there during the school holidays, but Mum will,' Cathy said, as Cara rose to lead the way out.

'Where are you parked?' she asked.

'In the driveway.'

'How is your father?'

'He's good, Mum. She's an interesting lady,' Robin said. He and Sally were driving that 'interesting lady' back to her London hotel.

'She flies home in the morning. I told her I'd look her and her daughters up at Christmas time.'

They'd lose him to Australia one day. Cara didn't want to think about that day. 'Drive carefully,' she said, kissed him, then turned and walked back to Cathy. She'd followed them out.

'Where's Morrie?'

'Saying goodnight,' Cara replied, shepherding her friend inside.

She hadn't lied about the uninvited guest, had explained Jenny away as the wife of the black sheep Hooper son. At the reception she'd warned Robin and Tracy not to feed Cathy more grist for her mill mouth.

A stressful day. A stressful week, but tomorrow there'd be peace on earth – and freedom.

Morrie knew what was waiting for him in the family room. For fifteen minutes they listened for him, Cathy geared up to give him the third degree. He could have gone for a walk – or crept in through the front of the house and gone to bed.

I should have stayed away from the library. I shouldn't have said what I said, Cara thought. But since seeing Jenny in the church, Cara had been determined to speak to her. Before the children pressured Morrie into talking to his mother, Cara had been waiting for her chance to go down and ask after Georgie. They were half-sisters, but more than that, they'd been friends with never a secret between them, or not until Cara's first wedding night.

Three men had shaped Cara's life. She'd used Dino Collins to fight her way free of suffocating parents. A rabid wolf would have been a safer choice. He'd killed her interest in the opposite sex – until Morrie, an English boy, in Australia only for a month or two.

They'd met when she'd been fresh out of teachers' college and holidaying in Ballarat with Cathy. She'd allowed herself to like him for the few weeks she'd been in Ballarat, but it hadn't ended there. For five years they'd had an airmail love affair.

She'd told Georgie about her English boyfriend, had told her parents less. He'd never met them. They'd lived in Sydney. She'd lived in Melbourne, and his visits to Australia had been brief.

Had she taken him to Sydney, would he have remembered Myrtle or the boarding house he'd called home for two years? Would Myrtle have seen in the adult the little boy she'd loved?

They'd married at Morrie's dying mother's bedside. Myrtle and Robert hadn't been there. To them, a marriage was no marriage unless sanctified by the Church.

Eight hours that marriage had lasted, long enough to conceive Robin, long enough for Cara to spill her biggest secret to her brand-new husband.

'I'm sort of adopted,' she'd said, then laughed while she'd explained how middle-aged, barren Myrtle and a pregnant lodger had pulled a swiftie. 'She was twenty years old and already had three illegitimate children,' she'd said. Then she'd spoken Jenny's name. He'd got out of bed, dressed, picked up his case and car keys and left his brand-new wife vomiting her heart out in the bridal-suite bathroom.

She'd been asleep when a surgeon had cut the lump of incest out of her. She hadn't looked at it, hadn't touched it. Myrtle had. Robin was eight months old before Cara had been forced to handle him, and born of incest or not, he'd been perfection.

As a tiny boy he'd had the voice of an angel. When he was fifteen she'd suggested voice training. He'd wanted to be a vet. He was eighteen when his interest turned to human patients.

Poor old Rufus needed to see a vet. He struggled each time he got to his feet and seemed to consider that struggle when he heard the back door open. The young pair ran to greet Morrie. Cathy got to her feet, eager to question him.

And he knew it. Cara lowered her head to hide a smile as his footsteps diverted to the rear stairs, the servants' staircase in some distant era. It led directly to their master bedroom beneath the roof.

'He's not going to bed at this time of night,' Cathy said.

'We've all had a long day.' Gerry yawned.

'It's not much after eight!'

'Some of us don't have your reserves of energy, Cath,' Cara said.

No one had Cathy's reserves. At her weight and age, her blood pressure should have been sky high. She should have had diabetes, arthritis in her knees. Cathy swallowed no pills, suffered no aches and pains – or migraines. She could go from daylight to dawn, and as she had when they'd roomed together at college, she exhausted Cara, who felt like old Rufus when she rose to follow Morrie up those stairs.

Queen Anne in the front and Mary-Anne at the rear, Morrie had said once of Langdon Hall, a crumbling, neglected Mary-Anne until old Leticia died and he'd inherited the estate. He'd hired a team of restoration fanatics more obsessive than he about the saving of crumbling history.

They'd dismantled and rebuilt most of the back walls. They'd rebuilt the servants' staircase but hadn't improved on its original design. It was steep and narrow, angling as it climbed.

Every rotting window had been replicated and replaced, every new beam carefully aged by those fanatics, and when they'd packed up their tools and gone on their way, only an expert eye might pick where the original ended and their restoration began.

The master bedroom had received its own improvements. Four rooms on the third level, low-beamed servant quarters squeezed in beneath the roof. The room Morrie had long claimed as his own could have slept six maids. It opened into a small room, perhaps the housekeeper's. The restorers had gutted it and transformed it into a bathroom. They'd done little to the bedroom and to the untrained eye it looked as it ever had. Its replicated windows now opened. Its floor now felt secure. A few of the massive beams supporting the roof were new, though not obviously so.

Light from the open doorway and the sound of splashing water told Cara that Morrie was washing his day away. She walked through the long room and into the bathroom, where she made a beeline for the cabinet that held her packet of migraine pills, which she preferred not to swallow. Tonight she washed down two.

'What are you taking?' he asked.

'If I thought it would work I'd take strychnine,' she said.

'She's Juliana Conti,' he said, water splashing.

'What?'

'Robin inherited her voice, you got her writing. She's Juliana Conti.'

'You're joking, Morrie,' she said, turning so fast her head threatened to fly from her shoulders.

'You said after that interview that she was a relative.'

'Her name,' Cara said. 'I've told you about Juliana and Itchy-foot.'

'You said she had your fingernails.'

'She did, and you're not serious, Morrie.'

'She writes as Juliana Conti. She spoke to Tracy about that convict woman book, which has now been autographed, *For Cara, with love, Juliana.* She said she'd posted a new manuscript to her publisher before she flew over here.'

'She's got to be eighty years old!'

'There's no retirement age for writers,' he said. 'That's why I married you – to keep me in my old age.'

'You sound . . .' She sighed, then turned to the vanity unit. 'I expected you to be as wiped out as me.'

'I feel spaced out,' he said. 'Did I know that Margot had a daughter?

'I didn't,' she said.

'She had a baby to Teddy Hall. I remember him.' He turned the water off. 'It's too much to process. Names and faces keep coming at me. We swapped eggs with Charlie White for groceries. I *can* remember him – and Maisy Macdonald too. She was Margot's grandmother but not mine. Elsie, Harry, Lenny. Names keep generating faces and I don't know if they're real or not.'

'What happened to it, to Margot's baby?'

'Jenny and my father adopted her. Trudy. She's got twin boys Leona's age.'

'I've met Trudy!' Cara said. 'The first time I went to Woody Creek she was a little pigtailed Alice in Wonderland. I thought she was Jenny's.'

'She's her granddaughter. My father is dead. He gave up his licence a couple of years ago and bought one of those electric trolleys. She said he lost control of it near the creek and rolled in. We used to swim in that creek. We used to harness a horse to an old barrel on wheels and hand-pump it full of water then pump it into Granny's tank –'

'That's why she's over here,' Cara said. 'Because Jim died.'

'She said he'd refused to travel.' He was beside her, a towel wrapped around his waist.

'A pity about the kilt,' she said. 'You've got the legs for it.'

He wanted the basin, wanted to brush his teeth. She stepped away.

The mirror over the vanity basin was long. She stood studying her face while cleaning away cloying makeup. 'Do I still look like her?' she asked.

'You never did,' he said, spitting toothpaste. 'Apart from your hair.'

'Can you see any resemblance?'

'Your hairdressers use a similar dye,' he said and spat again.

'The first time Georgie saw me, she guessed why I was in Woody Creek asking about a Jennifer Hooper. I used to be able to see what she'd seen.'

'Jenny told me that she recognised me in Melbourne by my father's hands,' he said, and he looked at his left hand, at his right. 'I remember a tall matchstick man – and his crutches but not his hands.'

'You look nothing like him,' Cara said.

'Did I know that Margot was dead?'

'It was all over the news at the time.'

'In the fire,' he said. 'That's right. I haven't thought about her in years, but I can see her tonight. We're in the backyard at Armadale and she's stamping her feet because I won't give her my trike. I can see them all in Armadale, almost smell Ray's leather jacket. He rode a motorbike. It's too much,' he said, then walked through to the bedroom.

She brushed her teeth, rinsed her face, creamed it then followed him.

'Did you know that Itchy-foot came from a long line of doctors?' he asked.

'I told you he used to be a ship's doctor – back when Robin decided he was going to study medicine. He was a writer too. After he died, someone posted a pile of his diaries to Jenny. Georgie read them. She said they put *Lady Chatterley's Lover* to shame.'

'Jenny told Robin that his grandfather used his doctoring on boats only to get from A to B. She said he had little interest in medicine but came alive on stage.'

'I'd never heard her voice before today,' Cara said.

'I've known it forever. It hit a raw nerve-ending,' he said. 'Robin is over the moon.'

'I noticed,' Cara said. 'And so it begins. I forget, Morrie. For months at a time I actually do forget who we are. Then one way or another, back it comes to haunt me.'

'You're Myrtle and Robert's daughter,' he said.

'You and I, Jenny and Georgie know different. Did she say anything to you about . . . our marriage?'

'Nothing.'

Cara didn't hang her frock. She tossed it over the back of a chair, pulled on the long t-shirt she'd hung over that chair when she'd dressed this morning, then joined him in their old four-poster bed. Its mattress and bedding were twenty-first century, as were the two lights on either side of the bed. She touched her own and the room darkened, though not enough. Mid-summer evenings were long.

They could have bought blackout drapes for the windows, but only passing birds could see in, and that long room needed all the light it could get by day. She lay on her back looking up at the shape of a heavy beam, her favourite beam, the original builder's rough axe cuts carved into time. It was high enough above the bed, but slanting down fast, was too low where it met the external wall. Morrie claimed to have suffered concussion for a month before he'd learnt when and where to duck his head in these upper rooms.

They had rooms with easier access. They had rooms Tracy advertised as palatial, but this one was their own. They'd slept beneath that beam when newly divorced. Cara had spent months here, editing *Rusty* by day, and by night, making sinful love beneath that rough-cut beam. A memory place this room. They'd keep climbing those convoluted stairs until . . . until the day they couldn't.

'She kept calling me Jimmy,' he said. 'No one has used that name since my grandfather died. It began to sound right.'

'Georgie always spoke of you as Jimmy. I never related my Morrie Grenville to her Jimmy Morrison. There's a part of me still that can't.'

'She told me that you knew the facts of my alleged "kidnap".'

'I told you what I knew years ago, and you didn't believe me.'

'During my denial period,' he said. 'Tell me again.'

Cara adjusted her pillow then lay back to stare at that beam again. 'You were burning up with some killer flu. A neighbour's son rode into town to get someone to drive you and Jenny down to the hospital. Lorna Hooper arrived. She took you but not Jenny. The Hoopers hated her. The next day Jenny was in hospital with pneumonia. She was sick for weeks, for years, Georgie once said. They never saw you again.'

'She told me tonight that my grandfather found out she'd aborted Ray's baby, that he'd blackmailed her into signing me over to my father. Incidentally, she ripped up my bill of sale.'

'I've been tempted to do that for years.'

'It's been a part of me,' he said.

'Not one of your better parts. That abortion is a fact,' Cara said. 'She had a nursing sister friend in Armadale who "fixed" unwanted pregnancies for the neighbours. She "fixed" two for Jenny.

The second one put her into hospital and when she was released her husband beat her to pulp. That's when she left him.'

'I can remember the day we left, coming home from school to a pile of cases and rolled-up bedding on the veranda. She'd forgotten my trike. We had to write a ticket to tie onto its handlebars.'

'What else do you remember?'

'Jenny squeezing milk out of a goat. Jenny frying a whole pan full of eggs. The taste of those eggs. She served them on pancakes.'

'Can you remember Lorna taking you?'

'Nothing. There's blank space. I was at Granny's then I woke up in a room with a light shade swinging overhead and Mum leaning over the bed.'

'You knew her before you went to live with her?'

'The Hoopers had always been around. They used to buy me presents. When we lived in Armadale, they sent me a train set that blew smoke. They bought me a bike with training wheels when I lived with them in Balwyn. I remember that house, those years. We lived in Balwyn until my grandfather died.'

'Was your father there?'

'Never. I can remember all hell breaking loose a few days after my grandfather died. He'd given Mum and Bernard control of his estate. Lorna went crazy and for some reason blamed her uncle, Henry. We put her on a boat to visit him.'

Silence, then he sighed and spoke again. 'Remember how the crowd used to throw streamers to boats leaving port?'

'No one I knew ever left port,' Cara said.

'They used to toss rolls of coloured streamers and someone on board or on the dock would catch them. Mum and Bernard kept throwing the streamers as if they were pitching rocks at Lorna. Then when the last streamer broke, they grabbed each other and started dancing. I thought they'd gone mad or thought the crowd down there would think they'd gone mad.'

'I would have danced too,' Cara said. She'd met Lorna.

'Everything changed then. They bought Lorna her own house in Kew and we moved down to a little place in Cheltenham. Mum loved the beach. Then Lorna came home and moved herself in with us, so we moved again, and again – until we came over here.'

'Why didn't she follow you to England?'

'Old Henry died while Lorna was over here, and to her last day, Aunt Letty swore that Lorna had put a curse on him. She used to call her *that black witch*. Had she come within a mile of the Hall, Aunt Letty would have had her burnt at the stake.'

'How old was your mother when she married Bernard?' Cara asked.

'Early forties, I think.'

'Life might have been very different for you if they'd had their own children.'

'Letty liked me – and life is what it is,' he said.

'Did Jenny mention me at all?'

'Robin asked her if she remembered your mother. She said she'd rented a room at her boarding house, that her landlady had a baby shortly before she left Sydney.'

'See,' Cara said. 'I was born three weeks before she left Sydney. She never lies, Morrie. I wished to God she had the night she told me that any one of five American sailors could have been my father.'

'I've known who she was forever but spent most of my life attempting to know who they told me she was. Mum used to call her an unfortunate girl. My grandfather told me I was better off not remembering her. Lorna told me she was the town trollop, shunned by every decent person in town.' He breathed in for a long moment while overhead the old timbers groaned. 'After Mum died and I found my bill of sale, I came up with my own description of a slut capable of selling her six-year-old son for two thousand pounds.'

'Mum loved her, and you. She told me once that God had sent one of his angels to her door so she might have her own baby to love.'

'*Angel at My Door?*'

'Yep. The first real image I had of Jenny was of a faceless girl who gave birth on Mum's kitchen floor, no doctor, no midwife. A girl who tied my cord with a length of used string, cut me free with blunt scissors, handed me to Mum, then put on her makeup and high heels and went upstairs to pull off her scam.'

'How did they do it?'

'We had an elderly spinster lodger who'd never been closer to a birth than the columns in her daily newspaper. She came down, saw Mum sitting in the mess of birth with me in her arms and that was as much as she wanted to see – Miss Matilda Robertson. I used to think that Mum had the backbone of a worm, until she told me the story of my birth. She had guts, just not of a type I recognised.'

'There's not much left of Jenny, but she's got a backbone of steel. You saw the mood I was in when the kids dragged me down there today. I wasn't pleasant. She told me I was like my grandfather, that being likened to him was an insult.'

'She loathed him,' Cara said. 'Georgie loathed him. She told me once that she stabbed him in the backside with a pair of embroidery scissors – when she was five or six years old.'

'Fearless Georgie,' he said. 'I remember one night in Armadale, being woken up by thumping and Ray yelling. Georgie opened our door. Jenny was on the floor, blood all over her face, Ray kicking her. I can see Georgie now, running at them, throwing herself on top of Jenny. She would have been seven,' he said. 'Jesus.' He shuddered.

'What?'

'Memories,' he said. 'That one raises goose bumps on my soul.'

Only the sounds of night then, the creaking of old beams until Cara spoke. 'It hurts,' she said. 'I know it shouldn't, but it does – her coming here to find you, not me. She carried me for the same nine months. She gave birth to me.'

'While I can convince myself that you're Myrtle and Robert's daughter, I can live happily ever after. She's convinced herself that you're Myrtle's daughter, so she could have her one day. That's all she wanted. One day. She flies home in the morning.'

'Did you ask her about Georgie?'

'I meant to tell you the second I saw you. She works for your Mafioso fiancé.'

'For Chris?'

'Yep. She's got a fourteen-year-old daughter – with hair as red as her mother's.'

'Is she married?'

'To a Paul someone.'

'Works for Chris, doing what?'

'Solicitor,' he said. 'She got into some university as a mature-age student, was forty-five when she graduated –'

'Paul Dunn?' Cara asked.

'Could be. It was a short name. Did you know him?'

'No, but it was a Georgina Dunn who got attacked by Dino Collins. I phoned Chris the morning after Cathy phoned to tell us that Collins was dead. He told me that an intruder had randomly attacked one of his solicitors in her garden, a Georgina Dunn. It wasn't random, Morrie. Collins couldn't get at me so he went after Georgie. My God. My God.' Nothing more to say but 'My God', until they heard water running and old pipes knocking.

'What time are they leaving?' he asked.

'After breakfast.'

'Think we could give breakfast a miss?'

'And have Cathy bailing us up in bed?'

'No hint of how long they plan to stay in London?'

'Until Tom and Gerry have to break up their first fight.'

'Do you think you could possibly refer to them as Gerard and Thomas, or Gerry and Tom?'

'It doesn't flow,' she said.

Once Henry's ghost started his knocking, he refused to stop until the water downstairs was turned off. He was still knocking, Cara drifting in that place before sleep, when Morrie sprang upright.

'What's up now?'

'Jenny gave me my father's war medals and I don't know what I did with them. Cover your eyes. I need light.'

'They'll be in your suit pocket.'

'They were in an envelope. I had it in my hand when I went for a walk. I could have dropped it.'

He found it, in his suit jacket pocket, and he brought it to the bed. 'It feels like aniseed balls. We used to buy aniseed balls when we went to the movies, used to see who could make one last the longest,' he said as he poured the contents of the envelope onto the quilt.

There were medals, half a dozen of them, but no bag of aniseed balls. There was a worn grey leather drawstring pouch. He pounced on it.

'Granny's beads,' he said unknotting the leather cord, then pouring the amber necklace into his palm. The bedside light insufficient, he took the necklace to the bathroom. She followed him with the envelope and caught him counting beads as a Catholic counted rosary beads.

'There,' he said. 'Granny's prehistoric mozzie.'

She needed her glasses to see it. She put them on, then beneath the strong mirror light saw the remains of an insect trapped in one of the larger beads.

'I can remember Jenny showing it to us. Granny was emptying out the old trunk so we could take it with us to Armadale. It sucked the blood from dinosaurs and cave men,' he said, then turned to her. 'I don't think I can let her go, love.'

'She's letting us go,' Cara said. She found a note inside the envelope, a tiny note written on a page ripped from a notebook, the writing by necessity, was small.

Dear Cara,

If you're reading this then it means that I've found my lost children and that I'm jubilantly happy. The amber beads belonged to Granny. They're over a hundred years old and were her only treasure. She would have loved to know that they'd gone to the woman Jimmy married.

With my love, Jenny. XXX

PART THREE

ROADS

*N*ight came down early in June, and as Jenny started up her car in the supermarket car park, she turned on her headlights. She'd picked up a few basics, all she'd need for tonight and tomorrow. She could have slept at Georgie's and done the trip in the morning, but so close to home and her car waiting for her on the lawn, she'd made the decision to drive and hadn't stopped until Willama. She'd be home before dark. She wanted to see Lila, wanted to sleep in her own bed. If nothing more, that tour had put her off anonymous beds for life.

Given the optimum driving conditions, Willama was thirty-five minutes from Woody Creek. The conditions weren't optimum at dusk, so she kept her speed down. A few truck drivers may have cursed her. She had a tail of trucks behind her when she crossed over the Mission Bridge. They passed her, one after the other when the road straightened out, but any kangaroos on the road that night may have thought twice before playing chicken with that convoy, so Jenny stayed on the tail of the last truck and got her speed up to the limit.

Harry knew she was coming. She'd phoned him before leaving Greensborough. He'd said he'd meet her at the house and have the kettle boiling. She needed her own mug, her own brand of tea, then her bed.

Five-twenty when she made the turn into Three Pines Road and drove that final kilometre to Hooper's corner.

The trees had leaves when she'd left. They wore their ghostly grey tonight, and the rose hedge appeared to have been pruned by a chainsaw, which would do it no harm. There was a light showing in her kitchen, and to a weary traveller, tonight that light looked like home.

The gate open, she drove in, drove down to her usual place and Lila was there to meet her, to greet her, lick her hands and her face when Jenny reached down for a cuddle.

'The conquering hero returned from the war,' Harry said.

'It was a war,' Jenny said. She handed Harry a supermarket bag, picked up the other and her handbag and followed him indoors.

*

Twenty kilometres west of town, two brothers and their mate got into a silver–green Mazda to begin the trip to Willama, and not via the Mission Bridge. Back in the horse and buggy days, when the railway line was the main artery feeding life's blood into Woody Creek, man and his beasts had forged a track that followed those lines as far as the Melbourne highway. They'd named that track Willama Road.

It was still there, dusty in the dry, impassable in the wet, but until the Mission Bridge and the sealed road leading to it were declared open, that track had been the only way for Woody Creek residents to access doctors and hospital.

The train lines crossed over the highway and continued on their way to the Big Smoke. Old Willama Road dead-ended when it hit bitumen. A left-hand turn and thirty kilometres would take a driver the back way into Willama.

Drovers and their herds still used that track, as did a few of the farmers who owned properties out that way. Enough used Old Willama Road to warrant a *Stop* sign where it T-intersected with the highway.

The driver of the silver–green Mazda had a girl waiting for him in Willama. Three times a week he drove that way, leaving a trail of dust behind him. He was too familiar with the *Stop* sign to heed its warning. Nine times out of ten when he turned left onto the highway, there wasn't a car on the road.

There is always a tenth time.

Black vehicles are not easily seen at that time of night. Its driver, unfamiliar with the big SUV, found the wiper switch instead of the headlights. He was cursing the flapping wipers when the Mazda shot out of the scrub. He attempted to find the brake, but his right foot out of action, he was driving with his left foot – never a good idea in an automatic vehicle.

The impact spun the smaller vehicle into the path of a fuel tanker, approaching fast from the opposite direction. The truckie took evasive action. The noise of his action had roosting birds screeching from their trees, but as those tankers are apt to do, his jack-knifed, then rolled.

The guardian of fools and thieves allowed the SUV to remain on its wheels. Its nose was in the scrub, but the driver rammed the stick into reverse and backed up. There was a tangle of wreckage barring his way, so he took his only option, that dirt track that followed the railway lines. He turned the wipers off, noticed that his front wheels were not responding as they should, but found the switch that turned on the headlights, one of which lit the track ahead.

The truckie hadn't been written down to die that night. He scrambled free of his over-turned cabin, saw a body wrapped in a tangle of metal, then looked for the third vehicle. He'd seen it coming. It had been big, dark. He'd seen the impact. He was thinking it must have ended up in the scrub when he smelt petrol. It shocked his legs into action. They ran him back in the direction he'd come from. They got him well clear of the accident before his load exploded.

Thunder on a night when the sky is clear, light where there should have been none, had farmer and motorist reaching for their phones. Willama dispatched a convoy of sirens, but fuel fed, the fire took the path of least resistance, towards the river, gorging on whatever got in its way.

Farm fences got in its way, small trees and large, timber power poles, a farm shed and stock got in its way.

The power poles had an important job to do and for a time continued to do it, but by seven-fifteen, Willama's twelve thousand residents were plunged into darkness, as were Woody Creek's five hundred.

'Bugger,' Jenny said. She was in the shower. Turned the water off blindly, found a towel where it was supposed to be, then, her hand against walls, she made her way down the passage to the kitchen where she opened the firebox, for its light. She'd pitched her plastic bag of candle stubs in the bin when she'd emptied the kitchen drawers. She had torches, the small one she kept in her car's glove box and the big one, which could have been on the hallstand.

'Sit down or you'll knock me over and make it a real homecoming,' she said to Lila. She'd never been an indoor dog, not until Jim died, when Jenny had started locking her in at night, for company.

Jenny added junk mail to the stove. Harry had delivered a pile of it with a rubber-banded wad of mail she hadn't yet got around to opening. She felt for the matchbox on the mantelpiece and by the light of matches, she found her nightdress, placed beneath her pillow the morning she'd left.

She undressed in the dark, then made her way to the hallstand where by the light of matches, she looked for the torch that wasn't there. She could get the one from her glove box, was considering it when she heard the shed door slam. The bolts had been rammed home before she'd left. Someone had been poking around out there.

Listened for a second slam. If that door did it once it would keep doing it until she went out there and bolted it. How many times had she got out of bed in the night to slide that bolt home?

'It can slam tonight,' she said to Lila, who refused to leave her heels. 'We're going to bed.'

She stoked the stove, closed it down for night burning, then her hand following the wall again, she felt her way back to her bedroom. The matchbox on her bedside table, she slid between familiar sheets and placed her head on a familiar pillow.

'Bliss,' she said, her bones settling on a mattress that was just right. 'Go to bed,' she said. Lila was scratching around in the dark. The shed door slammed once more, then either remained open or closed and Jenny's eyes closed. She knew no more until her bladder roused her at seven-thirty.

*

The power was still off, but her kettle was boiling and there was a nest of embers in the firebox, perfect for making toast in the old-fashioned way. She was buttering the first slice when Lila told her Harry was coming. He knew where to get a cup of tea in a blackout.

He knew what was causing the blackout. The transistor radio he'd been sleeping with since losing Elsie kept him well informed on the local news.

'There was a bad accident out where Old Willama Road hits the highway. A loaded tanker ran into a car full of kids.'

He spoke of the truckie who'd lived, of the youths who'd died, while Jenny impaled more bread on her fork. He knew the name of one of the dead youths. 'Young Cody Lewis, Walter's son. His brother told Teddy this morning at the newsagents.'

That was the way of this town, information exchanged where locals met, out the front of the newsagency, in the butcher's shop. They'd have the names of the other dead youths by midday. Jenny, only home for today, didn't want to hear of death.

'The fire would have done more damage if the tanker had been carrying a full load. That chap who trains racehorses out there lost a lot of fences and was lucky not to lose his house. They've been warning traffic all night about horses running loose on the road,' Harry said. 'Got any Vegemite?'

'In the fridge. It should be on the top door shelf.'

'You keep it in the fridge?'

'We don't . . . I don't use a lot of it,' she said.

'Young Harry said to tell you that he wants to pay you something for your fridge.'

'It was past its use-by date twenty years ago. Tell him he's saving it from the tip,' Jenny said. 'I was thinking on my drive home of how I had two cases, a tin trunk and a bit of bedding when I packed up in Armadale. It's amazing how little you can manage with when you have to.'

She spoke of the tour then and the aqua-blue case she'd left in Greensborough. She spoke of the secondhand man who'd said he'd be here between eight and eight-thirty this morning.

'You'll stay with Georgie for a while?'

'For a while, until I know where I want to be.'

'Down there, near the grandkids?' he said.

'I spoke to Trudy before I left yesterday. She was talking about moving back to Willama. Something big has happened between her and Nick.'

They spoke of many things, Lila content between them, Harry feeding her crusts, with Vegemite. 'I missed her this morning. She's been taking me for a walk up to get my newspaper.' She knew 'walk' and stood, head to the side, waiting for one of them to move. Harry gave her another crust. 'You can leave her with me, if you like – just until you get settled.'

'If the secondhand chap buys my bed, she'll have to stay with you tonight. I'll book into one of the hotel's cabins – or maybe the Gold Rush. I've got a ton of things I need to do down there, and I'll be on the spot to hand over my keys.'

'They've got no power down there either,' he said, then spoke again of the accident, or of the truckie who claimed that a third vehicle had sent the Mazda hurtling into his truck.

Lila heard the secondhand man's van backing in. She ran to the door to bark her disapproval when Harry let the interlopers inside.

They bought Jenny's bed, dressing table, bedside tables but wouldn't take the wardrobes as a gift. Pat and Mike might appreciate them – or chop them up for kindling. They bought her kitchen table and chairs, her old radiogram and vinyl records, for a pittance. They bought the large coffee table from the sitting room, then totalled their offers on a calculator, Jenny disinterested in the total or the notes the shop owner counted from his wallet to the table.

She picked them up before they picked up her kitchen table, and what was a kitchen without a kitchen setting? She swept the empty space of floor, then Lenny and young Harry came to collect the fridge.

Didn't want to watch it being moved, so she made a phone call to her hairdresser and got an appointment at three for a trim and to have her roots done.

Nothing left, or nothing that wouldn't fit into the green bin – and her small television and video player. She unplugged them. Harry loaded them into the Toyota's boot. She tied a dozen videos into a supermarket bag, placed the last of her bread, milk, cheese and butter into another bag, with her teabags and a jar of sugar. She'd spend the night at the Gold Rush and make her own breakfast in the morning.

One o'clock when she clipped on Lila's lead. Lila didn't want to walk with Harry. She wanted to patrol her land, bark at the shed. Harry led her away and Jenny went inside to walk the hollow rooms, to mop the floor where her fridge had been, wipe dust from the corner of her kitchen bench. She took one last look at the library and wondered if Pat and Mike might furnish it as

Jimmy's library had been furnished, wondered if they'd light its open fire and sit in here, watching television. She'd removed the newspaper from its chimney, from all of the chimneys.

A nice room this one, in a nice old house that had been Jim's and Trudy's and the twin's home but never Jenny's. She'd just lived here, because they'd lived here.

The sky to the west was looking dark. Woody Creek could have been in for a storm. The farmers needed rain. Jenny didn't. She didn't like driving in the rain.

Looked at her watch. If she left now she could book into the motel and make herself some lunch before her hair appointment. She might be able to pick up her photographs early. The chap at the photography place had said yesterday that they'd be ready in twenty-four hours.

Should have brought her overcoat. She'd meant to. In too much of a hurry to get away, she'd left it hanging in Georgie's guest-room wardrobe. She was wearing a sweater and cardigan, warm enough, but that cardigan wouldn't keep her dry if those clouds kept their promise of rain.

Her old parka was still hanging behind the laundry door. Half a dozen times she'd been going to pitch it in the green bin, but there'd been not a thing wrong with it – other than it made her look like the Michelin Man.

She picked up her handbag, her plastic bags, looked at her stove one final time. She'd miss it, though wouldn't miss stoking it. And a light came on in the hall. She turned it off, checked the bathroom cabinet one final time, checked the front door, then left via the back door, locking it and the security door behind her.

How many times had she locked and unlocked those doors? How many times had she walked those few metres to the laundry?

She took the old blue parka down from its rusting nail. Unworn in three years, it was probably full of spiders. She shook it, slapped it and, still slapping and shaking it, walked down Jim's ramp. It would be gone in a week. Pat and Mike hadn't liked it. They might be sorry in ten years' time – sooner than that they might be sorry they'd bought in Woody Creek.

The plastic bags tossed onto the back seat, the parka checked more thoroughly for spiders and then placed with her handbag on the passenger seat, she slid in behind the wheel.

Georgie had driven the Toyota for the weeks her own car was in the body shop. She'd had it serviced, had bought it a new battery and new front tyres. By no stretch of the imagination was it a new car, but it still looked new, still went like new.

Jenny had fallen in love with it the day she'd driven it home from the showroom. It was her first car with power steering, air conditioning and bucket seats that adjusted to suit the driver's size. Its fuel gauge was down to a quarter full, but a quarter of a tank was plenty to get her to Willama.

Shift in reverse, she backed up to where the nose of her car was level with the library window, where she turned her wheels hard onto the track she'd worn between house and shed. With less space to manoeuvre each year between the liquid amber and the crepe myrtle, she had to concentrate on her side mirrors, then make a second hard turn as the car mounted the cement driveway.

And her passenger side door flew open.

She hit the brake, wondering how she'd managed to leave that door open, and as she turned to close it, a black-clad male, his face hidden by a ski mask, flung himself into her passenger seat, pointed a gun at her and snarled, 'Drive.'

She didn't think. She didn't see. Her brain said, *Run*. If not for her seatbelt, she may have. She got her door open, but as she did, he hit her behind her ear with the barrel of his gun.

'Drive, you geriatric old bitch, or you're dead,' he snarled.

Jenny stared in open-mouthed disbelief as her car backed itself into the lavender bushes she'd planted to hide an old paling fence. No scent of crushed lavender in her car. Stink of Duffy in her car, stink of unwashed feet.

'Take the car,' she said. 'There's money in my bag. Take it.' She was too old for this. She had too much to do and too little time to do it. 'Please, just take my car and let me out.'

'Drive,' he said, and he pushed the barrel of his gun into her neck.

She didn't want to die in Woody Creek, be buried in Woody Creek. She wanted to do it drugged to the eyeballs in an old folks' home. Her foot found the accelerator and, taking half of a lavender bush with her, she reversed too fast out to Hooper Street, missing the right-side gatepost by a whisker.

No passing truck to stop her flight. No bike rider or wandering drunk. Not a soul to save her, and when had there ever been anyone to save her? Only Granny – who she was going to see a lot sooner than she'd expected.

The opposite kerb stopped her. One of her rear wheels hit it and mounted it, before her foot found the brake. He didn't want her to brake. He pushed the stick into *Drive*, turned her wheels away from Willama, ground the gun barrel into her ribs, then, from the mouth hole in his ski mask, familiar lips spat, 'Drive, you ugly old moll.'

She drove, her undercarriage grinding on concrete before all four wheels were back on Hooper Street. Too fast she turned right into Three Pines Road, her head throbbing where he'd hit her, her heart attempting to break free of her ribs. Her eyes searched the road for that pinch-faced constable, or a council worker, or Bernie Macdonald and his walking frame. Someone. Anyone.

Empty end of the world road in an empty end of the world town. She was getting out of it, though not the way she'd planned to. Should have locked her car doors as soon as she got behind the wheel. Jim used to tell her to lock her doors –

Drove by what used to be John and Amy McPherson's land to where the road used to curve left to the old bridge. No curve now. No old bridge. No McPherson's land. A new stretch of road led directly onto an ugly concrete bridge, designed by city men for city traffic that wanted to bypass tin-pot little towns.

Plenty of signposts where those roads intersected. The main road had right of way. Three Pines had a *Stop* sign. She attempted to obey that sign, but he hit her again, and in the same place, and the pain so intense the second time, she did something she'd never done in her life, she sideswiped a white post, hit it hard enough to fling the steering wheel from her hands.

Survival instinct saves us whether we want to be saved or not. Jim had known that. That's why he'd removed his prosthesis before taking his final ride. Survival instinct kept Jenny on the road, and at that moment, had she been holding that gun, she would have put a bullet between his eyes. He'd made her damage her perfect little car.

She was powerless. She had no weapon – only her car, and so thinking, she flattened the accelerator to the floor. The motor surged, the wheels skidded on gravel and bitumen, then all four became a team. Obedient to her foot, the Toyota took off over the bridge like a bat out of hell.

Big trees on the far side, nothing but trees, one of them marked by a Duffy utility that had attempted to climb it. Her passenger didn't want to climb a tree. He took the gun out of her face and grabbed for his seatbelt.

He'd sat on her parka and handbag, and unable to find the seatbelt clip, he dragged both from beneath him and pitched them to his stinking feet as her speedo crept past a hundred and twenty. She'd been doing a hundred and twelve when she'd got that speeding ticket, but the road beyond the bridge was straight and wide, so she increased her pressure on the accelerator and got the needle brushing a hundred and thirty, wanting another speeding ticket, praying for another speeding ticket.

He was wearing the Duffy uniform of windcheater and hoodie. For three generations, *Duffy* had been an obscenity in Woody Creek. They lived off the taxpayer, stole anything that wasn't tied down, and every generation bred better thieves than the last. His build was Duffy but something about him wasn't. Most of that rat pack's insults were four-letter words. *Drive, you geriatric old bitch*, he'd said. *Geriatric* had nine letters.

She glanced at him as she passed the old Bryant property. No more Bryants in Woody Creek, no more Monks or Hoopers. All three properties now belonged to a city company that ran dairy cows, hundreds of big black and white beasts that walked twice a day to modern milking sheds where machinery did the work of a hundred hands. The world had been a safer place when all men had laboured. The elderly had been respected, cared for. These days they were easy prey for this mongrel and his ilk.

*

In her office on the twenty-third floor, Georgie was thinking Duffy. She was with a client who made her skin crawl.

'Excuse me,' she said when her mobile vibrated. Few had that number. Katie's school had it. Paul, Jenny, Trudy and more recently, Harry, had it.

It was Trudy, and Georgie excused herself to take that call in the corridor.

'They found my car. He crashed it out near Broadmeadows. They're saying that he dragged a teacher out of her SUV at traffic lights then drove off with a little girl in the back seat.'

'Nick? Have they got him?'

'No. And they think that SUV was involved in that fatal accident near Willama.'

'Have you phoned Jen?'

'She's not answering, Georgie.'

'I'm with a client, Trude. I'll have to go.'

Her mind wasn't with her client – and she had another two this afternoon, one she'd transferred from yesterday so she could pick Jenny up from the airport.

She'd been determined to drive home. 'I'm so close,' she'd said. 'Off you go, and don't worry about me. I'm fine.'

She'd looked fine, had sounded fine and had been making her own decisions since she'd turned fifteen.

Only fifteen when she'd given birth to Margot – and in these days of enlightenment, a rape victim wouldn't be expected to give birth to her rapist's baby. Attitudes had been different back then. Males had ruled the world and girls weren't raped but taken advantage of – and apportioned more than their fair share of the blame. Jenny had run from baby Margot. She'd stowed away in the goods van of a night train.

In these days of enlightenment, a psychologist might explain why a fifteen-year-old girl had become involved with a twenty-six-year-old man, might explain Georgie's conception. Jenny had never attempted to. She'd said that Laurie Morgan had been kind to her, that he'd looked like Clark Gable with red hair, that he'd bought her beautiful frocks and shoes with heels four inches high, and glasses of magic lemonade, and if she drank enough of it, it made the world, the Macdonald twins and Margot go away.

The newspapers of the time had called Laurie Morgan *the redheaded water-pistol bandit*. Georgie was only a peanut in Jenny's belly when he'd been arrested, when a Salvation Army couple had returned an absconding fifteen-year-old to the loving arms of her parents. Jenny had run from them too, run to Granny.

There were sixteen years between Georgie and Jenny. Jimmy had been twenty months Georgie's junior. She had no recollection of him as a baby and little of Jenny, until she'd returned from Sydney with a three-year-old boy. He'd had a father, or a photograph of his soldier father and when she'd demanded her own father, she'd got one, a framed mug shot of Laurie Morgan, cut from a newspaper.

*

The last time Jenny had driven this road, Jim had been in the passenger seat and Katie in the back, holding on to two pups, Lila's litter mates, bought by old Paddy Watson. He'd wanted a breeding pair.

She wasn't thinking about those pups. She was thinking of Trudy and Croydon but mainly about the mouth behind that ski mask and the eyes. Her passenger was no Duffy. He was Trudy's parasite. He'd been missing since around the tenth of June. Today was the seventeenth – and if he'd washed his feet since he'd gone missing, she'd eat her hat, which she'd left in Italy. She'd left her blue skirt in Switzerland, her beige slacks in London. They'd stayed up since the elastic, but their backside seam had split with sitting, and she'd never liked beige anyway.

A signpost flashed by. It could have said N 60. Her speedo said a hundred and thirty, too fast to give her eyes time to focus on signs. She'd never seen Nettleton. Had known about it since infancy. The train used to go through Woody Creek to Nettleton, to be turned around and sent back to Norman's station.

No pinch-face patrolling this road. She wanted his siren and glanced at her passenger's ski mask. It had circles for his dead-snake eyes. She knew them well. She knew his stumpy hands too. And what the hell were they doing holding a gun?

Couldn't believe any of this. Couldn't believe she hadn't seen him. Too many trees, and her concentration had been on missing those trees and what movie might have been playing tonight at the cinema. She'd been carjacked in her own front yard by her gun-toting son-in-law.

It was probably a replica and, replica or not, he'd stopped pointing it at her. He was holding it on his lap and watching a truck approaching.

'He'll see your mask. If you think you're fooling me with it, you're wrong,' she said. No reply, and the truck driver was only interested in getting his load to wherever he was going.

The sky to the west was black. She was driving into that storm, but the road was straight, as were the train lines it followed.

'Slow down,' he said.

'Scared of dying? We all have to do it one day.'

She'd found Jimmy. She'd held his hand when he'd walked her to the car, and he'd kissed her goodbye. Her money was safe for the grandchildren. Juliana's brooch was safe with Georgie. Granny's beads were safe.

Trudy had been named beneficiary on her life insurance policy – if Jim had predeceased her. He had. Trudy would get that money, if the company paid up. They'd probably prove that speeding had been the cause of death and refuse to pay. They'd taken months to pay up for Jim's accidental drowning, but they had, while she'd been in Switzerland.

That damn road decided to curve away from the railway lines, and another loaded transport was coming at her around the curve and wanting the entire road. She was going too fast to give him what he wanted. Almost side-swiped him – and scared her passenger. He braced for impact, drew up his knees, and she caught a glimpse of what stunk. His right foot was bare and bloody. Dried blood.

'Shoot yourself in the foot with your gun?' she asked.

'Shut your flapping mouth, you ugly old bitch,' he said, and he pointed his gun at her nose.

'Shove it up your own and pull the bloody trigger,' she said.

It looked real. Laurie Morgan's water pistol had looked real enough until you saw its rubber-bladder handle.

All roads around Woody Creek were dead flat, but well beyond Watson's land now, that road had become a series of curves. Forged by a drunken bullocky on a dark night, Jenny thought, easing back on her speed and glancing in her rear-vision mirror. Hadn't seen a car behind her until those curves. She'd picked up a tail of cars and trucks, and one of them was almost riding her bumper bar.

'Get off this road,' he said.

'Show me another one,' she said, and hoped that the driver on her bumper bar saw his mask and phoned the cops. Her passenger must have had the same thought. He scrunched down in his seat and removed his mask – and he hadn't shaved for a week.

'What the hell has been going on while I've been away?'

They were passing her. Four cars and one truck, on a passing lane, strangers, annoyed that she'd forced them to slow down.

'Get off this fucken road!' he said.

'I'm going to Nettleton,' she said. There'd be a police station there. When she'd been a kid, they'd had a boarding school. A few Woody Creek farmers had educated their sons in Nettleton. They'd have a police station. She'd do a wheelie into its driveway and lean on her horn.

Glanced at his gun. Granny used to own one – a rifle. She used to keep a packet of bullets on her kitchen mantelpiece. As a youth, Jim had owned a rifle. His father bought it for his twelfth birthday. Jenny had never held a gun. Should have shot Vern Hooper with Granny's. I would have been out of jail by now, she thought, then noticed her fuel gauge. It was showing red. Should have taken the mileage. She'd had more than mileage on her mind at the time. *Kilometrage*, she self-corrected. The Toyota counted kilometres, not miles.

A big dusty ute beeped as it went by. It looked like young Paddy Watson's twin cab. Should have flashed her lights at him, given him the driver's SOS.

She passed a tractor attached to a trailer loaded with rams, passed two bike riders, pushing hard on their pedals to get to where they were going before the storm hit. It was coming at her. There was a curtain of grey rain ahead and she and those bike riders where heading straight for it.

What is it that turns some youths into bike riders and others into addicts? she thought. Why had Georgie become who she'd become – and Raelene?

She hadn't given birth to that girl, but she'd raised her from a three weeks' old baby, had raised her until Ray died, and loved the demanding little bugger. Blame Florence Dawson for who she'd become. She'd taken a seven-year-old brat and given back an out of control twelve-year-old.

And look at Jimmy. Whatever Margaret Hooper had been, she must have loved Jimmy. She'd raised a good man.

Morrison Grenville. It was a good name. A month ago, she'd told herself that she'd die happy if she could see him, touch him again. She didn't want to die today. She had pre-publication work to do on *We'll Meet Again* and she wanted to finish her *Parasite* file and find it a title.

Designer jeans, she thought. He was wearing his designer jeans. They needed a wash. His black hoodie might have come from Kmart.

And the rain hit, sheets of it. She turned on her wipers, eased back more on the accelerator and glanced at her fuel gauge. Never, in all of her years of driving, had she run out of petrol, or not since she'd been a licensed driver. She'd run out of petrol in one of Laurie Morgan's stolen cars. He'd been nursing a broken ankle, and in those days a driver had required two good feet to drive a car. At fifteen, she'd had the feet but not the knowhow.

Life is a circle, she thought. I've been around the block and returned to the beginning, driving a parasite with an injured foot – though there must have been a few good genes in Laurie. He'd given her Georgie.

Wiper blades flapping like frantic wings, doing what they could to give her vision. She sat forward, watching the white line, the white posts – like driving through a pea-soup fog, she thought. She wouldn't have seen a kangaroo. Maybe they had sense enough to find shelter during downpours.

Her speed was down to fifty before the rain eased off and she could see where she was going – and see a manmade structure playing behind the trees, dodging from one side of the road to the other.

His eyes were younger. They may have identified that structure before Jenny's could name it a silo.

'Turn,' he said. 'Turn here.'

There was a signpost at a T-intersection, *Nettleton 5*. She didn't see where that minor road was heading.

'Turn, I said!'

'I'm out of petrol,' she said.

There were three silos, big ones, but before they reached them, Nettleton started slinking out of a saturated landscape – a farmhouse, wet sheep, then another house, then a row of houses and overflowing gutters.

It was no Willama. It was an overgrown Woody Creek.

'Drive around the shithole,' he said, the gun barrel in her ribs.

'Whatever we're running from we'll need petrol to keep doing it,' she said, and braked to give way to the vehicle on her right.

Hotel on the corner, taller than Woody Creek's but as old. Two women with baby strollers sheltering from the rain beneath its veranda, a fat old Labrador waiting beside one of the strollers. No sign of a police station or a sign pointing to a police station, so she drove on, looking on both sides of the road.

Saw an IGA supermarket on her left, next door to a railway station. She was looking at the station, thinking of Norman's station and remembering waving trains on their way and being so happy when a passenger had waved back. She was thinking of the day Amber had come home on a train when the barrel of his gun dug in deeper. He'd seen petrol pumps.

She braked and turned left into a rundown service station. It had three pumps and a blue overall-clad chap working in a tin shed. She pulled in so that her tank was close to the lead-free pump, turned off the motor and unclipped her seatbelt, not to get out and fill her tank, but to run.

And he knew it. 'Move out of that seat and you're dead and he's next,' he said, *he*, the chap wearing blue overalls, now standing in his doorway, unwilling to get wet just for a few dollars' worth of petrol. No one else around.

What could she do? Call his bluff? Make him prove that his gun was real by committing suicide and murder? She looked at it. It looked real.

And that chap in blue overalls decided to get wet. 'Nice bit of rain,' he said, and half of his front teeth were missing.

Jenny wound down her window. 'I hope it made it to Woody Creek. Our farmers have been screaming out for rain.'

'Fill it up,' her passenger said, and as the chap removed her petrol cap and started pumping fuel, Jenny pointed to her handbag. His feet were on it. He didn't move to get it. The gun in her ribs didn't move.

'Unless you're paying, I need my handbag,' she said.

He didn't move until the pump kicked back and the petrol cap was on, when he aimed his gun at the chap who couldn't afford false teeth.

'Go, or I'll blow the rest of his fucken teeth out,' he said.

She stole that tank full of petrol. In one movement, she turned on her motor, yelled 'Sorry,' then took off in a spray of muddy gravel, because that toothless chap was better off robbed than dead, and because she'd got a good look at that parasite's eyes. He was on drugs. She'd seen his eyes that day in Croydon and had her suspicions. Today she knew why his eyes had always reminded her of Raelene's. Drugs killed the life in them, killed empathy, emotion. Dead snakes had more humanity in their eyes.

She turned off the highway the next time he told her to, turned left into a side street, a residential street, sealed, or its centre was sealed. She drove by houses for a long block, by a house or two in the next block, then no more houses and no more bitumen, only a potholed muddy track heading off into bush. She braked to turn around.

'Drive,' he said.

'There's nothing down here.'

'I said fucken drive!'

His gun damn near up her nose, she smelt its killing power. She might have loathed the sight of him but hadn't feared him. She feared that gun, and if she was going to end up dead, far better to end up bogged and dead close to Nettleton. There'd be more chance of her body being found.

Life's full of potholes, me darlin', Granny used to say. *If we keep our eyes on the track ahead, we can dodge the worst of them.*

Little Jenny Morrison had learnt late how to dodge the potholes of life. She'd been lucky to make it through infancy, very lucky to make it to her fifteenth birthday. She dodged a few more potholes while he helped himself to her handbag, to her red wallet. The secondhand man's notes were in it with a few English twenties and her red bank card. It would access around four thousand dollars – if he could access it. Her Visa and her other bank card were in her old wallet, still in Greensborough.

Her rings weren't. She'd zipped them into an inside pocket of her handbag. Had offered the diamond rings to Trudy. She hadn't wanted them – and he didn't find them. He pitched the bag back to his feet but put her wallet into his windcheater pocket and removed a glass bubble pipe.

GREENSBOROUGH

Georgie's mobile buzzed as she turned in to her driveway. She didn't pick up, not until the motor was turned off, when she sighed and reached for the phone.

'I've been trying to call Jenny for hours, on her landline and mobile. I called Harry, and he said she'd be at the Gold Rush Motel. She's not there, Georgie. They said she hadn't booked in.'

'She'll be at one of the others,' Georgie said. 'She's handing over her keys at eleven tomorrow, in Willama.'

'There's more to it. I should have told you. I should have told Mum yesterday.'

Georgie closed her car door, pointed her keys, then walked inside, the phone to her ear.

Katie and Paul were watching the news. She stood, bag over her shoulder, mobile to her ear, until a footballer's injury took precedence over a bad smash near Willama.

'I'll give Harry a call,' Georgie said. 'Paul's got a class tonight. I have to go, Trude.'

She didn't call Harry. She was moving her car to let Paul out when the landline rang.

'It's Vonnie,' Katie said, pushing the phone at her as she stepped inside. She'd turned the phone onto speaker.

'Harry said not to panic you, Georgie,' Vonnie said. She was long-winded. Time had always stretched longer in the country, but she finally got around to why she'd called. 'Jenny's car isn't at the house but there's a black SUV parked in her shed and it's been in a smash. I don't know if you've had a chance to see the news, but they've been talking all day up here about a stolen black SUV that was involved in that smash on the highway.'

'We watched it,' Georgie said.

'Well, why I'm ringing is, Harry wants to know if Jen's still got that hidden key? Teddy's gone around to get the police and Harry doesn't want them breaking down doors to get in. I mean not with the new buyers moving in tomorrow.'

Katie knew where to find Jenny's emergency key. They'd had to use it before Christmas, when they'd taken the twins for a walk and Pa had gone to sleep watching television.

The ABC had more news about the crash and the stolen SUV. They said that the owner of the vehicle had been dragged out of her car at traffic lights in Broadmeadows, that her seven-year-old daughter, buckled into the rear seat, had been driven thirty kilometres along the Hume Highway before the carjacker tossed her out.

At eight-thirty, Channel Seven showed a security video, a silent video, but worse for its silence. A masked robber armed with a metal rod was smashing up the office of a service station, the attendant backing away from him while pointing a gun.

'Why didn't he shoot him?' Katie asked.

'He would have ended up charged with murder.' He'd ended up in hospital with serious head injuries.

Georgie was showering when her mobile rang again. Katie took the call, hoping it was Jenny. It was Trudy and she was howling, and dealing with Trudy when she wasn't howling was bad enough. Katie took the phone to the bathroom door and, her finger covering the speaker, she relayed Trudy's news.

'The police are saying that Nick is the one smashing up that place on the video. That he's on the outside video filling up Trudy's car with petrol.'

Georgie turned the water off.

'She said that Nick's cousin and two of his mates have been arrested and she wants to come over here,' Katie said.

And Georgie was out, wrapped in her dressing gown. She took the phone. 'What's going on?'

'They arrested Nick's cousin and everyone's here. I have to get out, Georgie,' Trudy howled.

'Arrested for what?'

'They've been cooking ice, and Nick has been working with them. I thought they did gardening.'

'Cooking ice?'

'The police broke in today and caught them at it. If I get a taxi over there, can you pay for it? I haven't been out since the hospital. I should have told you,' she howled.

Georgie's landline saved her. It started ringing. She handed her mobile to Katie and took the call.

It was Harry. 'Jen's not in the house or the yard. The local chap has been onto his city mates and they're saying that it's Trudy's bloke, that Jen's driven him somewhere.'

'If she's with him, she hasn't gone willingly,' Georgie said. 'Make them understand that – or give them my number. I've got to go, Harry, my phone needs charging.' It was beeping its warning. She placed it on its charger, then took her mobile.

'Text your father, Katie,' she said, and then tried again to calm Trudy.

She'd always been a howler. She'd howled at Christmas time when she'd spoken of divorce – and if she'd gone through with it, it would have been finalised by now.

'Go to bed, Trude. It's no good dragging the boys around at this time of night. I'll call you if I hear anything.'

Then, with both phones silent, Georgie sat down and Katie picked up the remote to search for news. The world might end but the canned laughter would play on. She muted the laughter and flicked to the ABC. No commercials on the ABC but a talk show unfit for human consumption.

'Kill that,' Georgie said.

She wasn't ready yet to lose Jenny, and Jenny wasn't ready to go. She'd watched her coming through that door at the airport, expecting decrepit, but she'd looked younger than when they'd dropped her off a month ago.

'I've spent years claiming that the old bugger in the clouds had it in for me, and look what he gave me?' she said and she'd grabbed Georgie and kissed her within an inch of her life. 'And I told you not to bother coming all the way out here, that I'd get a taxi.'

She'd talked all the way home, about Jimmy, about Italy and about the secondhand man who'd said he'd be in Woody Creek early the next day. 'If I drive up there today, I won't have to leave at dawn tomorrow,' she'd said.

Katie flicked channels until she found the news. Channel Seven had a reporter on the spot. She didn't mention Jenny's name but got the basic facts right, that the fugitive was believed to be the son-in-law of an elderly woman, that it was believed he had taken her hostage and was now driving her early model white Toyota.

He is armed and dangerous. Do not approach.

'Where would he get a gun from?' Katie asked.

Georgie had a fair idea. She had a better idea when Channel Seven showed that security video in its entirety. The image was no clearer but given more information, she could see Nick in the movements of that masked, rod-wielding robber. They saw him smash that rod into the service station assistant's head, saw the assistant crumple down behind his smashed counter.

Georgie sat, her eyes fixed on the screen, watching that same old repetitive story, replayed too many times on Melbourne television – and when had she given a thought to those waiting at home within arm's reach of telephones? She and Katie were the waiters tonight.

Harry received a mention. *Mr Henry Hall, brother-in-law of the missing woman . . .*

'Henry?' Katie questioned, before questioning *brother-in-law*.

Georgie's mobile buzzing like an annoying mosquito, Katie muted the television.

'I burnt his passport,' Trudy said. 'I should have let him go.'

'Turn the television on to Channel Seven, Trude. They're calling Jen his hostage and he's got a gun, that service station's chap's gun.'

'He's probably killed her,' Katie yelled and Channel Seven cut to a commercial. The world might end but viewers would still need to know where they could buy the cheapest washing machine, what was on special this week at Woolworths, and who to call if they wanted to prepay for their funeral.

'Pa watched that thing,' Katie said, then she started howling.

'Stop that,' Georgie commanded. 'I don't need your tears right now – and she's indestructible. You should have seen her yesterday –'

'I didn't see her yesterday,' Katie howled. 'You made me go to school.'

A newsreader had news of another martyr blown away to paradise with six of his victims, just people, just kids. Australian boys were over there fighting an enemy that blended in with the general population. How did they know who to shoot, to bomb? You can't bomb an entire community. You can't do much against religious fanatics.

Can't speak your mind about them either. Tongues had been hobbled since the eighties, schoolchildren brainwashed, parliamentarians taught to mouth newspeak gobbledygook. Once there was a world and the world was good –

Paul came in at ten. A techno whiz, he'd taught Georgie how to use a computer. He also made good coffee, made three mugs of it, and tonight Georgie didn't comment on that third mug.

She needed Katie awake tonight and close, needed Paul on the couch beside her. They were all she had – and Jenny.

There was room for three on the couch. They sat bunched there, drinking coffee, Georgie thinking that fourteen-year-old kids were older than they'd been in her day, and younger too. She'd been a week shy of her fourteenth birthday the day she'd started working for old Charlie, had known nothing about the world, other than the importance of money and the power of men. She'd had three ambitions at fourteen, to get Jenny away from Ray King, to become as rich as Vern Hooper, and to find her father, dreams she'd never expected to achieve behind Charlie's counter. That job had been her first stepping stone.

But Ray died, Jenny left town, and Georgie had inherited responsibility for Margot. For another twenty years, she'd stood still on that first stepping stone – until the fire, which for some reason, she'd been allowed to survive.

Channel Seven showed a police roadblock on the Mission Bridge and a row of traffic lined up on both sides – as it may have been on the night of the fire.

A hot summer night that one. Tonight was cold. Five minutes ago the weather reporter had told them that the forecast for tomorrow was for heavy showers and a top temperature of twelve. Somewhere out there in the cold dark night, Jenny was . . .

'She likes driving,' Georgie said. 'Remember the night she turned up at the back door when we were eating dinner?'

That had been on a summer night. They'd had two air conditioners blasting when they'd seen her through their glass door.

'Just passing. Thought we'd drop in,' she'd said, and she'd laughed at their shocked faces. Jim had been behind her. He hadn't been laughing. She'd taken him out for a drive to cool down and when he'd nodded off, she'd continued driving. The temperature, sitting on forty for a week, their house would have been an oven. They'd been gone by daylight. She'd left a note.

Ta for bed. Have to get home before Trudy leaves for work. Jen XXX

From birth those boys had been her life, and Jim's.

'She'd spent her life pushing kids around that bloody town in strollers. She pushed Donny around in a wheelchair for eight years,' Georgie said. 'Then Trudy, then the twins.'

'What happened to Donny?' Katie asked.

'He died young, in a home for the retarded. She looked after him until Ray died.'

'Why would she take him back and look after his kids when he'd cheated on her with another woman, Mum?'

'She didn't, or not as a husband. I've told you. He lived in a back room.'

'Why would she look after the other woman's kids?'

Good question, Georgie thought. Guilt, maybe. Payback to Ray for the two babies she'd aborted in Armadale. That was the only reason Georgie had ever been able to come up with. 'She loved Raelene. I think that looking after her helped to get her over losing Jimmy.'

'What about Trudy?'

'She said once that being able to love her eased her guilt over not loving Margot.'

Trudy wouldn't receive a dollar from Jenny's will. 'Tie it up tight, Georgie,' Jenny had said on the phone that night. 'Make sure he can't break it.'

There was a copy of it in the concertina file with a disc Jenny had sealed into a manila envelope. *To be opened in the event of my death*, printed in red on both sides of the envelope. Georgie had no idea of what was in it.

Another commercial break, headed by a newsflash. Paul left the room to shower and shave. Katie flicked to a movie, an oft-played movie, the actor searching for his abducted daughter.

'Did your father ever come looking for you?' Katie asked.

'What?'

'You had a father. Did he ever go for custody of you . . . or whatever it was called in those days?'

'No.'

'Why not?'

'Lack of interest.'

'Is he dead?'

'Dunno.'

'Why not?'

'Lack of interest.'

'You're so frustrating when I ask you anything about him,' Katie said. 'He was my blood grandfather, Mum.'

'I didn't know him.' Didn't want to know him by the time she'd found him. She'd been in her mid-forties.

The movie broke to commercials, and another newsflash. Channel Ten showed Jenny's shed and the big dark vehicle parked in it.

'It's like watching one of those true-crime television shows, except we're in it, so it's a horror show,' Katie said. 'How could he drive that car in there without Lila hearing him?'

'She's been with Harry since before lunch,' Paul said, sitting down again.

'She wasn't last night. They said before that he'd been involved in that bad accident on the Melbourne road.'

'Shush,' Georgie said.

Police in two states are searching tonight for a gunman and an elderly woman, taken from her home this morning . . .

'She wouldn't like them saying *elderly*. When I used to ask how old she was, she'd say sixty and a big bit,' Katie said. 'Will the police phone us if they find out something?'

'Yes,' Georgie said.

Or they'd knock on the door.

GOAT TRACKS

The thump of the Toyota's undercarriage bottoming out in a water-filled pothole jarred Jenny's mind back to the present and made him drop his bubble pipe. He hadn't been blowing bubbles in it, but holding a disposable lighter to its bowl, making whatever he'd put into it bubble.

Her motor howled, her wheels sprayed mud, but the car refused to move forward. She'd never been bogged. She'd heard tales from those who had been, so rammed the stick into reverse and hit the accelerator again. And her good little car moved backward. It gave itself a mud bath but got out of that hole, and he unclipped his seatbelt to search for his bubble pipe.

She'd seen bongs for sale in the newsagency and had asked about them. The owner told her they were used for smoking tobacco, though everyone and their dog knew what was smoked in them. Her passenger wasn't smoking marijuana. Raelene used to smoke it. Jenny knew its smell. The twins would have loved his little pipe. They'd love blowing bubbles for Lila to chase.

Where were they tonight? Where was Trudy? What had gone on while she'd been away?

Her bladder, threatening to burst, wouldn't hang on much longer. She knew where to find every public toilet on the road to Melbourne, had pulled into most of them at one time or another. She'd chased a fourteen-year-old Raelene across an oval near one toilet and brought her down with a rugby tackle. Every couple of months, they used to leave home at dawn, hit the city by ten, get Raelene to her appointments with the child psychologist, case workers or other experts on child management, then get back into the car and drive home in the dark, no glasses necessary back then.

Needed her glasses tonight. Her bifocals were in her bag. She'd told him she needed them when the night became too dark to wear her sunnies. A black night now, her headlights cutting a narrow pathway through scrub land.

'Pull over,' he said.

She'd learnt obedience. She'd have a bruise on her ribs to prove why, and a sore spot behind her right ear. She braked and blinked her eyes into focus. He was going to get rid of her. She was going to end up roadkill for wild pigs – or maybe scrub kill. She'd watched enough criminal shows on television to know that killers usually made their victims walk a distance from the road before shooting them.

She wouldn't walk obediently. He'd have to shoot her on the run, or zig-zagging. She'd seen that done on television too. The actor had survived.

He didn't tell her to get out. She unclipped her seatbelt as he opened his door. She left the shift in *Drive* but kept her foot on the brake, her every muscle tensed to hit the accelerator hard as soon as his feet hit the dirt. She might knock him down with the open door or drag him with her. Didn't care if she ran over his head.

He didn't get out. He did what he needed to do where he sat, started adding his water to the goat track – and to her door lining.

His hands were occupied.

She killed the headlights, grabbed for the strap of her handbag, flung the door wide and hit the dark running. She didn't zig or zag as seen on television. She didn't run either, not as in really run. She told her legs to get her into the scrub anyway they could, and they did, his animal scream pursuing her – and her old parka. Its sleeve had caught in the strap of her bag. She could barely see a hand before her but could see the pale blue of that parka. She reeled it in, balled it and ran deeper into the scrub, giving no thought to the wild pigs she might disturb.

Or to low-hanging branches until one grabbed her hair and gouged her brow. It hadn't got her eyes and it didn't slow her pace. She didn't look back, not until she found something resembling a tree, not a big tree, but far enough in from the track for her to bare her backside in a semi squat and to wonder again why the male animal had been designed for convenience and the female designed for the male's convenience.

No moon, a few patches of stars breaking through a cloud-covered sky. Maybe the rain had moved on. She'd got her bearings earlier from a slim moon. Didn't know now if she was facing north, south, east or west, only that he was behind her, and that he'd been sucking on that pipe for hours and was stark raving crazy.

She'd left the shift in *Drive*. It had been in reverse when he'd got into the car and without her foot on the brake it had moved with no help from her. She'd expected it to move on down that track, but it was waiting for her like a faithful dog. Couldn't see it, but his screaming sounded too close.

She pulled up her pants and slacks and was stooping to pick up her handbag and parka when a night beetle buzzed past her left ear. In the split instant before she heard the *Crack*, she'd thought it was a beetle.

He'd shot at her. He'd damn near shot off her ear. He could see her, and faster, with an empty bladder, she zig-zagged deeper into the scrub, one hand feeling for the pearl-in-a-cage earring in her lobe. It was still there.

Crack!

No buzz of warning that time, and just when she didn't need it, that scythe of moon slid out from behind a cloud to paint the scrub and her parka silver.

She was heading north. That track and his gun were to the south and the bitumen highway around twenty kilometres east. Too far away. There could be a fence down here somewhere. She wanted a fence, a paddock, a house in that paddock.

Crack!

Kids always say, 'Bang, bang, you're dead.' Guns don't go *Bang*! They make a whip-crack, a loud whip-crack in the silence of this dead land where no bird, no frog, no cricket dared to breathe. She could hear her own breathing, hear every footfall. He was probably tracking her.

Probably wasn't, not with one bare and injured foot, not through this country.

She got in behind a stand of scrub to catch her breath and to put her old Michelin Man parka on. It might give him a target to aim at, but the night was cold and that parka had always been warm, and it had a hood. She pulled up its hood, found and tied the cords, fiddled with the zipper until she got it started, then pushed on by the light of the moon to find a fence.

No fence, no house, but she saw the glow of car lights on that track, her car lights, she hoped. He was going.

Crack!

Not yet, he wasn't. That was four shots. In the old cowboy movies, handguns only held six bullets. She and Jimmy used to count them so they'd know when the bad guy had to reload. Technology had done for the gunslinger's six-gun. These days, in television shows, guns had slide-in clips that held as many bullets as the producer or director required them to hold.

Her mouth was dry. She had a bottle of water in her handbag and could thank Rome for that. After their first day in that city, she'd never left the hotel without a full bottle of water in her handbag. She'd filled that bottle with Melbourne water before leaving Greensborough.

Heard her motor roar. Nick Papadimopolous, a city man, had been left stranded on a goat track, with an injured foot, midway between no place and nowhere.

Crack!

That was five, followed by a roar of pain from her Toyota's motor – and a pig's scream. That scream sounded close.

She'd seen three feeding on roadkill beside the bitumen road. His bullet must have hit one of their relatives.

She'd been bush-bashing towards the north and that non-existent fence. His gun was to the south, that screaming pig to her west. She turned east, towards that last bitumen road.

FIFTY-EIGHT KS
FROM HAY

'*D*id I wake you?' Harry asked.

       'I was catnapping. What's happened?' Georgie asked.

'A kangaroo got him. Jen wasn't with him,' Harry said.

Ten past four, Katie asleep on the couch, the television still playing. Paul had gone to bed at two. Georgie's eyes had been closed but her ears open to Yankee voices, a panel of them on the Yanks' version of a talk show. There'd been no news of Jenny, not for hours.

'Has he said anything?'

'He's dead. He was dead when a truckie called the accident in, fifty-eight kilometres from Hay. There's nothing on that road, or nothing but trucks and dead roos. The last time I was up that way I must have counted two dead roos a mile.'

'She wasn't in the car?'

'No and not flung out of it either, they say. She's been with him. They found her wallet on him.'

Harry still believed that he had to yell down a phone line to be heard. The average ear couldn't take one of his calls, or not against the ear. Katie stirred. Georgie wanted her to sleep through this night, so took the phone into the study.

'He hated her, Harry. She slapped his face before she went on her tour. He's killed her.'

'Trudy's not with you?'

'No. She's coming across in a taxi in the morning. Her sister-in-law has got a house full. They're burying his mother on Monday.'

'Lucky he's dead, or the loss of his mother would have probably got him off with a slap on the wrist. They're getting a search party up there at daylight to look for her,' Harry said.

'How are they going to search a few thousand square miles of nothing, Harry?'

'I'm going up there with Ted and Lenny – and Lila. We'll find her. We won't stop looking until we do, Georgie, so don't you go giving up on her. I've known her, girl and woman, and she never gave up.'

'She's damn near eighty years old, Harry.'

'That's a dirty word. Don't you go letting her hear you say it,' Harry said. 'As far as I'm concerned, she's alive until I know otherwise. Now you try to get some sleep.'

'When will you sleep?'

'I've been catnapping, and Lenny's driving us up there. I'll sleep on the way. We'll probably find her hitchhiking home.'

He ended the call and Georgie took the phone back to the charger. She'd been drinking coffee all night. Paul's wine was on the top shelf of the fridge. She rarely drank it but poured herself a waterglass full.

He's made himself a Jenny voodoo doll he spends his days sticking pins into, Jenny had once said of the old bloke in the clouds. *I thwarted him by living, Georgie, and the old bugger has been out to get me since.*

Keep thwarting him, mate, Georgie thought, and she took her wine back to the couch where she sat watching that Yankee talking-head show.

EPILOGUE

'*G*et up and walk,' Jenny said. 'Stand up, put one foot in front of the other, then the other in front of it. Now.'

She wasn't certain when she'd started talking to herself, but any voice in the dark is comforting and it was good advice. Had she been able to see where to put that one foot in front of the other, she might have taken her own advice. Couldn't see much right now.

The darkest hour always comes before the dawn, so they say. She'd had that slice of moon to guide her until shortly before she'd fallen. It had deserted her, as had those pockets of starlight. The sky was currently spitting at her.

She'd been rained on earlier, not heavy rain but steady rain. Hours since she'd last heard her car. Yesterday. Her mobile, which refused to pick up a signal, had battery power enough to tell her that Tuesday seventeenth had clicked over to Wednesday eighteenth, D-day, delivery day, the eighteenth. She wasn't going to be in Willama at eleven to hand over her keys. She'd missed her hair appointment yesterday, hadn't picked up her photographs, hadn't bought a new mobile. Her old mobile's battery died at 3:13, maybe an hour ago, maybe more.

There was no shelter out here. Any trees that had managed to scratch a living from this land long enough to grow old had grown stunted. She had her back to one. Its canopy was sparse.

Until maybe half an hour ago, she'd been walking, until she'd caught the toe of her left shoe on a stick and landed face down in the dirt.

'It could have been worse,' she said. 'I could have broken a bone. If I'd tried to save myself with my hands, I could have been nursing a broken wrist like that old New Zealand chap. He'd tried to save himself with his hands and ended up in hospital.'

She'd landed on her shoulder, which didn't feel good but still moved. She had a sore spot behind her left ear she couldn't blame on her fall, sore ribs too she couldn't blame on the fall. A few hours ago, she'd had a lump the size of a pullet's egg behind that ear. It was a patch of stiff hair now. It must have bled. The gouge in her brow had bled. If there was a bright side to that, it was that the branch had missed her eyes. Skin healed. Eyes didn't. Not that they could see a damn thing. She'd put her glasses on since she'd tripped. Still couldn't see anything.

'Get up,' she said. 'People die of hypothermia on nights like this. Do you want to end up pig food?'

It would sell a few books. *Juliana Conti, believed to have been eaten by wild pigs – after she died of hypothermia . . .*

She wasn't cold, or her top half wasn't. She could thank a few ducks for that; her old parka was duck-down padded, wind and shower proofed, and the warmest jacket she'd ever owned.

'It makes you look like the Michelin Man,' Trudy had said, and thereafter, it had hung behind the laundry door. She'd almost given it to the op-shop the day she'd cleaned out the laundry. Couldn't do it. There'd been too many good memories attached to it, and if she got out of this, she'd frame it. She'd found two crumpled tissues in one of its pockets and an unopened roll of peppermint Life Savers in the other. They would have been past their use-by date, but they'd saved her life – to date they'd saved her life.

'Do Life Savers have a use-by date?' she asked the night. These days everything did. Her mobile was well past its. She'd been going to buy herself a modern phone yesterday and get herself a new number. The Telstra shop was next door to her hairdresser.

That packet of Life Savers told her when she'd last worn her Michelin Man parka. She'd given up smoking a month after Trudy came home, or had given up buying packets of smokes. That's when she'd hung the parka on that nail behind the laundry door, so she could sneak out at night and walk around to Harry to beg him for a smoke. She'd quit officially three months before actually quitting, though Trudy and Jim had never known it. Used to crunch peppermint Life Savers all the way home, then pick a few leaves from the lemon tree to rub all evidence from her hands.

She used to do that when the kids had been small, when Granny wouldn't allow a smoker inside her house. Used to sneak down behind the fig tree, suck her smoke down to the butt, bury it then chew mint leaves and wash her hands with lemon leaves.

And Jimmy had remembered the scent of lemon leaves on her hands.

If Jim or Trudy had bothered to go into the laundry, that parka may have given up her secret walks in the night. She could almost smell a wisp of that last cigarette in the collar of that showerproof fabric.

She'd quit, for the sake of the babies Trudy had been carrying, and because passive smoke was bad for a non-smoker's lungs – according to Trudy and other experts, though tonight she might have disproved their passive smoke theory – last night. For hours she'd breathed in the fumes of whatever he'd been smoking in his bubble pipe. You can't see much when you're driving. She'd smelt it. Raelene's drug of choice had been heroin. His was probably ice. She'd read about ice that could turn a sane man crazy. A few of the Duffys were on it – and crazy enough without it.

'Although,' she said, 'I could have been passively ice crazy when I ran off into the middle of nowhere.'

She'd expected a fence, a farm, people, warmth, and found nothing and no one.

No disposable lighter in her parka pockets. If she'd had a lighter she would have been able to see the time on her watch, she could have lit a fire.

'Fires keep wild animals away,' she said, or they did on television. Australia had no wild animals – no four-legged wild animals. 'Nothing would burn anyway,' she said. 'Bugger the rain.'

Until last night she'd never seen a wild pig, or not in the wild. They were big. She'd seen one of them ripping the innards out of a dead roo with six-inch-long tusks. That's where she'd been heading when she'd tripped, back to that road, back to those pigs.

When she'd started her walk, she'd told herself that if she could do three kilometres an hour, she'd be there by daylight. If she'd been able to walk on that track, she might have done her three kilometres an hour.

He might have run her down too. Twice she'd thought he'd gone but he'd driven back. Not for a good while though.

'Probably miles away in my poor little car,' she said.

She'd done a lot of walking in her time, though little of it alone. Always had a dog at her heels or a kid in a stroller, or a couple of kids holding her hands. She'd walked Jimmy home from the city one day when the tram drivers called a snap strike, when she'd lived with Ray, in Armadale.

'That had to be a six-kilometre hike,' she said.

That walk had worn a hole through the sole of her shoe, a cheap shoe. She'd paid a hundred and forty dollars for the pair she was wearing tonight. They had a strip of metal between their rubber soles and their cushioned innersoles – which she hadn't known about until they'd made the metal detector beep at Tullamarine.

'Take your shoes off,' a woman in uniform had said.

'There are no knives or drugs in them,' she'd said.

'Take your shoes off!'

She'd taken them off.

She hadn't paid a lot for her parka. Had bought it at the end of a winter, eight or ten years ago, reduced to half price. Used to wear it all winter until the day of the Michelin Man. She'd bought a new black parka, not as warm but it looked better.

Her legs weren't warm. Her slacks felt damp, as did the dirt beneath her backside, cold and damp. She had to get up.

It was pure luck that she had that parka. She'd made a grab for her handbag, not thinking about her rings but her mobile – and the damn fool thing had refused to pick up a signal. Her bag's shoulder strap had got a grip on the sleeve of her parka.

'Pure luck.'

Didn't have a clue where she was – other than she was somewhere out of Telstra range. She could have been in the backblocks of Victoria or New South Wales. She'd crossed a bridge while diverting around a town. He hadn't liked towns and had gone screaming mad when her diversion over a bridge had led into another town. She'd seen a part of its name. *BAR*-something.

'*Bar*mah? *Bar*nawartha? *Bar*ham?'

One of Lila's litter mates had been bought by a chap from Barham. He'd driven a long way to buy that pup. The smartest dogs ever born, those red kelpies.

'So get home to her,' she said. 'Get up and walk. And go back to that track.'

It wasn't far off to her right. Three times tonight – this morning – she'd cut back through the scrub, just to make certain she was still walking east and not in circles.

'He won't come back again.'

Who knew what he'd do, and why bother anyway? She'd taken her first breath alone in scrub beside a railway line. Maybe the old bugger in the clouds had her written down to take her last alone in the scrub.

'We're born, we labour, and if we struggle through to old age, you give us arthritis or dementia, or both, you mean old coot,' she said. 'You're probably sitting up there, bathed in moonlight, having hysterics.'

Talking made her mouth dry and she had to stop doing it. She'd had a full bottle of water at 11:22. There wasn't much left now, not enough to swallow a Panadol. She needed one. Her shoulder was aching and her ribs. There was enough left in that bottle to dissolve an aspro, which might get her moving – or put her to sleep. She was tired enough. She'd been wriggling her feet until a while ago, as she had on the plane. Too much effort now to wriggle them, and they felt dead. Her legs were sufficiently alive to feel the cold and the weight of her handbag, which was doing what it could to keep her thighs warm.

She'd have aspros in that bag, and with her good arm she reached for it, then with both hands felt out the top zipper, which had developed a bad habit of jamming halfway open. She eased it past its jamming point, then felt for the inside zipper and her rings.

Still there. She hadn't worn them in three months, not since the day of the splinter. Rings and jewellery helped with the identification of bodies, or they did on TV cop shows – and her wedding ring definitely would. Jim had it engraved in Sydney with their names and the year she should have married him. *Jen and Jim 1942.* She'd worn it in Sydney, called herself Mrs Hooper. Had worn it on her right hand in Armadale when she'd married Ray – until she'd sold his wedding ring, so she could feed her kids – and put Jim's ring in its place. Not until '59 had it been sanctified by marriage, though in her mind, she'd been married to Jim since 1942.

She slid it back where it belonged, slid her engagement ring on, then her eternity ring, relieved that they were on her finger and not in his pocket. He'd taken her wallet. Had probably taken her pills. She'd packed aspros and Panadol in the front pocket of her bag the day she'd flown away. She'd swallowed a few but not all of them.

The side zipper slid open easily. Her hand found paper. It felt like a supermarket receipt. She pitched it. Found a business card. Maybe that of the London taxi driver. She pitched it too. Like a house, a handbag accumulated too much junk. She found a ticket stub. It could have been from the Venetian opera. Not much use to her tonight. It followed the business card and supermarket receipt.

Her seeking fingers found a mint, left by a hotel maid on her pillow. She'd been rationing her Life Savers. She didn't have to ration that mint and peeled the paper from it. Her dry mouth thanked her. She pitched the wrapper and smiled as she composed next week's or next month's news.

Searchers today found evidence that Juliana Conti sat in the dirt cleaning out her handbag before the pigs ate her.

The Panadol pills were there and easily identified in the dark. They came in sheets of ten and fewer than half were missing from that sheet. She considered them, considered crunching a couple with the mint. They'd spoil its flavour.

'Got you,' she said, her fingers identifying foil and the shape of two soluble aspros. She closed the zips, placed the bag on her thighs again, peeled the foil from the pills then reached for her water bottle.

'Aspros thin the blood,' she said. 'Is thinning frozen blood good for it or bad? It might give it easier access to my extremities,' she said. Then removing the lid from her bottle, she dropped both pills into what felt like maybe an inch of water.

She'd gulped down too much when she'd heard her car roar away, when she'd believed herself capable of walking twenty kilometres, but the maniac had come roaring back, the headlights blazing. She'd been rationing that water since.

'There's not much that an aspro or two won't fix,' she said, the bottle to her ear so she might listen for the fizzing to stop.

No noise out here. Still too early for birds, too late for crickets, too cold for buzzing mosquitoes. She shook the bottle to assist the aspro dance, then listened again until what was in the bottle became silent. The mint, grown smaller, she tucked in her cheek while sipping that lemony, slightly salty liquid. Didn't sip all of it. Screwed the lid back on and returned the bottle to her bag.

She was supposed to hand over the keys at eleven this morning. The keys were in her car, and God only knew where it was. Hadn't picked up her photographs – one hundred and forty-six of them plus double prints of Johanna's nine London shots she'd promised to post.

'What happens to photographs when their owner never returns to pay for their printing?' she asked, then replied to her own question. 'They get tossed in a bin.'

That photograph-shop chap wouldn't toss her memory card. He'd delete her grand tour, delete Jimmy and his family, and consider that card payment for time and effort spent.

She'd planned to go through them last night and remove the shots of Jimmy's family. Tracy had taken a good one of her and Jimmy, and a better one of her with her great-grandchildren. She could never have shown them to her girls, could never have mentioned Tracy, or Robin, or his voice.

He was the reason why she decided to buy a new mobile and get a new number. He'd added her old number to his contacts, so he could call her at Christmas time, meet up with her, meet her girls. It could never have happened. When she'd given Jimmy the medals and necklet she'd promised herself that she'd write the end to the Jimmy saga, and if that had meant learning to use a new mobile and giving up her familiar number, then she'd do it.

'Would a new mobile have picked up a signal? Its battery wouldn't have gone flat,' she said. 'Who would have believed when I was young that one day people would walk around with tele-phones in their handbags, that the entire world would be become reliant on computers?'

'Oh shit,' she said. 'That disc!'

She'd meant to bring that manila envelope home with her. She'd meant to chop that disc into a hundred pieces and bury those pieces deep. That's all she'd thought about on the plane, that disc and those photographs of Jimmy's family, and Georgie never finding out that her brother and sister had married.

And she'd forgotten to get that bloody disc!

It was all there. The heartbreak of her meeting with Jimmy that day in Melbourne, thirty thousand words of it, sealed into an envelope. *To be opened only in the event of my death.*

'Georgie will open it. She'll read what's on it. You can't die, you malingering old bugger. Get up!'

It took a while. She settled for her hands and knees for a minute, then using the trunk of the tree she'd leant against, she got her feet beneath her. Stood leaning on the stick that had tripped her and holding on to the tree while stamping life back into dead feet.

They weren't dead. Nor was she. She got the strap of her handbag over her hooded head and across her breast, then, using that stick as a blind man used a white cane, she put one foot in front of the other, then the other in front of it.

And that old bugger in the clouds released his grip on the moon. 'Let there be light,' he said.

And there was light. A little light. Enough.